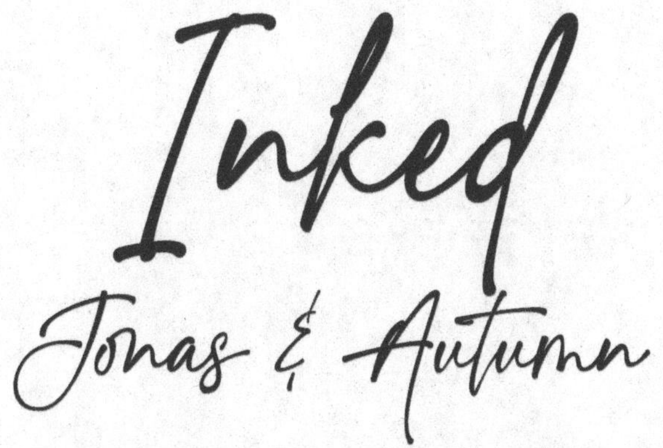

A SINGLE MOM, SECOND CHANCE AT LOVE ROMANCE DUET

USA TODAY BESTSELLING AUTHOR

PERSEPHONE AUTUMN

BETWEEN WORDS PUBLISHING LLC

Books by Persephone Autumn

Lake Lavender Series

Depths Awakened

One Night Forsaken

Every Thought Taken

Devotion Series

Distorted Devotion

Undying Devotion

Beloved Devotion

Darkest Devotion

Sweetest Devotion

Bay Area Duet Series

Click Duet

Through the Lens

Time Exposure

Inked Duet

Fine Line

Love Buzz

Insomniac Duet

Restless Night

A Love So Bright

Artist Duet

Blank Canvas

Abstract Passion

Novellas

Reese

Penny

Stone Bay Series

Broken Sky—Prequel

Shattered Sun

Fractured Night

Standalone Romance Novels

Sweet Tooth

Transcendental

Poetry Collections

Ink Veins

Broken Metronome

Slipping From Existence

Poisonous Heart

Beneath Wildflowers

PUBLISHED UNDER P. AUTUMN

Standalone Non-Romance Novels

By Dawn

contents

FINE LINE

Prologue 5
Chapter 1 13
Chapter 2 22
Chapter 3 33
Chapter 4 44
Chapter 5 52
Chapter 6 61
Chapter 7 69
Chapter 8 77
Chapter 9 87
Chapter 10 96
Chapter 11 110
Chapter 12 117
Chapter 13 128
Chapter 14 137
Chapter 15 145
Chapter 16 153
Chapter 17 163
Chapter 18 171
Chapter 19 181
Chapter 20 189
Chapter 21 199
Chapter 22 210
Chapter 23 225
Chapter 24 233
Chapter 25 245
Chapter 26 253

LOVE BUZZ

Chapter 1	261
Chapter 2	270
Chapter 3	279
Chapter 4	289
Chapter 5	297
Chapter 6	307
Chapter 7	317
Chapter 8	329
Chapter 9	341
Chapter 10	350
Chapter 11	357
Chapter 12	364
Chapter 13	371
Chapter 14	379
Chapter 15	390
Chapter 16	401
Chapter 17	407
Chapter 18	417
Chapter 19	425
Chapter 20	432
Chapter 21	442
Chapter 22	449
Chapter 23	459
Chapter 24	468
Chapter 25	476
Chapter 26	483
Chapter 27	490
Chapter 28	498
Epilogue	506
Thank You	513
More by Persephone Autumn	515
Inked Duet Playlist	517
Acknowledgments	519
Connect with Persephone	521
About the Author	523

Fine Line

BOOK ONE

To every person who pined for someone who would never belong to them.

prologue

JONAS

Fuck, she is beautiful.

My best friend. The woman I have loved for years. The woman walking down a sandy aisle in a stunning black lace wedding dress. To another man. A man she has been in love with since high school. A man I will never compare to in her eyes.

And although he broke her heart at sixteen, she never fell out of love with him. Gavin Hunt. The luckiest fucking man on the planet. The man at the end of the aisle holding his breath as she steps closer.

I close my eyes and duck my head. "Can't watch this," I whisper to myself. Because watching the woman I have loved for nearly ten years marry the love of her life is… painful. No, not painful. Debilitating. Excruciating. Crushing.

Fuck, I can't breathe.

Don't get me wrong, my heart holds so much happiness for Cora. Glad she reconnected with the one person who puts a permanent smile on her face. The person who constantly sparks her laughter. Who fulfills her in a way no one else has been capable of for years. As gut wrenching as it is to admit, Gavin is Cora's soul mate. Her *person.*

Once upon a time, I filled the role. For a phase of her life, I was her person. Was the only guy she leaned on for comfort or support. The one person she laughed with and spilled her heart to.

Cora is my best friend.

But she isn't mine.

And as much as it hurts, she never was.

I dreamed of the possibility, but she always tossed out those "you really are a great friend" lines with such ease. Every time she did, it twisted the knife in my heart a little more. Tore away another piece of my soul that I willingly handed her.

The day I met Gavin, the day we all hung out and I witnessed their chemistry for the first time, I threw in the towel. The energy in the room shifted and I witnessed it ebb and flow and magnetize them closer to each other. Cora and I have an undeniable bond, but it paled in comparison to the connection she and Gavin share.

In her own way, Cora loves me. Just not the way I love her.

But now, I have to let her go. Finally let go of the daydream. Let go of the possibility I stood a chance.

Snapping my attention back to my best friend, I memorize her happy, tear-stained face as she speaks her vows to Gavin. Tells him he was her first everything. *Twist.* Jokes how their middle names are similar—another sign they're meant to be. *Deeper. Twist.* Explains how life isn't worth living without him at her side. *Shattered. Split in two.*

I stop watching. Stop listening. My heart balls into a fist, clenches hard, and crumbles to ash beneath my ribcage.

Fuck, this hurts.

As badly as I want to rise from my seat and walk off, I won't. I will not ruin my best friend's wedding with my own selfishness. Won't squash her happiness with my sorrow. I am not that guy. Not an asshole. Or a prick.

Everyone laughs and cheers. I follow suit, not knowing the reason. My laugh floats off with the Gulf breeze, hollow and empty. Like my heart.

I chance a glimpse at my best friend. Bad timing. The moment I choose to look up, Gavin envelops her in his arms and kisses her the way I have always imagined doing. The way that haunts my dreams often.

The next hour trickles by in a fog. Shelly and Erin hang out with me. I remember to smile and laugh and joke at the right times. I hide the fact I am a withering mess inside. People scurry into the reception hall and tell everyone to prepare for the newlyweds. Reminding us to hoot and holler as they enter the room.

I clutch my stomach. *Think I am going to be sick.*

Cora and Gavin enter the room and everyone erupts in cheers and wolf whistles. I mimic with an empty smile plastered on my face.

An emcee announces the newly married couple before soon inviting everyone to eat. I fall in line with Shelly and Erin. They must sense my mood. Neither of them has said a single word to me. Can't blame them, I am shit company right now.

Shortly after everyone eats, Cora and Gavin share their first dance as husband and wife. I struggle to keep my meal down, but I do. I refuse to make a scene. Refuse to ruin this for her.

Shelly elbows me and I peer over at her. "What's up,

Shell?" But the moment I look up at her, I realize why she nudged me.

Cora.

The most stunning bride I have laid eyes on is standing beside me with a glowing smile. "Hey you," Cora says. She extends a hand out to me. "Will you dance with me?"

Fuck. *Fuck, fuck, fuck.*

I swallow and work to dislodge the lump in my throat. "Yeah," I choke out before coughing to clear my throat. "Yeah," I repeat.

She smiles as I take her hand and follow her to the dance floor. At the center of the room, she spins around and holds me like we are at senior prom. All too briefly, serenity blankets me. Cora in my arms has always felt *right.*

But she isn't mine. And I need to continue to remind myself of such facts.

"Are you okay?" she asks as we sway back and forth.

I won't lie to her, but the truth hurts like a motherfucker.

"Not so much." I lock eyes with her. "But I'm working on it. Promise."

"Jonas…" Cora smiles, but it doesn't touch her eyes. "Sorry. I wish…"

She doesn't continue. The way she holds my gaze tells me everything she wants to say, but can't articulate the words. How she wishes things could have been different. How she hopes I find happiness like she has. And how much she loves me. *Like family.*

I shake my head and close my eyes. "You have nothing to apologize for, Cora. Life has happened how it's meant to. You're my best friend," I whisper the last line and she lays her head on my shoulder. Closing my eyes, I soak up her warmth and relish the moment. "And no matter what, that will never change."

"Good." She laughs, but it isn't the unrestrained laughter I have heard countless times. "Because you're stuck with me, mister."

For the first time in months, a genuine smile stretches my cheeks and I chuckle. "Glad to hear it." I take a deep breath and swallow my pride. "Sorry if I haven't been the best party guest."

She lifts her head from my shoulder and I hide the disappointment threatening to flash across my face. "Jonas, you're here. That's all I care about. I don't give a damn what anyone else thinks. We've been through a lot over the years. If you're sad" —she studies my eyes for a minute— "you're entitled to feel how you feel. I'm sorry if this is hard for you. Being here."

The song changes and we continue to sway around the dance floor. Her sparkly green eyes stay on my hazels. The sweet, earthy floral notes of her perfume float in my nose. I will miss this. Miss the little pieces of her I have familiarized myself with over the years. But I need to do right by her. I need to remove the guilt she holds captive because of our bond.

I need to let her go.

For her. For me. For our future friendship.

Swallowing down the pain, I vow to myself to never let her feel guilt or sadness because of me. If I can't have her any way except for friendship, I need to accept it. Accept it and move on. Accept it and allow her to be happy.

"Cora..." I stroke my knuckles over her cheek and sigh when she closes her eyes. "It isn't easy." When I remove my hand, her eyes open and lock on mine again. "But I wouldn't miss this day for anything. The day you told the world you found love and grabbed it by the horns." She giggles and my pulse jump-starts. "Glad I could be here to witness this day. I will always be here. Even if we're just friends."

She lays her head on my shoulder again and snuggles closer to me. "My best friend," she whispers. "I love you, Jonas."

My eyes glaze over and I am damn glad she isn't looking at me right now. Glad she won't witness the dam of tears threatening to unleash. I hug her tight. "I love you, too," I croak.

We dance for the rest of the song in silence. When it ends, Gavin walks over. "May I?" he asks. He fucking asks. If I were in his shoes, I would probably yank Cora out of my arms. But he doesn't because he knows her heart. More than anyone.

I step back and smile. "Yeah, man." I offer Cora's hand to him. As she breaks from my embrace and glides easily into his, I take a deep breath and release her. "Congratulations. Not gonna lie, I'm envious as hell. But I'm happy for you both."

Gavin glances down at Cora and the smile on his face tells me he knows he is a lucky son of a bitch. And he will never fuck this up with her. He faces me again. "Thanks, man. Means a lot. To me and Cora. Don't give up." I flinch for a second and he registers my confusion. "Hard as it is to believe right now, the right woman is out there waiting for you. You're a good guy. Fate won't fuck you over."

Okay. Wasn't expecting that. And I have no clue how to respond. So, I remain tight-lipped.

Cora lays her hand on my bicep. "How could no one love you." She meant it as a rhetorical, so I don't answer her. "I have a sneaking suspicion you'll meet her soon."

"Her?" I ask.

"Yeah. The one. The girl who will seal all the cracks and make you whole again."

This conversation is one of the most awkward of my life. The woman I have loved for almost a decade, the woman I am trying desperately to let go of, is telling me I will soon find the love of my life. Which is supposedly not her.

I nod. "Hope so. I'm gonna head out." I hug Cora and memorize her one last time. We will see each other again, but it won't be the same. Then I extend my hand to Gavin. He shakes it, then surprises me when he pulls me in for a hug.

"Thanks for taking care of my girl when I didn't," he whispers in my ear. "Don't give up, man. Your girl is out there, waiting."

We break apart and I smile softly. "Congrats again." I turn on my heel and head for the exit, keeping the torrent of emotions at bay.

Outside, I bend at the waist and slap my hands to my knees. *"Your girl is out there, waiting."* Yeah, I don't see how that's possible. I hop in the Jeep, crank it to life, and let the tears fall.

I hope you're right.

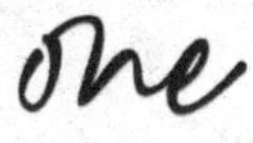

AUTUMN

The flashing yellow arrow torments me as I patiently wait for a break in the oncoming traffic. With everyone and their mother out shopping, on the hunt for the deal of a lifetime, the roads are busier than usual.

Black Friday has never really been my thing. People swarming like agitated bees. Fighting over electronics and shoes and kitchen gadgets. Don't get me wrong, I love shopping. Love buying cute new dresses, fun graphic tees, and endless accessories. But you will never find me throwing punches for *things*.

"Caution" by The Killers spills out the speakers as the traffic breaks. I turn onto the side street and hook a sharp right into the tattoo shop parking lot. Driving to the far rear corner, I back into a space, hop out, and enter through the back door.

"Hey, chicky. Busy?" I ask Penny as I wander over to my booth.

She smacks her strawberry bubble gum and shakes her head. "Nah. But it'll pick up soon. You have a packed schedule today."

Mentally, I throw devil's horns with my hands. A busy schedule equals a kick-ass payday. "Awesome. Thanks, Pen."

"Just doing my part," she says as she ambles over to my booth. Penny gives me the rundown on my appointments as I resanitize my workspace. The distinct smell of disinfectant fills the air as I wipe everything down. For years now, this has been my favorite smell. Most of my appointments today are small jobs. A name here, a symbol there, and a couple photos to etch in ink.

"Well, I appreciate you."

Penny curtsies, tilts her head, and smiles wickedly. She is a freaking nut, which is why we are such great friends—and roommates.

"How was the wedding?" Penny asks.

She met the bride and groom months back when they came in to get tattoos. When they invited me to their wedding, she frowned. Think she was a little butt hurt, especially when I didn't RSVP with a plus-one. She will get over it.

"Gorgeous," I say with a green man on my shoulder. "Lots of black." I laugh. "But mostly beautiful. They're so sweet together. I envy their connection."

The green devil pops back up on my shoulder as I recall Cora dancing with a man other than Gavin. Remember the way he held her. The glints of his profile in the dim, shimmering lights. He held her closer than a typical friend. But the exchange didn't faze Gavin whatsoever.

A balloon swells in my chest as I reminisce over the way he held her. I ache to be wrapped in someone's arms like Cora was his. To feel wanted and loved without effort.

"Yeah, they seemed pretty inseparable when they came in. How does one nail down a guy like that?" Penny asks as she rests her thumb and forefinger against her chin, inquisitive.

"Not sure. If you figure it out, let me know."

I finish organizing my booth and Penny goes back to her seat at reception. Soon, the bell hanging over the door chimes and the bodies flood in. Reznor strolls in and starts cleaning his booth after he throws me a wave. I toss one back before Penny hands me my first client's paperwork.

Name—Sean. Age—eighteen. Tattoo—the name "Nina." Placement—over his heart.

I avert my eyes to the floor and roll them. *Kids*… will they ever learn to not tattoo names on themselves? No. Fingers crossed Nina is his mom. But, deep down, I know it isn't.

My guess? Nina is the bouncy girl on his right, gripping his hand like a vise. The girl smiles at Sean as if he is the reason she breathes. Hope she feels that way for many years to come. Him, too.

"Sean," I call out as I wander over to the couches in reception.

He kisses her knuckles and hops up. "That's me," he says. "Can she watch?"

I nod. "Sure. Come on over." I wave them over to my booth, then point at the chair. "Have a seat." Scanning over the paperwork one last time, I review his tattoo with him and verify the placement. After he agrees on a font, I print "Nina" on the transfer paper, moisturize his young, hair-free chest, and apply the stencil.

The next hour is full of minor flinches and loud hisses. When I set the tattoo gun down, he sucks in a lungful of air. I spray a paper towel and wipe it across the fresh ink as I explain tattoo care to him. He nods at all the right times and smiles feverishly when I hand him a mirror and he stares at the tattoo for the first time.

When he rises from the chair, he wobbles in place. "Be

sure to grab a bite to eat when you leave here." I point to who I still assume is Nina. "Please don't let him drive until he eats." She nods and they head over to Penny to pay, leaving me a gracious tip.

The day trickles by much the same as usual.

My next appointment wants an old photo of her grandparents tattooed on her bicep with dates and the single word "forever" underneath. The memorialization is sweet, really. I press the pedal and the gun vibrates to life in my hand.

As I engrave her grandparents into her skin, the woman shares their story. How they met in a hospital during the Vietnam War and her grandmother nursed him back to life. How her grandfather could no longer fight on the front lines because he was too severely wounded to stand with his comrades. How pissed her grandfather was and how quickly he got over it because he saw a "pretty nurse lady" every day.

The way she conveys the love story of her grandparents, there was no doubt she heard their story firsthand hundreds of times.

Far too often, I dream of a love like theirs. One I hug close to my heart and brag to others about. *Maybe one day*, I mentally profess.

Halfway through, the woman closes her eyes with a smile on her face and remains silent for the rest of the session. While she zones out, so do I.

Every time a person sits in my chair or stretches out across my table, I mentally prepare for all or nothing. Clientele come in mixed bags. From nervous to somber to never-ending bursts of energy. Some talk your ear off for days. Others never speak a word. Then you get the ones who do a mix of both. Those who talk because they are nervous or shy, then quiet down once the initial buzz wears off.

I love it. Love my job. Love all the wonderful—and crazy—stories I hear. It's kind of like reading a new book every couple of hours. Living in someone else's shoes for a snippet of time.

When I finish up my second appointment, I clean and prep my station for the next—who Penny said is already here. After I wipe everything down, I pick up the clipboard with his paperwork and scan it.

Great. One of those. Lucky me (insert sarcasm anytime you would like).

My next client—male—wants the word "heaven" inked into his skin. No big deal, right? Sure, if he was getting it in any other location. I roll my eyes and lay out the narrow massage table in my booth. Because my next client is getting "heaven" tattooed an inch or two above the base of his penis.

Dumbass. Arrogant dumbass.

Penny waltzes over and sniggers as I lay paper gowns on the table. "Hope he's hung, otherwise a lot of people will be disappointed when they don't reach heaven as indicated."

I slap her arm and laugh. "Shut. Up." I shake my head. "How am I supposed to concentrate and act professional when you say shit like that?"

Penny shrugs, pops her pink bubblegum, and skips back to the reception area. Halfway across the store and I still hear her giggles.

Walking over to the waiting area, I retrieve Mr. Heaven and bring him to my booth. Without shame, I admit he is hot. Inches taller than me. Tan skin like he just left Clearwater Beach minutes ago. Bulky muscles showcasing his arms and legs.

But as I have learned, not all those qualities add up to

"heaven" in the bedroom. I cough into my elbow to cover the laugh bubbling up my throat.

Get it together, Autumn.

"Any particular font you were looking for?" I ask.

He shakes his head. "Maybe old English. Something masculine."

I show him a few variations and he chooses one. Once I have the transfer paper ready, he shoves his sweatpants down until he exposes his hairless skin and I glimpse the base of his penis.

Ugh, this is going to be a long—ha ha—and awkward session.

Mr. Heaven raises his arms and tucks his hands under his head. He has the audacity to smirk at me. Cocky bastard. Can't wait to wipe the smirk from his face when the gun bites his skin.

An hour and a half and an H-E-A-V later, Mr. Heaven isn't as suave as he thought he was. *Ha! Take that!* A sick pleasure floats in my veins each time he jerks or flinches or hisses. *Hope it is worth it, buddy.*

As I am midway through the second E, the bell over the door jingles. When I lift the gun away from Mr. Heaven's skin and wipe the excess ink away, I glance up and spot Penny chatting with the guy who walked in.

I stop breathing. Stop thinking. Stop everything.

"You good?" Mr. Heaven asks.

Snap out of it Autumn. "Yeah, sorry." Mr. Heaven glances to the man up front. "Thought it was a friend of mine," I say to cover up my flounder.

"No worries," he says as I finish working on the end of his tattoo.

Every now and again, I peer up and see the man is still

here. Currently, he sits on one of the couches as he flips through the artist's albums. He studies the photos with obvious interest. From my vantage point, I sporadically—and, fingers crossed, inconspicuously—survey him.

He hunches over an album as he flips the pages. His milk chocolate hair sticks out in different directions on top of his head—the underside buzzed short. When he swaps albums, I spot some of the ink between the bottom of his shirt sleeve and his elbow. Sacred geometry. Interesting.

I focus on Mr. Heaven as I finish the last of the N. As soon as I set the gun down and glance over at Penny, album-flipping guy waves at her and walks out the door. All I got was his backside.

But what a glorious backside it was.

Mr. Heaven rises from the table and hobbles over to the floor-to-ceiling mirror and inspects his fresh ink. He smiles like the cocky bastard he is. Penny cashes him out and he tips me well.

"At least Mr. Heaven was good for something," I say with a giggle as Penny heads my way.

"Yeah. But, girl, I'd climb that stairway to heaven." As if on cue, "Stairway to Heaven" by Led Zeppelin plays through the shop's speakers.

We both fall into a fit of laughter as I play slap her arm. "Shut up. You're sick." She shrugs without care. "Who was the guy?" I point to the door as if it explains who I am referencing.

When Penny deciphers who I am talking about, she smiles. "Your final on Wednesday. Hottie, huh?"

"Only saw the top of his head and a few inches of his bicep," I fib and pray she doesn't notice. Now is not the time for me to go into my starry-eyed moment. Fact is, I noticed so much more. But if Penny hears that, she will give me shit until Wednesday.

"Well, he'll be the cherry on your hot fudge sundae." Penny fans herself. "Let me just say it was hard not staring the entire time he was here."

Tell me about it.

"Stop," I tease. Couldn't place it, but something felt oddly familiar about him. "What's his name?"

Penny studies me a moment as I go through my usual sanitizing procedure. *Spray. Wipe. Repeat.* "Jonas. Why?"

I shake my head. "No reason. Just looked familiar. But I don't know a Jonas." I shrug and continue as if unfazed.

"You will," she teases and walks off.

I will. But something tells me I already do.

My last client is quick and easy. A young woman. I tattoo the kanji symbol for fierce on the back of her neck. The entire time I have the gun in my hand, my mind wanders to the tall, chocolate-haired man. His stature and sullen demeanor. Somehow, someway, I know him. Just can't place from where.

In my line of work, I see thousands of faces a year. Is there a possibility I inked his skin before? Maybe. But I would remember him. His broad shoulders and creamy brown locks. His long legs and strong hands. His stare-worthy ass as he strode out the door.

Jonas.

Don't remember a Jonas. And I would *definitely* remember him.

When I finish cleaning up my booth for the night, I walk over to Penny. "See you at home. Drive safe."

"You, too. Love you."

"Love ya, chicky."

I unlock my '57 Bel Air, slip inside, and spark the engine

to life. Scanning my music, I tap on a rock playlist and sing along as I roll out of the parking lot. The entire drive home, I sing the songs I have heard hundreds of times, but don't hear now. Because my mind is stuck. Stuck on the future. On Wednesday, and a mysterious man named Jonas.

Consider me screwed.

JONAS

I pick up Spartan's leash and he yaps, running excitedly in circles around the living room. "Come here, nut. Have to put your leash on if you want to see Grandma and Grandpa."

Spartan drops his front legs to the floor—his hindquarters still up as his tail swats the air. I step closer to him and he pivots sideways. We do this a few times, mixed in with more barking. The same game happens every Wednesday when we head to my parents' house for dinner. I grab the leash and my goofy as hell, three-year-old fur-child loses his shit.

At least he brings a smile to my face.

"You want to see Grandma?"

Woof, woof, woof.

"Well, we have to put on your leash." I flick the clasp a few times and he jumps. "Get over here, dude."

Woof, woof, woof.

I rest my hands on my hips and give Spartan the look that says *we are not going anywhere until you put on your leash.* And just like that, he wags his tail, steps forward, and stands tall at my side.

Once I lock his leash in place, we head out the front door

and hop in my Wrangler Sahara. When we are both in the cab, I connect his collar to a safety harness in the car. Last thing I need is my little man jumping out of a moving car because he spots a cat. His crazy ass would, too.

Windows down, I drive down the street and head toward my parents' house. Spartan hangs his head out the window with his mouth open as he squints at the oncoming wind. The temperature in our part of Florida is still warm—a toasty eighty-two degrees at four thirty—but you can feel a shift in the air. Not just the cooler days as we transition to Florida's version of winter.

Something else lingers in the air. A new beginning, maybe. Whatever it is, it terrifies and invigorates me.

I stick my arm out the window and shift it up and down in a wave motion. Glancing over at Spartan, I soak up a little of his boisterous energy. Smile at his silliness as he tries to bite the wind. Every time I peek over at him, I am grateful he is in my life. If not for this crazy as hell husky, I would be drowning in alcohol or in a hole somewhere. He keeps me going.

Thirty minutes later, we park along the street at my parents' house in St. Petersburg. I jump out and Spartan barks at me as if I forgot him. Opening his door, I loop the leash around my wrist before unclipping his car harness. Once I do, he flies out of the car and yanks me toward the house. I barely get the car door closed.

"Who's excited to see Grandma?" I announce as Spartan drags me inside.

"Where's my good boy?" Mom calls back. "Where's my Sparty?"

I drop Spartan's leash and he scrambles across the floor in her direction. Mom has her arms open as she squats down and waits to hug Spartan. He bolts into her arms and it is a hugging and licking contest between the two of them. Spartan's the only one doing the licking, obviously.

Wandering into the kitchen, I step up behind my older sister, Jasmine, and peek over her shoulder. She is so focused on stirring the hamburger meat on the stove, she doesn't hear me come in. *Perfect.* Slowly, I bring my hands to her sides before going all in and tickling the hell out of her.

"Ah!" she screams, dropping the spatula. "Stop, stop, stop." I tickle her harder. "Jonas! Please…" She laughs so hard she snorts. "Please."

"Mommy, Mommy, Mommy!" My nephew, Lex, comes barreling around the corner. "I save you from Unkie Jonas." Lex is armed with his favorite stuffed animal and ready to whack me with it.

I drop my hands and step back. "Whoa, buddy." Scooping him off the floor, I twirl him in a circle. "I stopped. Please don't get me."

Lex stares over at Jasmine with the most serious expression I have ever seen on his face. "Okay, Mommy?" Such a protector at two years old.

She ruffles his hair and kisses his forehead. "I am now. Thanks for saving me from Uncle Jonas."

He nods with enthusiasm and I set him back on the tile. "Hey, buddy. Why don't you go play with Grandma and Spartan. I'll help Mommy in the kitchen." Without so much as another glance in my direction, he bolts from the kitchen and calls across the house for Spartan.

"We're making tacos tonight, if you want to dice onions and tomatoes and slice up some lettuce," Jasmine says.

I hug her from behind and kiss the top of her head. "On

it." Grabbing the produce from the fridge, I step up to the counter beside the stove and get to work. "Anton here?" I ask.

Anton, my big sister's husband, doesn't always make it to Wednesday night dinners. Depending on his work schedule, sometimes he doesn't beat the Tampa traffic when he leaves work. If he runs too late on Wednesdays, he heads home and Jasmine brings him leftovers. Nine times out of ten, though, he makes it. For the most part, investment banking has a set schedule. Only time his schedule changes is when the firm gets a new client.

"Yeah, he's out back with Dad."

Garlic, peppers, and smoked paprika float in the air and my mouth waters. "Hey, we having grilled onions and peppers?"

"If you cut 'em, I'll cook 'em."

My sister and I work in the kitchen like a well-oiled machine. When we were growing up, oftentimes we cooked dinner for everyone. Dad sometimes got stuck at the shop late, while Mom was wrapping up her latest words of wisdom for the local newspaper's advice column. And sometimes our baby sister, Jillian, got hungry earlier than everyone else. Mom taught us early on how to fend for ourselves and help around the house. We didn't always have to, but we loved giving her a break from the kitchen after a really long day.

I chop up large chunks of onion and bell pepper for Jasmine. She rotates between all the burners on the stove, stirring the taco meat, a pot of beans, another with corn, and now the onions and peppers. On the fifth burner—whoever came up with that idea is brilliant—is Tex-Mex rice. Once I finish with the veggies, I shred a big bowl of cheddar cheese and lug out the other toppings. Just before everything is ready, I lay the taco shells on a tray and toast them in the oven for a minute.

A moment later, I wander to the sliding glass doors that lead to the back patio and pool and poke my head out. "Dinner's ready."

Dad and Anton pop their heads up simultaneously as Dad rubs his hands together. "Perfect timing. I'm famished."

Everyone piles up their plates—Anton helps Lex with his—and we all sit down at the table built for six, but extends out for ten. We all wait to start eating until Jasmine has Lex situated in his booster chair. We have never been a religious family, but Mom always likes to say a few words of gratitude before we eat.

"I'm so glad everyone could be here tonight." Spartan barks in the living room and we all laugh. "You, too," Mom says. "Seriously, though. I'm grateful to have all three of my kids here, plus Anton and my baby boy, Lex. You all are the highlight of my week."

Smiles and *awe*s spread throughout the room. Moments like these are my favorite. Of course, we banter. What family doesn't? But these moments are the ones I hold close when I have a bad day. Like watching my nephew make a hot mess of his tacos and hearing my Mom laugh when my dad leans in and whispers in her ear. Truly the best.

"So, what's new with you, oh quiet brother of mine?" Jillian teases.

Jillian was a surprise baby. But she is the best little sister anyone could ever ask for. She keeps me levelheaded with her jokes and nagging. Where Jasmine is two years older than me, Jillian is seven years younger. For a mature young woman, sometimes she still acts like a teenager. She gives me clarity when I am stressed and makes me laugh when I am down.

"Nothing exciting," I answer. "Same stuff, new day. What about you? How's the wild world of fashion?"

She rolls her eyes. "Nice avoidance tactic, big bro. The store is great. Just got a glimpse at the spring line. We're putting in out just before Christmas."

I cock my head and stare at her. "It's not even winter, technically. Why so early?"

"You have so much to learn, dear brother. It's kind of like when car dealers put the next year's model out months before the year begins. Sales tactic." Jillian taps the side of her head as if her brain holds all the secrets.

Jillian is smart. Not like Mensa-smart, but pretty damn close. Her IQ is stellar. She graduated Salutatorian of her class in high school and graduated two years early—with honors— from college where she studied business and marketing.

At least she went to college. My path has been carved in stone since I picked up a wrench in Dad's garage. You don't need college to be a mechanic, but I did attend a trade/vocational school. I wanted the merits under my belt. Plus, school taught me more of the computerized auto information Dad occasionally searched for online. This way, we both brought something to the table.

And one day, when Dad finally decides it is time to retire his coveralls, I will take over Thompson's Garage and Body Specialists. Dad put a lot of time and energy and grease into our shop. I want him to be proud when I take over.

"I will never understand fashion," I tell her.

"True. And you're still avoiding my question," she repeats and I hang my head. The table goes silent and Jillian leans in closer. "If you don't want to talk about it, just tell me to shut up."

I laugh and she backs away. "You're fine. Just been a

rough week. But I'll be okay. And if not, you can tease me more." Off in the living room, Spartan barks. "You, too, buddy," I shout.

The rest of dinner goes by a little quieter. Conversations and laughter still carry on around the table, but the mood has tapered. They all know about Cora. Hell, they have met her and invited her to dinner a few times. They knew we were just friends, but thank god they bit their tongues about more. It has been obvious for years I had feelings for Cora, but no one ever shed light on those feelings. Which makes this whole new awkwardness a little less weird. Only a little, though.

Once everyone finishes eating, I help clear the table. "Hey, Mom?"

"Yeah, honey." She sidles up next to me and wraps her arm around my waist.

"You mind if I head out? Know it's early, but I have an appointment at eight."

She squeezes me harder for a second, then releases me. "Sure thing. What's the appointment?"

"Time to brighten up the canvas," I say with a smile on my face.

It is no secret Mom isn't a fan of tattoos, but she never judges. "Just don't understand the desire to sit in a chair for hours, in pain, while someone paints lines on your skin."

I laugh. "Maybe one day I will better explain it to you, but I need to head out so I'm not late." I kiss her forehead and she hugs me as close as humanly possible.

"See you next week. Love you."

"Love you, too," I tell her.

After I make my rounds, I leash Spartan and drive home to drop him off. Thankfully, the tattoo shop is close to the house. I check the time on the dash as we drive away from

Mom and Dad's. Spartan barks his goodbye before resuming his usual car window position.

~

I arrive at the tattoo shop with ten minutes to spare. Perfect amount of time to fill out paperwork and mentally prepare myself for being in the chair for more than an hour.

A bell chimes when I open the door and step inside. The same woman sits behind the counter. Her hot pink hair reminds me of the color candy companies give artificial watermelon. Nothing like the actual color of the fruit. She twirls a finger around the locks on her shoulders while she pops her bubble gum.

All I do is laugh internally. She is a strange mix of pinup girl and grunge princess. Hair to the nines. Clothes casual and baggy. I wonder if she dresses like this outside of the tattoo shop?

I step up to the counter. "Hey," I say, giving a small wave. "Jonas. I have an appointment."

Bubble gum princess peeks up at me and sits a little straighter. "Hey, Jonas." The way she says my name insinuates she holds secrets about me. She grabs a clipboard and hands it to me. "Fill this out and I need to make a copy of your ID."

Fishing my license out of my wallet, I hand it to her before sitting on one of the couches and filling out the standard paperwork. Once I finish, I hand it back to her and she hands me my license with a smirk.

"She'll be with you in a minute, sugar."

While I wait to be called back, I mindlessly stare at the funky art on the walls. Each drawing and painting has one of the shop's artist's name below with a price tag. Kind of cool the artists put work on display to show their individual talents.

"Jonas?" a soft, cheery voice calls out.

"That's…" I spin around and stop short at the petite brunette staring at me. Clearing my throat, I try again. "Sorry. I'm Jonas."

She smiles and the room brightens instantly. "Autumn. Follow me." I follow in her wake as she leads me to her booth.

Unabashedly, I check her out as she walks in front of me. Autumn is roughly six inches shorter than me, but leggy as hell. In a pair of black and white plaid-like skinny pants which hug every curve and a black top with straps looping around her neck and a dangerous dip at her cleavage. Her hips sway slightly when she walks, and I remind myself to keep my eyes at a gentleman's level—up. As we reach her booth, I notice the bandana in her hair. It matches her pants and is a simple accessory to her pinned-up locks.

"Have a seat," she says, gesturing to the chair in her booth. "Your paperwork says you're wanting to continue one of your half sleeves."

I nod and search for my voice. *Use your words, Thompson.* "Yeah. I brought the drawing with me." I hand over a folded paper.

Autumn takes the paper, unfolds it, and studies the intricate artwork. Artwork I spent weeks drawing. This piece is my right arm. The left is similar in design, but not the same. Only a true enthusiast would detect the dissimilarity.

She examines the lines, dots, and shading on the paper, then peers over at my arm. After several back and forth examinations, I wonder if it would be easier for me to take off my shirt. My shirt sleeves block at least half of the current art on my skin, and she is probably gauging where to start.

"Need me to take off my shirt?" I ask.

Her eyes lift from the paper and meet mine. *Fuck.* The most delectable glass of cognac stares back at me. Dark chocolate rims her irises, softening from brown to a golden, bold orange near her pupils. A light rouge pinks her pale cheeks.

"Um." She swallows. "Probably a good idea," she mumbles. "So I can see what's already done, of course."

Is she nervous? If so, it is adorable as fuck. Seriously, she has to have seen hundreds of people in her line of work. Work in the oddest places and a plethora of designs. I cringe mentally at the idea of her tattooing some asshole in awkward places. But pricks like that exist.

"Of course." I smile and tug my shirt over my head. If possible, her cheeks darken from a gentle blush to the soft petals of a pink rose and a surge of excitement floats beneath my sternum.

She swallows again and blinks rapidly. Her eyes drop back to the paper as she tucks her cherry red lips in her mouth. Is she fighting off a smile? When she keeps her eyes downcast too long for my liking, I lay my shirt over my chest in the hopes she will look up again. I need another shot of her cognac irises.

As soon as my torso is covered, she sighs. *Sighs.* The sound a mix of disappointment and relief. Dear god. This is going to be one of the longest tat sessions in history. And she won't even finish the rest of the design tonight.

Studying the current ink on my skin against the drawing, she bites the corner of her lip. I avert my gaze to the ceiling and pray to someone holier than me.

Please let me get through tonight unscathed. Please let me get through this without the embarrassment of a hard-on. At this rate, there's a high likelihood. I beg you, please.

"Be right back," Autumn says as she rises from her stool and strolls out of the booth. Once again, my eyes wander to her backside until she is out of sight.

I slide my shirt down and expose my skin to the cooler air. Let it temper my overheated skin as I take a few deep breaths.

But the fire Autumn created still burns hot. I love and hate how it simmers in my veins.

What the fuck is happening?

three

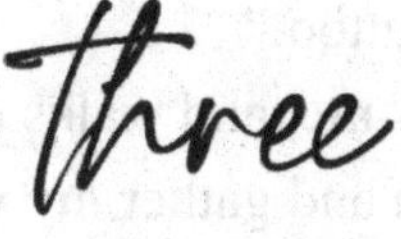

AUTUMN

Jonas's eyes scald me as I walk out of the booth. For the first time in years, I enjoy male attention. Jonas's attention. His eyes on me make my blood pump harder, faster.

As I make copies of his design to cut and put on transfer paper, Penny sneaks up from behind. "I was right, he is a hottie."

I jump and slap a hand to my chest. "Jesus, Pen. Don't do that."

"Do what?" She feigns innocence while smacking her bubble gum. Why didn't I hear the distinctive smack of her lips as she came up behind me?

"Scare the shit out of me."

She throws her head back and laughs. I glance over at Jonas—who seems oblivious to Penny's obnoxious chortle— then back at my friend. I narrow my eyes at her and she lifts her hands in surrender. "Sorry, not sorry. But I wasn't lying. He is hot."

I focus on my task—Jonas is a paying client, after all. "Yeah, I guess." A heatwave spreads across my skin.

Penny leans in closer and scrutinizes my every move.

"You guess?" Keeping my head down, I peek up at her. She smiles at me with wicked intent. "Girly, you must be blind if you don't recognize a good-looking man when you see one."

The printer finishes and I grab the transfer paper. "I'm not blind. Okay? Just trying to breathe through the next two hours of my night. So" —I point to her chair— "go back to your desk and do what you do. And don't pester me. Last thing I need is to fuck up his tattoo."

She giggles, salutes me, and walks off. "Yes, dear."

I take a deep breath and gather my wits.

You can do this, Autumn. He is just another guy in your chair. A hot guy. Shut up!

When I turn the corner of my booth and glance over at Jonas, I stop breathing. Since I left, he has pushed his shirt down his chest and sits perfectly still with his eyes closed. Is he sleeping? Stepping over to my stool, I set the papers down on the counter. His eyes remain closed as I start prepping for our session.

Part of me wants his eyes open. A big part.

As if I professed it aloud, Jonas opens his eyes just as I glance up at him. My stomach flips and I swallow. I have never seen eyes like his. Such fascinating shades of blue with a burst of sunshine at the center. As if his DNA couldn't decide whether to make his eyes blue or hazel. I prefer the indecision.

"So, I printed off more than what I'll actually work on tonight. Some of what I printed, you already have done. But I did that so I could line it up."

Jonas nods. "No problem. You know what you're doing. I'm not concerned."

He closes his eyes and lays his head back again. My whole body sags at the loss. "I need to shave your forearm.

Thankfully" —I trace the corded muscles in his forearms with my fingertips— "most people won't notice the difference." His eyes pop open and lock on mine. I try swallowing the lump in my throat. "Your arms aren't really hairy. It won't look weird when I shave it, is what I mean."

He smiles and a dimple accentuates his left cheek. A dimple I want to kiss.

Shut up, Autumn. He is your client.

"I don't care either way."

When I think he is going to close his eyes again, he surprises me. Instead, his eyes drop to where I lather soap on his arm. I dry off the gloves and pick up a disposable razor. Inch by inch, I swipe the razor over his skin. Finished, I wet a paper towel and wipe away any excess soap.

After I rub a thin layer of natural moisturizer on his skin, I line up the stencil on his forearm and press it in place. I peel back the paper and smile at the purple lines on his skin. On the small rolling table next to my stool, I set his original drawing next to the small ink caps filled with black ink.

Jonas closes his eyes again as I go through the process of opening the sterile needle pack and loading it on my gun. I run through my usual routine and make sure I have everything ready before I start. Once everything is set, I pick up the gun and press the pedal on the floor.

When the gun buzzes to life in my hand, the old familiar joy of why I do this kick-starts my adrenaline.

As a child, I always loved to color and draw. The older I became, the more I honed my craft. I took every possible elective art class in school. Somehow, I also managed to coerce the art teacher during my sophomore year to give me art lessons outside normal class hours. We worked at the school, of course, and she gave me extra credit—which I didn't mind, but also didn't ask for. Through Ms. Gibson's lessons, I learned to love art over everything. She taught me every medium and how to open my imagination beyond what the human eye sees.

I took those lessons and the skills I learned, and eventually discovered my preferred canvas. Skin.

Leaning forward, I stretch the skin near Jonas's elbow and press the buzzing needle forward. He startles, then relaxes. "Okay?" I ask, not looking up.

"Yeah," he answers, voice scratchy. "No matter how many times I've been under the needle, when it first hits my skin, I jump."

I nod but don't look up. "Me too."

For the first ten or fifteen minutes, I work in silence and locate my rhythm. Every person you work on is different. Depending on their age, how often they are in the sun, and how well they take care of themselves determines how easy or difficult it is to work on them. Skin is skin. But at different stages of life, it has different density and elasticity. The older you are, the thinner your skin is. It is a natural progression. Also, the more exposed to the elements—sun, wind, level of humidity, and so on—you are, the more your skin is impacted.

Jonas has nice skin. Slightly tan. Not the type of tan you get from regular visits to the beach. Jonas's tanned skin is from everyday activity—mowing the yard, jogging outdoors, driving with his arm out the window or the top down. For a moment, I picture him in a lush, green yard. Black shirt stretched taut on his broad chest. Khaki cargo shorts hanging low on his hips. A bright smile and that adorable dimple on his face as he pushes a little girl on the swings.

I lift the gun from his skin, turn my face away from him, and cough into my elbow.

Stop it, Autumn.

"Grab some water," Jonas says as I spin back his way.

"I'm good. Just a tickle." I play off the softball-sized lump of emotion in my throat. What I need is a distraction. "So, Jonas…" His eyes shift from my hand dipping the needle in the ink cap to my eyes. "Tell me about yourself."

His Adam's apple bobs in my periphery before he sits a little taller. "What would you like to know?"

I bring the gun back to his arm and spark it to life again. "Girlfriend? Wife? Kids? All the good stuff."

"The good stuff, huh?" He snorts and I peek up at him for a second before refocusing on my work. "I'd laugh, but I don't want to throw you off." Out of the corner of my eye, he points to where I am currently working on a flower of life pattern.

"I appreciate that. No way I'd be able to sleep if I jacked up your tat."

"Good stuff," he mumbles then goes silent for a moment. "No girlfriend or wife." And I can tell—without looking up— his face is turned away. It piques my curiosity. "No kids. Unless fur children count. If that's the case, then I have one. Spartan. He's three."

"Spartan. He a fighter?" I ask.

He laughs, but not enough to jostle his arm. "Nah. He's a big softy. Fifty-seven pounds of pure energy. Loves hugs and barking."

Now it is my turn to laugh. "What kind of dog is he?"

"Husky."

I pause and meet Jonas's eyes. "So, a fur baby. But no fur baby mama?" My retort is meant to be funny, but a gray cloud suddenly masks his joy.

"Nope. No fur baby mama."

I hate how sad he sounds right now. Hate that I wrecked his mood. "Want to talk about it?"

First and foremost, I am no therapist. But far too often, people sit in this chair and spill some of the craziest details of their life history. Some fascinate me. Others… not so much. But I have learned over the years to just go with the flow. If people need to get things off their chest, I let them. Not like I am the gossiping sort.

"Yes. No. I don't know." He looks away and I slump at the obvious discomfort I spurred.

Instead of pestering him, I continue working on his tat. If Jonas wants to divulge whatever is bothering him, he will. A few minutes pass and neither of us says a word. But I feel his eyes on me. Not on my hand as it holds the gun and carves intricate black lines into his skin. No, his eyes are on *me*. A buzz ripples through my body. A buzz that has absolutely nothing to do with the tattoo gun vibrating in my right hand.

"My best friend just got married," he whispers. Voice so soft I almost miss it.

I stop working and gauge his expression. Eyes sad. Smile absent. Shoulders low. Everything in his body language tells me he is upset or disappointed over this marriage. "Not my place to ask, but shouldn't you be happy for him?"

"Her," he corrects.

Ah. There it is. The fine line detail. His female best friend just got married. And he isn't too keen on the idea.

"Shouldn't you be happy for her?"

He nods. "As painful as it is, I am happy for her. She's with the one person she can't live without. They've known each other since high school, but his family moved away when he was in high school. They reunited this past spring."

There is a peculiar familiarity to the story he tells me.

Could be sheer coincidence. But it might not be. What are the odds?

"This might be weird." And suddenly, I have his full attention. "But is your best friend Cora?"

His eyes widen at the mention of her name and a ball of jealousy forms beneath my diaphragm. His expression tells me he considered her more than a friend, but she never did. Most women would cringe at the notion. Me? I bask in it.

Bask in the fact he never overstepped his bounds with her. As quickly as my jealousy formed, it melts away.

Over the last seven months, I got to know Cora. Mostly through text and the occasional girls' night, where we had dinner and a movie at her house. She is super sweet. Told me about this guy she had known for years—who she had given the same title. Best friend.

Don't know the dirty details of Jonas's life, but I do know Cora thinks highly of him.

"He just needs to find the right woman, you know. Someone who will make him smile and laugh. Someone who will hug him tight and make every day better than the last."

Her words come back to me from a couple weeks ago at her bachelorette party. I had no clue who she was talking about, but she wanted to make it her life's mission to see her best friend happy.

Now I know why.

He swallows. "Yeah. You know her?"

I lock eyes with him and nod. "Yep. Did her and Gavin's tattoos back in April. We've chatted and hung out here and there. Attended their wedding." His eyes sparkle at this fact. "She never mentioned your name. And, obviously, we never all hung out at the same times."

"Obviously." He averts his gaze and mumbles, "I would definitely remember you."

I smile at the words I am sure he didn't mean for me to hear. "Back atcha."

He faces me again with a soft smile on his lips. "It hasn't been easy seeing her with Gavin, but I keep telling myself everything happens for a reason. Keep reminding myself she was never mine to keep. Not in the way I originally intended."

I continue working on his tattoo. "Sometimes, people come into our life to teach us something. Not necessarily like an actual teacher. In your case, maybe Cora taught you how to open your heart. How to love someone in a nonfamilial way. She may not be the person you're meant to love, but she helped teach you what love *feels* like."

He sits quietly in the chair for a few minutes as I get closer to the center of the flower of life in the middle of his forearm.

Did I say too much? Go too far?

From what Cora told me, her "best friend"—aka Jonas—has crushed on her for years. Several years. Honestly, I lived vicariously through her. The fact she had one man pining over her while she was in love with another… color me jealous and envious and dark, dark green.

Just as I start to apologize for stepping over the line, Jonas speaks up. "I never looked at it like that. Actually puts it in a whole new perspective." He hums. "Not as if it concerns you, but I've been slowly working on letting her go. Not fully. She is my best friend, after all. But I've been trying to disconnect myself from her romantically. See her more like a sister or one of the guys. Know what I mean?"

"I do," I tell him. "But it's easy to say 'you are my friend.' The difficult part is accepting it."

"Yeah. Weeks before the wedding—which I did not see you at, by the way—I repeatedly told myself she was never mine to have. That I needed to find a way to get over her. Move on." I feel his eyes on me again. "I'm getting there," he whispers.

"I'm getting there." What exactly does that mean?

"You think?" I glance at him as I dip the needle into the ink cap.

Eyes locked on mine, the corners of his mouth tip up the slightest bit. "Yes."

Dear God. Please forgive me. But I really want to sin with this man.

I am the last person in the world anyone would consider to be religious. My history could sway the decision either way. But this man makes me want to drop to my knees, hold his gaze, and pray for him to let me make his life better.

I may not be a miracle worker, but I could do many miraculous things to this man.

"W-well that's great," I say with a little too much enthusiasm.

In turn, he laughs. And since I don't have the tattoo gun anywhere near his skin, he laughs harder than earlier. Deeper. Throatier. Louder. So loud, Penny and Rex—another artist in the shop—glance our way. Penny's eyebrows waggle and I roll my eyes at her.

When I sleep tonight, I will dream of his laugh and the way my insides swirl at the sound. The way my body sparks to life.

"Glad you think so," he teases. "Your turn." I cock my head to the side and narrow my eyes. "Tell me about you," he clarifies.

"Ah. Tit for tat, huh?"

He smirks and I realize the innuendo he has created from my words. "If that's what you want to c-call it." I love his slight stutter at the end. His jitters as we tease.

"What would you like to know?" I prompt.

He taps his chin with his free hand. "Boyfriend? Husband? Kids?"

Keeping my face down as I work on him, I stop breathing for a minute.

You can do this, Autumn. Baby steps.

I smile at his arm, but, if he saw my face head-on, he would know the smile is forced. So, I keep my head down. "No boyfriend or husband. Most guys I've dated were grossly immature. Don't get me wrong, I love silliness every once in a while. But some guys don't know when to be serious."

"I hate how I'm automatically lumped into this category because of the extremity between my legs." For a moment, I glance at his groin. No doubt he notices. *Great.* "But I get where you're coming from. I know plenty of guys who act exactly how you're describing them."

"Not trying to harp on the male species. Just noting the history I've had with them. Hasn't really worked in my favor."

I sit up straighter as I wipe excess ink off his arm. When he remains silent for a minute, I meet his gaze. He just… looks at me. Looking at me like no one else has. As if trying to read more into what I say. Tapping into my brain and digging for unanswered questions. Answers I am not ready to divulge yet.

"Sorry to hear. But you shouldn't give up."

I cock a brow at him. "No?"

He shakes his head. "Definitely not."

His words are laced with more. Emotions left unsaid. The

sentiment weighs heavy and I blink rapidly to snap myself back to reality.

Is he suggesting what I think he is? When he says I shouldn't give up, is he inviting me to give him a shot? *"Definitely not."* His answer repeats in my head over and over. Unsure how to process it, I change the subject.

"What do you think?" He scrunches his brow. "Your ink? It's done. Well, done for tonight. What do you think?"

I grab a fresh paper towel and the alcohol blend I use to clean it up. Squirting some on the paper towel, I swipe the damp cloth over his skin and clean up the fresh tattoo.

"Perfect," he whispers.

And for a moment, I wonder if he's only referring to the tattoo. When I peek up, his eyes aren't on his forearm. They are on me.

The intensity of his stare sends a shock wave of heat across my flesh. Under the thin material of my bra, my nipples harden. At the apex of my thighs, dampness slicks my skin. I press my legs closer together and pray he doesn't notice. Pray he doesn't call me out. Because if he studies my reaction hard enough—pun intended—he will know exactly where my head is at.

Why has it been so long? Why the hell have I denied myself for so many years? And why has it worked until now?

"Thanks," I whisper back.

The answer to all three questions is simple. Because I have been waiting. For the right guy. For a guy like Jonas.

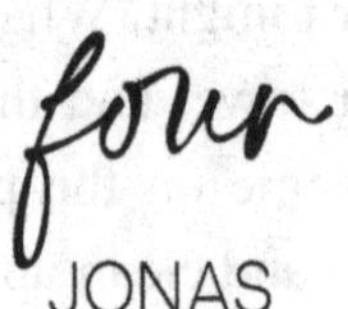

four

JONAS

I soak up every line and curve of Autumn's profile as she cleans the new addition to my sleeve. Never thought I would say this about another woman, but damn, she is beautiful.

Autumn has a classic beauty, not one born of facials and layers of makeup. A heart-shaped face with a slender button nose and full lips. Scarlet paints her lips while a thin black wingtip accentuates her eyes. The only additions I note. We may be surrounded by beaches, but her alabaster skin tells me it isn't a place she frequents. A full sleeve of flowers and vines is inked on her right arm. And the style of her clothes and how she has her hair pinned… she reminds me of a modern-day pinup girl.

My pinup girl.

The errant thought catches me off guard, but I don't dismiss it. Not yet.

Autumn is a breath of fresh air. The fresh air I didn't think would filter through my lungs ever again. A new breath of life. Invigorating.

Beside me, she adheres a thin film to the new ink. Lifting her eyes to mine, I hold her swirly cognac gaze as she explains the new product. "Not sure if you've used this yet, but it's called Saniderm." I glance down at the clear film on my skin for a beat. When I shake my head, she continues. "It's a new, breathable way to protect your tattoo while it heals." She goes over the specifics and I get lost in the sound of her voice.

How have I not seen her until now?

The answer sits on the tip of my tongue. I won't say it. Not even in my thoughts. Let's just say I was otherwise distracted.

Now, though… I see clearly. The curtains over my eyes have been shoved to the wayside. The light of a new day shines bright. Has me seeing the world I have ignored for years.

When Autumn stops her spiel on tattoo care—which she knows I am obviously familiar with because of my previous tattoos—she stands and leads me back to the front desk. Call me a pig, but I eat up every inch of her as she walks in front of me. How can I not?

"Hey, Penny," she says, talking to the pink-haired woman behind the front desk. "Will you add Jonas on my schedule for next week. Wednesday or after." Autumn leans on the counter, pops her hip out, and faces me. *Someone rescue me from my depraved thoughts.* "If that works for you."

I nod, not trusting my voice yet. After I swallow a couple times, I pray to not sound like a prepubescent boy. "Yeah." *Thank fuck.* "Thursday might be easier, though."

"It's a date," she says as her face flushes rosy. She tucks both her lips in her mouth and clamps down before releasing them. "See you next week."

"Next week," I reply.

She scurries off to her booth and it's fucking adorable how

flustered Autumn is. *Me too*, I want to tell her. Because this is the first time I have felt so immediately enamored by a woman. Although I undoubtedly loved—still love—Cora, my heart never hummed with her. Never galloped. Nor did I forget to breathe around her.

Maybe Autumn was right. Maybe Cora was a lesson. The lesson which taught me nonfamilial love.

Cora was never mine to love. I know this now. She was just a star in the constellation leading me to where I belong. And the constellation shines brighter than any other star in the galaxy now.

My constellation.

Penny cashes me out and I hand her a tip to give Autumn. "I'll make sure she gets it, sugar. What day works best for your next appointment?"

Getting here tonight after the weekly family dinner was cutting it close. I would rather get here a little earlier, so I am not here until ten at night. Although I don't need to be at the garage until eight each morning, I usually arrive between six and seven to help Dad catch up on invoices.

"Is Thursday at six available?"

Penny leans close to the computer monitor, rests her chin on her palm, and clicks the mouse a few times. Her eyes flick across the screen as she scrolls down. She pops her bubble gum once then looks up. "Six is all yours, sugar." Her fingers run across the keyboard. "Probably another two-hour appointment."

I nod. "Thanks. See you next week."

She leans back in her chair, pops her gum, and gives me a spirited wave goodbye.

As I reach the door to leave, I glance over my shoulder toward Autumn's booth. She stands frozen in place, eyes on me, with a new wave of crimson on her cheeks at being caught ogling. A wide smile tugs at my cheeks as I raise a hand and wave her direction. She timidly lifts her hand and returns my smile with one of her own.

I turn just in time to not smack into the door and make a fool out of myself.

Walking out of the shop, I head for the Jeep, hop in, and crank it to life. I sit in the lamplit parking lot for a few minutes and stare at the steering wheel in a fog. Although nothing extraordinary happened over the last two hours, the most mysterious and alluring woman blipped on my radar.

How the hell am I supposed to function for the next week? On a shitload of caffeine and daydreams, that is how.

Daydreams of an exquisite, petite pinup woman named Autumn.

The alarm squawks on the bedside table. I roll over and slap the snooze bar as Spartan vaults onto the bed and licks my face.

Swinging my arms in the air, I jerk my face left and right. "Spartan." I laugh at his relentlessness. "Stop, stop, stop." I cover my face with my hands and he starts licking my ear. "Argh! Okay, I'm up."

I wrap my arms around Spartan's belly and wrestle him on the bed for a minute before I slip out of the covers and turn off the alarm clock. He jumps off the bed and bolts for the front door, barking. After a quick trip to the bathroom, I throw on a hoodie, sweatpants, and sneakers, then hook Spartan's leash to his collar.

Out the door, we wander in the dark around the neighborhood. Houses on the street only illuminated by porch lights. Most of the windows still dark as residents continue to sleep.

Spartan sniffs and marks as many patches of grass, bushes, and signposts as possible. Cool air whips through my hair and, for the first time ever, it invigorates me. For years, I gravitated toward all things sunny and warm. Now, I discover a new appreciation for the opposite.

The cool breeze reminds me of fresh starts and new beginnings. Something I am in desperate need of.

"Spartan," I call out. He glances back at me a second, but doesn't stop tugging me forward. "I met someone." Funny enough, he barks.

I laugh. "You'd like her, buddy. Real pretty." He stops, sniffs at something I can't see on the sidewalk, and I run into him. "Whatcha got there?" But before I get close enough to see what caught his attention, he drags me forward again. "Anyway. She's really pretty. Like the women in fashion magazines or something." He barks again and I shush him. Last thing I need is for an angry neighbor to complain my dog woke them up at five in the morning.

So, for the rest of our trip around the neighborhood, I stay quiet while Spartan takes me for a walk.

Once we get back home, I jump in the shower. The instructions for this new tattoo cover say I shower normally with it on, just not to scrub it. Tattoo innovations—gotta love 'em. Out of the shower, I scramble a couple eggs, fry up a few pieces of bacon, and butter some toast. In no time, breakfast fills my stomach.

I secure Spartan in his crate, turn on the radio to our favorite rock station, and head out the door.

It's no surprise Dad is already at the garage when I arrive.

Parking my motorcycle behind the building, I stroll into the office and greet him with a thermos of coffee.

"Morning, Dad."

He pops his head up, checks the time on the clock over the door, and smiles at me. "Up early today?"

I set the thermos in front of him and grab his mug from the small dish rack and hand it to him. When Dad bought this garage in 1980, he cleaned it up and changed a few things around before opening. Dad had worked in several mechanic and body shops prior to owning Thompson's Garage. He knew the ins and outs of daily activity. Knew what made a shop dysfunctional and what made it flow with ease. Taking bits and pieces of all the things he loved, he set up this garage.

Thompson's Garage and Body Specialists has four bays total. One bay is used for bodywork, unless we have no body-work to work on. Each bay is only separated by the occasional pillar and larger machines. Along the back wall of the garage is section after section of chrome and black industrial automo-tive cabinetry. Every tool we possibly need inside. And if we don't have it, Dad orders it.

He also added a small kitchen dinette and a couch and small table in the office space of the garage. One thing he said bugged him at most shops he worked at was how they didn't have simple necessities—a sink for dishes, a fridge, and a small table for lunch (and breakfast for the early birds). Or a place to sleep on exhausting days. Dad made sure Thomp-son's had all of those, plus some counter space and a few cabinets.

Our garage was voted top family-owned mechanic of the Bay Area ten times. And we take pride in our work.

"Nah. Just moved faster than usual." I laugh and he joins in. "Best night of sleep in a while, I guess."

He fills his mug with coffee as I grab the creamer from the fridge and sugar on the counter. Setting it down, I pour my own mugful. We both add cream and sugar, and sit in silence a moment as we take the first few sips. Something Dad and I have in common is our morning routine. Maybe it's because I am the only son and I wanted to be just like him growing up. Or I could chalk it up to the fact we both wake up crazy early Monday to Friday and share the same job.

"What changed?" he asks after sufficiently caffeinated. I furrow my brow. "What happened after dinner last night? Said you slept better."

I smile and bring the mug to my lips. He studies me when I don't answer and shakes his head, following it up with a smile that matches my own.

Dad and I, for as long as I can remember, share a secret language. As a child, I dubbed it the *Boys Only Club*. That's how I kept my older sister away. Jillian was a baby during the age of *Boys Only*, so I never worried about her. Over the years, it evolved and I learned Dad and I just shared the same mindset. He is simply an older version of me.

I lift my arm and show him the new addition to my sleeve. "Went to the tattoo shop last night."

"Son, tattoos don't make you smile." He points at me as he shakes his head. "Not like an idiot, anyway."

Slapping a hand to my chest, I gape at him. "You wound me."

"Dumbass." He laughs.

I finish off my mug and set it down. "Met someone. A woman," I clarify. "She works at the tattoo shop."

"And?" Dad drawls out the one-word question.

"And I don't know. Couldn't stop looking at her. Or

thinking about her. We talked the two hours I was there. Not sure, but I don't think the feelings are one-sided."

He nods, drinks the last of his coffee, and looks me square in the eyes. "Well, it's nice to see you smile again." Rising from his chair, he goes to the sink and washes out his mug before setting it in the rack. "Time to get to work."

And just like that, the conversation ends. Another great thing about the relationship Dad and I share is how we don't need all the nitty-gritty details. If either of us wants to disclose something, we will.

One day, I hope to have more to share with him.

five
AUTUMN

"Leaving the mall now."

I pin the phone between my shoulder and ear as I fumble through my purse for the keys. "Find anything good?" Penny asks on the other end. In the background, I hear my favorite sound ever. Little girl giggles.

"Show you when I get home. Just need to stop and pick up a few more ingredients for the lasagna. Anything else we need?"

I unlock the door, slide into the car, and toss my bags on the passenger seat. Cranking the ignition, I pull the phone away when the engine lags and rumbles rougher than usual. I shrug as the roar settles in its typical hum.

Bringing the phone back to my ear, Penny rambles on. Who knows what I missed. "And will you grab Twizzlers, popcorn, M&M's, Red Hots, and Mike and Ike's. Oh, and ice cream." God, she probably rattled off twenty other different forms of junk food before I paid attention. Oh well.

"Are we serving sugar comas for dessert," I joke. "We do not need all of that."

"Hey," Penny says in a stern motherly voice. "We *need* them for movie time. Don't be a Debbie Downer, Auti."

I laugh. "Alright, I'm hanging up now. Should only be another thirty minutes. You guys okay?"

More giggles. Tickle-fest giggles. "We're fine. Drive safe and see you soon."

Disconnecting the call, I toss my phone in my purse and back out of the space. Two miles down the road, the car idles high at a red light. I check the gauges and note nothing looks off. No warning lights light up the display. Giving the dash a gentle tap, I tell the car we are almost done for the day.

Inside the grocery store, I snatch up the final missing ingredients for our Sunday night lasagna. Reluctantly, I grab a handful of sugary snacks for movie night per Penny's request. After checking out, I head back to my car, slip inside, and go to start it.

But the engine doesn't turn over.

I crank the key again. Nothing. No ticking or whining. Not a single sound.

"Well shit," I say, slapping my hands against the steering wheel.

Digging my phone out of my purse, I call Penny. "Are they out of Cherry Garcia? Please tell me they aren't."

"Pen, my car won't start."

The television mutes in the background. "Won't start? Does it sound like it's trying?"

I shake my head, then remember she can't see me. "No. It sounded off when I left the mall, but nothing bad. Just louder."

"Need me to come get you?"

Giggles erupt in my ear. "No, stay with her. I'll call for a tow truck. Hopefully it won't take long."

"You at our usual store?"

"Yeah, why?"

When Penny doesn't answer right away, I pull the phone away from my ear to see if the call dropped. Nope, still connected. "Sorry," she says when I bring the phone back to my ear. "Was looking up tow places nearby. Looks like there's one a couple miles away. I'll text you the number."

A second later, my phone pings with an incoming text. "Got it, thanks."

"Sure thing. Keep me posted."

"I will."

After hanging up with Penny, I dial the number she sent to me. A gruff voice answers and I explain my situation and ask if he can tow my car. Thankfully, I am met with a resounding yes. The man tells me he should arrive within thirty minutes.

While waiting for him, I turn the key one click in the ignition and listen to the radio. *At least it's not the battery and I don't have to wait in silence.* Five songs and two commercials later, an older man pulls up behind me with a flatbed.

As I step out of the car, he strolls forward staring at my Betsy and whistles. "Where'd you get a beauty like this?" he asks.

"Long story short, it was my granddad's. He restored it and passed it on to me."

"Well she's a beaut." The man extends his hand my way. "Name's Aaron."

I shake his hand. "Autumn. Thanks for coming to my rescue."

"Tell me what seems to be the problem."

I explain to Aaron what happened earlier when I left the mall and at the traffic light. Then how it wouldn't start when I walked out of the store. Thank goodness I didn't buy any perishables.

"Mind if I give it a try right quick?" Aaron asks.

I shake my head and gesture to the driver's side door. He sits in the car a moment and turns the key a few times, leaning closer to the dash. He listens intently, trying to locate the source of the issue. A minute later, he hops out and closes the door.

"Not sure what's wrong with her, but I'll give it a full rundown at the shop in the morning. Anything you need to grab out of the car before I get it on the flatbed?"

"Just a few bags."

After I collect my bags and purse, Aaron loads Betsy up on the truck. Soon, we are driving down the road toward his shop. A mix of gasoline and pine-scented cardboard trees fills the cab. Aaron whistles along with a country music song on the radio as he taps his fingers on the steering wheel.

I glance over at his profile and can't help but think he looks familiar. Not sure how, but his profile gives me déjà vu. But I shake it off and stop scrutinizing him.

Just as another song starts on the radio, we pull into the parking lot of an auto repair shop. The exterior a bright and bold blue with an oval white sign in the center. Thompson's Garage is swirled in the same blue on the white sign. Several cars are parked on the side of the building, shaded from the afternoon sun by a handful of various trees.

As Aaron circles the lot and starts to back up to one of the white bay doors, it rolls up. I look in the side mirror, but don't see anyone and assume Aaron must have pressed a garage door opener.

When the truck stops fifteen feet from the bay, I glance over at him and he gives me a warm smile. "Time to get your girl inside. Then we'll do paperwork. Do you need a ride home?"

"No, I'll request an Uber. Thank you." We hop out and I hear him talking over the Diesel engine on the opposite side. I walk around the front of the truck, ready to ask him to repeat himself. "What was…"

Words fail me as I round the tow truck and none other than Jonas is eyeing my Betsy with a giddy expression. He says something to Aaron, and I can't quite make it out. He starts to say something else, turns his head to face Aaron, and spots me.

A brilliant smile lights up his face and Aaron notices. "Hey," Jonas says as he walks past Aaron, heading straight for me. "Is this you?" He points up at Betsy.

I nod. "Yeah. She won't start."

"Dad just told me." *Dad?* Now the déjà vu makes sense. Similar profiles because they are from the same gene pool. "Sorry she's being stubborn. We'll fix her up for you."

I smile. "Thanks, I appreciate it."

Aaron sidles up to us. "Jonas, you know this pretty lady?"

Before Jonas answers, I speak up. "We just met. I work at the tattoo shop a few miles down the street." I point to Jonas's forearm. "Worked on his newest addition."

A wide, toothy smile stretches from ear to ear on Aaron's face. "Huh." Aaron glances to Jonas then back to me. "Well you did a great job, sweetheart." He throws a wink my way. "Gonna unload your girl here. Shouldn't be long."

"Thank you." Once Aaron is out of earshot, I face Jonas again. "That's your dad?"

"Yep. And this is our shop."

Oh, wow. Suddenly, I am wondering if there were any

photos online of the shop owners when Penny chose this place. Sneaky wench. Not sure if I should hit or thank her.

Not sure what to say, I glance up at the sign on the building. "So, has your dad owned it since eighty?"

Jonas follows my gaze. "Yeah. He'd been saving for years. Worked as many hours as he could to still pay the bills plus save. Lucky for Dad, the bank took over the place from the previous owner and he purchased it cheaper than expected. Kismet, I suppose."

"Kismet," I mumble.

I had never given much thought or energy to the term. Fate. Destiny. Devine providence. Fate had its place in the world, I suppose, but the idea of some outside force steering me this way or that way didn't sit right with me. I liked believing I was in control of my life. That I made the rules and held the power. The notion of being in control, I could apply it to so many scenarios from my past.

No one held power over me.

But the idea of kismet is starting to grow on me. How else could I explain meeting Cora and Gavin, and, by proxy, Jonas? Did they just stumble into a random tattoo shop? Or did some invisible force guide them my way? Not sure I will ever know the true answer. And the more I think about it, the more my head hurts.

What I did know for certain was Jonas walked in. He sat in my chair. And my heart somersaulted like a gymnast for hours. By the way he looks at me right now, I would venture to guess Jonas's heart is flipping and twirling too.

"While Dad unloads your car, we can step into the office and start the paperwork."

"Okay."

Jonas leads us into a spacious room on the south side of

the building. As we step inside, I scan the room and see a couple rows of chairs next to a table with a Keurig and coffee fixings. A large window consumes half of the south wall and brightens the room naturally. A rack of magazines sits beside the coffee station and a small flat screen hangs near the ceiling. The large window is partially cut off by a wall, which looks to be an addition to the original structure. That specific wall is painted with a mural of the shop, I assume, when it first opened.

Jonas leads us through a door and into an office, where the large window continues. Two desks sit butted up against one another. There is a small kitchen/dinette area and a plush couch with a coffee table. The walls have a coat of beige paint with several framed photos—which I can't make out without closer inspection. Cozy—for an auto repair shop.

"Have a seat," Jonas says, gesturing to a chair near one of the desks. "Let me just grab the paperwork." He sits at one of the desks and rummages through a drawer. Retrieving a triplicate form, he puts it on a clipboard, grabs a pen, and leans back in his chair. "Just a few questions and then you can head out." Then he glances up from the form. "Do you need a ride? I can take you home, if you want."

I shake my head. "Nah. I'll grab an Uber. Only live a mile or two from here, so shouldn't cost much."

He nods, then prattles off a handful of questions. Name. Address. Phone number. When he asks for my number, I stumble for a moment. *Your phone number is for the paperwork, idiot.* At least that is what I tell myself. He continues the questionnaire as if he fills them out a thousand times a day. Most of it was simple maintenance history on the car.

After all the questions, I sign the bottom and he gives me

a copy. "Once we get a look under the hood in the morning, we'll call you and let you know what we found."

"Sounds great." I rise from the chair, grab my purse and shopping bags. Retrieving my phone, I open up the Uber app and request a ride.

"Sure I can't give you a ride?"

I shake my phone in front of him and smile. "Already got one. Thanks, though."

"Mine is better," he teases.

No doubt about that. Heat crawls up my neck and blazes across my cheeks. "What if my Uber driver pulls up in a snappy sports car?" I joke.

He rolls his eyes and laughs. "Mine would still be better."

We wander out of the office and back into the sticky, Florida fall weather. Just outside the building, we pause under an awning. The sun still shines down from above, but is slowly fading as afternoon drifts closer to evening.

Beside me, I *feel* Jonas's eyes on my profile. Tracing the angle of my jaw to my chin with his hypnotic eyes. Skirting them up to my lips and honing in on them. I tuck my lips in my mouth for one, two, three before I pop them back out. And I don't miss the soft groan from him.

"Can I call you?" he asks.

I peek up at him and his eyes are exactly where I knew them to be. "About the car?" I play innocent, but know his question has nothing to do with the car.

In slow motion, he shakes his head and meets my gaze. "You know I'll call about the car." His eyes drop to my lips for a split second before returning back north, and my heart skips. "What I mean is, can I call you" —he pauses and licks his lips— "and take you out sometime?"

Every atom inside my tiny five-foot-five frame jumps up

and down like I just won a million dollar lottery. Because Jonas is definitely a prize. A prize any woman would be lucky to hold in her arms. So why am I hesitant? What is stopping me from blurting out *yes, yes, yes* at the top of my lungs. I know the answer to this question. It's a question I have had to answer several times over the years. But it's an answer I keep to myself.

"Jonas… I-I don't know…" His eyes wilt as his shoulders sag. *Damnit.* "It's not that I don't want to."

And just like that, hope glints anew in his eyes.

This is going to be so much harder than I imagined.

Six

JONAS

She likes me. I see it in the upward curve of her lips. In the extra sparkle in her eyes. How her breathing changes. The way she automatically leans an inch closer. She likes me, but is afraid to admit it.

"What is it then?" I run my fingers through my hair. "Am I too pretty for you?" I tease.

Autumn throws her head back and laughs. The sound bubbly like a fountain-style cherry cola. "Maybe." She waves her hand up and down my body. "I mean, how's a girl going to compete with this?" Her words are meant as a joke, but they heat me from head to toe.

When I finally get my wits about me again, I say, "Swear I'm not always this pretty."

She laughs again and shakes her head. "You're persistent, aren't you?"

I shrug. "Only with people who count."

At this, her smile softens. Becomes more shy. "Jonas…" She steps closer to me and I pick up hints of vanilla and something fruity—cherry, maybe. "I really would love to talk more and go out sometime, but…"

At the tattoo shop the other day, she said she wasn't seeing anyone. Right? "But?"

"I- I have other obligations."

What does *other obligations* mean?

Maybe she has a sick family member she helps when not at work. Or maybe she works more than one job. I never really took that into consideration. Could be something completely innocent. She could be a volunteer at a shelter or attend school during the day.

But does she have said obligations every day of the week? I wouldn't think so.

"Well, if you ever find yourself free of said obligations for a teeny, tiny minute, I would love to take you out. I'm willing to beg, if necessary." I glance over at Dad who continues to ogle Autumn's car. "Dad would never let me live it down if I got on my knees and groveled. But I'm willing to live with the incessant teasing."

She laughs again, and I press record in my mind. I love the carefree sound and want to play it on repeat. A white SUV pulls into the lot and Autumn glances down at her phone.

"My ride is here." She locks her phone and drops it in her black, white, and red purse which looks strikingly similar to a bowling bag, only smaller. "Let me see your phone."

I glance down at her outstretched palm. Without hesitation, I pull my phone from my back pocket, unlock it, and hand it over. Polished nails matching the rouge on her lips tap with efficiency over the screen. Seconds later, her phone pings in her bag and she hands me back my phone.

"Gotta go." She salutes me. "Talk to you later."

My head drifts in the clouds. I watch as she gets in the SUV and buckles up. I wave as the car drives off and just stand there like an idiot. Hand still up a minute later. Snapping out of my fog, I unlock my phone and stare down at the screen where she messaged herself from my phone.

> Can't wait for you to call.

A smile slowly creeps across my face as I fixate on the simple text. *Me either*.

"So, that's her, huh?"

I jump. "Argh! Dad, you scared the shit out of me."

He laughs. "Guess there's a first for everything. She must have you all kinds of twisted up if your old man scared ya."

"Guess so."

He points to my phone. "If my instincts are right—which let's get real, they always are—she's a keeper."

Yeah. But how do you keep something not yet yours? "Couldn't agree more."

After parking my bike near the back of the lot, I enter the pub, wave to the hostess, and weave through the crowd to our usual table. Twenty feet away, I take a deep breath and throw on a smile as I approach Cora, Gavin, and Shelly.

More than a week has passed since Cora and Gavin's wedding. And so much has happened in that small blip of time.

Tonight will be the true test. To see whether or not the love I have had for Cora over the last ten years has changed. If it has really transitioned from romantic to friendship. Most people wouldn't be able to set aside such potent feelings. But when something else—someone else—clicks in place, you see the world a little different.

As I step up to the table, Cora laughs at something Shelly said and I absorb her laughter. Test how it makes me feel. See if it strikes me as it did weeks and months and years ago. It echoes across the table, has the corner of my mouth perking up for a beat, then settles.

The first thing I realize is it doesn't sink in. Her laughter doesn't seep into my pores, bleed through my veins, and root itself in my marrow. It just floats through the air and settles. The only reason I smile is because it's natural. Her happiness makes me happy.

"Hey, man," Gavin says as I settle on a stool next to Shelly.

"Hey." I raise a hand and nod at Chris, the bartender. He throws me a thumbs up. "Any good ones hit the stage yet?"

For years, Cora, Shelly, and I came to this bar at least once a week. The local bar and grill hosted karaoke several nights a week. If it was a slow night on non-karaoke days, the manager would let people go on stage and sing for the hell of it. The more drinks people consume, the more interesting the singing. Definitely some memorable performances.

Cora perks up. "You just missed the Momma Train Gang."

I glance over at her and *see* her for the first time. No doubt, Cora is a beautiful woman. But in a strange twist of events, I no longer see her how I once did. I don't study her eyes or lips or smile with too much depth. Don't feel the urge to stare at her for hours and pine over what I can't have.

The day I met Cora, I remember how her smile made me sweat a little. Made me a little fidgety.

Now when I look at her, a familiarity settles inside me. Still a form of love, but more comparable to what I feel when Jasmine or Jillian are around. Sibling love.

Maybe this is how close friendship should feel. Like family.

"Momma Train Gang? Dear lord, dare I ask?"

Shelly snort-laughs just as a beer is set in front of me on a coaster. "Thought I'd seen it all." She slaps her hand on the table. "Boy, was I wrong."

I glance between the two women, both of which laugh uncontrollably, then to Gavin. "Care to fill me in since these two are obviously incapable."

Gavin tilts his head and eyes me for a beat. Once he satisfies the question in his head, he tells me what I missed. "Four women, probably in their mid-to-late forties, jumped on stage and mutilated 'My Humps' by Black Eyed Peas. Mix the singing with the way they shook their… assets, let's just say it was memorable."

We both take a sip of our beers and shake our heads. "You guys eat yet?" I ask him.

"Nah. Thank god. Might've come back up. Not sure how you guys have been doing this for years. Some of these people make me want to gouge my eyes out."

I throw my head back and laugh. Shelly and Cora join me. "Dude, the first time was a total accident. But it wiped the stress of the day away. So, we kept coming. Call it tradition. Need a good laugh? Come in for karaoke night." Scanning the bar for our server, I spot my oldest friend, Trevor. "Be back in a sec."

Slipping off my stool, I walk over to the bar and sidle up beside him.

"Hey," he says as soon as he notices me. "What're you doing here?"

I point over to the table I just abandoned. "Hanging out.

Drinking beer. Listening to shit karaoke. Grabbing a bite. You?"

He stares down at his glass, rounds his shoulders, and sags. "Just broke it off with Christine."

Well, this throws me off. "Seriously, bro? What the hell happened?"

Trevor and Christine have been connected at the hip for the last three years. Went everywhere together. If we had a guy's night without her tagging along, we were lucky. So hearing that they are no longer together shocks the hell out of me.

"Got off work early on Friday. Thought I'd surprise her. Get home before her and make a nice dinner."

"Okay…" I drawl.

"When I parked at the complex and spotted her car home early, I was bummed I couldn't surprise her. But excited she was home early." Trevor pauses to down the last of his drink. Something tells me this tale is about to go south real fast. "I heard it before I unlocked the door." He cringes. "Her screams. The ones she only makes when…"

Fuck. His pain is so out of my element. But like a good friend, I listen and give him a shoulder.

"I walked into the bedroom. Saw *everything*." He taps the bar before peering up at me. "Dude, it's burned into my retinas. I can't unsee it and it pisses me off. So, I'm trying to forget," he says as the bartender sets another Jack and Coke in front of him.

What the hell do I say? How does a friend comfort another when something like this happens? Fuck if I know.

"Wish I could say or do something to make this better, man."

Trevor slaps the back of my shoulder. "You're a good friend, brother. Thanks for that."

I glance back at my friends across the bar and battle internally where I should be. With them? Or Trevor?

Why choose.

"Trev, come hang out with us." I point over to the high top. "We'll help take your mind off things for a bit."

He stares across the bar at the laughing trio and gauges what to do. "I don't know, brother. Not sure I'm in the mood."

"Exactly. Which is why you need to."

I grab hold of his arm and drag him off the stool. He stumbles beside me through the bar.

Fuck, he has had a lot to drink already.

When we reach the table, I plop his ass on a stool and sit next to him. Gavin scrutinizes every visible inch of Trevor then glances over to me with a silent question. Asking if Trevor is good. Subtly, I nod.

"Shelly, Cora, you remember Trevor?"

They chime in with a unified yes, followed by a bout of laughs.

"Trevor, this is Gavin. Cora's husband. Gavin, this is my oldest friend Trevor. We go back to the days of BMX bikes and when boys thought girls were gross."

Gavin laughs and it thins the bubble of intensity surrounding us. "Sometimes," Gavin says as he side-eyes Cora, "girls are still gross."

"Hey!" Cora play slaps him. "Take that back or you'll regret it."

For the next couple of hours, I sit in the middle of a bar surrounded by a group of people I care about. Smiles and laughs and banter bounce back and forth the entire time. Happiness hovers in the periphery when I catch Trevor smile for a moment. Because if anyone can come out on the other side stronger after something shitty like cheating happens, it is Trevor. And I will help him however possible. Maybe lug him to Wednesday night dinners for the foreseeable future.

Whatever it takes.

The only person missing from this semi-perfect moment is a petite brunette with stormy, cognac eyes and scarlet lips. Maybe I will get lucky. Maybe one day, she will sit on the stool beside me.

seven

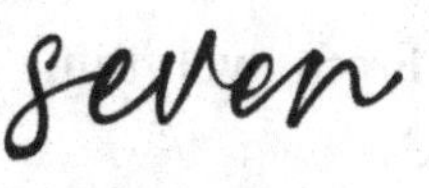

AUTUMN

Two days. Two days have passed since I pushed past my doubts and insecurities. When I, for the first time in years, handed out my phone number to a guy.

And he hasn't used it. Not once.

What the hell?

Jonas threw out every hint. Practically begged to call me. So why hasn't he?

And why the hell am I being such a *girl* about the fact he hasn't called or texted? This is one reason why I don't put myself out there. Why I haven't dated in years. Because I can't get my hopes up. Not when my heart isn't the only one on the line. Relationships—no matter the type—don't involve just me. Others have to be taken into consideration.

Penny plops down on the couch and lays her head on my shoulder as I sip my coffee. "Whatcha thinking about?" she asks.

I lean my cheek on her crown and shake my head. "Ridiculous nonsense."

Her body vibrates with laughter, but she contains the

sound. "Just call him already. Pull a Sadie Hawkins and woman up."

I laugh at her reference. Penny is always so gung ho and dives in headfirst. Her energy and enthusiasm boost the parts of me I squander. Like reaching out to a guy who is seemingly interested in me, but has been radio silent since I gave him permission to call.

"But…"

"But what, Auti? From everything you told me, the guy is interested. So no buts."

I roll my eyes, sit taller, and spin to face her as she falls from my shoulder into the couch cushions. Drama queen. But I wouldn't want her any other way.

"What if I'm reading him wrong?"

"What if you're not?" Penny garbles into the couch cushion before sitting up and swiping her hair out of her face. "I saw the way he looked at you last Wednesday. Girl, you can't fake the way he reacted. He wants you. Probably more than either of you cares to admit."

"Say you're right." Penny waves her hand in the air and rolls her eyes. I ignore her antics and trudge on. "Why hasn't he called me yet? If he is as interested as you suggest, why am I sitting here questioning it?"

Penny crisscrosses her legs and lays her hands on my knees. "Because he's a guy." I shake my head as she continues. "And because he's probably working all day to fix your car."

I hadn't thought about Betsy or the fact Jonas has his hands all over her. Is it weird to suddenly be jealous of a car? That she's getting more action than I have in years. Hope she isn't too broken. Hope it won't cost a fortune either.

"Forgot about Betsy," I admit.

Penny lifts her hands to clutch my shoulders. "Then use Betsy as a reason to call. Ask how things are going with the repairs. Throw out a little charm. No way he'll resist."

I inhale a deep breath and tuck my hair behind my ear. "Say I call. Besides Betsy, what else do I talk about?" I drop my eyes to my lap. Study a nonexistent loose thread on my pants. "You know how long it's been."

"Yeah, I do. And I question your sanity." I go to interject and she holds her hand up to stop me. "Hear me out. I know *why* you haven't dated or gotten close to anyone in years. But it has been *years, Auti.* Enough time has passed. It's okay to do what makes *you* happy. No one will fault you for that." Penny picks up my hands and envelops them in hers. "Give yourself permission to live. To find happiness."

Although I hate to admit it, she is right. But owning the truth in your head is wholly different than speaking it aloud. Because once the truth leaves your lips, you can never rein it back in. The words can never be unsaid.

"How?" I whisper. "How do I *live* when…" I trail off and she squeezes my hands.

"You let us help. Just as we always have. Me, Reznor, Iliana, Rex. We may not be conventional, we may not share the same genetics, but we're family. And family always sticks together. Through thick and thin."

I nod robotically. Times like this, I wish my actual family gave a damn. Wish they actually loved me for who I am, instead of hating me for the choices I made over the years. Choices I wouldn't change if given the opportunity. Because all my choices led me to where I am now. To Penny and my tat family. To happiness and potentially more. To so much love.

I reach for my phone and Penny claps like a lunatic. "You

need to leave the room. I can't call him with you sitting in front of me, judging every word or gesture."

Penny sighs like the drama queen she is and rises from the couch. "Fine." She huffs and wanders down the hall. "If you need me, I'll be in the tub, reading and soaking up lavender bubbles. I expect a full rundown after."

"Yeah, yeah."

Once the bathtub faucet cranks on, I bite my lip and scroll through my text history. I tap on the message I sent myself from Jonas's phone and read it for the hundredth time. *Can't wait for you to call.* And it suddenly dawns on me. If I read this as the recipient, it sounds as if *he* is waiting for *me* to call.

Shit. Has he read this message over and over, wondering why *I* haven't called?

I tap the top of the message and stare at the different options below his phone number and blank contact image. My finger hovers over the small phone icon as I suck in a deep breath.

Now or never, Autumn. Just tap the screen.

Swallowing, I press the phone icon and lift the phone to my ear. One ring. Two. Three. Just as I consider hanging up, the line connects.

"Hello?" Jonas's low, throaty voice floats through the line and settles deep in my bones. A flutter stirs in my belly. My tongue suddenly thick. "Hello? Autumn?"

Did he add my name to his contacts? A new wave of excitement washes over me as I clear my throat. "Yeah, sorry," I answer.

"Everything okay?"

No, because I am a complete moron. "Yes. Just calling to check on Betsy." And ask why you haven't called me yet.

"Betsy's doing just fine," he answers with jubilance in his

voice and I picture a smile brightening his face. "Should be done with her in time for Thursday."

"Thursday?"

"My appointment." Right, he will be back in my chair in two days. My belly does another flip. "Thought I'd bring the car to you. If that's okay."

I nod, then remember he can't see me. "Yeah, that's fine."

The line goes silent for a moment as I pick at the chipping polish on my finger nails. *Need to repaint them later.*

The longer the silence stretches, the more I wonder why I am so bad at this. Years ago, I never had issues talking to guys. Hell, most of my friends are men. Always have been.

So why am I struggling to find a single thing to say? Why is it so difficult to ask him how he is doing? Or if he would like to hang out sometime. Penny's words from minutes ago repeat in my head. *Give yourself permission to live. To find happiness.*

Is Jonas the happiness I have been missing all these years? Maybe. But I will never know until I put myself out there. Until I ask.

Just as I open my mouth to ask if he would like to get together sometime and get to know each other, a bang on the other end of the line breaks the silence.

"Shit," Jonas mutters. "Sorry, but I need to go. Some people can't be left unattended." He doesn't sound angry. Amused, maybe. "Glad you called."

"You are?" I slap my hand to my forehead and close my eyes.

"Definitely. But I really do need to go before *someone* breaks shit." I pick up on the humor in his voice. "See you on Thursday."

I nod. "See you Thursday."

"And Autumn?"

"Yeah."

He stays silent a moment. "Nothing." I hear his dimpled smile in the single word. "Bye."

"Bye," I whisper as the line disconnects.

I keep the phone at my ear long after Jonas hangs up. What was he going to say? Doesn't he know my mind will spin with endless possibilities until I see him again? Until I ask him.

Holding on to the phone, I drop my hands to my lap and stare at the screen. Stare at the generic contact image and the number beneath it. Tapping the top of the screen, I click on the info icon and add Jonas's contact information. Somehow, I need to figure out a sneaky way to get a picture of him. I hate not having images to associate with my contacts. Just a weird preference.

"Why aren't you in here telling me all the juicy details?" Penny yells from the bathroom.

Rising from the couch, I head down the hall. When I reach the bathroom, I peek in and laugh at Penny as she bobs in the middle of a two-foot tower of bubbles. "You're a freaking nut," I tell her.

"And you're avoiding a conversation. Better luck next time."

I roll my eyes, walk into the bathroom, and plop down on the closed toilet lid. "There's not much to tell. I called him, he was busy at work, there was awkward chitchat about Betsy, then silence, and goodbye."

"You should've been in here with it on speakerphone. Then I could decipher all the things you're leaving out."

Forever wanting all the dirty details. "There was this one thing," I trail off.

She sits up taller in the tub, sloshing water over the sides and flashing me her boobs. I cover my eyes with a hand and she laughs.

"First, you've seen my boobs a million times. No need to be prude now."

"But we weren't talking about guys then."

Penny shrugs and scoops bubbles closer to her chest to appease me. "Anyway. Elaborate. What does *this one thing* mean?"

I huff and lean back on the toilet tank. "There was this one point when it sounded like he wanted to say something. Maybe ask me something. But then he just blew it off and said bye."

During the call with Jonas, that moment of silence dragged out for hours in my head. I filled it with daydreams of my hand cradled in his. Of his cheek pressed to mine as he whispered sweet words in my ear. Of his soft lips brushing mine while his stubble scraped my skin.

Did his mind wander much the same? Did he picture the possibility of us?

Penny shrugs and the bubbles flatten a little in the tub. "Maybe he was going to ask you something, but didn't want to over the phone. Have you ever considered the idea he may be just as nervous as you are?"

Have I given the idea consideration? No. I pictured most men as forward and cocky. Majority of the men I ink represent the notion well. Hundreds have asked for my number. When they do, I just hand over my business card for the shop.

Except for Jonas.

Granted, he has my phone number on an invoice in Thompson's Garage. But I never picture him abusing the privilege. He asked for my number because he was raised to be a gentleman. He asked for my number because he wanted to give me the choice. To say yes or no. When I said yes, I assumed he would use my number sooner rather than later. Most men don't have the patience to sit idle and wait for the woman to make the first move. Obviously, Jonas has many redeeming qualities I have yet to learn.

"Actually, I haven't. Suppose you could be right."

"Could be? Girl, I'm right ninety-nine point nine percent of the time. And you know it."

"Alright, conversation is officially over," I tease as I stand up and head out of the bathroom. "Finish your bath and we'll head out."

"Yes, mother," she teases back. "Be out in a jiff."

I amble into my bedroom and sift through my closet. Tugging a shirt from the hanger, I toss it on the bed and grab a pair of jeans. Mindlessly, I dress and replay Penny's response to Jonas's silence.

Is Jonas nervous? If he is, I am curious as to why. He doesn't come off as timid. At least not to the degree where he would be nervous asking a woman out. In some respects, he already did. So why would he be nervous to ask again? Is it the simple notion of being rejected twice? I hope that is not the case. Because if Jonas asks me again, my answer will be different.

If he asks me again, I will say yes.

eight

JONAS

I crank the Bel Air to life and smile when it purrs like the beauty it is. Dad wanders over and I roll down the window.

"She sounds good as new." He wipes his hand with a red rag then stuffs it in his coveralls. "Tell Autumn I say hello."

I laugh under my breath. Since Autumn's car arrived at the garage and she went home, Dad has given me a ration of shit every single day. Teases me about wanting another grandchild. Asking me over and over if I called Autumn yet. If I asked her on a date. Sometimes, I swear he is worse than Mom.

And when she called on Tuesday, Dad knocked a fender off the workbench as he snuck closer to eavesdrop. Always lurking about. Hence why I ended the call abruptly with Autumn.

"Will do." Dad taps the roof before I throw the car in reverse.

Since the trip to the tattoo shop from the garage is short, I take the 'scenic' route to listen better to the car. Thankfully, nothing major was wrong with the engine. Just typical wear and tear on easy-to-replace parts. Cars like the Bel Air can be more challenging to repair if it's a major component. Engines just aren't made how they once were. When this car was manufactured, the engine didn't rely on hundreds of little computers and motherboards. They were solid and metal and everlasting. And their parts weren't easy to find nowadays.

Five miles later, I roll into the back parking lot of the tattoo shop. Shutting off the engine, I sit in the car another minute, study the silver and black upholstery, and inhale the peculiar Coke float scent.

Every inch of this car screams Autumn. Fits her personality and the way she carries herself.

Question is, do I? Do I fit into her lifestyle? Who she is and the life she leads.

Because I want to. Desperately.

Other than Cora, I never thought it possible to feel so intensely for a woman. And I never thought I would feel it so soon and easily.

Exiting the car, I lock it up and head for the front entrance. The bell jingles when I walk in and I love the smile on Autumn's face when she peeks up and notices my arrival. Her smile brightens the room instantly. *Hey* I mouth and her cheeks pink.

I wonder if she blushes this much with other men. Hopefully not. I would like to believe she reserves the crimson heat just for yours truly.

After I check in with the Bubble Yum queen, I pace the lobby and stare at the art on the walls. I scan each image but pay closer attention to the artist's names on the bottom. I stop at the third piece and study it intently. The eleven-by-fourteen heavy cream paper penned with millions of small dots. Up close, I spot each pinpointed speck of ink on its own. Stepping back, the dots form the image of two people holding hands and strolling down the sidewalk. Of the two people, you only see their hands and half their forearms. When I glance down at the artist's name, it doesn't shock me when I see Autumn's next to a hefty price tag.

But the art is worth every penny.

A finger tap on my shoulder interrupts my fascination with the art. I spin around to find Autumn. Her smile bright and shy. One-hundred-percent adorable and addicting.

"Nice piece," I say, pointing over my shoulder.

Autumn glances around me and eyes the art. "Thank you. Took months to finish." A fresh blush paints her cheeks and I love her bashful nature more.

"No doubt. Wish I had the patience to create something so priceless."

She tucks her lips in her mouth and bites down to fight against her smile. Then she pops them and I can't look away. Don't want to look away. Her crimson lips an invitation I want to answer with a resounding yes.

"You ready?" she asks.

I nod. "Yeah."

Autumn leads us to her booth, and I don't miss the way Bubble Yum winks and smiles as we pass. Interesting.

I sit in the chair while Autumn preps everything. In no time, she places the stencil on my forearm. After it's in place, I remember I still have her keys and pull them from my pocket. I set them on my lap and chance a look at her. She has been quiet. Too quiet.

"Sorry I didn't hand over the keys before you gloved up."

"No biggie," she says and shrugs. "Why was Betsy being temperamental?"

I love how she refers to her car as a person with an ill

temper. Yet another quality to add under the adorable category. An ever-growing list.

"Just needed to replace the starter and a couple other small parts."

Autumn slumps and sighs before meeting my eyes. Her brows pinch slightly and accentuate her swirly cognacs. "Sounds pricey."

General automotive repair racks up over time. Certain parts and repairs costing more. But repairing Autumn's car was simple. Easier than most newer cars. The beauty of older cars is how spread out the engines are. How you don't have to remove half or more of the engine to get to one part. Whenever Dad and I get to work on older vehicles, we savor it. Drool like idiots. Take our time to have it around longer.

"Not at all, actually."

She perks up at that. "Great. Let me know how much I owe you, and we can settle up when we're done."

After Dad and I finished up Autumn's car earlier, he followed me into the office and closed the door. As I finalized the paperwork for Autumn's car, jotting down what repairs we had done, Dad walked over and slapped his hand on top of the invoice. "*No charge*," he'd said. He looked me in the eyes and shook his head. His decision was final and not up for debate.

Honestly, I was happy to not charge Autumn. But I didn't have the final say in waiving payment. Dad still holds the power where Thompson's Garage finances are concerned.

"Not a dime," I tell her. "Dad insists. He says hello, by the way."

Autumn slouches and pouts.

Fuck me running. If I don't look away now, I will embarrass the hell out of myself. Nothing like sitting in a chair next to a beautiful woman with a hard-on while her eyes focus less than six inches away.

Think, think, think.

Images of my sisters pop in my head and is exactly what I need. Nothing like siblings to kill any sort of mood.

"Well, I'll have to repay him. Bake him a cake or brownies or cookies. Does he like any of those?" she asks.

"All of the above. He's not picky and will love whatever you make. Thanks."

"For what?"

For existing, I want to say, but bite my tongue. "It's a generous thing to do. Most wouldn't."

She nods. "Well, I'm not most people."

This much I have figured out.

For the next twenty minutes, I close my eyes and lay back while she starts on my tattoo. For the first time, I don't enjoy the silence. I want to talk to Autumn. Ask about her life. What she does for fun. What she does when she isn't working. Ask her to have dinner with me. Or do something she enjoys.

For obvious reasons, I haven't had an actual girlfriend in years. I tried. Tried to date other women while I pined over Cora. But it never worked out. Never got past the first kiss on the doorstep after our date. Because I never wanted it to.

But now… I want it more than anything.

Want to take her out and share a meal together. The food or restaurant doesn't have to be fancy as long as Autumn is there. I want to hang out with friends and have her hooked on my arm. Feel her warmth against my skin and bask in her sweet perfume and infectious laughter.

I peel my eyes open, lift my head, and glance down at her. Hunched over my forearm, she shifts my skin and runs the gun over the purple lines. I study her every move. The way she cocks her head when she scrutinizes her own work. How she leans back to see the tattoo from farther away. The way she tucks her lips in her mouth when hesitant—like she is right now.

"What are you thinking about?" I croak.

She sits up straighter and meets my gaze. Her eyes tell the tale of struggle. Struggle to do one thing versus another. A battle of wills.

Her lips pop out and I swallow. "What were you going to ask me the other day?"

I furrow my brow and tilt my head to the side. "When?"

"On the phone. Sounded like you were going to ask me something, and you didn't."

Ah, yes. Because I did have a question on the tip of my tongue. Until I caught Dad snooping. The plan was to ask if I could take her to dinner. But I chickened out when I spotted Dad ten feet away with his head leaning in close as he picked up the fender.

"Um." I rub the back of my neck with my free hand. "Was going to ask if you wanted to maybe grab dinner sometime."

I get drunk on her cognac irises as she doesn't blink or look away. Sweat a little from the intensity of her gaze. Stop breathing when she doesn't utter a single word in response.

A guy such as myself would strike gold if Autumn agreed to go on a date. I still have so much to learn about her, but from what I have seen so far, she is a rare gem. Sparkling in the sunlight and stealing your breath.

She parts her lips to respond, but snaps them shut a moment later. When she does it again—and again—I perk up at her speechlessness. Before I have the chance to tell her to not worry about it, she dips the gun in the ink cap and works on my arm again.

Rejection washes over me—for a second time—as I slump in the chair.

What exactly stops her from saying yes? This is the single, most important—and frustrating—question rattling inside my brain right now. The one that makes me question her bashfulness and blushing and frequent eye contact. The reason must be huge. Has to be. Because the chemistry between us is off the charts. At least it feels off the charts from where I sit. And there is no way this attraction is one-sided. Can't be.

As I lean back and rest my head against the chair, I get a quick glimpse of her smile and a blush smattering her cheeks. I close my eyes and smile like a fool—not giving a damn who sees. She may not respond verbally, but her body language gives so much away.

The next hour breezes by as I daydream of taking Autumn on a date. Where we would go. What we would do afterward. Her warm, slender fingers woven with mine. My arms holding her close as I hug her good night. Her sweet perfume swathing me in a cocoon as I lean in to press my lips to hers.

A chill snaps me out of my daydream as Autumn cleans my finished tattoo.

"So jumpy," she teases. "Might start to think you're a virgin." Autumn laughs, then stops once she realizes what she said. "Sorry," she mutters. "That was inappropriate."

Tattoo virgin is what she meant. Not a virgin in the sex department. My virginity had been surrendered long ago in both areas. For obvious reasons, she knew I wasn't a tattoo virgin. But Autumn had no clue about my sexual history—which isn't extensive, but exists.

Which is the exact reason her cheeks are currently one shade lighter than her rouge-painted lips. And I love how the intimacy of this conversation makes her squirm. Her semi-shy nature is not something often seen nowadays.

"Would that be a bad thing?" I mean the question as a joke. But a joke she isn't privy to yet.

She tucks her lips in her mouth and clamps down. I want to reach forward and release her lips from their prison. But I stop myself. We don't know each other well enough for me to do such things.

"Um, no," she answers softly.

Although my tattoo is as clean as it will get right now, she continues wiping it to avert her eyes. "Autumn…"

"Yeah?" she says, eyes still laser focused on my distal forearm.

"Look at me," I whisper.

She licks her lips. "Mmhm?" Slowly, she lifts her gaze and locks it with mine.

"There's no need to be embarrassed." The desire to touch her expands like a hot air balloon in my chest. And I don't want to deny myself any longer. I reach forward with my free hand and graze the skin of her forearm near the black glove edge. Her momentary gasp trips my heart. I swallow and say, "Was only kidding." The corner of my mouth kicks up as I draw circles over her skin with my thumb.

"You were?" she asks, voice cracking.

I nod and she exhales. Her bashful nature continually takes me by surprise, but I love how flustered she gets when we are near. Because she has my stomach flipping on a trampoline nonstop. "About being a virgin, yes." She snorts quietly. "But not about wanting to ask you out."

Autumn peels off her gloves and tosses them in the trash. She rises from the stool and stretches. I study her a beat before standing up on stiff legs. Taking a moment, I stretch my limbs and arch my back, working out the kinks.

Please tell me I didn't scare her away.

She steps in front of me and moves to exit the booth, then stops and spins to face me. Tipping her head back slightly, she homes in on my lips. When I lick them, her lips quirk up at the corners as she nods.

"Yes," she whispers. "I would love to."

What? I stop myself from sticking my fingers in my ears and wiggling them. "Yes?"

She nods slowly as her nervous smile grows bolder and brighter. "I need to check my schedule, but yes. Can I call or text you later?"

I want to jump on the chair and scream *hell yes you can.* But like the proper gentleman my parents raised me to be, I keep my feet planted firmly on the floor and answer her as levelheaded as possible. "Of course. Wednesday is family dinner night, just so you know."

"Cool."

"Cool," I repeat and suddenly feel as if I am fifteen all over again. "Talk to you later."

She bites the inside of her cheek and nods. "Later." After a cute wave, she spins on her heel and wanders back into her booth with a little extra sway in her hips.

After I pay at the desk, I walk out the door and smile when the bell jingles. Who cares if I need to walk two-plus miles back to the garage to get my bike. Who cares if I forgot to bring a hoodie to the shop. Winter is still a few weeks away —not that the first official day of winter equals cool weather in Florida.

The only thing I *do* care about is the fact Autumn said yes to a date. And the promise of a date with Autumn is enough to keep me warm and has me walking faster. Has me smiling like an imbecile. Makes my heart beat faster and my breath stutter.

Today marks one of the happiest days of my life. A day I will never forget.

nine

AUTUMN

Jonas leaves the shop and I stand like a fool staring at the door for who knows how long. Staring at the place he last stood. Imagining him walking back in for no other reason than to see me.

I agreed to go on a date with Jonas. Me. A date. An actual doll-yourself-up-for-a-guy date.

Oh my fucking god. 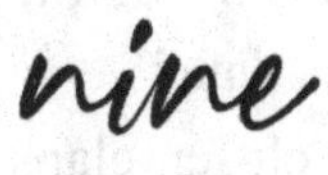

I want to cheer and scream and jump and puke all at once.

When was the last time I was on an actual date? I would have to consult a 2013 calendar to determine the answer. And that little fact makes my stomach ball into a fist and squeeze tight. I may have sequestered myself for all the right reasons, but in doing so, I lost part of who I am. A spontaneous and vivacious woman.

Not as if those elements aren't still inside me. But now they have been tamped down by other qualities. Traits which currently reside in the spotlight for good reason.

"What just happened?" Penny asks as she skips into my booth.

I snap out of my daze and start cleaning my workstation.

"Not sure what you're talking about," I reply, working hard to hide the smile painfully stretching my cheeks.

"Don't toy with my emotions, Auti. Spill. I know something happened."

After I drop the needles in the red bin, I peer up at her and shrug my shoulders. She widens her eyes when I hesitate and torture her a little longer. When she grunts, I decide to alleviate the torment. Because if I don't, Penny will make a scene.

"Jonas asked me on a date."

"And?" Penny steps closer, claps her hands in prayer position, and bats her eyelashes. Utterly ridiculous.

"And…" I drag the word out and count to five before continuing. Last thing I need is Penny strangling me because I am not forthcoming. "I said yes."

She gasps and leans back. Slaps a hand over her heart. "You said yes," she says in disbelief, voice decibels higher than normal. "Did I hear you correctly?"

I ball up the paper towel in my hand and toss it at her face. "Shut up." I laugh. "You heard what I said. Don't be a doofus."

"A doofus? Really? You sound like a five-year-old." Penny puckers her lips and cocks a brow. "Whatever." She blows a bubble and pops the pink gum with a loud smack. "So, where's he taking you?"

Her question has reality setting in a little more and a buzz hums low in my belly. *Jonas is taking me on a date.* A real date. Out in the world. Where other people exist. Where other people sit together and eat meals and laugh.

Holy shit.

"Not sure," I whisper before clearing my throat and finding my voice. "Told him I needed to check my schedule and I'd call or text him."

Penny rolls her eyes. "Check your schedule? Girl, you make your own schedule."

"True. But I'd be an asshole if I told him a day and someone was booked on my schedule already. Not cool. Someone would end up disappointed, and you know how I feel about that."

She nods. "Guess you're right. So..." She drags the single syllable into a ten-letter word. "What are you going to wear?"

Her question stops me in my tracks. For the first time in almost a decade, restlessness blankets me. Any other day of the week, this question wouldn't bother me. Could prattle off my ensemble in the blink of an eye. But something about dressing myself when I know it's for a set purpose—what I imagine will be the most amazing date of my life—has me stumbling in my tracks.

Jonas makes me stammer. For all the right reasons.

"I have no clue." I stare at Penny dumbstruck.

Stepping closer, she lays her hands on my shoulders and shakes me. "Snap out of it. That's what you have me for." I nod. "Okay, you finish cleaning up. I'll check your schedule for the next week and then we can game plan. Sound good?"

"Yes." I still can't believe this is real.

"Auti, I'm so excited for you."

I glance up at her and soak up her sunshine of a smile. Her enthusiasm has me smiling back. "Thanks. Pen?" She lifts her brows in question. "I'm going on a date," I squeal.

Reznor pops his head up from his client and smiles. "You know we all need to approve of him. Right?"

Stepping up to the wall between our booths, I prop my elbows on the ledge. "Yes, big brother. But let me have a date or two first. Before you and Rex scare him away."

Reznor dips the needle in an ink cap and leans back over

his client's posterior ribcage. "Sure, little sis." He smiles and returns his focus to his work.

Once my booth is sanitized, I sidle up next to Penny. It surprises me when she tells me my Saturday night is free. Saturday is generally a busy day at the shop. Although not everyone works Monday to Friday, nine to five, majority of our clientele comes in on Friday and Saturday nights. So it blows my mind when she says my Saturday is bare.

When I question it, she winks conspiratorially and tells me all my other days are jam-packed. I narrow my eyes, but don't push the topic. Penny has been dying for me to get out in the world for years. She accepts why I haven't, but reminds me to live my life. *"How can you ever be happy if you never live outside the same four walls?"* Her words from over the years float through my thoughts.

Penny and I get home an hour later. Iliana is stretched out on the couch, asleep. *Gilmore Girls* plays quietly on the television. When there is nothing new to watch, we watch *Gilmore Girls*. Might be up to our seventh visit to Stars Hollow now. Never gets old.

I pick up the remote and press mute before sitting down next to her. Laying a hand on her forearm, I gently jostle her. "Ili. Wake up," I mumble.

She groans and squints. "What time is it?"

"Little after ten. Everything go okay tonight?" I ask.

"An angel, as always." Iliana scoots herself upright. "You guys finish up early?"

"Yeah. Rez still had someone in his chair, but said he'd be cool if we headed out."

Penny comes up behind me and rests her chin on my shoulder. "Auti has a date."

Iliana's jaw drops. "I'm sorry, but did you just say she has a date?"

Dear, god. Will I ever hear the end of their mockery? In short, no. No, I won't. My two closest friends will surely poke fun at me for quite some time. But I don't care. Wouldn't want them any other way.

"Well, more like the promise of a date. The actual day hasn't been determined yet. Although" —I turn and face Penny for a second— "my Saturday schedule is magically vacant."

"People must be out holiday shopping," Penny tosses out. "Can't help where people go to spend their money."

"Whatever." I roll my eyes, then refocus on Iliana. "I have to reach out to him and let him know what days I don't work."

Iliana leans forward, wraps her arms around me, and surprises me with a hug. "So happy for you," she whispers in my ear. Before I can squeeze her back, she releases me and rises from the couch. "I'm gonna head out."

"You're welcome to crash on the couch if you're still tired."

She smiles. "Thanks, but I'll make it home okay. Rather sleep in my bed, no offense."

After we exchange hugs and goodbyes, Iliana heads home. A second after the lock clicks in place, Penny hauls me to the couch and plops us down. She stares at me, expressionless, until I squirm under her scrutiny.

Why is she looking at me like that? Like a stern mother. Or a perturbed friend. She almost looks… bored. God, she confuses the hell out of me.

"What?"

"Auti," she says, more earnest than ever. "This is very serious."

My brows bunch together and I try to decode what the hell she is talking about. "What is, Pen?"

"Him. Jonas."

I nod. "Yeah," I whisper.

"I can't begin to tell you how excited I am for you." She glances at the hallway, down toward our bedrooms. "But this is big. Not just for you."

"Why do you think I haven't dated in years? Not like I've never wanted to. Believe me, I *miss* it. But, over the years, I made the right choice."

She nods. "You did."

Solemnity settles between us for a few minutes as we sit quietly on the couch. It isn't just the fact I haven't sat across from a good-looking man and shared a meal in several years that weighs heavy. But also the emotions and expectations which usually come with said scenarios. Emotions and expectations I have no idea if I am ready to handle.

The occasional blip on my radar isn't love. Love takes time. Is substantial and messy. Swallows you whole and never lets you leave.

Thirst is what currently consumes me. Thirst and hunger. My years without companionship have left me starved. Practically emaciated. But my attraction to Jonas isn't some attempt to fatten the ravenous fiend living inside me. My attraction to him is pure and mystical. Makes the organ beneath my breastbone swell and gallop wildly. Has my lungs burning for breath and my stomach topsy-turvy.

Never have I experienced the sensations Jonas induces. Emotions and energy and a gravity that hauls me into his atmosphere.

"Enough with the heavy," Penny announces quietly. "We have more important things to discuss."

"We do?"

She nods. "Like what you'll wear. How you'll fix your hair. What color you plan to paint your nails. The important stuff."

Eyes meeting hers, I pucker my lips and wiggle them side to side. "Oh my god, Pen," I whisper-scream. "Oh. My. God. I have a date."

"What about…?" Penny glances down the hall.

I peek over my shoulder and follow her gaze. "Can you? Please?"

A smile kicks up the corners of her mouth. "I got you covered."

"Thanks, Pen."

Penny and I gossip and giggle on the couch for another half hour before she heads to bed. She mothers me and suggests which top I should pair with which bottoms. What shoes I should wear. How to pin up my hair. I cut her off when she tells me to paint my nails a different color besides my typical cherry red. Polish and lip colors don't get messed with. Ever.

When I hear her bedroom door click shut, I dig my phone out of my purse. Opening up the text history between Jonas and I—where I texted myself from his phone—my fingers hover over the keyboard. Where to begin?

I check the time on the top of the screen and realize how late it is. Almost midnight. He is probably in bed already. No doubt the garage opens early.

I will send a quick message. If he doesn't answer, we can talk tomorrow. If he does answer, well… we shall see where it leads.

Hey. You still up?

My finger hovers over the arrow to the right of my message. *Press send, Autumn. Just. Press. Send.*

I drop my finger and slump into the couch when the blue bubble populates the screen and it says *delivered* beneath. To my surprise, a small bubble hovers on the lower left side of the screen. Three tiny dots dancing as he types a response. My stomach dances alongside the dots.

Still up. Too wired to sleep.

Is he ramped up from the adrenaline of getting new ink? Most people find it difficult to sleep shortly after getting a new tattoo. The adrenaline keeps them buzzed for hours afterward. Or is he riled up because I agreed to go on a date with him?

Hopefully it's the latter.

Me too.

You just finish work?

I smile. Why does him asking about work make me smile?

No. You were my last victim. Pen and I got home an hour ago.

You guys live together? Must be interesting.

This makes me laugh, and I slap a hand over my mouth. He barely knows Penny, yet has already deemed her a fascinating creature. Which is more than true. Penny is a sassy diamond in the rough.

She keeps life interesting.

I bet. You get to check your schedule?

Eager. I love it. More than I thought possible.

I did. Somehow, the gods have shined
down on me and I have Saturday free.

Perfect. Would it be okay if I pick you up?

Yes.

My cheeks sting from the broad, permanent smile plastered on my face. Why can I not stop smiling?

Six?

Can't wait.

Although he could dig it up from my paperwork at the garage, Jonas asks for my address. I give it without hesitation. He bids me good night with the promise of picking me up at six on Saturday. Less than two days from now.

I hug my phone to my chest like a preteen. After I swim in the sea of serenity a moment, I rise from the couch, flick off the light, and head down the hall.

Slipping into my bedroom, I quietly change into a tank top and boy shorts. I peel back the covers and ease into bed. Head on the pillow, I follow the moonlight as it dances on the wall and ceiling through the blinds.

I fall asleep with a smile on my face and gentle, sweet snores beside me.

Ten

JONAS

I change my shirt for the seventh time.

Somehow, going on a date with Autumn has turned me prepubescent again. I have never cared so much about my clothes or hair a day in my life. Never lifted my arms so many times to check if I put on deodorant. In the last thirty minutes, I have probably sniffed my pits more times than in the last three months.

Someone send help.

I decide on a long-sleeve, black Henley, jeans, and my leather boots. Staring at my reflection in the bathroom mirror, I brush my hair left, then back again. Regardless of my efforts, the few inches of hair atop my head stays a mess. So I give up, comb my fingers through it, and abandon my reflection.

Spartan barks and zooms around the kitchen island like a bewildered maniac.

"Come on, nut. Let's get you dinner before I leave."

He barks in approval and drops on his haunches in front of his bowl. I scoop a cup of food into his bowl and make him wait with a hand signal. For a spaz, he obeys every command

I give without hesitancy. Thank you obedience classes for all you do.

While Spartan vacuums down his dinner, I fetch my keys, wallet, phone, a couple blankets and my leather jacket.

Done with his dinner, Spartan runs up to me and barks. I shuffle my hand back and forth over his head, roughing up his fur. "Good boy. Let's go outside really quick. Then Dad has to go."

I open up the door to the back yard and let him loose. He runs the perimeter, finds several patches of grass he hasn't marked as his, then runs back into the house. I secure him in his kennel, turn on the radio, and head out the front door.

After stowing the blankets in the back, I crank the Jeep's engine and set the heat to low. Yesterday's cold front finally brought cooler temps to our part of the state. The air isn't frigid, but for us natives, it is on the cooler side. Especially once the sun goes down.

A second after I park the Wrangler in front of Autumn's apartment, her front door opens and she steps out. I swallow and all but choke on my own saliva.

How the hell am I supposed to focus all night?

Autumn stands in front of her door in a dress hugging every curve beneath her bust to her knees. The dress bolsters a snug but loose red top and a slim-fit black skirt. The sweetheart neckline accentuated with a small black bow. Her dark, rich locks frame her face in soft waves.

I swallow again and remind myself to breathe. Remind myself to not be an idiot or say the wrong thing.

Cutting the headlights, I step out of the Jeep and we meet in the middle. A jacket drapes over one of her arms while a small black purse hangs on the other.

"Hi," I rasp. "You look… wow."

She giggles. "Hi. And thank you." Reaching forward, she traces her fingers over my bicep. "You look great too."

The corner of my mouth kicks up. "No one will give me the time of day with you in the room." She peeks up at me from beneath her lashes. "Shall we?" I gesture toward the Jeep and resist the urge to lay my hand on her lower back.

Not yet. Soon, but not yet.

Both of us buckled in, I flip the headlights back on and drive. We sit in the dark cab with only the low volume of my rock playlist floating around us. The air weighted with thrill and anxiety as neither of us speak. And for once, the silence kills me.

"Are you warm enough?" I ask to break the constant quiet.

Out of the corner of my eye, she swivels to face me slightly. "Yes, thank you. Where are we going?"

"Well..." I glance at her a second before returning my eyes to the road. Damn, she robs my every thought. "Wasn't quite sure what you liked to eat, so I aimed for variety. Hope that's okay."

"For future reference, I eat just about everything. Well, at least everything I've tried."

I don't miss the start of her words. *"For future reference."* Three simple words have me soaring high as a kite on a summer day.

"Good to know." I tuck away the new information for safekeeping. "Hope you're hungry. You'll want one of every-thing. Guaranteed."

"Now I'm intrigued." I hear the smile in her voice and wish I could take my eyes off the road.

Minutes later, I park and help Autumn out. This time I don't resist the urge to rest my hand on her lower back as I steer us to the front door of the restaurant. We may be at the start, but the simple touch feels more than natural. Right. The second we step inside; it feels as if we stepped back in time. Back to the 1950s.

Black-and-white tiles checker the floor. Pops of red and chrome accent backless stools and the lengthy diner counter. Fountains line the counter like keg taps in a bar. The back wall loaded with vintage metal signs for cola and floats and items more popular during a different era. Shelves packed with glassware for milkshakes and sundaes and banana splits. Red and black vinyl booths line the windowed walls, while small two-seater tables sit nestled between the booths and fountain counter. Each booth has its own jukebox. A handful rest on the counter for patrons who sit near the fountains.

A young woman seats us at a booth, hands us menus, prattles off the evening specials and reminds us breakfast is served all day.

"How did I not know this place existed?" Autumn asks and I shrug. Her eyes float around the room. Awe and delight twinkle in her eyes as she takes it all in. "I think I'm in love."

When her eyes circle back and land on me, she tucks her lips in that cute way she does. A flush paints her cheeks. And I bite back the urge to say what is on my mind.

Me too.

"Wait until you taste the food. This is nothing," I say as I wave around the bustling mom-and-pop diner.

Silence falls over us as we study the menu. After a beat, the server returns to take our order. Autumn orders first and I bite the inside of my cheek at the amount of food she orders. She is either really hungry or had difficulty deciding. Either way, the notion is adorable.

Once both of us order and the server leaves, I laugh.

"What's so funny?" Eyes trained on my face, her brows lift incrementally.

"Hungry?"

My new favorite shade of red tints her cheeks. "There were a hundred different things on the menu I wanted. You're lucky I only ordered what I did."

"Autumn, if you wanted to order the whole menu, I wouldn't care."

And I didn't. As long as I get to sit with her, talk with her, have her in my presence, consider me a happy man. I believe in the simple things. That life doesn't need to be full of miracles, money, and endless *stuff* to discover true happiness. Moments matter more than material possessions. Moments can't be taken away.

"Well, damn. I should've ordered more." She laughs and I join in. "So, Jonas…"

"So, Autumn…"

"Tell me all there is to know about you." She leans forward, sets her elbows on the table, and rests her chin in her palms.

Damn, she is lovable. I mentally shake my head. Shake off the ease at which I fall so easily for a woman I barely know. Am I fortunate or cursed? Fate has yet to decide.

"All of it?" I tease.

"Don't leave anything out."

If possible, I would share my entire life with her in a split second. But light speeds aren't possible when it comes to relationships. The good ones built over time—marinate. Any great relationship starts with friendship. And friendships start with details and trust.

"Alright. Let's see how much I can spew before our food arrives." Just as the words leave my lips, the server drops off my cherry cola—a newfound favorite—and Autumn's vanilla milkshake. She plucks the cherry off the whipped cream and pops it in her mouth. "Uh, where to start…"

Her lips wrap around the cherry as she pops the stem off. Liquid cognac and red lips swirl my vision. The bright lights, bopping music, and bustle of the restaurant fade in the background as I stare at her mouth. How the hell am I supposed to speak basic vocabulary when she inadvertently teases me.

As if unaware of her influence, she suggests, "Tell me about your family. I already met your dad."

Family. A safe place to start, I suppose. I sip my soda to wet my throat and start somewhere near the beginning.

"Dad and I are a lot alike. I don't know if it's because I inherited more from him than Mom. Or if it's because I'm the only male child."

Autumn sits up straighter and sips on her milkshake. "So you have sisters?"

I nod. "Yep. Two. Jasmine and Jillian." She giggles and the sound spreads warmth in my chest. "What?"

"Do your parents have a thing for the letter J?"

"Never asked, but often wondered myself. Maybe it's because of Grandpa and Uncle John on Mom's side. Not sure."

She leans forward and resumes her position with her chin on her hands. "Continue, please."

"Jasmine and I are two years apart—she's older. But Jillian is seven years younger than me. And because Jasmine and I had more years together before Jillian was born, we're closer. We're all close, though. Mom made sure of it. Hence our weekly family dinners."

Across from me, Autumn sits back against the booth and sighs. Her bright spirit from seconds ago fades as she speaks.

"Wish my family mirrored yours. I'd give anything for a close-knit, kind family."

Something in her tone stings when matched with her words. At times, my family annoys the heck out of me. Always in my business or making suggestions on how I handle this or that. As if they know what is best for my life. But I wouldn't trade them for anything in the world. And honestly, I might be lost without them.

"Want to talk about it?" I ask. Because I don't want to pry something out of her that she isn't ready to share.

She shakes her head. "Not tonight. Too heavy for a first date." A smile curves the corners of her mouth, but it doesn't reach her eyes. This moment is the most solemn I have seen her.

And I don't like it. One bit.

"Well, maybe sometime you can meet the rest of my family." Her eyes widen and I fear I have just sunk the evening deep at sea. "If that's something you'd like. Eventually."

The more I correct myself, the bigger her smile gets. "I'd like that."

The server stops in front of our table and sets the tray on a stand. Plate after plate, I laugh as the server keeps setting dishes on our table. When finished, she glances between the both of us and winces. "Anything else I can get you right now?"

I want to laugh because I know she is just doing her job. After looking at Autumn, I shake my head and relieve the poor girl. "Nah, we're good." When she walks off, I stare at the five plates in front of Autumn and laugh. "This will be interesting."

"Don't worry, I plan to have leftovers."

"Good to know. Because I don't imagine *I* could even

scarf down mozzarella sticks, a plate of onion rings, potato skins, a double cheeseburger with all the fixings, fries, and coleslaw. Plus a milkshake."

She giggles and it vibrates across my skin and warms me more than the summer sun. "I plan to sample it all. But I have to save room for dessert, too."

"Dessert? Dear god, woman. How can you even think about dessert already?"

With a shake of her head, she says, "Dessert is the first thing I think about."

Something about the way she eyes me as she says the word dessert has me wanting to box everything up and leave. But Mom would smack me across the back of my head if I did. Lecture me until her voice scratched and my ears fell off.

I eat my BBQ-style double cheeseburger and fries while watching Autumn in awe. Surprisingly, she demolishes a third of the food without breaking a sweat. We ask the server for a couple to-go boxes before Autumn orders a banana split made with toasted marshmallow and Smurf-flavored ice creams.

When her dessert arrives, I gape at the heaping mound of sugary cream and fruit. Blue and white ice cream sits sandwiched at the base between a split banana and under a mountain of whipped cream, sliced strawberries, pineapple nibs, chocolate syrup, colorful jimmies, and three maraschino cherries.

"Holy shit," I spit out. "Are you going to eat all that?" Jesus. What is that, a thousand calories?

"Nope." I blink away from the mammoth-sized dessert to catch her expression. "You're going to help."

"I am?"

She slowly nods. Picking up one of the spoons, she scoops some of the confection up and brings it to her lips. I follow the spoon with my eyes and swallow when it disappears between her lips. She closes her eyes and hums. The sounds go straight to my groin.

"Here," she says as her eyes pop back open and she scoops more on the spoon. "You need to taste this."

My gaze locks on to her lips and I imagine better ways to taste dessert. More intimate ways. She holds the spoon inches from my mouth. The whipped cream and blue ice cream melt together as a piece of strawberry dips slowly in the middle. I lean forward, lift my eyes to hers, and open my mouth as she feeds me dessert. I haven't even tasted it yet, but know it is—and forever will be—the best damn dessert to hit my tongue.

The sweet confection melts over my tastebuds and I moan. As messy and funky as it seemed, it tastes damn good.

"Was I right?" she asks. All I do is nod.

We take turns feeding each other until we have scraped every last bit of dessert out of the small glass boat. It is the most innocent and provocative meal I have eaten. A meal I won't soon forget. After I pay the check, we walk out to the Jeep and I start it up.

"Is it okay if we are doing something else, too?" I ask.

As much as I don't want the evening to be over, I don't know how she feels after eating half her weight in food. Not that I could tell when she stood from the table.

"I'd love to. What'd you have in mind?"

I tap my temple and smile. "Top secret."

"Fine," she huffs out and rolls her eyes. "Take me on your top secret adventure."

I laugh and put the Jeep in gear. Music floats in the cab and Autumn asks if she can change it. I hand her my phone and tell her the code to unlock it. "Sure. The app should be open already."

Out of the corner of my eye, I see her gawking in my direction. I want to ask why, but I think it's because I just gave her the code to my phone. If something so simple surprises her, it breaks my heart. But I have nothing to hide. Hell, I already told her about Cora the first day we met. The only skeleton I had in my closet has come out.

Trust is a big deal in every relationship. As of now, I have absolutely no reason to not trust her. I don't know much about her, but I hope to change that. Hope whatever keeps her from opening up—her avoidance on discussing her past—can be ripped to shreds. But everyone exposes themselves in their own time, and I need to give her the space to do it at her own pace.

She scrolls through the app and selects a song. An upbeat rock tune spills from the speakers and I can't help but bop to the sound. After the next song, I pull into a parking lot and weave through the rows until I locate a spot.

"The park?" she asks.

I cut the engine and glance over at her in the dark. "Yep. Tonight is *Movies In The Park* night." She bites her lip and shrugs. "Every two weeks, the park hosts a movie night after the park closes to foot traffic. You bring your own blanket or chair and they supply the movie."

"Really?" There is a lightness to her voice. A level of wonderment. And I love that I put it there.

"Really."

I slip out of the Jeep, open the back door to grab the blankets and my jacket, and round the back to help her out. A man in a bright orange vest wielding a flashlight approaches and directs us down the path for the movie. We walk across the lawn in silence, weaving between the people already set up and waiting for the movie to begin. Twenty feet on the lawn, my knuckles graze hers and a jolt of energy zings me head to boot. My pulse whooshes behind my ears and I remind myself to breathe.

If she affects me this easily from a single graze of the hand, it's unimaginable how I will feel when we kiss.

"How about there?" Autumn points to an open spot on the lawn since I have obviously stopped focusing.

"Perfect."

We weave between more blankets and finally reach the vacancy. I ask her to hold the extra blanket and my jacket while I spread the one for us to sit on. Once set up, we plop down and kick off our shoes.

"What movie are we seeing?"

"Not sure. I didn't look up the schedule. Mom and Dad have come to a few of these. That's how I knew about them."

"Fun. I like surprises."

You are the best surprise of them all.

A few minutes later, the movie flickers on the temporary screen. One I haven't seen.

"Oh god."

"What?" I ask.

"I'm going to cry."

Shit. Is this bad? Should we leave? "We don't have to stay," I suggest. Although every atom in my body screams to stay put.

"No." She presses her hand to my chest and I stop breathing. "It's a good movie."

About five minutes in, the title *A Star Is Born* pops up in red on the screen. Now I understand why she said she will cry. Jasmine told me she and Anton saw this in the theater and she bawled like a baby, but it was worth every tear.

We slip on our jackets as the movie rolls on. I lay back on

my forearms while Autumn sits up, leaning back on her hands. My attention shifts between Bradley Cooper and Lady Gaga to Autumn. I follow the lines of her profile as her eyes remain glued to the screen. The slim line of her nose. The voluptuous curves of her lips. Down to the slight dip in her chin. I would rather watch her for two hours than this movie, but I force myself to alternate between the two.

Halfway through the movie, she shivers beside me. "Cold?" She nods. "Here." I unfold the second blanket and go to wrap it around her.

"What about you?" she asks as she mimics my position.

"I'll be fine."

She shakes her head and sits back up. "Sit up."

"What? Why?" She gives me a pointed look. "Fine."

When I sit up, she cocoons us both with the wool blanket. My mind thinks a hundred different ungentlemanly thoughts and I tell myself to shut up. Slowly, she starts to lie down and I get the hint.

We lay on the blanket—my front to her back—and I stop watching the movie altogether. All I can focus on is the way her body molds to mine. How she pulled my upper arm down and wrapped it around her waist and laid hers over top. How her fruity, vanilla scent wafts from her hair into my nose. And how perfect she feels in my arms. Like she belongs there. Like she has always belonged there.

With Autumn in my arms, I close my eyes and get lost in my imagination. Lost in the fantasy of what kissing her will be like when it finally happens. Because it will happen.

I keep my eyes closed as I splay my fingers on her belly and she weaves hers between mine. Everything about this moment, about us, continually comes together with comfort and ease. Without difficulty, I envision Autumn in my arms often. Imagine her lips pressed to mine daily. Believe this rhythmic rush beneath my sternum will only get stronger the more I see her. Spend time with her. Hold her.

Hopefully, she believes and feels the same. That she reciprocates this unfamiliar rush of emotions.

Before long, the movie ends. I mentally whine at the fact I have to unravel her from my arms. But I do. We fold up the blankets, hop in the Jeep, and head back to her apartment. The entire ride back, neither of us says a word. The silence isn't uncomfortable, but seems like a missed opportunity to learn more about each other. Soon, too soon, I park in front of her apartment and cut the engine.

We sit in the dark a moment before I finally open the door and walk around to her side. Out of the Jeep, we take slow, measured steps to her front door. Not that I have a professional dating degree, but if I am reading the signs correctly, neither of us wants tonight to be over.

When we reach her front door, she spins to face me. But she doesn't look up. Not yet.

"I had a really nice time," she whispers into the darkness.

Lightly, I brush my knuckles from her temple down to the angle of her jaw. "Me too," I whisper. Her gaze lifts to meet mine. "Can I kiss you?" Her eyes dart between mine for a moment before she subtly nods.

Thank fuck.

I lift my other hand and frame her face with my palms. She sucks in a breath as I lean down, but doesn't exhale. The red cotton covering her breasts brushes against my chest and my heart bangs its fists against my ribcage. Less than an inch from her lips, she closes her eyes just before I do the same.

And then my lips press to hers and nothing else exists.

The faint porch light fades away. The occasional roar of a

car engine or pitter-patter of an animal scurrying across the grass in the dark disappears. I lick her lower lip and she opens up like a flower blooms. Every sense I own homes in on her.

The residual taste of ice cream on her tongue. Her sweet perfume in my nose. How warm her body is as it presses flush with mine. The small whimper from her lips when I break the kiss. How her cognac eyes slowly open and beg for more. And how I *know* this will not be the last time our lips meet.

I lean in for one last peck and love how she whimpers again when our lips separate.

"Thank you," she whispers. "Best date ever."

I hold her gaze. "Hopefully I can top it next time."

"No doubt about it." I step back from her and a slight frown mars her face. I brush my thumb over her cheek. "Good night, Jonas."

"'Night, Autumn."

eleven

AUTUMN

Jonas walks back to his Jeep, and I want to run after him. I press my fingers to my lips and reminisce in the fire he set moments ago. A fire I don't want extinguishing.

"Wait," I holler then jog out and meet him by his car door. "Please don't think I don't want you to come inside."

Although he never made such a suggestion, part of me feels the need to confess this aloud. To share what I desire, but am not ready to explore. For him to hear it from my lips—not only the words, but the subtle message behind my tone.

"Autumn, I would never assume anything." He caresses my cheek with his knuckles again and I melt into his touch as emotion dances like carbonation in my chest. "Much as I would love for you to invite me in, I don't think either of us is ready for that step. Not yet." He inches forward, the proximity of him hot on my skin. "I will wait until you're ready."

I peek up at Jonas from under my lashes and wonder where the hell he has been all my life. Why I hadn't met him sooner. A man with endless patience and unshakable kindness. A man that looks at me with gentleness and ardor.

"Jonas…"

Another shuffle forward, his lips now a breath away from grazing my own. Oh, how I want to taste him again.

"Please don't feel like you owe me an explanation. Because you don't."

Our eyes meet and my throat goes dry as I soak up the intensity of his gaze. The magnificent swirl of blue and green and gold, but a hint darker. They remind me of an incoming rainstorm at sunset. Not a storm worthy of fear, but one that lures you outdoors and begs you to get lost in it. To dance in the rain rather than try to escape the waterfall.

God, how I want to kiss him again. More than I want to breathe.

"Thank you. For telling me I don't owe you anything." My eyes drop to his lips and I tell myself to look back up. To focus on what I should say. To use my words. "There is so much I want to tell you. So much. But I need things between us to go slow. Not because I don't want you. I do, believe me." *You're rambling, Autumn.* Rambling aside, Jonas gives me his smile. One full of contentment with a dash of humor. "But my past has roots. Roots I need time to dig up. And it may take time."

He frames my face in his hands. "Hey." When he knows my attention is solely on him, he continues. "Like I said, we go at your pace. I'm not in any rush. I'm not going anywhere."

I really hope his words hold truth. Because what I haven't told him could be the one thing which scares him away. Jonas doesn't seem the type to scare easily, but it is best not to assume. Some people surprise you.

"You're the first person I've dated in a really long time," I confess. He cocks his head, toys with a strand of hair, and waits for me to continue. "Years ago, I dated this guy who swore he'd always be there for me. But" —I swallow and hang my head— "when things got more serious than he wanted, he bailed. It threw a wrench in everything. With my parents and my sister, and other parts of my personal life." I glance over my shoulder at the front door. Picture who is on the other side. "If it weren't for Penny and everyone else at the shop, I would've stayed on the street."

Jonas drops his hands from my face and the immediate loss sends a chill across my cheeks. But before I dwell on the absence of his touch, he slips his arms around my waist and envelops me in a hug so potent, emotion stings the back of my eyes. He holds me close to his chest, shushes the tears threatening to fall, and whispers how everything is fine now because he is here.

And I believe him. Right here, right now, I believe him. Regardless of how little I know Jonas, some facts are undeniable. Jonas is a good man. A good man raised by another good man.

I sense it when he hesitates to do things other men would assume is normal and acceptable. Like resting his hand on my back or taking my hand in his. Like asking for my phone number or address when he had the means to get it without my consent. Or when he asked, only minutes ago, permission to kiss me. Most men don't ask, they just take.

Jonas isn't like most men. He is levels above.

Not sure which of us initiates, but we slowly pull back from each other. Jonas lifts his hands back to my face and swipes his thumbs over my cheeks before leaning in and pressing a sweet, chaste kiss to my lips. "Although I don't like why you were crying, you look more beautiful than ever."

I close my eyes and get lost in the gyroscope of emotion spinning in my chest. Before Jonas, no man ever had me so tongue-tied and wobbly. Although I have walked on my own two feet for years, with Jonas I feel as if I am truly learning how they work. How they will carry me where I need to go. Toward him.

"Only you would think I look beautiful with mascara staining my cheeks."

He shakes his head. "You don't get it." No, I don't. Though, I won't admit such things aloud. "It's not that you have tear-stained makeup. It's the reason why. That you're exposing a piece of yourself and letting me see the parts no one else gets to."

When he explains it like this, I understand better. Little did I realize, I unintentionally opened myself up to him. I let him in when I never let anyone else in. With the exception of Penny. Reznor, Rex, and Iliana know minor, rough-around-the-edges details, but they don't know anything with depth. Penny, on the other hand, knows everything. Not because I favor her over the rest of my tattoo family, but because we live together and there is no possible way around it.

I drop my gaze from his eyes to his lips again. He won't make me ask permission, but I want to taste him one more time before we say good night again. Taste the sweetness of our shared dessert mixed with a flavor I define as distinctly Jonas. When my eyes remain on his lips, he makes my wish come true.

He leans forward and the space between us disappears. I close my eyes and fist his shirt as his lips press mine with unprecedented tenderness. He kisses me once. Twice. On the third kiss, I sweep the tip of my tongue along the seam of his lips. A low groan rumbles in his chest. I tighten my grip on the cotton as he slips his fingers into my hair and opens up to let me in.

Then I taste him again. Hot and sweet and addictive on my taste buds. The heat of his tongue tangling with mine is a shock wave throughout my body, waking all the parts once dormant. Loosening my hold, my hands trail up his chest, cup his cheeks and revel in the gruff grain against my soft palms.

He groans at my touch, drops his hands to my hips, and draws me impossibly closer. Close enough for the bulge beneath his zipper to brush my abdomen. The temptation to invite him in multiplies tenfold seconds before he breaks the kiss.

"You might be the death of me. But it'd be a good way to go," he says, gasping.

"Back atcha."

"As much as I don't want to leave, I should go."

I fight the urge to disagree, and nod. "Yeah," I whisper. "Will you call or text me?"

"Better believe it."

I smile and peek up at him. "Good night, Jonas."

He sweeps a stray hair out of my face, tucking it behind my ear. "Good night, Autumn."

As I walk back to the front door, he gets in the Jeep and starts it. We keep our eyes on each other until he backs out and drives away. For a moment, I stare at the space where I last saw his taillights. Absorb every moment of the evening, now that I am alone. Well, alone for a minute longer.

I take a deep breath and dig for the house key in my purse. Just as I go to insert the key in the lock, the door swings open and an overzealous Penny yanks me inside.

"I want details. Now."

I stumble over my own two feet as she closes the door and drags me over to the couch. "Pen." I laugh and plop down on the middle cushion.

"Don't you *Pen* me. And don't pretend like you weren't just outside kissing a hot-as-fuck man. Twice."

Biting the inside of my cheek, I fight the smile and laughter dying to burst free. But I lose the battle.

"Do you want a complete rundown of the evening? Cause I promise the entire date wasn't like what you witnessed out front, Peeping Tom."

"Girl, you better tell me everything. Beginning to end. And don't you dare leave a single detail out."

I kick off my shoes and tuck my feet beneath my butt. Penny draws her legs to her chest, rests her chin on her knees, and listens to every intricate detail about my date with Jonas. From the cutest retro diner I ever set foot in to the movie in the park where he held me close and I stopped paying attention to the screen and focused solely on his warm body curled behind mine. How his fingers splayed my belly and held me close. How I never wanted to miss a single moment of his breath on the back of my neck. She already witnessed the two separate kisses out front.

As I tell Penny how I broke the barrier and told Jonas a little about my past, she slaps a hand over her mouth. Me explaining an ounce of my past to anyone—no matter how big or small the detail—is a huge step. Penny knows I wouldn't tell just anyone. Which means I believe Jonas and I could become far more than just two people dating for the sake of dating.

"Auti, I'm so happy for you." I give her a half smile. "Seriously. It is way past time you did something for yourself. Be a little selfish for a change. Be happy. It looks good on you."

"Thanks, Pen." I yawn.

Although I have been awake much later than this countless times, the exhilaration from the evening is slowly fading and exhaustion is taking over.

"Go." Penny throws a thumb over her shoulder toward the hall. "Wash up and go to bed. We'll go out for breakfast in the morning. My treat."

I squint at her and she shakes her head. Rising up from the couch, I snatch my shoes off the floor and kiss the crown of Penny's head. "Thanks for always being the best. Don't know where I'd be without you."

"Love you too, Auti. Sleep tight."

After stowing the leftovers in the fridge, I go about my normal nightly routine before bed. As I brush my teeth, I zone out and replay my evening with Jonas. Recall the buzz zapping every inch of my skin and the hum deep in my belly as he laid behind me and pressed his palm to my lower abdomen. Jonas encasing me in his arms... I never felt more at home.

Flipping off the bathroom light, I tiptoe into the bedroom, change into my pajamas, and quietly slip between the sheets. I curl onto my side and face the opposite side of the bed. Face the angelic form beside me. Chest steadily rising and falling in the darkened room.

"I'm not going anywhere." Jonas's words creep back in from earlier. And as I take in the most important person in my world, the little girl less than a foot away, I pray his words stick when I tell him.

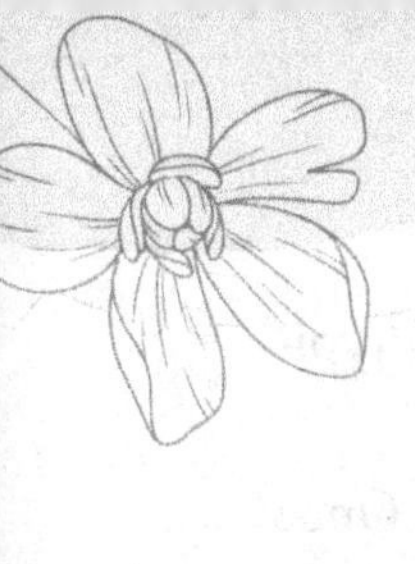

twelve

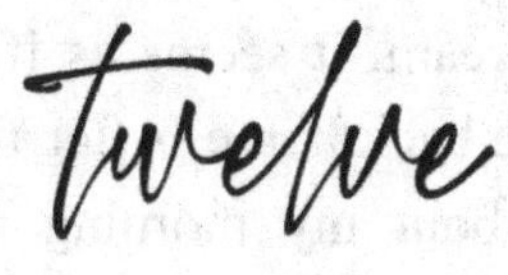

JONAS

I lay awake in bed, eyes on the ceiling but not really seeing it. Spartan twitches and dream barks at the foot of the bed. For once, it doesn't bother me. Nothing could right now.

When was the last time I felt like this? Lighter. Carefree. Happy. Like the future has a million possibilities and I can't wait to explore them all.

Easy. I haven't.

Date night with Autumn was literally one of the best in my life. Hell, I spent all day yesterday smiling like a goddamn idiot. I never enjoyed doing housework so much. Never enjoyed tearing up the back yard to landscape it like I did yesterday. Spartan ran around the yard, barking incessantly at squirrels and hunting for lizards. But it didn't irritate me as per usual.

The alarm blares on the bedside table and I slap the snooze button to shut it up. Spartan pops his head up from the mattress and yips.

"'Morning, buddy."

He yips again. I like to call it his quiet voice. As if he knows it's too early to use his full bark yet. Either way, it's adorable how quiet he is until I get out of bed. Then his typical, boisterous bark commences.

We get out of bed and ready for our morning walk. Once we step out the door, Spartan leads us down the street and along our usual morning path. Glad he can focus and lead the way because mentally I am still standing in front of Autumn's apartment, kissing her.

Lost in my daydream, it seems as if only a few minutes pass before we arrive back home. After filling Spartan's bowl with kibble, I go about my morning routine. I slip on a Thompson's Garage shirt and a pair of jeans before heading into the kitchen to make breakfast. Belly full, I slip on boots, secure Spartan in his kennel, and head out the door. A moment later, I zip through Clearwater on my bike, relishing the sharp sting of wind on my cheeks, and arrive at the garage early again.

When I walk into the office, Dad glances up from the stack of papers in front of him to the clock and shakes his head. "You keep this up and I might start setting your schedule earlier."

"Ha ha, old man." I brew a fresh pot of coffee before sifting through the invoices on my desk. "Looks like a busy day."

Dad doesn't say anything for a moment and I wonder if he didn't hear what I said. When I glance over at his desk, he stares at me with the biggest shit-eating grin on his face. The type you see when people know something you don't. I cock a brow and he shakes his head.

"Interesting," he says, cryptically.

"What?" I drop my head and scan my shirt to see if my breakfast is still hanging around. Nope.

"How was your weekend, son?"

My weekend? Why the hell would Dad ask about my weekend. Not that we never chat about how we spend our time apart, but it isn't an automatic Monday question. I think back and try to remember if I told him I was going on a date with Autumn.

Think, think, think.

No, don't think it ever came up. Especially after his snooping while I was on the phone. He means well, has a good heart, but it suddenly feels as if I'm a teenager all over again.

"Great. Why?"

His grin widens further. "Great, huh? What'd ya do?"

What the hell is this? Twenty questions of obscurity? Dad isn't the type to be evasive. At least, not from past experiences. Then again, I have never openly discussed my interest in someone. Does he know what I did this weekend? I mentally shake my head. Not possible.

"Went out. Did stuff around the house. Why?"

"Where'd you go?"

Okay, game over. Between him skirting around what he wants to say and the devious smile on his lips, I am about to explode from curiosity. "Why don't you just spit it out, old man."

He tips his head back and laughs. A full belly laugh. Similar to the thousands I have heard over the years. He's yanking my chain and he full well knows it. Even enjoys the slow torment with a wicked gleam in his eye.

"Back at ya, son." He points to my face. "Only reason I'm giving you a hard time is that."

"What?" I swipe my palms over my face and feel for the evidence he refers to. But I don't find it.

"Your permanent smile." My cheeks heat. "Don't be

embarrassed, son. The smile suits you." He gets up, walks to the coffee pot, and pours us each a cup. "Plus, a smile like that could be good for business."

"Alright." I laugh. "That's enough from you, old man."

He hands me a mug while he fishes the creamer out of the fridge. After he pours some in his coffee, he passes it my way.

"In all seriousness, it's really great to see you happy, son. And if a certain female car owner has anything to do with it, then I approve."

I pour cream in my cup then spoon in a little sugar. "Thanks, Dad. Means a lot."

We drink our coffee and work for the next hour in silence. But it isn't awkward or filled with the expectation to spill more details. Although, if I keep dating Autumn—which I have every intention of doing—Dad will dig for more. And I won't hold back.

The Thompson family is an open family. We don't hide anything from each other. We were all raised—Mom and Dad included—with the belief it is better to be open and honest from the get-go. Just saves from stirring up future problems.

After I finish paperwork in the office, I head to the garage bays and start on the first clients of the day. As of now, most of the morning is filled with appointments for routine maintenance. I step up to an SUV and match the vehicle to the invoice then get started on the oil change.

As I wipe my hands clean after finishing, my phone pings in my pocket. Pulling it out of my coveralls, I smile down at the screen. Two bays down, Dad laughs and points between my face and my phone. *Yeah, yeah, old man.*

Morning. Hope the rest of your weekend was good.

Her text has me smiling for two reasons. One—she sent me a text. How can I not be happy over that small fact? Getting a text means the other person was thinking of you. Two—her actual text. The message is sweet, but also makes me think she had no idea what to say. She simply wanted to text me, but didn't know how to initiate conversation. It reminds me how she said she hadn't dated in years. She didn't go into great detail, but someone probably didn't treat her right.

> Good morning. Best weekend in years.

> Yeah. What made it so great?

Is this Autumn subtly flirting? And why does every single word from her lips—and her fingers, I guess—make my cheeks sting? Heat me head to toe. Make my mind wander to places it never has. Places which include her in every facet.

> Oh, you know. A night on the town with a beautiful woman. Being domestic at home.

> Domestic, huh? *screenshots for future reference*

And there it is again. *Future reference.* The term sinks deeper into my marrow every time I hear—see—it. I love how she sees us beyond a single date or moment in time. How she wants more between us, even if she doesn't openly say it. Little indicators such as saving something I say for *future reference* means more to me than imaginable.

> What can I say... My parents raised me to be self-sufficient. Want to know a secret?

steeples fingers and leans in close Dish it
out already.

I laugh as my fingers fly over the screen.

Mom taught me how to sew buttons when I
was 5. Said every man should know how.

And now I'm in love with your mom.

A small tornado swirls in my chest—flipping things
upside down and causing my heart to beat violently. *Don't
take it out of context.* Her text is meant to be funny or cute.
That she loves my mom because she taught me things the
general populous deems a female activity. But Dad taught my
sisters how to change their own oil and swap out a flat tire.
It's just how the Thompson family rolled. Being self-sufficient is a life skill, not a gender skill.

Is it too soon for me to tell her that? She
might replace me with you. The third
daughter she never had.

Did that come out wrong? I reread my text and mentally
wipe my brow with the back of my hand. *Whew.* For a second
there, I thought maybe I insinuated something else. That our
relationship would lead her to becoming my mother's
daughter—in a sense.

Aaron already knows me. Wouldn't bother
me if you told your parents we are dating.

Dating. Not "went on a date." I glance up and across the
garage. Dad leans against a silver pickup with a knowing
smile on his face as he watches me text Autumn. Time to

wrap this up, otherwise Dad will tease me until the end of time.

> Hate to cut this short. Dad's giving me the side-eye.

Sorry 😊 I'll bring him cookies later.

> No need to apologize. And sprinkles are his favorite.

Sprinkles. Check. See you in a bit?

> I'll be here.

I tuck my phone back in my pocket and look over at Dad. "What're you smiling at, old man?"

"Ah, to be young and in love again," he says and I stop breathing.

Autumn is gorgeous and funny and downright lovable, but I never indicated I was *in love* with her. Did I? I mean, Jesus, I have only known her just shy of two weeks.

"Dad…" I warn. But he just waves me off. "By the way, since you wouldn't let Autumn pay for the repairs, she's bringing you cookies later."

"Really?" I nod and his grin brightens. "Well, son, I approve."

An hour later, I hear the telltale sounds of a classic car. Rolling out from under the sedan I currently work on, I sit up and swallow at the woman walking toward the bays with a bag in her hand.

Autumn strolls up in an off-the-shoulder, black-and-white striped top under dark denim overalls folded up to land just below the knee. Her black-brown locks are pinned up high on the back of her head while a folded bandana loops from the base of her skull up into a bow at her crown. Lips painted scarlet, as are her nails. And today she wears dark-tinted, black-framed, wingtip sunglasses.

I swallow harder with each step she takes in my direction. This woman will be the death of me. No doubt about it. Dad steps out of the bay next to me and meets Autumn five feet away from where I still sit on the ground.

"Hey there, sweetie. My son tells me I get cookies for being a nice guy."

Autumn slides her sunglasses up to rest on top of her head. "And I hear you love sprinkles."

Dad smiles down at me before meeting Autumn's gaze again. "You hear correct. Honestly, haven't met a cookie I don't love. Sprinkles just make them fun."

She laughs and hands Dad the bag. "Well, I didn't have time to bake. But there's lots of sprinkles plus some other flavors, in case anyone else wants cookies."

Without asking permission, Dad leans forward and side hugs Autumn. Doesn't seem to bother her one bit. "Very generous of you." Dad hands me the bag and I rise from the ground. "Son, why don't you take lunch and put these cookies in the office."

It's a suggestion, and one I appreciate. "Yeah, sure."

Walking over to a shelf, I set the cookies down and slip out of my coveralls. And I don't miss, in my periphery, the way Autumn ogles me as I disrobe. Although I am fully clothed beneath, she looks me up and down as if I stripped bare.

"Hungry," I croak out as I lead us into the office and set the bag of cookies on my desk.

"Starved," she whispers. But her response seems weighed down with so much more.

A foot between us, I keep my arms tucked at my sides and hold her fiery, cognac gaze. "Wish I had more than an hour for lunch."

Autumn steps closer, leaving a breath between us. "Any amount of time is better than none at all."

I nod and take a deep breath. My time with her now is limited. Lunch dates are not the same as dinner and a movie and her lips pressed to mine. Lunch dates are time crunched and light conversation and hugs until next time.

"C'mon. There's a sub shop up the street. My treat."

We walk out of the office and into the lot. "Well, if you're buying, I'm driving."

"I have no qualms about riding shotgun. Besides, I rode my bike to work."

"You own a motorcycle?" I nod as I slip inside the car and she cranks the engine. "Never been on a motorcycle before. Maybe sometime soon."

What is it about Autumn that lights my soul on fire? With a simple suggestion, my chest swells and my stomach ties knots faster than a sailor. Hell yes, she turns heads everywhere she goes. But her heart-shaped face and curvy body are just the tip of the iceberg. Autumn is so much more than the physical sum of her parts. All her remarks about the future, I ink them into my memory for later reference.

"I'd love to take you for a ride. Early morning works best on the weekends. Less traffic."

A couple miles down the road, I point out the sub shop and she pulls in. We head inside, order, and sit at a table while we wait for our sandwiches. I tell Autumn about some of my favorite places to ride during the early hours of the day. On a few occasions, I left town earlier than I leave the house for work and drove north. An hour or two north, the roads have fewer commuters and there are several small towns with attractive scenery. If the opportunity ever presents itself, I would love to take Autumn on one of those day trips.

"It'd be nice to visit these places you're telling me about."

"Well, if you're ever up for it, let me know."

A man deposits lunch on the table and walks off with the numbered plastic tent. We dig into our sandwiches and eat in silence for a minute. For some reason, a weird vibe bounces off Autumn. Not sure if it is because I mentioned going out of town on the bike or if it's something else altogether. She never mentioned how the rest of her weekend went.

"Sorry I didn't get to ask earlier, but how was the rest of your weekend?"

She finishes chewing the bite in her mouth, but still covers her mouth with her hand when she speaks. "Good. Went out for breakfast yesterday. Then binged on snacks and Netflix. I was definitely not productive." She laughs and it is music to my ears.

"Love those kinds of days. I try to have one at least once a month. Spartan and I spent most of the day digging up old flower beds in the back yard. Previous owners had a thing for cementing pavers together. Was probably a great idea thirty-plus years ago, but now it's just horrible."

The rest of lunch goes by way too fast, and before I know it, we have to head back to the garage.

At the traffic light two blocks before the garage, I lean my back against the passenger window and soak up every inch of Autumn. I want to kiss her again. Soon.

"Are you busy tomorrow night?" I ask.

She peeks up at the red light then over to me. "Haven't checked my schedule for work yet. Why?"

"I'm meeting friends at the bowling alley. Cora should be

there. We get together at least once a week. Tomorrow, we're bowling. Wanted to know if you'd care to join."

She tucks her lips between her teeth and I want to reach over and pop them out. But I don't.

"When I get to work, I'll check my schedule. What time is everyone meeting up?"

"Seven. We usually bowl a couple games and call it a night."

"I'll tentatively say yes, but let you know if there's a schedule conflict."

She steers the car into the garage lot and stops parallel to the storefront. I unbuckle my belt and lean toward her. Her eyes drop to my lips and I take it as a sign of permission to kiss her.

The moment my lips graze hers, the cooler December temperatures vanish. Our slow and sweet kiss ends far too soon. "I'll text you the details for tomorrow night when I'm off work."

Our lips a breath apart, her eyes shift back and forth between mine. "Look forward to it," she says, voice drug laced and lips parted.

One last chaste kiss and I force myself to exit the car. "See you tomorrow." She nods, and I love how I struck her speechless.

I turn on my heel and walk back to the garage bay with an ear-to-ear smile. Dad spots me. "Good lunch?"

Best damn lunch in the history of lunches.

thirteen

AUTUMN

Is this a mistake?

I turn into the parking lot of the bowling alley. Since when are bowling alleys this busy on a Tuesday night? Sure, it has been forever and a day since I have set foot in one, but it was always a weekend day. And every place is busy on the weekend.

Winding through the lot, I park Betsy and cut the engine. Facing the entrance of the bowling alley, I scan the sea of faces standing outside. Among them is Jonas. With his messy chocolate strands, broad shoulders, and booming laughter, I will always be able to pinpoint him in a crowd.

He stands with two other women—a dirty-blonde nearly as tall as him and a curly redhead closer to my height. For a moment, I observe how he interacts with them. By the ease at which they interact, it's evident they all know one another. They smile and laugh and look completely comfortable with one another. When the blonde pushes at Jonas's chest and the trio laughs in unison, the little green monster perks up on my shoulder as a rush of jealousy spikes my bloodstream.

"Get it together," I chide myself. "Men and women have non-romantic relationships all the time."

Nothing but truth. After all, the same can be said about some of my male friends. Then why does seeing Jonas so casual and relaxed with two other women make my jaw clench? More than likely, it is the result of not dating or being in a committed relationship for years.

Taking a deep breath, I open the door and exit the car. Seven steps forward and Jonas homes in on my presence. Locks eyes with me. Stops listening to the two women at his side. Smiles so wide, the dimple I love makes an appearance. Pushes off the wall and walks my direction. Meets me a few feet from the paved walkway around the building.

"Hey," he says as he steps into my space.

"Hi."

When he drops his lips to mine, I don't stop him. If anything, I encourage him to give me more. His tongue sweeps over mine and I moan. He tastes of cherry cola and desire. Far too soon, he breaks the kiss and chuckles under his breath as I lean into him.

"If we keep this up, we'll never see the inside of the bowling alley." *Sounds good to me*. He laces his fingers with mine. "C'mon. Let me introduce you to Shelly and Erin."

Hand in hand, we walk back to where he stood earlier. Where the two women he chatted with stand. "'Kay," I whisper.

A few strides forward, he pauses. "Everything alright?"

I nod and tighten my hold on his hand. "Yeah. Just nervous. Don't hang with new people often."

He drops my hand and I pout until he frames my face with his palms. "It'll be okay. Promise. Everyone is pretty chill.

Plus, Cora and Gavin will be here too." He plants a chaste kiss on my lips and I silently beg for another.

We step up to the two women and I paste on a polite smile. If I thought they were attractive from a distance, I was sorely mistaken. Attractive isn't the proper term. Because up close, they captivate and hold my attention more. And the wicked green monster pops up on my shoulder again, swinging its legs and whistling. *Shut up.*

"Shelly"—Jonas gestures to the blonde, then the redhead—"Erin, this is Autumn. Autumn, this is Shelly and Erin. Shelly and Cora have been friends since boys were gross. And Erin works with Cora."

I extend my hand to each of them. "Nice to meet you both."

Shelly performs a quick scan. "You are fucking cute." I laugh and peek up at Jonas who chuckles under his breath. "Really dig your vibe."

"Thanks." Although we just met, it's easy to see Shelly is a hoot.

Jonas wraps his arm around my shoulders. "Ladies, let's head inside and grab lanes. Everyone else should be here soon."

We stroll through the automatic doors and are immediately hit with the cacophony of Tuesday nights at the bowling alley. Colorful globes of resin clash against wooden pins. Upbeat dance music booms from the overhead speakers. Patrons hoot and holler and cheer each other on. Claps and whistles. Middle-age adults jumping off the floor when they manage to knock all the pins down.

The energy is boisterous and infectious.

We pay for shoes and get assigned two lanes. On our way to the lane, we pass the bowling alley's food bar. Melted cheese and baked bread and cinnamon sugar waft up my nose. My stride falters and Jonas pauses beside me.

"You okay?"

I point over at the neon lights highlighting every party food known to man. "Yep. Just swallowing down my hunger."

He laughs. "After we get everything set up, we'll order food."

After swapping out our shoes, Shelly, Erin, and I venture off to find a ball. Can't remember the last time I bowled, let alone what weight ball I used when I played. Once I decide on a lime green, eight-pound ball, I head back to the lane where more bodies have congregated.

Cora and Gavin stand near the seats of the left lane we rented. Arms wrapped around each other; she looks up at him as if no one else is here. Maybe it holds true for them. Their happiness makes me smile and spreads warmth in my chest.

I set my ball down and sidle up to Jonas. He curls his arm around my waist. "Everyone else is here. Let me introduce you." I nod and bite the inside of my cheek. "Hey guys." Six sets of eyes glance over at us. "This is Autumn." Although I have met four of the six, the attention from all of them makes me wilt into Jonas's side. "Autumn, this is Cora, Gavin, Shelly, Erin, Micah, and Trevor." With each name Jonas prattles off, he points to each person.

Lifting a hand, I wave to the obviously tight-knit group as heat crawls up my neck and lands on my cheeks. "Hey everyone. Nice to meet you." I am not necessarily a shy person. Hell, sometimes I am pretty outgoing. Just don't prefer the spotlight. Especially around new faces.

"Let's order food while everyone finishes getting ready," Jonas suggests.

Three pizzas, two pretzels, a basket of loaded fries, and

two churros ordered later, we head back to the lanes with two pitchers of beer and glasses. The young girl at the counter told us they would bring the food to our lane soon.

We settle in the chairs at the lane. Jonas places an arm around my shoulder and inches closer to me while I snack on the churros. As we wait for Trevor and Gavin to come back with a ball, I people watch the group Jonas calls family.

The dynamic between all of them is fascinating. If I had to guess—strictly by appearances and the way they interact—Shelly and Micah must be siblings. Same dark blonde hair. Same dark blue eyes. And they tease each other in a way only brothers and sisters do. When Gavin winds his way back over to us, I follow his every move until he sits down next to Cora. Who is staring at me. With piqued intensity.

Nothing in the way she watches me feels malicious or worrisome. If anything, she studies me with intrigue. Beside me, Jonas talks to Trevor—who I hadn't realized returned—with his arm still around my shoulders. A small smile perks up the corners of Cora's mouth. But her smile amplifies when Jonas stops talking to Trevor and he presses his lips to my temple.

Cora is happy for me. For Jonas. And her silent interest says more than any words could express.

Jonas drops his lips lower and his breath heats the shell of my ear. "Ready to bowl?"

You have no idea. "Yes."

One by one, we roll our ball down the oil-slicked lane and occasionally knock down pins. Early on, I learn Jonas, Shelly, and Trevor play a decent game. The rest of us are mediocre. The first game ends and I land a whopping seventy-eight points. Thankfully, I don't stand alone in my meh score. And I didn't score the lowest.

I snag a third slice of pizza and laugh when Jonas catches me scarfing it down. "What?" I ask around a mouthful of dough, cheese, ham, and pineapple.

He steps up to me, rests his hands on my hips, and draws me close. "Nothing. You're just so damn cute." I swallow my bite just before he leans down and kisses me.

Not sure if it's because we are surrounded by hundreds of people—and a handful of Jonas's close friends—but this kiss feels different. Loaded. Intense. Powerful.

Jonas brings both his hands to my cheeks and holds me reverently as our lips move in time and his tongue dips inside my mouth. I reach forward and grip the hem of his shirt, bringing him closer. Warmth radiates off his chest and seeps into every one of my pores. Heats every molecule in my body and fevers my skin. The cacophony surrounding us vanishes. Bursts of red and orange splash the backs of my eyelids like fireworks in the night sky. The pericardium encasing my heart swells and constricts with each frenzied swipe of his tongue against mine.

I drag him impossibly closer. Deepen the kiss. Sink my nails in his hips. Moan against his lips.

Until someone coughs behind Jonas and dumps a bucket of ice water over us.

"Sorry to interrupt, man. You're up," an embarrassed Gavin says.

If anyone should be embarrassed, it sure as hell shouldn't be him. It should be me. He wasn't making out in the middle of the bowling alley like a hormonal teenager. Nope, that was most definitely me.

Jonas inches back and meets my eyes. His palms still pressed to my cheeks; I swelter beneath the swirl of his irises. Like two thermal hot springs, they smolder as the blue and gold and orange devour me. I can't look away. Won't look away.

He places one last, all too brief kiss on my lips. I visibly pout when he retreats and he chuckles. "Be right back."

Stepping up to the ball return, he picks up his ball, positions himself, and follows through. The ball whirls down the lane and knocks all the pins down with a loud *whack*. He returns to my side and kisses my temple.

"You're up," he whispers against my skin.

I bowl my turn and knock down nine—which is better than most of the frames in the first game—and slap a few high fives on my way back to Jonas. A few more frames pass with *oohs* and *aw mans*. The laughter is nonstop and I quickly love this group of people. They remind me of my tat family. Not conventional by any means, but everyone cares about each other. How real family should be.

As Jonas refills his beer, my phone vibrates in my pocket. I tug it out, glance at the screen, and let Jonas know I will be right back.

Stepping away from the lane, I head near the entrance where it is somewhat quieter. Covering my left ear with my palm, I lift the phone to my right. "Hello?"

"Hey, someone wants to say good night," Penny says.

I step a little farther from the noise. On the other end, the phone changes hands and a sweet voice filters through the speaker. "Hi, Mama. Are you having fun?"

"Hey, pumpkin. I am. Are you and Auntie Penny having fun?"

"Yep. We watched *The Nightmare Before Christmas* again."

I laugh internally. Penny groans every time Clementine

wants to watch it. Probably because she has seen it a hundred times. "Was it good?"

"Better than last time," she announces. "What time will you be home?"

"In a little bit. My friends and I are almost done playing our game. Then I'll be home."

"Okay, Mama. I love you."

I smile into the phone. "Love you too. I'll kiss you when I get home."

"M'kay. Night night."

"Good night."

As I disconnect the call, I look up and spot a confused Jonas a few feet away. *Shit.*

Is there ever a good time to tell someone you're dating you have a seven-year-old daughter? Nope. Because no matter the reason, Jonas will be upset I haven't told him about her. Which will end in one of two results. One—he will drop me faster than a hot pan. Or two—we will stay together, but his trust in me will diminish for a bit until I can prove myself again.

Either way, it sucks.

"Who was that?" Jonas asks, pointing to my phone.

I want to tell him. Want to let him in on this part of my life. But it's too soon. We still have so much to learn about each other before I let him know this other part of my world exists. And I don't let many people know Clementine exists for one reason. Hurt.

If Jonas decides to stop seeing me because I have a daughter, I can suck up the pain that will undoubtedly consume me with his absence. But my daughter, she doesn't need to feel hurt or pain or sadness. It's horrible enough her own father has never been around. Never seen her face or heard her precious laughter. I don't need Clementine to suffer the loss of a pseudo-father.

"Penny called," I say.

He purses his lips and breaks eye contact. "Does she often call for a *love you* and *good night*?" His tone isn't angry or spiteful. But he knows I am not telling him the whole truth. And this is not the right time or place.

But before the end of the night, I will have to tell Jonas about Clementine. Hopefully afterward, he won't hate me for keeping the biggest secret from him.

fourteen

JONAS

Am I an asshole? Because right now it is difficult to tell.

A minute ago, I heard Autumn tell whoever she was talking to that she loved them, would kiss them when she got home, and wished them a good night. When I asked her who she was talking to, she said Penny called. Is her relationship with Penny more than friends? Because I didn't sign up for that.

But here I am, lipping off like a douchebag. Throwing accusations at my girlfriend when I haven't given her the chance to explain anything. Going against everything my parents taught me—which is to never assume. All assumptions do is cause harm and way too much stress.

Yep. Official asshole.

We walk back to the lane in silence. Usually, silence with Autumn is easy. Comfortable. Pleasant.

This new version of silence sucks.

Every few steps, I peek over at her out of the corner of my eye and berate myself mentally. Autumn hangs her head—not sure if she is embarrassed, angry or upset. Regardless, I hate how I put her in a foul mood. How I am the reason she went from enjoying a night out with me and my friends to probably wishing she wasn't here.

Before I buck up the courage to apologize, we reach the lane. She lifts her head, smiles, and pretends like the last few minutes never happened.

For the next five frames, neither of us speaks. We don't whisper to each other, kiss or remotely touch. And I hate every single second. It sears my heart like a branding iron. Except this brand doesn't mark me as hers, it just keeps pressing on and scalds until I black out from the pain.

When the game ends, Cora sidles up beside me as Autumn puts her ball back on the rack.

"Everything okay?" she asks.

This is beyond awkward. The woman I thought was the only person I wanted, who recently married the love of her life, is asking me about the woman I have been dating for almost no time at all. Funny thing is, it feels as if I have known Autumn for years. As if she has always been mine. What Cora and Gavin have, I get it now.

"Not sure." I glance toward the wall with the ball racks and spot Autumn chatting with Shelly. A smile sits on her face, but it isn't genuine. I have seen the genuine smile. "She was on the phone earlier and I overheard part of the call. Then I said something dickish."

Cora smiles subtly. "Your relationship with her is still very new, Jonas. But the way you both look at each other… it's deep. You guys need time. Don't rush it. Get to know each other. Autumn is a sweet woman. But we all have history and baggage. The older we get, the more we have."

I stare at my best friend straight-faced. "When did you become so wise?"

She slaps my arm and laughs. "Jerk. I've always been wise." Another laugh. "It just takes everyone else way too long to realize it and catch up."

"Ouch," I say, and it has nothing to do with the playful smack a moment ago.

Autumn walks up to us with a shy smile on her face. Without permission or announcement, Cora hugs Autumn. Cora squeezes her tight and whispers something in Autumn's ear. Too quiet for me to hear. When Cora lets her go, she braces her hands on Autumn's shoulders and gives her a pointed look. Autumn's lips curve up and she nods.

"Have a good night. See you next time," Cora says to Autumn before turning to me. She gives me a hug and whispers in my ear next. "Assumptions are the death of relationships. Ask, but be patient. Because I love the way she makes you come to life."

Before Cora pulls away, I whisper *thank you* in her ear.

Everyone else leaves before me and Autumn. As if they wanted to give us privacy to talk. To hash out whatever changed both our temperaments three-quarters of the way through our night out.

On the way out of the bowling alley, I desperately want to wrap Autumn's hand in mine. But I don't. I feel as if I don't deserve her hand right now. Not after how I behaved earlier. How I accused her of being dishonest.

It was super shitty and I wish there was a way I could take it all back. Take it back and say something different. Or not say anything at all.

But instead of giving her time to slowly divulge her past to me, I ripped the proverbial bandage off and basically forced her to explain herself. My parents would be pissed with my juvenile behavior. I am.

Her conversation could have been completely innocent. But instead of allowing her the opportunity to tell me in her own time, I snooped and jumped to conclusions. Mom always taught my sisters and I that snooping never accomplished anything except for causing more problems. And I have learned, over the years, Mom always steered me down the correct path.

A couple cars from Autumn's, I reach for her hand and she lets me take it. *Thank goodness.*

"Hey" —I halt us at the back of her car— "I'm really sorry about earlier. I shouldn't have been such an ass."

Autumn closes her eyes and essentially cuts me off from her sweet, addictive cognac irises. And the loss of her eyes on me sends a sharp pain through my chest. Slow, yet steady and debilitating. I don't like it.

"Jonas…" She says my name as if it causes her pain. The ice pick in my heart twists and deepens. "Please don't make me choose."

I shake my head, confused. "Choose?"

She opens her eyes and my pulse silences for one, two, three beats. "Jonas, I…" She swallows and peeks up at me. Tears stand on the ledge of her eyes, thinking of jumping. And I hate how I have put her in this place.

"What is it, Autumn? Please tell me. I… I hate that I did this. I hate that I upset you." I wipe away a tear that escapes and rolls down her cheek. "That I made you cry. I will never forgive myself."

She leans into my touch and I take it as a good sign. "Thank you. But, Jonas…" Autumn kisses my palm, then stands straighter. "I need to tell you something."

I bend at the knees and lower myself to her height so we stand eye to eye. "You can tell me anything," I say.

Her eyes dart between mine. She swallows and nods. "Jonas, I have a daughter." Her confession comes out barely audible.

What did she just say? Did I hear her correctly? Did Autumn just tell me she has a daughter?

Dumbstruck, I have no clue how to respond to her confession. Does it bother me that she has a daughter? A child? No. But the only thing I know about kids I have learned from being around my nephew. Which isn't often enough to say I have knowledge. He is cute and fun and says the craziest shit sometimes, but I don't spend long periods of time with him.

"Jonas?" Autumn asks after I don't say anything for far too long.

"Sorry. I'm just…"

"Terrified?"

I shake my head at her. "No. But I don't know what to say or do next." Her phone call earlier makes perfect sense now. And I hate how I reacted. Ugh, I am such a prick.

"There's nothing to do," she says. And the way she says the words adds a new wound. But this one feels different. Deeper. Harsher. One which will leave a vicious scar. "I think we should take a break."

Shaking my head and pinching my brow, I stumble back from her. "Wait, what? Why?"

Is she really doing this? Breaking up with me before we even begin. I can't fucking breathe. Can't hear anything except buzzing white noise. Can't see anything except Autumn's face slowly fading in the darkness.

Please tell me I misheard her. Please tell me this is all a farce.

"This is why I never dated, Jonas. Because it just gets in the way."

Seriously? How on earth is this reality? Two hours ago—hell, even an hour ago—everything was perfect. We were perfect. And now…

"Is that what I am, Autumn? In the way?" Anger seeps into my veins and coats the hurt residing there. Because anger is easier to manage than heartache. Heartache and I seem to be besties nowadays.

"Jonas, that didn't come out right."

I throw my hands in the air, ready to go to battle. Hours ago, I would fight to the death for Autumn's happiness. But this stubborn rejection she tosses at me for shits and giggles… it's bullshit.

"Then please, clear it up for me. Explain it so I understand."

She rolls her eyes. "Please don't make this harder than it is."

I laugh without humor. "Why? Because you like me? Because I like you? Breaking up a relationship shouldn't be easy, Autumn. Not when both parties feel the way we do." Part of me wants to drop to my knees and grovel. But I won't. Not here. Not tonight.

"It's just easier this way."

"For who? You? Me?" I step within an inch of her face and lock eyes with her. "Losing you will never be easy," I whisper. "Never."

Autumn closes her eyes as if it pains her to look into mine. Good. It should hurt. Breaking off what we have, what we could have, should hurt. Nothing has ever crippled me like hearing Autumn tell me she no longer wants me.

A tear rolls down her cheek and, this time, I don't reach for it. Don't swipe it away with my thumb while muttering sweet reassurances. Words which tell her everything will work out. That we will be okay. That we will survive this.

Because I don't believe it myself. How can I?

"As great as we are… were…" Tears spill from her eyes more easily now. Pain floods every line and curve and dimple of her face, but she won't admit the pain this causes her. Not aloud. Not when she believes being alone for her daughter is the right thing to do. "I can't do this, Jonas. It wasn't a good idea."

I bite the inside of my cheek to prevent myself from saying something I will later regret. As determined as Autumn is, I will find a way to make this better. I have to.

"If that's how you feel," I say before swallowing down the wad of cotton in my throat. "If this is what you want, I guess there's nothing I can do to change your mind."

I take a step backward. Then another. And another.

With each falter back, the pain on her face intensifies. Each move away from her, she flinches. But I refuse to be a punching bag for someone. Refuse to stand on the sidelines while she lives her life as if I don't matter to her. Because I do. I do fucking matter.

She won't admit it to herself, but she cares. Maybe a little too much. And perhaps therein lies the problem.

"Jonas," she mumbles.

I take another step away from her. And another. Then I spin around and stride toward my bike. After I slip on my helmet, I rev the engine louder than appropriate. I am in no condition to ride, but I can't be here any longer. Not after everything that has happened here tonight.

How do I go from being on the cusp of slipping the infamous *L*-word to breaking up with the one woman I can't imagine life without?

Fuck.

I smack the handlebar as I fly down the highway. As I ugly cry for a woman for the first time in my life. As I feel my life crumbling into a pile of ash.

fifteen
AUTUMN

Jonas revs his motorcycle louder than polite several spaces down from me. Still standing at the back of my car, I stare glassy-eyed at him as he backs the bike out of the space then zips out of the parking lot and onto the highway faster than safe.

And the moment I no longer see him, when I no longer hear the angry growls of the bike engine, I start shaking head to toe. My heart hammers in my ribcage. My breath coming in short bursts.

What have I done?

I reach behind me and brace myself on the car. Slowly, I guide myself to the driver's side door as a torrent of tears spills down my cheeks. I fumble through my purse—frustrated as hell with my oversized bag—until I locate my keys. Drop the keys from my trembling fingers as I try to unlock the door.

Once I finally get the door unlocked, I fall into the seat and slam the door shut. Tossing my purse on the passenger seat, I white-knuckle the steering wheel as I rest my forehead on top.

My chest wrenches violently as the sobs continue to come. I can't catch my breath. Can't think clearly. And there is an ever-expanding hollowness beneath my breastbone.

It fucking hurts. Hurts more than anything I have ever known. The exponential pain unbearable.

I lean back into the seat with my grip still firmly on the wheel and scream at the top of my lungs. Slightly cathartic, it only serves to exacerbate the emptiness taking over my heart.

"Why," I scream at the windshield. "Why did I do this to myself? Why did I do this when I knew it would be a bad idea? When I knew it would end badly."

Simple. When your heart is involved, your brain no longer makes rational decisions.

And Jonas was definitely in my heart. Still is.

But doing this, breaking things off, before either of us becomes too heavily invested, is for the best. At least that is what I keep telling myself.

How could it be for the best if it hurts this much?

Shouldn't I be relieved? Now I don't have to worry about the awkwardness of being a single parent and trying to fit another person into my life. Don't have to worry about my daughter becoming attached to a man who won't stick around. Don't have to worry about her little heart being crushed by losing another person in her life.

I should be relieved, but I am far from it.

Minutes tick by as I work to cease the dam of tears spilling from my eyes. Once they subside enough for me to see clearly, I pop the key in the ignition and start the car. I ease out of the space and exit the lot.

The drive home is a blur. Not because I can't see, but because I go from point A to point B on autopilot. No music to distract me. No visual stimulation to spark my brain back to life. And somehow, I make it home safely.

After I cut the engine, I sit in the dark for a moment and try to compose myself. Surely, I look like shit. There will be no hiding what happened tonight from Penny. Nothing except time will erase the pain on my face and in my heart. Quite a bit of time.

I suck in a deep breath and tug the handle to open the door. Each step toward the front door feels like a step closer to my demise. Where I will have to relive everything all over again. A vicious cycle of hurt on repeat.

As I unlock the front door, the television mutes inside. When I swing the door wide and Penny sees my face, her smile vanishes as she bolts from the couch.

"Oh my god, Auti. What's wrong?"

And I lose it. Again.

Penny wraps her arms around me and holds me in a death grip hug. I cry into her neck. On her shoulder. And she gently strokes my hair and shushes me, telling me everything will be okay.

Before I realize it, Penny has walked us to the couch and is sitting us down. She lets me cry until I am ready to stop. Doesn't ask any questions and just lets me sob uncontrollably.

When I finally compose myself enough to speak, everything comes out broken and stilted. "I broke up with Jonas." A new torrent floods my eyes. Penny rises from the couch, disappears down the hall, and returns with a box of tissues. She pops one from the box and hands it to me before settling the box on the couch in front of me.

Penny brushes fallen strands of my hair out of my face as I swipe my eyes dry. "Want to talk about it?" she asks, her tone soft and cajoling.

I blow my nose and try to rein in my sobs so I can explain how everything unfolded at the bowling alley. When the tears settle to a lesser flow and the sobs quit wracking my body so heavily, I dive headfirst into how everything went from fantastic to shit in the blink of an eye.

"Let me start by saying, the night had been perfect up until your phone call."

Penny scrunches her brow. "My call?"

Nodding, I continue. "We bowled. Ate all the junk food from the food bar. Had some beer. Shared smiles and laughs with his friends." I suck in a breath. Futz with tissue between my fingers. "He kissed me in front of everyone like no one else existed. It was perfect," I whisper. "And then a couple of frames later, you called and I stepped away."

She reaches forward, takes my hands in hers, and gives them a little squeeze. Encouragement to continue, but also to remind me she is here. That no matter what she says, she has my back.

"I guess he saw me walk off and followed. But I had no idea. He overheard part of my conversation with Clementine. After I hung up and saw him watching me… Pen, you should've seen the look on his face. It's like he didn't trust me. He asked who I was talking to and I told him you had called."

Penny snorts and shakes her head. "Truth and not."

I nod. "Yeah. Well, I guess he heard me tell Clementine I love her and that I'd kiss her when I got home. I never said her name. And when I told him you'd called, he flipped on me. Got upset and thought I was lying. Asked if you called for a good night often. I'd backed myself into a corner and had no idea how to get out."

"You should've told him about her then."

"I know," I say as I hang my head. "But he was acting like such a jerk. And I didn't have the energy to go into explanation right then. Plus, his friends were all waiting on us to return. When we did, they all knew something was off."

I go on to tell Penny how we finished the rest of the game in the thickest cloud of tension. How I got more and more frustrated with each passing moment. How I decided, when the night was over, that I would break things off with Jonas because it seemed like the right thing to do. To just cut out the heartache now. To eliminate the need to skirt around the truth. That I had a daughter and she was my world. Clementine would always stand front and center in my life, no matter how much I cared for someone else.

"When we got ready to leave, Cora came over to me and gave me a hug."

"Cora? As in Gavin and Cora, Cora?"

"Yep. She and Jonas have been friends for years. He supposedly had the hots for her."

"Had?"

"Until he met me," I whisper.

Penny stares at me wide-eyed. "Wow."

"Yeah. Well, when Cora hugged me, she whispered something to me."

"What?" Penny asks, leaning in closer, hungry for all the details.

"She told me she'd never seen Jonas so happy. And she hoped he made me happy too. When she pulled out of the hug, all I could do was nod. Because I knew I was about to rip it all away."

A new onslaught of tears pours down my cheeks as Penny tugs me forward into her arms. God, I have never cried this much in my life. And it fucking sucks.

I thought getting this all off my chest, spilling all my pain out, would help. That talking with Penny would alleviate some of the devastation coursing through my veins. Bring a sense of comfort and slowly wash away the heartache I know will reside in me for days or weeks or months to come. But it isn't. If anything, it only serves to amplify it. Spark it with new life.

Penny eases her embrace and leans back to swipe at my tears. "Auti, do you really think what you did was the right thing?"

What? Why is she asking me this? Of all the people who I assumed would be Team Autumn, I pegged Penny at the top of the list.

"What kind of question is that?"

She shakes her head as she cups both my cheeks and locks eyes with me. "Don't be upset. It's a fair question. If you thought breaking up with Jonas was the right thing to do, you wouldn't be crying like this. Not after dating for such a short period of time. Neither of you knows much about the other. Your relationship is, was, still in the beginning stages. You're getting to know one another. Finding the quirks and kinks. Learning about pasts as well as likes and dislikes." She drops her hands from my face and leans back slightly. "Please don't take this the wrong way, Auti, but you didn't even give him a chance."

I narrow my eyes at her. Did she really just say that? Or did I mishear her?

"Let me clarify," she says.

"Please do."

"Auti, you left him high and dry not explaining the phone call. Then, when you finally do go into explanation, when you finally tell him about Clementine, you break it off with him.

You never gave him a chance to register any of what you told him. You never gave him a minute to comprehend what you'd just told him. To grasp the fact you are a mom. It's a lot to process. I hate to say it, but it isn't fair to him. It isn't fair for you to have dropped a major bomb and then run for the hills."

When she says it like that, it dawns on me how much of a jerk *I am*. She has a point. Without considering Jonas's feelings, I dropped a whopper of a bomb and then told him we would be better off apart. A knee-jerk reaction, but now I am slowly seeing the error of my ways.

Since my pregnancy with Clementine, all I wanted was to do what was right for my daughter. Give her a good home. Shower her in love and smiles and laughter. And have good people around her. Her father and my family may have severed ties with us, but she has never felt unloved or unwanted a day in her life.

"How do I fix this?" I whisper-ask as fresh tears spill from my eyes.

"Give him a little time. And then, reach out to him again. Spill your heart out to him. Let him know you're sorry. Grovel, if necessary." I laugh at the last bit. "Just don't wait too long, Auti. Because men like Jonas only come around once."

Shit, shit, shit.

Did I royally screw myself by jumping the gun? I made a decision in the heat of the moment without really thinking things through. I made a decision based on the people of my past and how they hurt me and, by proxy, Clementine. But Jonas isn't like Clementine's father. Nor is he like my own mother and father, who disowned me.

Jonas is this sweet and wholesome guy. One who holds your hand and sets your body on fire at the same time. Who kisses me breathless as if I hold the key to a life he never thought he would possess. Who looked at me as if no one else existed.

What have I done?

Penny rises from the couch and kisses the top of my head. "I'm headed to bed. Try to get some sleep. It'll all work out, Auti. Just believe it will and it will."

"Thanks, Pen. Love you."

"Love you too. Night."

"Night," I whisper as she walks to her room.

I turn off the television and the light before heading to the bathroom. When I flip on the bathroom light and see my reflection in the mirror, I immediately flick the light off.

Looks as if I have been at a funeral for ten days straight. My eyes are veiny and angry, red and puffy. My cheeks and throat blotchy. And the mascara streaks down my face could double as clown makeup.

After I finish my nighttime routine in the dark, I slip into bed and kiss Clementine on the forehead. Turning so I face away from her, I cry silently into my pillow.

Cry for the loss of a good man. Cry for the mistake I made in assuming he would no longer want me once he found out I am a single mom. And cry for myself. For the throbbing ache in the center of my chest. The ache which only grows stronger with each passing second. The ache I deserve after what I did tonight.

But I will make this right. I have to. Not just for selfish reasons. Also because I need Jonas. More than I thought possible after such a short period.

I only hope he still wants me when I crawl back and beg for forgiveness.

sixteen

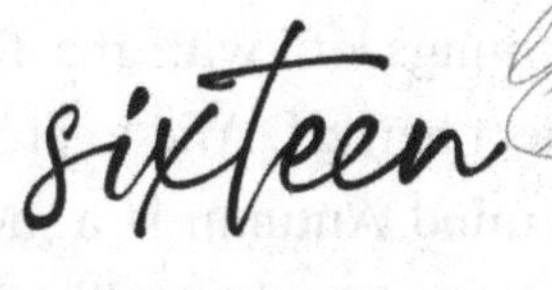

JONAS

The entire day at work sucks.

I slept for shit last night. No matter which way I had lain in bed, sleep was impossible. I tried counting backward from one hundred. That only lasted to eighty-five, when my brain sidetracked and I had to start all over again. Tried listening to calming music, but it only fired me up more. Even tried a meditation app I downloaded at three this morning. Nothing.

Dad knows something is wrong. He sees the complete one-eighty in my demeanor. But he won't ask what has me on edge. When I feel ready to tell him, he knows I will. Our entire lives, that's how he and I operated.

So, he will wait patiently for me to explain why I can't focus on one goddamn thing. Why I have yelled and cursed more times today than I have in the last decade. Why I slam the tools down instead of carefully put them in their place. Why I have stormed out of the garage and into the office more than a dozen times in the last three hours.

It might be a while before I mention anything to Dad, though. My ego is littered with bruises while my heart lies scattered in bits.

She didn't even give me a chance. Not having a chance stings the worst.

Last night's conversation in the parking lot cycles through my mind for the thousandth time. Each time I recall what she told me, a new wave of emotion rolls through me. Anywhere from anger to frustration to agony to understanding. And then it starts all over again.

Autumn broke things off with me for one reason. Well, maybe two. To protect herself. And to protect her *daughter*.

Still blows my mind Autumn is a mother. Not because it was inconceivable to picture her with a small bundle in her arms. Picturing her that way is actually quite believable. But because she thought hiding a major piece of herself was the right choice. She once told me she hadn't dated in years. Is her lack of dating because she is a single mother?

Another stab to the heart.

I only got a small glimpse at life with Autumn on my arm. With her lips on mine. And I miss every second of it.

The hurt on her face last night flashes in my memory. She didn't want our evening to end the way it did. She didn't want *us* to end. But she did it anyway. To protect the only life she has known. To shelter her heart and the heart of her daughter.

How do I fix this? Fix us?

Because I refuse to believe there isn't still an us. I refuse to believe what we have is beyond repair. All I have to do is figure out how to go about it.

Minor relief washes over me when the Harley-Davidson clock in the garage reads five and I can call it quits for the day. But the day is far from over. Because today is Wednesday. Family dinner night. And family dinner night equals several sets of eyes and ears homed in on me. No doubt Dad will go home and tell Mom something is up. If my sisters arrive before me, the *what's-wrong-with-Jonas* gang will be in full effect upon my arrival.

Might be a good night to hang on the back patio with Anton.

When I get home from work and let Spartan out of his kennel, he mauls me as if I have been gone days and not hours. He licks my face and jumps excitedly around the living room.

"Well, I'm glad to see someone is happy to have me around," I tell him as I rough up the fur on his head. "You ready to see Grandma tonight."

Woof, woof.

I love how Spartan answers me as if we are having a genuine conversation. He has always been this way. Makes me laugh at times. Who knows, maybe he does actually understand what I say. Never underestimate the intelligence of your fur-child.

We go out in the back yard for a little bit. Spartan trots along the fence line and sniffs every possible tuft of grass to make sure no one else has marked his territory. I sit on the small outdoor couch set up on a paver patio I laid months ago. The L-shaped couch can easily seat five and has a matching lounger and two chairs. A canopy spans the entire patio and shades the seating while protecting the gas fire table set up in the middle.

Occasionally, I will sit out here and get lost in a book or the flicker of the fire. Being out here is a great place to unwind after a long day. Plus, Spartan gets extra outside time when I hang out here.

After Spartan alleviates a tenth of his energy, we hop into the Jeep and drive over to Mom and Dad's. I watch Spartan as he finds happiness in the little things—such as riding in the car or biting the wind or barking at a passing car—and do my best to soak up some happiness of my own.

The moment we walk in the door, Spartan runs off and Mom is on me as if I am three years old and fell from the tree-house again.

"How's my baby?" She frames my face and twists it left and right as she examines me.

"Fine, Mom," I say as she hauls me against her for a hug. I wrap my arms around her, close my eyes, and soak up her hug more than normal. Mom has always been a great hugger. Warm and giving and soothing.

"Don't you lie to me. Your father says you've been in a sour mood all day."

She releases me from the hug and holds me at arm's length. Her scrutiny is somewhat unsettling, but I know it comes from a heartfelt place. Even when I felt sad about all that happened with Cora, my parents never reacted this way. They checked in more often, but otherwise let me be.

"Well, he wouldn't be wrong. But I don't want to talk about it right now."

Her eyes scan every fine line and detail of my face. Judge my eyes and lack of smile. "Just don't keep it bottled up. Okay? Never solves a thing if you keep it to yourself."

I raise my right hand and press it over my heart. "Promise."

In a flash, she grabs my hand and drags me into the kitchen. "Now that that's out of the way, let's make dinner." And just like that, Mom makes me laugh.

Joining Jasmine and Jillian in the kitchen, Mom and I chop potatoes for cooking and mashing, and vegetables for salad. Garlic, garden-fresh rosemary and lemon waft through the kitchen, and it isn't hard to guess we are having Jillian's favorite—lemon and herb roasted chicken. We all work in synchronicity until dinner is ready.

As much as I wanted to seclude myself to the back patio earlier, it was better being in the kitchen with my sisters and mom. We worked as a unit and nothing needed to be said as we went about our individual tasks. Without a word, the women in my life helped lift me up. And I love them more for it.

Dinner went on much like it normally did. Lex flung bits of salad at my dad as he tickled the bottoms of his feet. Jasmine scolded Dad and told him to quit teaching Lex food was a toy instead of something you eat. Anton laughed with Dad and egged him on. Mom asked Jillian about work and when the next batch of new fashions would hit the racks.

The only exception to the usual conversation was me. I sat quiet and shuffled the cut pieces of chicken around my plate. Stirred the mashed potatoes more than ate them.

As plates emptied, Mom went into the kitchen and grabbed dessert. Apple cobbler and vanilla bean ice cream. My favorite.

Dad must have called her during the day and forewarned her of my mood. Because the cobbler would've had to be in the oven long before the chicken. Plus, she would've had to shop for the missing ingredients I know weren't always in the house.

Jasmine scoops out a helping of cobbler. "What's the special occasion, Mom?"

She glances at me briefly before peering at my sister. "No special occasion. Just thought it'd be nice to have. Been a while." Shock must register on my face when Mom looks back at me because her eyes widen. All I do is smile in return.

Neither Mom nor Dad told Jasmine or Jillian about today.

About my adult-sized temper tantrum. They really do love me. If my sisters don't know the nitty-gritty details, my parents get how bothered and upset I am.

After we all have our fair share of cobbler, my sisters and I go out on the back patio while Anton and my parents stay inside with Lex. We sit on the poolside loungers in silence for a few minutes and enjoy the soft glow from the twinkling lights around the yard. A breeze kicks up and Jillian shivers in the lounger on my right.

"Want my jacket?"

"Nah, big brother. But thanks."

"So, what's up with you?" Jasmine asks a moment later. I know she isn't asking Jillian, but I play coy anyway.

"Me?"

"Yes, you. You've been acting *off* all night."

Jillian sits up and spins to face both of us. "You do seem more bummed than usual."

Great. Mom and Dad may not have said anything to my sisters, but they are more intuitive than I give them credit for.

Maybe talking with them—two women I trust, and from different ages—will help. Fingers crossed.

"I recently started dating someone…" I trail off, trying to figure out what else to say.

"And?" Jillian drawls out the single-worded question.

"Jesus. Give me a minute." I pause and stare up at the stars. "Last night, she told me she has a daughter." To my left, Jasmine gasps. "Then she said we need to take a break."

"What? Why?" Jasmine asks.

As I continue to stare at the stars, I secretly hope I get the opportunity to sit under a starry sky with Autumn in my arms. Somewhere far from the city, where there is less light pollution and only the stars brighten the night sky. Where we can point out different clusters and tell each other what we see.

"Not really sure. I think she's just scared to let anyone in. She's a single mom. And from what I know, it's been that way for a while. She told me I was the first person she's dated in years."

Now Jasmine sits up and faces me. It feels as if I am stuck in a sisterly vise. Except they won't squeeze the life out of me. They will just pump me full of advice. But their words of wisdom may be exactly what I need.

"Brother, if you're the first person she's dated in years—possibly the only person she's dated since her daughter was born—she had to have broken it off because she's scared. Letting someone in is probably huge for her."

I lift my head from the lounger and turn to my left. "Yeah, I get it, Jas. But why would she let me in to drop me five seconds later?"

"Easy," Jillian says, and I turn to face her. "She wants to see if you're worthy."

"If I'm worthy? What does that mean?"

"It means" —I turn back to Jasmine, almost dizzy sitting between my sisters— "she wants to see if you'll just let her go. Or if you'll step up and fight for her."

Okay. If I thought women were complicated before, now the ideal has been solidified. Women are the most complex and confusing creatures on the planet. They say one thing and want something completely opposite. How is any man supposed to grasp this concept? Or know when they are doing something right or wrong?

"And how am I supposed to do that? How do I fight?"

"Little things," Jillian says. "Leave notes where you know she'll find them. Send her flowers. Nothing major, just small tokens to let her know you're still thinking about her. As complex as we seem, big bro, we are simple creatures. Those little things add up over time. Women are more sentimental. Sure, we all love gifts. But when it comes down to it, we want the reason behind the gift, not just the trinket."

At the word trinket, I run my fingers over the Eisenhower dollar in my pocket. A token I have carried with me for years. Something Grandpa John gave me just before I started kindergarten. *"Keep this close by and it'll always give you luck."* Since he slipped the large coin into my small palm, I never left home without it. It was either in my pocket or my wallet or somewhere close by. It wasn't only special because Grandpa said it was a good luck charm, but also because it was a gift from him.

"So, if you were in my position, what would you do?" I ask them both.

"This all went south last night?" Jasmine asks and I nod. "Give her a couple days to breathe. Give her time to process everything. She asked for a break so she could think clearly about how you fit into her world. And her daughter's world, too. If you don't give her the time she needs, she'll push harder."

"Okay, I get that. But how much time is enough?"

"Maybe wait until the weekend. I like Jillian's idea with the notes," Jasmine states.

"Thank you." Jillian tips her head in gratitude.

"Write her a note. Tell her how you're feeling. It's easier to say things when you're not face to face. Then leave it somewhere she'll find it."

This is something I can get on board with. Writing her notes. Love letters. Something short and sweet which lets her know she is still on my mind. But for how long?

"How long would you suggest I do this?"

"Forever," Jillian says at the same time Jasmine says, "Until your hand falls off." We all laugh.

"Seriously, big bro. If things pan out with her, keep doing it. She'll love it."

Good to know. But it still doesn't answer my initial question. Maybe I need to rephrase.

"Okay. When do I take the next step? When do I move from letters to something more?"

Jasmine shrugs. "Whenever it feels right to you. If you leave her the first note and she reaches out to you, angry, back off. Otherwise, use your best judgment. Women like to be wooed. All of us. Woo her."

Woo her. Notes and flowers and standing on her front porch singing old love ballads. I got this. Maybe.

My sisters pile on top and hug the hell out of me. For a moment, I fake cough as their weight presses down. But as they lift off me, I wrap my arms around them and hug them tighter.

"Thank you both. I love you."

"Love you, big brother."

"Me too. Now make things right. Cause I want to meet her."

I laugh and sit up. "On it."

We all wander inside the house and exchange hugs before heading out for the night. Although I was hesitant to be here tonight. To deal with my family as they breathed advice down my neck. Being here was exactly what I needed. To be reset back to what matters. To get clarity only my family delivers.

As I head out the door with Spartan on my heels, Mom hands me a container of leftovers. "Extra cobbler." A gentle smile lifts the corners of her lips.

"Thanks, Mom. Love you." I hug her again.

"Love you too. See you next week."

The ride home has me thinking nonstop. Of what messages I want to write Autumn. Of what else I want to do to show her how much I care. A small list fills out in my head and I am excited to begin.

Once home, I get to work. Writing notes. Whipping out my sketchpad and my pencils, I draw for hours. Get lost in the notion of wooing Autumn. Of getting her to see I still want her, even if I have to share her.

seventeen

AUTUMN

The last week has been miserable. Well, not completely miserable, but not really good either.

I miss Jonas. A lot. How the hell do you miss someone you barely know? But how do you not miss someone who walked off with a chunk of your heart? Because Jonas definitely took a piece of me with him on the back of his motorcycle. Hopefully bits of my heart aren't strewn all over the highway.

Although I have a feeling he would never do such a thing.

Clementine asked to set up the Christmas tree and decorate the apartment. The temporary distraction was needed, but only lasted for a few hours. In no time, the tree was up and littered with a mix of homemade and store-bought ornaments. Stockings hung from the far side of the breakfast bar we never sit at. Sporadic glittery Santa's and elves and snowflakes were spread throughout the living space.

Everywhere you look, there is a splash of holiday cheer. The apartment oozed festive and fun.

Difficult as it has been, I kept a smile plastered on my face. The last thing I want or need is Clementine wondering why or what has me upset. To ask questions I don't know how to answer. The timing isn't right. Not yet.

Over the last five days, when I left the shop, I discovered a folded piece of paper under my driver's side windshield wiper. At first, I was leery. I'd heard stories about criminals who place things on cars to distract the owner before attacking them. With Reznor and Rex close enough to hear my screams, I scanned the lot, took a breath, and plucked each paper from the wiper blade. Then, I unfolded the page and saw who it was from. Warmth instantly spread through my limbs to my chest when I read it.

The first note, on Thursday, was short.

Autumn,

I'm sorry. I miss you.

Jonas

The note said so much with only a few words. Not just an apology. Not just to say he missed me. But to remind me he was still there. And he was thinking about me after everything that happened.

On Friday, the paper on my windshield was bigger, the stock heavier. When I unfolded it, I gasped. Jonas had drawn what I assume was the two of us, curled up on a blanket in the park, watching a movie on the makeshift theater screen. His arm around my waist and body snug against mine. When I showed it to Penny, all she said was *"He's got it bad."*

Saturday, Sunday, and yesterday each ended with another note. Typically, I had two days off during the week. Plus, the shop closed on Sunday. But with everything that happened last Tuesday between me and Jonas, I came into work on my days off. Worked some. Hung out mostly. Even brought Clementine with me on Sunday while I worked on two desperate clients. Although the shop was closed, it was better than sitting at home. Chores only distracted so much of my time.

The other notes were much the same, but each got a little longer. Sweeter. Made me miss him more.

> *Autumn,*
> *No matter what it takes. No matter how long it takes. I will fix us.*
> *Jonas*

> *Autumn,*
> *The first time I saw you, I forgot how to breathe. How to speak. How to function. But then you smiled and the world righted itself again. Because you make the world, my world, a better place.*
> *Jonas*

> *Autumn,*
> *On our first date, I constantly wanted to hold your hand. Touch your skin. Kiss your lips. But I was raised a gentleman. Raised to respect women and wait until they're ready. When I kissed your lips for the first time... I never want to kiss another woman. Never want to taste anyone other than you. Because you're the perfect mix of everything I have ever wanted. Breathtaking and genuine and funny.*
> *Jonas*

I may not have seen Jonas in a week, but he still held my heart in his clutches. Don't think he will ever let it go. Not that I want him to. If anything, I want him to hold it closer. Longer. More tenderly. I want to hear him whisper the words on these pages—the ones secured in my purse, that go everywhere I go—in my ear. To say all these sweet words with his warm breath on my skin.

With each note I receive, Penny cradles her heart and coos. Begs me to call or text him. Give him another chance. And I want to. God, do I want to. I want his arms around me again. Want his lips on mine again.

But after how I behaved last week, I'm terrified to show my face again. How do I begin to fix this? Fix us. I harbor most of the blame with why we aren't together. Past insecurities gnaw at my happiness. Tell me romantic relationships aren't in the cards. So, how do I let Jonas in? How do I introduce Clementine into the mix? This is all so new to me—dating as a grown woman and single parent. The idea of us not working out, of Clementine getting hurt, terrifies me to no end.

Twenty minutes in with my current client—an eighteen-year-old getting her first tattoo—the front door jingles. Automatically, I peek up to see who walks in. The blonde from the bowling alley—Shelly, I think—ambles in with a cheery smile on her face. She glances over at me and her smile glows lumens brighter.

But it isn't her or her smile that surprises me. No, it would be the bouquet in her hands which has me stunned. Because I know who the arrangement is for and who sent it. Shelly delivers the bouquet to Penny and hangs out at the front desk until I finish the small script tattoo.

After I clean up the girl's tattoo and give her instructions for aftercare, she pays and leaves.

Now I have to deal with Penny *and* Shelly. Yay me—insert sarcasm.

"What's this?" I ask, feigning ignorance.

Penny rests a hand on her hip, pops it out, and cocks her head. "Really, Auti. Gonna play stupid?"

"You know what they say about assuming." I laugh and both of them stare at me as if they don't know. "It makes an ass out of you and me. Please tell me you both have heard that saying before."

Penny rolls her eyes and Shelly laughs. "Yes, dippy. I've heard the saying. And you know what I meant."

I ignore Penny and look up at Shelly. "Jonas?"

She nods slowly. "He's a mess, Autumn. I've never seen him like this. *Ever*. Not sure what happened last week, and I don't expect you to tell me. But please talk to him. Give him a chance. Give your relationship a chance." I subtly nod. "You make him smile. Like really smile. And I miss seeing his smile."

I miss seeing his smile, too.

I take in the arrangement. Unique and beautiful. A handful of soft pink roses. A vine of pale pink and white orchids. Small white flowers at the base. Light green and lavender succulent buds. Pulled together with curly willow and blue thistle. A blend of rustic and opulent.

Not too flashy. Not a typical floral arrangement. Perfect.

"Thank you, Shelly," I whisper.

Out of nowhere, Shelly hugs me. "See you soon," she says so only I hear her. Then, she releases me, pivots away, and walks out the door.

Penny tips her head toward the front door. "One of his friends?"

"Yeah. She was at the bowling alley last week."

I pick up the arrangement, turn on my heel, and head back to my booth. Attached to the bouquet is another note, and I would prefer to read it without Penny hovering over my shoulder. Not like I won't show it to her later, but I want to read it on my own first.

Leaning forward, I inhale the subtle perfume from the flowers. Understated and delicate, yet exemplary. I pluck the note from the plastic tong in the center and unfold it. Taking a deep breath, I scan the page and absorb each of his words.

> *Autumn,*
> *There is something so classic about your beauty. You ravish me. Without doing anything extraordinary, you shine. Brighten the darkest night sky. Ignite a fire inside me. And without you, the fire has extinguished. My true north has vanished, and I'm wandering alone in the dark.*
>
> *If you can find a place for me in your heart, I would love another chance. A chance to show you more than one person can love you. And when you're ready, I would be honored to meet the little girl who holds your heart captive. Because if she is anything like her mom, I already know how I will feel about her.*
>
> *Please give me—us—another chance. I will do whatever, give whatever, you need. Time. Patience. As*

*long as you are in my life. All I ask is that you call
me. Talk to me. Let me back in.*

Yours always,
Jonas

I read the letter again. And again. Then crush it against my chest and start crying. Reznor glances over the wall separating our booths, then over at Penny. Seconds later, Penny is in my booth and trying to snatch the letter from my arms. I fight her tooth and nail.

"If you won't let me see the letter, then you better start talking. I've seen enough tears from you over the last week to last a lifetime," Penny says, frustration lacing her tone.

"Pen, it isn't bad. Quite the opposite, actually. So, stop mothering me."

She extends her hand between us, flexing her fingers in a *give-me* motion. "If it isn't bad, let me see it."

"Can I have just this one to myself? Please."

Tilting her head to the side, she gives me a sad smile. "I guess. But if he makes you cry again, I'm cutting his balls off."

"Ouch," Reznor says. "Little extreme, don't you think, Pen?"

She shrugs. "Just telling it like it is." Reznor shakes his head and continues working on the guy face down in his booth.

I fold the letter up and tuck it away in my shirt—close to my heart and where Penny can't reach it easily. She harrumphs and leaves my booth. In a slight fog, I clean my workstation up and prep for the next person on my schedule.

Two more clients and then I am done for the day. Two more clients and I can leave work and call Jonas. Hear his voice again for the first time in a week. Although, with every note he has left me, I have read them with his voice in my head. Heard each and every word in his low baritone. Felt comfort with each letter. With the fact he was still nearby. Seeking me out.

The next three hours go by slower than any other time in my life. It didn't help that both my clients had no idea what they wanted inked in their skin. But it didn't shock me to find out they came in together. Eventually, the first decided on a rose. And although the second could have figured out her tattoo while number one was getting hers, it took her fifteen minutes past her session start time to realize she wanted the exact same thing. And it wasn't as if they had never gotten a tattoo before. Hell, they had them everywhere.

Finally, I finish up the night. Clean my workspace faster than any previous shift. Shoulder my purse, cradle the bouquet in my arms, and bolt for the back door. Once alone in the confines of my car, I inhale the gentle bouquet perfume one more time before setting it on the passenger seat. Then I dig my phone from my purse and open up Jonas's contact info.

The screen illuminates my face in the dark as my finger hovers over the call button. I suck in a deep breath and tap the screen.

eighteen

JONAS

Shelly called me hours ago and said she delivered the flower arrangement and note to Autumn. I have been on pins and needles since. Yes, I realize she was working when the delivery arrived. But I really hoped I would have heard from her already.

Either Autumn has been crazy busy with work. Or she is avoiding me. Hopefully, it is the former.

Spartan noses my elbow and whimpers before running to the door which leads to the back yard. I ignore him the first two times. When he noses my elbow a third and barks at me for good measure, I rise from the couch, grab my phone off the coffee table, and head for the door.

As soon as I open the back door, Spartan bolts down the three short steps and races through the grass toward the back fence. His energy is off the charts and I wish I had a fraction of it.

"Ya freaking whacko," I call after him.

Sitting on the lounger on the patio, I light the fire bowl and lean back. Eyes closed and head against the cushion, I absorb the world around me. The still night air—cool and crisp. Perfect for the second official day of winter. The soft hum of an airplane as it flies overhead toward Tampa. The flames flicker in the rock-filled fire bowl, a faint smell of propane floats through the air. Spartan trots nearby, his coat brushing against my elbow as he passes me to scavenge in another section of the yard.

I love this small slice of heaven I created. But it isn't quite perfect. Not yet. And only one thing could make it perfect.

Autumn. And the echoes of young laughter and pitter-patter of small feet.

A wad of cotton clogs my throat and strips it dry as I daydream—well, night dream—of a future I hope happens. So strange, but I never imagined the future so in depth until Autumn. Sure, I wanted to land the woman of my dreams and build a life with her. But until Autumn, I never had vivid pictures in my head of the end result. Small Kodak moments captured in time, printed on matte photo paper, and wedged between glass and wood.

But I see it all so clearly now. See her beside me, for years to come.

My cell phone rings in my pocket and startles me from my fantasy. I bolt upright, fumble to get it out of my pocket and answer it just before it goes to voice mail.

A half second glance at the screen has me smiling from ear to ear. "Autumn?"

"Hi." Her voice wispy and muted. I melt back into the lounger and close my eyes.

Just the soft resonance of her voice settles every anxiety I have endured over the last week. Every questionable minute where I wondered if she would give us another chance.

"Hi," I say back. "How are you?"

As much as I don't wish Autumn to feel any sort of

anguish, I secretly hope the last week has been as equally challenging for her as it has been for me. Although I only flaunted my emotions the day after, they ate away at me the entire week. With each note I wrote, I took pause. Stared at the paper for hours with pen in hand. How do you express yourself with so few words? How do you not slip up and say the words you feel will scare someone away?

I loved writing her the notes and letters, but they weren't so simple.

The drawing, on the other hand, was easy. Like extracting a strip of movie reel from my memory and scrawling it across paper with pencil. I could have drawn us together with my eyes closed. The subtle curves of Autumn's body as she lay on the blanket, her back to my front. My arm around her waist. Her warmth heating every inch of me.

I swallow and shake off the real-life fantasy floating in my thoughts.

"Okay, I guess." She says the words, tries to believe them, but the slight crack in her voice tells me she doesn't. Pain pierces my chest and I pinch my eyes tightly as she continues. "Thank you. For the notes and the d-drawing" —she sniffles — "and the flowers. They're all so beautiful."

Her heartache bounces through the air and smacks me like a bullseye in the chest. Settles deep. Liquifies and sheathes the rapid pulsing organ between my lungs. I clench my hand into a fist and press it over the sensation robbing me of breath.

"You're welcome," I croak out. "Meant every word. Every line and smudge."

On the other end, Autumn goes silent. The only indication the call hasn't dropped is her occasional sniffle in my ear.

What is going through her head? Why is she so quiet? Is she battling what to do next? Where we go from here?

God, I hope she wants to try us again. Give us another chance. With her biggest skeleton out in the open, and me still fighting for her, she has to know where I stand. That I still want her. Want more with her. Want more of us.

She has been silently sniffling on the other end for minutes now. But I don't break the silence. As many questions as I want to ask her, as much as I want to pour my heart out, I stay tight-lipped and give her however much time she needs. Time to formulate whatever it is she wants to say to me. Because I will wait as long as she needs me to.

"I miss you," she whispers. Three simple words. But how they swallow me whole and hug me fiercely. "A lot."

I inhale deeply, hold the air in my lungs for one, two, three before exhaling. Opening my eyes, I stare up at the inky night sky and land on the brightest star. Hold it in my sight and watch it brighten and dim as if pulsing.

"Me too. So damn much."

During the last week, Spartan has even grown frustrated with my temperament. Since he sees every side of me, he has sat grumpy beside me on the couch. Curled up with me at night. Groaned when I didn't want to throw his ball in the back yard. And licked my face when I spent too much time in bed or on the couch.

"Jonas…" My name leaves her lips as a plea.

My pulse kicks into fifth gear. "Yes?"

"I…" she starts, then pauses briefly. I don't dare interrupt her silence. Don't push her to say the words waiting in limbo. When she speaks again, it's not what I expect. "I'm sorry."

Why is she apologizing? If anyone should be apologizing, it should be me. I was the one who misconstrued things. Got frustrated with her evasion and lost my cool. I was in the wrong. She was merely protecting her daughter. She has every right to protect her daughter.

"Autumn, please don't apologize. It should be me saying sorry, not you."

"Maybe we were both in the wrong. I could have been more honest about the call when you asked. But I was scared. It still scares me."

"Will you tell me why? Help me understand."

She remains silent for a beat, then sniffles again. "Jonas, I haven't dated anyone since Clementine's father."

Clementine. How charming and sweet and totally Autumn. I wonder if Clementine is anything like her mother? Beautiful, charming, and someone I always want close. If so, consider me double screwed.

"How old is Clementine?" Not that it matters in my eyes, but I am curious how long Autumn has deprived herself of happiness. How long she has dedicated herself solely to this little girl. Not that I assume her daughter doesn't bring her joy.

"Seven."

To be honest, I am glad we aren't having this conversation face to face right now. Because seven was not what I expected to hear. Maybe a number closer to three. Not seven. Seven years is a *really* long time to not have any sort of romantic relationship. I understand her desire to be dedicated to her daughter, but as a woman—hell, as a grown human being— she has needs. Not necessarily sexual, but basic human desires. Companionship. Love. Having an intimate relation- ship—sexual or not—is basic human nature.

"Wow," I whisper. She starts to speak, but I cut her off. "Autumn, seven years is a really long time to rob yourself of love. Love other than the one you share with Clementine."

"Well," she starts. I picture her tucking her lips between her teeth a moment. "Her father and I separated before she was born. Being a parent wasn't in the cards for him."

In the blink of an eye, red pricks the backs of my eyes as I close them and grind my jaw. *Piece of shit. Fucking asshole.* I take a minute to simmer my boiling blood. Not only did this douchebag leave her, he left her high and dry when she needed someone most. Not to mention the prick abandoned his child. No wonder she has steered away from a relationship.

Breathing deep, I exhale and speak as calmly as possible. "Autumn, I'm so sorry. Can't imagine what that must've been like for you."

"Everything happens for a reason, right?" She says it with such nonchalance.

"Guess so." She has a point, though. Because if she was still with him, we might not have met. Might not be having this conversation. Might not have the possibility of getting to know one another and growing close.

"Can we save this topic for another time?"

"Of course."

"Jonas, will you forgive me?"

Her request renders me speechless for a moment. She is asking *me* to forgive *her*. The concept seems backward. Wrong. Just because Autumn had yet to tell me about her daughter, she wasn't the one out of turn. Protecting your child is never wrong.

"Only if you'll do the same. I shouldn't have been so harsh. Shouldn't have lost my temper. Should have let you tell me when you were ready. It was wrong of me to be upset over something so private."

"It's done then. All is forgiven." For the first time during this conversation, Autumn has a sliver of happiness in her voice. "Jonas?"

"Yeah?"

"I want to see you."

I sit up on the lounger and Spartan glances up at me from his spot on the patio. *She wants to see me?*

This is good. Really good. Because, fuck, I miss her. Her sweet smile and laughter that settle in the left chamber of my heart. Her fiery cognac irises which have me drunk in seconds. The warmth of her touch that fevers every molecule in my veins.

"Yes," I answer, too dumbstruck to form a proper response. "Would love to see you. More than anything."

She giggles and my chest swells in delight. "Glad to hear. Wasn't sure you would."

"Autumn, do you know how difficult it was to slip notes under your windshield wiper and not walk in the shop to see you? To sneak a peek at you through the windows? Walking away each night got more and more punishing. A couple times, I wanted to wait by your car and hand the note to you personally. But I knew it wouldn't be received the same. So, I left. As difficult as it was, I walked away and gave you time to think."

The first three nights I left notes and the drawing for Autumn, I stood next to her car for at least ten minutes. Stared at the driver's seat and pictured her behind the wheel. Imagined opening the door and her stepping out. Dreamed of her in my arms again. Of my lips on hers.

"Thank you," she whispers. "For giving me time to sort this out. To sort us out."

Us. Hope soars in my chest. "I got some sisterly advice," I confess.

"Well, your sisters are wise women." She giggles again. Each musical note of it lightens the weight I have felt over the last week. "Jonas, if you're open to it, I'd like you to meet Clementine."

Wow. This shocks me more than anything. Only because she has protected her daughter so fiercely over the last seven-plus years. Because she has forfeited her own happiness to make sure her daughter doesn't get hurt. Has dedicated her life to her daughter so she doesn't feel any less loved because her father abandoned her long before she took her first breath.

"Autumn…" My voice is barely audible. "I would like that very much. But only if you're comfortable with it."

"Wouldn't suggest it if I wasn't. But Jonas?"

"Yeah?"

"This is a really big deal for me. Me introducing you to Clementine… this has never happened before. I wasn't kidding when I told you I haven't dated."

The gravity of her repeated confession strikes me in the solar plexus. The words engulf me. Tell me how much I mean to her without actually expressing them in the terms most do. This is Autumn's way of saying she wants me more than a fling. Wants permanence. A life.

"Don't know what to say. I feel like an idiot."

"You're not an idiot. Just let me know you grasp how big this is for me."

"I do. Honestly, it's a big deal for me too. Just for a different reason."

For a moment, neither of us says anything. We sit in comfortable silence as the magnitude of what is happening between us evolves. Autumn wants to introduce me to her daughter. Wants me to meet her. And for her to know me. This isn't a baby step. It's a leap. A headfirst dive into uncharted waters. It invigorates me and scares the hell out of me in equal measure.

"Is Thursday okay?" she asks. "Or do you have plans with your family?"

I want to remind her Wednesday is when I have family dinners. But then it hits me. This is Christmas week. And Thursday is Christmas Eve. A day when most families gather and celebrate traditions other than exchanging gifts. Now that my sisters and I are grown, we don't get together until Christmas evening. So my oldest sister can celebrate with her husband and son however they choose.

"Thursday is perfect."

"How do you feel about pizza and a G-rated movie?"

I laugh. Never has greasy cheese-coated dough and animation sounded so wonderful. "Well, I've never met a pizza I didn't like. And I watch G-rated movies with my nephew now and again, so I'm up for it."

"Awesome," she says with enthusiasm. "If it's okay with you, I'll figure out the where and when and what to see then text you."

In this aspect of her life, Autumn needs full control. And I will happily give it all to her. Give her whatever she needs so long as I get to be by her side.

"Sounds great. Can't wait to see you. And to meet Clementine. Thank you."

"Why are you thanking me?"

How in depth do I go? How do I tell her I am just thankful for another chance with her? The answer has so many layers, and tonight isn't the time to unravel them all. "Because you deserve it. Because you didn't completely dismiss me or my silly notes."

"They're not silly," she whispers.

"No, they aren't. But I've never written notes to anyone, and I felt like a teenager again. Felt like I was asking the girl stuck in my head if she likes me or not."

"Well, this girl likes you very much."

"Good to know." My cheeks sting from smiling. Only Autumn makes me this way. Happy like this.

"I should go. Been sitting in the parking lot behind the shop this whole time. Kind of need to head home."

"Head home. Sorry I kept you so long."

"No worries. I'll text you. See you Thursday."

"Thursday. Good night, Autumn."

"'Night, Jonas."

The call disconnects and I fall back against the lounger again. Spartan pops up on all fours and nudges my elbow. But I ignore him for a minute as I stare up at the night sky. As the stars stare back at me with more twinkle.

I get to see her again. Hold her. And meet the little lady who is the most precious part of her existence. Hopefully that little girl approves of me too.

nineteen

AUTUMN

"Ready, pumpkin?"

"Yeah, Mama." Clementine picks up her small red purse and tosses the strap over her shoulder like any other day. Like any other night out for pizza and milkshakes.

Yesterday morning, while we sat down for breakfast, I told Clementine about Jonas. About the man who was a friend, but who I like more than a friend. The whole conversation with my seven-year-old daughter was awkward to say the least. Honestly, it felt like I was the child and she was the adult. I only imagine how weird and uncomfortable it will be to have the birds and bees conversation with her.

Although Clementine acts older than her age at times, she still holds so much innocence inside. And I take the blame as well as pride. Nowadays, too many kids grow up too soon. At every turn, I try to give my daughter a chance to remain a kid. To be spirited and not worry about things children shouldn't be burdened by—including my love life. Past or present. Most girls her age go out and do things I didn't until my preteen/early teen years. But I have done well at preserving her innocence as long as possible. Every once in a while, her sassy, trying to be older side comes out. Most of the time, though, she acts like seven-year-olds did before tablets, computers, cell phones, and online games stole their attention —and I am grateful.

We only get eighteen years to be a child. Adulting lasts three or more times longer.

When I asked Clementine if it was okay to share pizza and watch a movie with Jonas, her excitement shocked me. She jumped off the couch and started dancing. I bet it was a happy dance for pizza and a movie, but at least she wasn't perturbed by meeting Jonas.

"Let's go." We shuffle out the front door and soon buckle up in the Bel Air.

Part of me is happy Penny is at work, while part of me wishes she was home. Her constant attention would be both annoying and desirable. Her dating words of wisdom. Her constant nagging and mothering. Asking if I have my lipstick in my purse. If I put on deodorant. Reminding me to spritz perfume on my clothes and not my skin, in case Jonas kisses me. The little things which drive me crazy on a normal day, but would love tonight.

I back out of the space and drive toward the Italian restaurant we agreed to meet at. It butts up against the movie theater and makes pizza-movie night easy whenever I take Clementine.

In the passenger seat, Clementine bops to the song on the radio. Singing the lyrics she knows and humming the ones she doesn't. As on edge as I am about Jonas meeting Clementine, seeing her so at ease with the whole evening tapers the anxiety a smidge. I bask in her carefree existence. Her lack of fear or worry. Use that spirit to calm my nerves with each passing minute.

A few songs later, I steer the car into the lot. For a Thursday evening, the lot is fuller than expected. Granted, school is on break right now and parents are probably trying to find ways to amuse their children, so the crowd isn't a shock.

As I search for a place to park, I spot Jonas on his motorcycle in the next row. I swallow and clamp down on my lips. Clementine continues to sing, completely oblivious to the sudden panic attack creeping through my veins.

I pull into a spot and throw the car in park, but leave the engine and heat running. Clementine unbuckles her belt, but doesn't go to open the door. She knows if the car is still on, she stays inside.

When I glance in the direction of where I saw Jonas on his bike, he is no longer there. Instead, he slowly walks toward the car. I close my eyes and take a deep breath. *You've got this. Don't chicken out now. Not yet.*

"Mama? Are you okay?" Clementine rests her hand on my forearm and I open my eyes.

"Yeah, pumpkin. Will you please stay in the car a minute? I want to speak with Jonas before you meet him."

She nods. "Can you leave the radio on?" I love how something as simple as leaving the radio on will keep her happy.

"You bet. Stay here. I'll be back in a second."

"Okay, Mama."

Now or never, Autumn.

I open the door and step out. Jonas is a few cars away. I step around the front of the car and meet him at the rear of the car parked in front of me. Clementine still within sight, but far enough away she doesn't hear anything. Just want to gauge Jonas's mood before I open the floodgates.

God, he steals every practiced word from my lips and

renders me speechless every time he is near. We haven't seen each other in nine days, but those days feel like months. Years. How is it possible he looks a hundred times more appealing? Taller. Broader. More handsome.

Two more strides and he stands inches from my touch. "Hey," he whispers. As if speaking too loudly will shatter our reunion.

"Hey." I lock on to his magnetic hazel eyes and swallow. Before I formulate what to say next, Jonas steps into me and wraps his arms around my center.

I melt into his embrace. Inhale deeply and pull in the scent of him—a distinct blend of sunscreen, gasoline, and the smell of Thompson's Garage. Bask in the warmth and strength of his arms snug around my waist. I would stay in Jonas's arms forever if given the opportunity.

Far too soon, he slips his hands to my hips and breaks the hug. But before I can pout, he dips down and presses his lips to mine. Shock registers for a split second, then slips away as my lips move with his.

Every anxiety-ridden minute I have suffered since we last saw each other vanishes. His lips brush against mine, slow and measured. Each move calculated and perfect. He swipes the tip of his tongue against my lower lip and I open up for him. His hands snake up the sides of my torso and frame my face as we memorize each other again. Memorize our individual tastes. The way our bodies curve in exactly the right places against each other. And the way we cannot get enough of the other.

Lost in the feel of Jonas pressed against me, in his taste, I audibly pout when he breaks the kiss. He chuckles and presses a chaste kiss to my lips again. "You have no idea how much I love it when you pout."

I fist his shirt, tug him closer, and rest my forehead in the crook of his neck. "Well, I missed you."

"Missed you too." Jonas slips his arms back around my waist and holds me close. His embrace is the most at home I have felt in a long time. He kisses the crown of my head. "Are you nervous?"

I nod into the collar of his leather jacket. "Definitely."

"Me too," he whispers. "But also thrilled."

I lean away, tip my head back, and take in his expression. He smiles, but his dimple I love so much doesn't pop up. His eyes are as soft and brilliant as always, but his pupils are dilated. And every few seconds, he looks toward my car. Where Clementine sits patiently, singing songs.

Taking a step back, I slip my hand down to his and lace my fingers between his. I lock eyes with him and smile. "You ready?" He nods but doesn't say anything.

Slowly, we walk hand in hand toward my car. Jonas's fingers squeeze mine slightly every other step forward. I weave us over to the driver's side. When we stop, I give him another kiss before opening the door and ducking my head inside. "Hey, pumpkin. Thank you for waiting."

"You're welcome, Mama."

Behind me, Jonas's fingers tighten around mine. I give him a gentle squeeze of reassurance. I reach in, cut the engine, and pull the keys from the ignition. "Grab your purse and crawl across the seat. Let's go get some pizza."

"Yay, pizza!" She slides her purse on her shoulder, locks her door, and crawls across the seat to exit through my door.

As Clementine steps out of the car, Jonas inches away from me. Not in fear. More like he doesn't want to give Clementine the wrong impression. But Jonas doesn't realize Clementine doesn't have any set impressions of anyone or relationships. Unfortunately, she hasn't witnessed many. Penny never brings dates home per my request. Just so Clementine doesn't feel uncomfortable with a stranger in her home.

"Pumpkin, this is Jonas." I glance up from my daughter to look into Jonas's eyes. "Mommy's boyfriend." Jonas tightens his grip on mine as a cute smile pops up on Clementine's face. "Jonas, this is my daughter, Clementine."

He squats down to her height and smiles so bright. "Hi, Clementine." Jonas extends his hand to her. "It's nice to meet you."

She looks at his hand as her brows bunch together. Jonas meets my gaze and I shrug. And then Clementine launches forward and hugs him. When he loosens his grip from mine, I let him. I let him hug her back as I smile like a fool. I forgot to warn him Clementine is a hugger.

When she lets him go, she smiles at him. "Nice to meet ya." She glances up at me. "Can we get pizza now? I'm hungry."

And just like that, the awkward stage of the evening ends.

Jonas walks on my right, Clementine on my left. All of us connected. We stroll through the lot toward the pizza shop, Clementine swinging our connected hands and talking animatedly about all the holiday décor on the buildings. The sparkling reindeer and glowing lights and shimmering tinsel.

She asks Jonas if he has a Christmas tree up at his house. If he has cookies and milk for Santa and the special sparkly oats for the reindeer. I shrug and let him answer on his own. Clementine knows not everyone celebrates Christmas, but can't help her own enthusiasm for her favorite holiday.

"I don't have a tree up at home. Spartan would knock it down and eat the ornaments," he answers.

We arrive at the entrance of the packed restaurant. Jonas gives his name and our party info. A high school–age boy hands him a buzzer and lets him know it will be a ten-to-fifteen-minute wait.

The three of us sit on a bench just outside and bundle up close. "Who is Spartan?" Clementine asks.

"Spartan is my dog."

Clementine bolts up from the bench and stares at Jonas with wide eyes. "You have a dog?" Jonas nods and chuckles. Clementine turns her attention in my direction. "Mama, can we meet Spartan sometime?"

One thing you learn about children, especially younger children, is they speak their mind. It isn't until we grow older —somewhere around puberty—that we learn to taper our reactions and the words we say. Hopefully, I can continue to teach Clementine to voice her thoughts, but just be mindful of how she says things so as not to hurt anyone's feelings.

"We'll see, pumpkin."

Jonas leans closer to me, his breath hot on my ear. "He's good with kids. Licks my nephew to death." I hear what he says, but my brain won't react. Can't with his lips so close to my skin. As if he senses my debacle, he kisses the soft skin beneath my ear and sits up. "So, Clementine, what's your favorite part of Christmas?"

I shake my head and snigger. "You asked for it," I mumble.

Until the buzzer goes off, Clementine prattles on about her favorite parts of Christmas. All with hand gestures and full exaggeration. About her love of decorating trees and hanging the stockings. Squishing her fingers in the sugar cookie dough, licking the extras off the spoon, and frosting them after they cool. But most of all, she loves Christmas movies. *The Polar Express* and *The Nightmare Before Christmas*.

Jonas play-argues with her for a bit. Debating whether or not *The Nightmare Before Christmas* is a Halloween or Christmas movie. Clementine cocks her head as her brows pinch at the middle, settling the debate with a resounding "both."

As we walk to the table and sit in the booth—Jonas and I on one side, Clementine across from us—I can't help how *normal* this feels. How wonderful it all is. How jovial my daughter is in the company of Jonas. More so than I expected. But it warms my heart. Fills me more than I ever thought it could. To have my daughter happy in the company of someone I am growing more and more fond of with each passing day.

How could life possibly get any better? I don't see how it can.

twenty

JONAS

Mini-Autumn—aka Clementine—is the cutest little girl I have ever laid eyes on.

Not only is she a spitting image of Autumn—hair, eyes, ensemble—but she has an addictive personality. With her little hands flailing in the air as she tells me about the sparkly snowflakes her class made before the holiday break. And that she has never seen real snow before.

Part of me itched to tell her I would take her and Autumn to see snow one day. But I bit my tongue and listened to all her stories. Tales about her schoolmates—and the one boy who seems sad all the time, but who she makes laugh.

The more she says, the more I fall for Autumn and her mini, Clementine. God, even her name is fucking adorable.

We order pizza—a mini cheese for Clementine, while Autumn and I split a medium; ham and pineapple for Autumn, and supreme on my half. Nothing about sitting in this pizza shop with Autumn and Clementine—surrounded by several other parents and children—feels wrong. If anything, nothing has ever felt so *right*.

Autumn rests her hand on my thigh and I set mine over

hers. I haven't dated a lot of women. Most were one-night stands. Only there to fulfill a primal need while I pined for another woman. A woman whose heart belonged to someone else. Until Autumn, I didn't comprehend the connection Cora and Gavin share. Now, I get it.

When Gavin first flew in from Los Angeles to work, he had no clue he would see Cora. Actually, hoped he wouldn't because of how he left things with Cora. But the moment they saw each other again, it was like they never parted. That's how bonded they are. When Cora tried to explain it to me, I couldn't grasp how she still wanted him. How it was possible to be in love with him after so many years apart. After what he had done.

But now, I recognize the bond. Their constant need to be near each other. Because I feel the same thing with Autumn. Clementine is an added bonus. The little girl I never knew or saw coming, but has filled some gap in my heart in less than an hour.

Autumn rests her head on my shoulder and sighs. "How ya holding up?"

I turn and press a kiss to her forehead. "Fantastic. She's perfect, Autumn. You've done so good with her." She smiles into my neck. "Seriously. She is the cutest thing ever."

"Cuter than me?"

I chuckle and shake my head. "No. No one will ever be cuter than you." I kiss her forehead again and note the flush pinking her cheeks. "But since she is a mirror image of you, she takes second place."

The pizza arrives and we all go quiet as we scarf down our pieces. Clementine starts talking with pizza in her mouth, and I laugh when Autumn corrects her. Citing why it isn't ladylike to talk with her mouth full of food. Where most kids, including my nephew, would argue, she doesn't. She simply finishes chewing then picks up where she left off.

When we finish eating, I pay the bill and we head toward the movie theater. But stop short when we see the ticket line a mile long.

"How set are you on watching this movie?" I ask.

Autumn tucks her lips in her mouth a minute then releases them as she squats down in front of Clementine. "Hey, pumpkin. There's a really long line to get into the movie. Can we do something else instead?"

Clementine glances between the two of us. "Like what?"

"I have an idea," I say as Autumn stands up. "What about the arcade down near Park?"

"The Fun Center?" Autumn asks and I nod. "That might work. Pumpkin, what if we go to the arcade. We can play all kinds of games and win tickets for prizes."

Clementine claps rapidly. "Yay! Prizes. Let's go." She grabs Autumn's hand and starts dragging her toward the parking lot. But Autumn digs her heels in.

"Hold on a minute, pumpkin." Autumn spins to face me. "Want to ride together?"

I shake my head. "Nah. I'd rather not leave my bike here. It's okay, we can meet there. Only five or so minutes up the road. Let me walk you to the car."

We all walk hand in hand back to Autumn's car. After Clementine gets in and her door is shut, I walk around to the driver's side with Autumn. Before she gets in, I draw her in close and kiss her. Deeper and slower than the kiss we shared earlier. She tastes sweet and salty and something distinctly Autumn. When she fists my jacket lapels and moans into my mouth, I reluctantly break the kiss.

"We're like horny teenagers," I say against her lips.

She giggles. "I really like kissing you. Will that be an issue?"

"Nope. Not at all."

"Good." She inches back. "We should get going if we want to get there before closing time."

"See you in a few." I kiss her again before jogging over to my bike.

I spark up the bike and put my helmet on. Glancing over my shoulder, I see Autumn back out of the space and drive away. Rolling the bike back, I fall in line behind her. We roll down the street and a sense of serenity fills me.

I may not be in the car with her, but I have never felt closer to her.

And Clementine… she is a hoot. I was so nervous to meet this little girl. God, I don't ever remember being that nervous before. Where I was completely riddled with anxiety. Meeting Clementine felt more powerful than meeting parents. That little girl's approval could have possibly made or broken our relationship.

But from how everything went over dinner, I am positive Clementine approves of me and my relationship with Autumn. That little girl's approval means the world—not just to me, but also Autumn.

We pull into the parking lot at the Fun Center and I park the bike next to Autumn's car. When Clementine gets out of the car, she runs up to me and spreads her arms wide.

"You have a motorcycle?" she asks with wide eyes. "That's so cool!"

I laugh and squat down in front of her. "Maybe one day, you can sit on it with me." Autumn stares at me wide-eyed and mouth agape. "But only if it's okay with your mom." I stand back up and lean into Autumn, whispering so only she can hear. "The bike would be parked. No actual riding until adulthood."

"Thank god. I was freaking out for a minute there."

I want to tell her it was written all over her face, but I don't. "No need to panic." I kiss her temple. "Believe it or not, I know better."

She hums. "But I still want to ride on your bike."

In an instant, I picture Autumn snug behind me on the seat, her legs clamped around mine. Her arms wrapped around my waist. Hands under my shirt and grazing my abdomen. The trail of fire her touch would leave on my skin.

Fuck, I need to stop thinking about that right now. *Focus, Thompson.*

"Let's head inside and play some games. Clementine, have you played arcade games before?"

She shakes her little head. "Nope, just the games on Mama's phone. But not a lot."

"Well, you're in for a treat. Because arcade games are way more fun than games on the phone. Plus, you get tickets when you play. Then you turn in your tickets for a prize."

"What kind of prizes are there?"

We walk through the front door, music blares around us as kids run left and right to different games. Heading over to the check-in counter, I swap out twenty dollars for tokens. The girl behind the counter hands us each a small cup to carry our tokens and tickets in.

After we step back and organize our tokens, I show Clementine the various display cases and huge wall with prizes pinned to them. Anything from plastic vampire teeth to nail stickers to stuffed animals and everything in between. She oohs and awes over each item she sees.

She points to a small makeup set. "I want to win *that*."

"Okay, well let's go find what game we want to play so we can earn tickets."

Clementine bounces in place on her toes. "Let's do this," she announces and Autumn and I both laugh.

For the next hour, we play various video games, but Pac-Man seems to be her favorite. Autumn and I try our hand at Skee-Ball and the basketball game. Both of us trying to find easy games for us to win as many tickets as possible.

When we tally up all of our tickets, we don't have enough for Clementine to get the makeup kit—which Autumn doesn't seem too upset over. But Autumn and I both still have tokens. So, we pass our tokens on to Clementine and follow her around as she tries different games.

By the time all the tokens run out, we have hundreds of tickets. I walk us over to the ticket feeder to redeem them in for a receipt. Clementine laughs when she feeds the long strip of tickets into the machine and it sounds as if it's chomping them up. Like a monster lives inside the ticket machine.

With her tickets, she chooses a stuffed animal. A rainbow unicorn with shimmering hair. She hugs it close to her chest and it warms my heart.

As we stroll out to Autumn's car and my bike, Clementine stops us in our tracks. "Mama, can we meet Mr. Jonas's doggy tonight?"

I smile, but keep my eyes straight ahead. Kids are the cutest creatures in the world. They say whatever pops in their head. Whether it be wanting to meet a dog or if they don't like someone's clothes or talking about body parts. They literally have no filter and I love it. I wish that little piece of humanity existed among all ages. But somewhere along the line, we are taught certain things are inappropriate to say in front of other people. Although, once you find your circle of people, that filter slips away.

"Not tonight, pumpkin. But I'm sure we can meet Jonas's doggy soon."

"Really?" she asks, hopeful.

"Promise, pumpkin."

We reach the car and Autumn unlocks it and starts it. I squat down in front of Clementine. "It was really nice to meet you, Miss Clementine. See you again soon."

She wraps her little arms around my neck and squeezes me as if I might run away. *Never*, I think to myself. "'Night, Mr. Jonas." I want to kiss her head, but don't. It's too soon.

Clementine hops in the car and slides over to her seat, buckling her seat belt without being asked.

"Thank you for tonight," Autumn says. "I had a really nice time."

"Me too." I step into her, rest my hands on her hips, and bring her flush to me. "Can't wait to see you again."

"Soon," she whispers a breath from my lips.

I close the space between us and press my lips to hers. Warm and sweet and inviting. She instantly opens up for me, and I brush my tongue against hers. When she moans against my mouth, I deepen the kiss. I could kiss her for hours and not tire from it.

Her lips on mine intoxicates me. Makes me drunker than her cognac eyes. The more I kiss her, the harder I fall. Fall for this astonishing woman. A woman I never saw coming. A woman I don't want a day without.

We kiss in the parking lot, against the side of her car, as if no one else exists. I frame her face in my palms. Draw her into me. Press my hips to her belly. Her hands slip beneath my jacket. Under my shirt. Graze the skin just above the waistband of my jeans.

I hiss and break the kiss. My lips still hovering a fraction above hers. "Autumn…" Her name a plea. A prayer. An urge for more. But I know there is nothing more we can do right now. Not in the middle of a parking lot, out in the open, with Clementine less than five feet from where we stand.

"Jonas," she moans. My name painful, but not in a bad way. More like she wants me just as badly as I want her, but knows this moment won't go much further than where it is now.

I lean my forehead against hers and breathe in her cherry vanilla scent. It inebriates and soothes me in equal measure. Settles every anxiety or fear I have experienced. Soothes me more than any other person ever has.

No doubt about it, Autumn is my balm. The remedy to any ailment I possess. As if made for me.

"Much as I want to stand in this parking lot all night and kiss the hell out of you, we should probably leave."

God, I don't want to let go of her. Don't want to stop kissing her. Or stop touching her. More than anything, I don't want her to stop touching me. Her fingertips on my skin elicits the most exhilarating sensation. Leaving a trail of sparks wherever she touches. Embers burning in their wake.

"Probably. But I don't want to," she confesses. "I wish I could invite you back to my place."

Me too. But even if Autumn offered for me to join her, I would be the gentleman. I would tell her it's too soon. All good things come to those who wait. At least that is what everyone says.

So why does that old adage feel like a line of crap right now?

All I want is to hold her in my arms all night. Sex would be great, but neither of us is ready for sex yet. Not mentally or emotionally, anyway.

"Yeah. But not tonight. Baby steps. Tonight was a big leap. For all of us. Let's ease into the rest of it. We have time."

She nods. "Lots of time." And I love the way the words leave her lips. Like more than a promise. A commitment.

I pocket her commitment and seal it away for safekeeping. Hold it close to my heart. Let it warm my bones.

Taking a deep breath, I slowly inch away from her. Give us both room to breathe. To cool off in the chilled winter air.

I open her door for her, peek my head inside, and look over at a singing Clementine. "'Night, Miss Clementine. Be good for your mom."

She waves at me. "'Night. I will." She draws an X over her heart. "Promise."

Autumn slides into her car, but doesn't shut the door immediately. I lean down and kiss her innocently. With Clementine's eyes on us both, I won't do more. A sense of inappropriateness washes over me like a cold shower.

"Night, Autumn. Text me when you get home so I know you made it okay."

The corner of her mouth kicks up. "I will. 'Night."

Reluctantly, I step back and close her door, tapping the roof. I walk over and straddle my bike, watching as she backs out. Clementine waves and I return the gesture with a smile.

As soon as they disappear from sight, I stare up at the night sky and smile at the brightly lit dark backdrop. Tonight, more stars appear in the skyline. Each moment with Autumn seems to add another star. Hopefully one day, the night sky will glow so bright, I won't need additional light.

The entire ride home goes by in a blur. A slideshow of

memories of the evening. Memories I will never forget. And what I pray is the start of a million more memories. After I park the bike in the garage, I step into the house and tell Spartan all about Clementine. The little girl who will win his heart faster than she won mine.

twenty-one

AUTUMN

The past two weeks has been nothing short of bliss.

Jonas and I have seen each other several nights a week. Dinner at his house or my apartment. Although, Clementine prefers going to Jonas's. The second she laid eyes on Spartan; my daughter forgot I existed.

I didn't take offense to it. In fact, I found it downright adorable how the two of them hung out together. Clementine would hug or pet him. Talk with him—because yes, Spartan barked back when you spoke to him. They were like a dynamic duo.

Each time we had dinner at Jonas's house and had to leave, Clementine wrapped her small arms around Spartan and hugged him tight. Kissed his head and wished him a good night. Adorable didn't even begin to cover how they interacted together.

When dinner happens at the apartment, Clementine asks if Jonas will bring Spartan along. Bless his heart, he always finds a valid excuse as to why he can't come along. Tired. Grumpy. Had a bad day. As the list grows, it makes me laugh harder.

On a few occasions, Penny joined us for dinner. But for the most part, she goes and hangs with friends or chills in her room.

I told her it was cool if she hung with us, but she laughed it off and said, "It's pretty much a date, Auti. I will not be a third wheel." She makes a valid statement.

A couple nights ago, we watched a movie after dinner. Our nights together have been some of the best moments of my adult life, but they were also a strain. The more Jonas and I see each other, the less time I spent at the shop, and the more I considered it wise to shift my work schedule. Honestly, I don't know why I didn't do it sooner. It works better with Clementine's school schedule. Now, I work fewer hours in the evening and she spends less time with a sitter. It's a win win. More time with Clementine and Jonas.

And although we have been seeing each other almost nonstop for the last two weeks, we have yet to do anything beyond some serious kissing and light petting. Not that either of us doesn't want to do more. The perfect opportunity just hasn't presented itself yet. But it feels fast approaching.

Tonight, we are having dinner at Jonas's house. Clementine is bringing her favorite movie with her for us to watch afterward. This tends to be the trend with each dinner we share. The only night we don't see each other is when he goes to his parent's house for their weekly family dinner. It gives us both a night apart to do anything we want.

I park in Jonas's driveway and cut the engine. As soon as I do, Clementine unbuckles, grabs her purse with the movie tucked inside, and hops out of the car.

"Sparty," she hollers as she runs for the door. "I'm here, Sparty."

Her enthusiasm to see Spartan cracks me up. But what's

even funnier is Spartan on the other side. Jonas has told me each time we pull up, after our first visit here, Spartan sits at the door and whimpers until Clementine walks in. Their instant connection is so freaking precious.

Clementine bolts up the three steps and turns the door handle, walking into Jonas's house as if she lives there. I laugh and shake my head.

As I step up to the front door, Jonas greets me with a chuckle. Both of us bewildered by his fur-child and my human one. "Hey, scarlet," he says, kissing the hell out of me as I shut the door.

Sometime over the last two weeks, Jonas started calling me scarlet. The first time he said it, I cocked my head in question. Wasn't sure if he was calling me someone else? Then, he explained between my lipstick, nail color, and my overall fashion sense, it fit. It didn't bother me. If anything, I loved it. Quite a bit. The term of endearment made my cheeks heat. Scarlet, of course. And since, he says it more often.

When he breaks the kiss—because let's be honest, I will never break our kisses—I sigh and lean into him. "Hey. What's for dinner?"

We wander from the living room—where Clementine and Spartan sit on the couch and cuddle together as Clementine tells him about her day—to the kitchen. I could easily stare at the two of them for hours and not tire of how darling they are. Two peas in the cutest pod.

"Thought we'd have homemade chicken tenders with macaroni and cheese and corn on the cob."

"You really are domestic," I tease as I hug his middle and stare into the large pot of cheesy noodles. A girl could really get used to this. Her guy cooking dinner nightly. And if I get lucky, he will let me help with the dishes.

"My momma taught me right. Wanted to make sure we were all self-sufficient. Either that or so we could pull our weight in a relationship."

When I get the opportunity to meet Jonas's mom, I plan to thank her. She raised a wonderful man. No doubt his sisters are equally amazing. From what he has told me, during their weekly dinners, Jonas and his sisters usually make most of the meal. The only exception is when they have something which takes more time to cook.

"Look forward to meeting her," I say.

He stops stirring the pasta and I stop breathing. Did I go too far? Suggest meeting the parents a little too soon. Meeting Jonas's mom—since already meeting his dad—seems inevitable, but I don't expect it by any specific time.

Jonas sets the spoon on the rest and spins to face me. He clasps my hands and wraps them around his waist, drawing me near. My hips press to his upper thighs. He sweeps my long flowing hair off my cheek and tucks it behind my ear before cupping both my cheeks in his palms. Slowly, he closes the space between us and kisses me.

Fevered and intense. Lips smacking. Tongues tangling. Hips grinding. Moan emitting.

His fingers slip into my hair and curl in my locks. He draws me closer. Kisses me deeper. Kisses me as if I am his oxygen.

Over the last two weeks, I learned to wear my hair down more with Jonas. Otherwise, it ended up looking like a hot mess in less than an hour. At least with my hair down, I didn't spend every five minutes trying to fix it. And Jonas really loved my hair down. A lot. Oftentimes, his fingers toyed with the strands. While we cooked dinner. During movie time, while we spooned on the couch. Every possible chance he got.

When he breaks the kiss, I gasp and work to catch my breath. He rests his forehead against mine, eyes closed. We stand absolutely still for a moment, absorbing our exchange.

"Can't wait for you to meet her, and my sisters, too. Think they'll love you and Clementine. Plus, Clementine can play with Lex and Spartan. Whenever you're ready, of course."

I nod. "We should talk about it. Everything you've told me about them, it feels as if I already know them."

An angry beeping fills the room as the timer on the stove interrupts our little moment. In the living room, I hear Clementine tell Spartan dinner is ready. And just like every other time she says this to him, he yips and bounces around the house. Because Spartan is trained to know the word dinner equals food. Same goes for breakfast. Clementine giggles every time she says it and Spartan flips out.

Jonas presses the buzzer and shuts it off. Then removes the lightly breaded chicken strips from the oven and sets the tray on trivets. After they cool a minute, we portion our plates then feed Spartan.

Just like we have several times over the last two weeks, we sit at the breakfast bar and eat our meal. When we finish, we settle on the couch and watch Clementine's movie. She lies on the end of the couch with a chaise—Spartan sprawled at her feet and facing the television. Jonas and I lay on the longer section of the sofa. Him behind me, his front to my back. Hand on my abdomen, toying with the hemline of my shirt. Knuckles brushing back and forth across my skin just beneath my navel. His breath hot on my neck below my ear. On occasion, he lightly kisses the sensitive skin there.

And every time he does, I groan as quietly as possible while grinding back against him.

As big a fan of foreplay as I am, this level of teasing may

soon be my demise. Weeks of titillating torture. I love it and hate it at the same time. All I know is, is when we eventually have sex, it will be mind blowing.

Slowly, I turn around so Jonas and I lie face-to-face. I brush his fallen hair off his forehead and lean into him. As I weave my upper leg between his, he draws me closer and throws his leg over my hip.

Weeks ago, it would have freaked me out to do this with Clementine in the room. But now, things have become more comfortable with all of us. One, her eyes are on the movie as she combs her fingers through Spartan's fur. Two, she has seen Jonas and I kiss so many times now, it is normal. Natural. Nothing to bat an eye at.

I brush my lips over his then retreat. "God, I want you," I confess. His hand on my lower back holds me in place as he slowly rocks his hips forward. My eyes roll back then close.

"Right there with you, scarlet. Not tonight, though," he whispers. "But soon."

I nod and bring my lips back to his. For the remainder of the movie, we make out like teenagers. Jonas tucks his hand between us and explores my skin beneath my shirt. He doesn't dip beneath my bra or push it to the side. And hell if I don't have lady blue balls by the time the movie ends.

As the credits scroll up the screen, neither of us moves. Clementine doesn't say a word about the movie being over, which means she recently fell asleep. But the moment we move, she will wake. It happens every time.

So, we stay right where we are. Cuddled in each other's arms. Lips locked and tongues a tangled mess. Hands traveling the others' body. Squeezing and groping. Taunting and teasing.

When Jonas's fingertips graze the elastic band of my

panties, I gasp and tip my head back. He trails his lips and tongue down the column of my neck. I rock into him, needing to feel him against me. Even if we are both still completely clothed, I need the friction.

"Oh god," I whisper-moan.

Jonas's hands are in a frenzy—kneading my hips harder, driving us together over and over. He sucks at my skin, at the dip below my collarbone—from sternum to shoulder— nipping my skin when he reaches the end point. He rocks our hips together, again and again. The friction rubs me in all the right places. Sparks fire beneath my skin. A light sheen of sweat coats my skin. Energy swirls throughout my body, like a river from head to toe, and slowly converges beneath my navel.

His lips travel up my neck, across the line of my jaw, then return to mine. He devours me as if I am his last meal. Hips rocking in time together as his hand trails along my abdomen and lightly scrapes my flesh.

I moan against his lips, fist the fabric of his shirt, just before my body stutters and releases. He sucks on my lower lip as my orgasm consumes me. Swallows me whole.

"Fuck, that was sexy as hell," he whispers against my lips.

Clementine groans and I stop breathing. "Mama," she says, her voice thick with sleep.

"Yeah, pumpkin," I answer, hoping I don't sound too far off from normal. Jonas smiles wickedly in front of me and I resist the urge to slap him.

"Are we going home soon?"

"Soon, pumpkin."

She doesn't say anything else for a minute and I wonder if she dozed back off. When I lift up and glance over at her, her eyes are closed but her fingers are moving in Spartan's fur again.

"I feel bad," I tell Jonas.

He furrows his brow. "Why?"

Glancing down between us, I rock my hips against him and hear him groan. "Because I can't return the favor now."

He nods and kisses the tip of my nose. "Please don't worry about that. I'm a saint in the patience department."

"Still feel bad."

A wide, toothy smile spreads across his lips and his dimple makes an appearance. "Just remember it for when you *can* make it up to me."

I lean back in and kiss him, but he breaks his lips away far too soon and leaves me wanting. "Fine. Guess I better go. Not that I want to."

Jonas softly brushes his knuckles over my cheek. "More than anything, I want you to stay. But not tonight."

Pushing out my lip, I pout and laugh when Jonas drops his face in the crook of my neck and grunts. "Please stop pouting. You have no idea what that does to me."

"Oh really…" I kick the corner of my mouth up in a devilish smile. "Note to self. Pouting is my weapon."

"Yeah, that may be true. But I'm sure I have a few up my sleeve too."

I narrow my eyes at him and he laughs quietly. When he doesn't budge or say anything else, I shift to roll off the couch, but Jonas stops my momentum. Rolls me back to him and proceeds to tickle the sides of my abdomen. I shriek and twitch beneath his hands. Clementine wakes up more at the other end of the couch and sits up, watching as Jonas tickles me.

"Tickle Mama party!" she announces, way more awake than she was a minute ago.

And then Clementine crawls over and drops on top of us both. Her little fingers dig in near my belly and wiggle around. Jonas laughs as he and Clementine continue to torture me.

"Stop," I shriek. "P-please. Pr-pretty please." No matter how hard I try, I can't stop laughing.

Eventually, Jonas stops tickling me and suggests they *give Mama a break to breathe*. As much as the whole tickle fest made my abdomen sore and my throat dry, I wouldn't trade out this moment for anything. Jonas and my daughter tag-teaming me in the name of fun. Joining forces to make me laugh. Seeing Clementine jumping in the game with Jonas, it jolts something in the center of my chest.

My little girl has a father-type figure in her life. Someone she is fond of and loves spending time with. As this realization hits me, I stare at the man lying in front of me. Really look at him. Study the kindness in his gaze. The way he looks at me. And the way he looks at my little girl. How thoughtful and generous he is toward us both.

And at this exact moment in time, reality dawns brighter than ever. A truth I can no longer ignore. But a truth I am not ready to confess aloud.

I am in love with Jonas Thompson. Madly.

Leaning back in, my eyes open and locked on his, I kiss him tenderly. He closes his eyes briefly and exhilaration bleeds from his lips to mine. The surge amplifies and pulses through my veins. Wakes every nerve ending and lights me on fire. Spreads from my lips to limbs and comes back to center where it fuses together and forms a life all its own.

My pulse goes into overdrive and I breathe shallowly.

When Jonas breaks the kiss, his eyes pop back open and he sees it. The intense emotion alive between us. What I feel. What I know he feels too. But we both stay quiet.

This is not the time or place. But soon, without a doubt, I will tell him.

"Mama, is it time to go home?"

My eyes don't leave Jonas's. "Why don't you pick up what you brought over. We'll go in a moment." But my eyes tell Jonas leaving is the last thing I want to do. A slow nod of his head, he then kisses the tip of my nose.

Reluctantly, I sit up and fetch my shoes. In less than five minutes, Clementine and I are ready to go. I wish for a valid excuse to stay longer, but it's late and Clementine is tired. And I should do what is best for her.

We walk out the front door. I unlock the car and start it up so the heat will warm the cabin. "Give me just a minute." Clementine rests her head against the door and nods. She will be out before we get home.

I close the door and turn to Jonas. We don't say a word. He holds my face in his palms and leans in closer. When his lips touch mine, he is so tender. More tender than I have ever felt before and I mold my body to his. Thread my fingers through the loops of his jeans and pull him against my waist. Hold him flush to me as we express all the emotions we aren't saying aloud.

Because Jonas feels it too—how deeply I have fallen— and matches the emotion.

When he breaks the kiss all too soon, he swipes both his thumbs over my cheeks and places one last kiss on my lips. "Drive safe, scarlet," he says, soft and gruffly.

"I will. And I'll text once we're home." The sentiment—

those three words—almost slips from my lips, but I catch it. Catch it and remind myself now is not the time. Soon.

"If you really meant it when you said you'd like to meet my family, I can see if they have room for two more on Wednesday."

Placing one last kiss on his lips, I smile. "Yes, I would love to."

"I'll double-check. Not that I think it'll be an issue." He kisses my forehead. "'Night, scarlet. Get little C in bed."

"Night." I get in the car and back out of Jonas's driveway. On the drive home, with my baby girl in the passenger seat passed out, I recall my eureka moment. The exact moment in time when I realized I am in love with Jonas.

Sure, we haven't been dating very long. Maybe a month altogether. But does love have rules? Is there some hidden decree which dictates how long you have to know someone before you can realize the depth of your affection for them? No. Because love has no rules. Never has. Never will.

Society may deem it odd to do or say or feel certain things in a relationship when it is still new. But societal rules were made by people who feared being vulnerable. And love is one of the most vulnerable emotions in existence.

Now, I just have to find the right time to tell Jonas of my revelation. And be ready to hear it in return. Because I see it in his eyes. Jonas Thompson loves me. Unconditionally.

twenty-two

JONAS

After talking with Mom—who I knew would freak out in the best way—I open my text history with Autumn to let her know Wednesday is a go. I also mentally prepare her for the onslaught of questions she will get. Because as much as I love my mother and sisters, they are curious women. Especially since I have never brought a woman home. Ever.

The moment I get off the phone with my mom Saturday morning, I text Autumn.

Autumn and I chat a little longer. She and Clementine are going to the park with Penny and Rex, from the tattoo shop. From everything Autumn has shared with me so far, everyone in the shop is pretty close. More like family. When she first mentioned it to me, but didn't say anything about her actual family, I tucked that little tidbit away for the future. A conversation for down the road when Autumn is ready to tell me more about her past.

Reluctantly, I let her go so they can enjoy the park. Spartan and I head out to the back yard where I work on the flower beds more. Spartan lays in the grass and soaks up the sunshine for a while.

I add new fertilizer to the beds in the area I work on and plant the small shrubs and flowers I had Clementine help me choose. Last weekend, I told her I needed her help to make my back yard pretty. She stood tall, more than willing to assist.

We walked around the home improvement store for an hour and stared at rows and rows of options. We narrowed down her twenty choices to four, for now. When we got back to the house, she helped me plant the first flower plant. I told her I would do most of the rest and make the flower beds pretty for her to look at when we were outside.

In a matter of no time at all, this little girl abducted my heart. And honestly, I don't care if she never gives it back. She is the sweetest little human I have ever known. Mom, Jasmine, and Jillian will have a field day with her. And without a doubt, they will fall in love with her just as quickly. As well as with Autumn.

Halfway through planting, my phone rings in my pocket. When I pull it from my pants, I roll my eyes and answer. "Hey, Jas. What's up?"

"Mom says you're bringing your girlfriend and her daughter to dinner Wednesday."

Her words are a statement and leave it wide open for me to mess with her. "Do you have an actual question for me?"

"Don't be a jerk, Jonas. Anything you want to tell me before Wednesday?"

What? "Uh… I don't understand what you're asking. Is this a trick question?"

"Sorry, bro. Just didn't know if there's anything I shouldn't bring up. Never been in this situation before."

Alright, my sister is being dramatic. I roll my eyes and laugh. "Jas, she's not an outcast or something. She's a wonderful person. I really like her. She really likes me. And it just so happens she has a daughter. But you'll love her too. Both of them."

"Okay, brother. Just elbow me if I start acting weird."

I laugh. "Can I elbow you no matter what?"

"You're an ass."

"Love you too. See you Wednesday."

"Bye."

The call disconnects and I shake my head. Of my two sisters, I knew Jasmine would be the one to freak out more. Jillian has always been more laid back about life. Sure, she will ask questions, but it won't feel the same as when Mom and Jasmine do.

I finish putting the last of the plants in the soil and head back into the house. After washing up, I plop down on the couch and lay where Autumn and I do every time she visits. The fabric smells like her. Like vanilla and cherry and the distinct scent of Autumn.

Like a weirdo, I press my face into the cushions and inhale deeply. Only a few more hours and I will see her for dinner. I set an alarm on my phone and take a nap with my nose against the cushion where her scent is strongest. Fuck, I love her....

~

Autumn wanders around her apartment in search of a specific bandana she wants to wear in her hair. I offer to help, but stop after a minute when it seems I am only in the way. Clementine tries to tell her the last place she saw it, but steers clear of Autumn while she scours the apartment.

Five minutes later, the bandana is secure in her hair. But she fidgets more. Bites her lips frequently. Checks her hair. Questions what she wears. And I can't help but adore how nervous she is about meeting my family.

Her anxiety says more than any words. Says how much she cares—not just about me, but also wanting my family to like her. And Clementine.

I step up to her and rest my hands on her hips. "Autumn." She stops for a minute and stares up into my eyes. "It'll be okay." Her eyes dart between mine and don't calm down. At this rate, there is only one way she will calm down. So, I dip down and kiss her. Kiss her so deeply, I steal her breath.

When I break the kiss, she stares up at me as her body sags. "Thank you."

"Any time." I scan down the length of her. "You look great. Ready to head out?"

She stares down her front, then meets my gaze again with a sigh. "As ready as I'm going to be." Spinning away from me, she calls down the hallway. "Clementine, time to leave."

The cutest girl in the world comes barreling down the hallway with Spartan as her sidekick. I swear he has never been so loyal to a person before. Not even me. But any time Clementine is near, he switches to this whole new dog. Yes, he is still silly and wild, but he is also gentle and attentive with her. The two of them in the same room is the strangest and most interesting sight to witness.

When Clementine and Spartan stand a few feet away, I cock my head and take in the new accessory around his neck. A bright red bandana, folded into a triangle, and hanging proudly around his neck. And no joke, I swear Spartan smiles.

I bite the inside of my cheek. The last thing I want to do is laugh and let Clementine think it's about her. But I do want to laugh at Spartan's new attire. Especially since I tried to make him wear several similar items over the last three years and have failed. Put him in a room with Clementine for five-plus minutes and bam. Done.

"Spartan." He jerks his head my way. "Ready to go see Grandma?"

Woof, woof, woof.

"That is hilarious and cute as heck," Autumn says.

"Just wait, it'll get better when we get there."

The ride from Autumn's apartment to my parent's house passes quickly. Autumn bounces her knee in the passenger seat more often than not. Each time it bobs, I give her thigh a gentle squeeze to reassure her everything will be fine. Then again, can't say I have ever been in her shoes.

Sure, I have hung out with friends' families several times over the years. But meeting them was different. Cora is the only friend whose parents I met that made me semi-nervous. But they were hosting a Memorial Day BBQ and invited everyone. But she was the only person whom I ever had a romantic interest in as an adult where anxiety would apply.

It surprises me, though, how not nervous I am about tonight. Will my mom and sisters probably probe Autumn with a hundred awkward questions? I hope not, but wouldn't be shocked if they did. But I am driving the two most important people in my life right now to my parents' house—to our weekly family dinner—and I have never been calmer in my life.

Huh. No doubt this could be psychoanalyzed for days.

When I turn onto Mom and Dad's street, Autumn grips my forearm. And when I park the Jeep in the driveway, she practically digs her nails into my pulse point.

Spartan barks like the lunatic he is, dying to get out and run for the door. Clementine bounces in her seat with obvious excitement. While Autumn stares at my parent's four-bedroom house with lips tucked between her teeth and eyes scanning every flower and shrub along the exterior.

I lean over and kiss the soft spot beneath her ear. "Hey." Slowly, she rotates her head to face me. Our mouths a breath apart. "Breathe. There is absolutely nothing to be nervous about."

"Says you," she whispers.

"Promise I'll keep you safe. Just stick by my side." I close the space between us and kiss her sweetly. "Okay?"

She nods. "Yeah."

Both of us hop out of the Jeep. I fetch Spartan from the back, while Autumn helps Clementine down. As soon as we are close enough to the door, I let go of Spartan's leash and he bolts. Before he can bark for Mom to open up, the door flies open and he leaps into her waiting arms.

"Who's my favorite grandpup?" Mom asks Spartan. His responding bark makes me laugh per usual.

"Mom, he's your only grandpup," I say.

She rises back to her normal height and looks me square in the eyes. "True, but he doesn't know that."

I laugh as we step up onto the porch. "Mom, this is Autumn and her daughter, Clementine. Ladies, this is my mom, Irene."

"Autumn, it's wonderful to meet you." Mom lifts her hands and silently asks permission to hug. When Autumn leans in to reciprocate, I exhale.

"Nice to meet you, Irene." The hug lasts for two breaths, but Autumn relaxes the second Mom's arms wrap around her. "Clementine"—Autumn peers down at her daughter—"say hello to Miss Irene."

Clementine lifts her hand and waves. "Hi, Miss Irene." Then she leaps forward and hugs Mom's midsection. "Nice to meet you."

Mom laughs at Clementine's spunky nature before throwing a smile my way. A smile I have never seen before.

Once Clementine breaks her hold, Mom escorts us into the house. "Your sisters aren't here yet, but we can start prepping dinner now."

We step past the foyer and into the formal living room. The sofa, matching chairs, and table are like new, only because my parents hardly use the room. Usually, we sit in here during Christmas or other big gatherings. Otherwise, we sit in the family room.

I let Autumn know where she can set her purse and tell Mom I'm going to give her a tour before we start dinner. Mom agrees to keep an eye on Clementine, who is currently talking to Spartan. No doubt they will entertain each other most of the evening.

As we wander down the hall, I slip my hand around Autumn's and walk backward so I can face her. "Still nervous?" She has been silent—with the exception of introductions—since we left her apartment.

"Yeah," she says with a nod. "God, I've never been so anxious to impress people."

I lead us into the bedroom at the end of the hall on the right. My old bedroom, now a guest room. Shutting the door behind us, I steer us to the bed and sit us on the edge. "Hey, you don't need to impress anyone here. We don't operate that way."

"You know, I got that vibe from your mom right off the bat. But I think your sisters will be more critical."

Autumn may not know Jasmine and Jillian yet, so I get her concern. But if either of my sisters make Autumn uncomfortable or give her the third degree, I won't be the only person giving them a ration of shit. Mom and Dad would both jump in the ring and defend her too.

"They won't be. If either of them so much as says something off-putting, you'll have three people in your court." She smiles, but it doesn't reach her eyes and falls away as quickly as it appeared. "Hey." I pinch her chin in my thumb and forefinger, lifting her line of sight. "It'll be fine, scarlet. Promise."

She nods, eyes still swirling with apprehension. I hate how her nerves are eating her up. How they hinder the great night to come.

Leaning forward, I lower my mouth to hers. Kiss her slow and sweet. Part her lips with my tongue. Taste her distinct flavor, a flavor I cannot pinpoint but also cannot get enough of. Her hands trace my jawline. Nails scrape my scalp until they reach my longer strands and take hold. Drawing me closer. Deeper.

My hands drop to her hips and fist them as I step back, sit on the bed, and haul her onto my lap. Her legs straddle mine as if they have done it hundreds of times before. We kiss as if another opportunity won't arise. As if our lips won't have contact for days or weeks or months. Our passion is a firestorm. Unrelenting. Building. Flourishing into something primal yet unexplainable.

Autumn rocks her hips against me. Moans down my throat. The bulge beneath my zipper thick and swollen and starving for her. I break the kiss and trail my mouth over the soft line of her jaw, nipping and licking. Down the column of her throat as she throws her head back and gasps, fingers clutching my hair and locking me to her skin.

When I reach her shoulder, I stop and lay my forehead on her. Inhaling her delicious scent, I close my eyes and bask in her weight on my lap. If I keep this up much longer, every adult in the house will know what we are up to. Which will only serve to stir up more discomfort.

Our rapid breathing floats in the room as our pulses slowly settle. I lean back and trail my eyes up her neck until they lock on to her intoxicating irises. So many words pass through her eyes without a single word leaving her lips. And I feel it. Deep down in my bones, I feel all her unspoken thoughts. Because those same words trickle through my every vein and artery like DNA.

Neither of us has brought up the extent of how we feel for the other. But staring into her eyes right now, the way she refuses to look away, it is obvious she is in just as deep as I am.

Some men would be unsettled by this revelation—falling in love. Me? I indulge in it. Take it and tuck it safely inside the cage surrounding my heart.

I brush my fingers from her temple down to her lips. "As

much as I'd like to stay in here the next several hours, we should finish the tour and help with dinner."

Autumn kisses my fingers before sliding off my lap. "Suppose you're right. Last thing I need is your family thinking we're in here having sex."

I laugh to cover my sudden choking. She pats my back a few times then laughs too. Rising off the bed, Autumn straightens her shirt and runs her hands down her thighs to smooth her jeans.

Once she finishes, Autumn steps between my legs and combs her fingers through my hair. "If we walk out with your hair like this, everyone will know what we were up to in here." She giggles as I roll my eyes closed and sit perfectly still.

Her touch is the cure to every ailment I will ever have. My remedy. Created for only me.

When she stops fixing my disheveled strands, I open my eyes. "Thanks," I whisper. "Let me show you the rest of the house. Oh"—I wave my hand around the room as I stand— "this was once my room."

"Fitting." She hums and nods.

Taking her hand in mine, I lead us back into the hall. I play tour guide through the rest of the house and finish up the circuit in the kitchen. Which is where my mom and sisters reside.

The moment we step into the room, all three of them look to us. Autumn's grip tightens and I kiss her temple. "Jasmine, Jillian, this is Autumn. Autumn, these are my sisters. Jasmine"— I point to my older sister, then to my baby sister—"and Jillian."

Jasmine picks up a hand towel and wipes her hands before extending one to Autumn. "Wonderful to finally meet you,

Autumn. My son, Lex, is playing with Clementine in the family room. She's a doll."

"Nice to meet you. And thank you." Autumn smiles like a proud mom. A smile that warms me throughout.

Jillian steps forward and Autumn extends her hand. But Jillian takes us all by surprise when she hugs Autumn. Not that my family doesn't hug. We just don't generally hug new people. Especially Jillian.

"Wow, Jilli," I say when she releases Autumn. "Feeling extra affectionate today?"

She play-punches my bicep. "Ha ha, big brother. And so what if I am. Can't I be happy and want to hug people?"

"Forget I asked," I say, throwing my hands up in surrender. "Mom, what can we help with?"

Mom directs me to the cutting board to help with the salad. She frequently gives me the task and I wonder if my slicing and chopping skills supersede those of my sisters. While I slice carrots, Mom asks Autumn if she will help her with dessert—magic brookie bars. If there is one thing my mom is master of, it is dessert. And her magic brookie bars are to die for.

The kitchen fills with chatter as everyone catches up. Jasmine tells us how Lex heard someone say the word shit the other day and he won't stop saying it. I laugh, probably harder than I should, because my sister is adamant about raising Lex to be a proper young man. Mom chimes in and tells her about each occasion when we all said our first bad word. It only serves to make me laugh harder.

After Dad and Anton set the table, we all carry out dishes while Mom puts the magic brookies in the oven. We take our seats at the table and start passing around food from one to the next. Beside me, Autumn relaxes more. Clementine is the life of the party. And I spend the entire hour at the dinner table with a wide smile stretching my cheeks.

"Irene, I need this recipe," Autumn says as she chews her last bite of magic brookie bar.

Mom smiles at the other end of the table. "I'll jot it down before you go. Let's clean up and sit out back for a little bit before everyone goes."

And just like that, everyone rises from their seats and shuffles around to clean up. Then we all sit out back on the loungers near the pool while the kids watch a movie on television. Autumn sits between my legs and chats with everyone as if she has been here several times before. Her earlier nerves nowhere to be found.

When I check the time, I suggest we head out so Clementine can get a good night's sleep before school. We collect the goody bag Mom made us, give hug after hug, and say our goodbyes.

Once Clementine and Spartan are secure in the back seat, Spartan lays down and rests his head on Clementine's lap. Autumn and I hop in, and soon we head for Autumn's apartment.

Tonight went better than expected. Mom and my sisters didn't probe Autumn with questions. Thank god. The conversations in the kitchen and around the dinner table flowed naturally. And Autumn smiled often, as did I.

A few miles from the apartment, I stop at a red light and look in the rearview mirror to see Clementine asleep. I nudge my head toward the back seat. "She passed out."

Autumn glances back at Clementine briefly and smiles. "Was a busy night for her. But she had fun."

"Did you enjoy yourself?"

She nods before I face forward again and drive. "Yeah."

She reaches across the console and rests her hand on my thigh. I swallow. "Your family is wonderful," she says wistfully.

"They are," I mumble as I envision her and Clementine as part of the family out of nowhere. Crazy how my mind jumps from point A to point Z before stopping at any of the other points in between. But I can't help how Autumn makes me feel. How she makes me long for more. To fall asleep with her in my arms and wake with her curled to my torso and tangled in my limbs.

A block from her apartment complex entrance, I strike up the nerve to propose an idea to her. After double-checking Clementine is still asleep in the back, I take a deep breath and swallow. I reach over the console and rest my hand on her leg.

"Autumn, I want to ask you something. But I don't want you to freak out."

She turns in the seat to face me better. In the process, my hand slides farther north and stops inches from the junction of her thighs. She doesn't lean back or shift it away.

"Okay," she drawls out.

"Keep an open mind and don't shoot me down right away." I glance over at her as I steer us into the complex. "Will you stay at my place?" I park the Jeep and take in Autumn's wide-eyed, frozen state. "Obviously not tonight, but one night soon."

Autumn looks to the back seat out of the corner of her eye. "Jonas, I don't know."

"Think about it. No rush. And Clementine can stay over too. The couch doubles as a bed too."

"Jonas..." I lean toward her, press a finger to her lips, and cut her off.

"All I ask is for you to think about it. No pressure. If you decide it isn't a good idea, I'll understand. But at least give it a day." She slowly nods, and I remove my finger from her lips.

I open and close my door quietly and meet Autumn on the passenger side. Before we open Clementine's door and I carry her in, I cage Autumn against the front passenger door. Her arms wrap around my waist, beneath my shirt. The heat between us wiping away the evening January chill.

Her nails softly dig into my skin as I lean down and press my lips to hers. The kiss starts off slow and steady, but heated. I paint her tongue with mine as soft moans echo in her throat. I deepen the kiss, shifting my hands to the back of her neck and the curve of her hip. My groin presses into her lower abdomen. Unhurried, her hands dance across my skin from back to front. Skimming up the length of my torso with purpose.

I hiss and our lips part for a second. In the darkness of the parking lot, Autumn kisses down the side of my neck. Claws down my chest. All but unmans me against the Jeep. *Sweet fucking Christ.* I drop my other hand to her hip, hold her steady, and rock mine forward.

"Fuck, scarlet," I whisper toward the heavens.

She kisses back up my neck until her lips reach mine again. We stand tongue-tangled like teenagers for I don't know how long. When I'm on the verge of ripping her clothes off in public, I tear my lips from hers. Her pouty lip makes an appearance and I laugh.

"We should stop, I know," she says.

Hesitantly, I step back from her and grunt. "Yeah, we should. Just consider what I said before. About staying over. Promise if you say no, I won't be upset."

"Swear I'll think about it."

After I give my body a moment to cool off, I open Clementine's door slowly, unbuckle her, signaling Spartan to stay while I carry her inside. Once I lay her in bed and slip off her shoes, Autumn walks me out. Kisses me again, but this time more tenderly. Every ounce of affection poured into the gesture before we say our good nights.

On the way home, one constant thought swirls through my mind. The possibility of soon not having to say good night to Autumn as one of us leaves. A man can only hope.

twenty-three

AUTUMN

"Earth to Autumn."

I snap my head up to find Penny staring me down, hand on her hip and brow cocked. "What?"

"Said your next appointment is here. I'll let them know you need a few more minutes to get ready." She scrutinizes my expression. "You alright? Haven't been yourself all day."

I sigh heavily and nod. "Yeah." Curling my finger, I beckon her closer. "Jonas asked me to stay the night. Clementine, too."

Penny steps back with the most wicked smile on her face. "And?"

"And nothing. He asked and told me to think about it." Now me spending the night with him is the only thing occupying my mind. My clients are lucky I haven't jacked up their art today.

She plops down on my client chair. "You are going to say yes, right?"

Herein lies the dilemma. Every atom in my body, every firing live wire zapping my skin, tells me to say yes. I *want* to say yes. But one thing still has me hesitant. Not Jonas. He is the best man to enter my life. The piece which has me mulling it over, to death, is Clementine. Not because I would bring her, but the possibility of her getting attached to Jonas.

What if our relationship is all smiles and laughter for a bit, but then something changes and it no longer is? What if Clementine falls in love with the idea of always having Jonas around, and then he isn't? These are the thoughts which have me uncertain. It's one thing for me to hurt, but I never want that for Clementine.

"Pen, I want to. Badly. But…"

"But what, Auti? Jonas is a good man. Everyone sees it. And I know you see it. So what has you second-guessing?"

I huff, hating that this conversation has to happen. Being put on the spot sucks, as does my uncertainty. "What if it doesn't work out with Jonas and Clementine gets close to him?"

Penny tilts her head to the side and pops her gum. "Honestly?" I nod and tuck my lips between my teeth. "Think you're more scared of you and Jonas staying together." My forehead scrunches and she holds up a hand to stop me from rebutting. "Auti, you haven't had the best relationships in the past. Clementine's birth father was the last person you were with, and he was an asshole. Any person who tucks their tail and runs when shit gets serious is a piece of shit. Especially after what went down with your parents."

Wiping down the counter and chair, I nod as Penny continues.

"Jonas is not Leo, Auti." I meet her eyes and she holds strong. "He isn't. And the way Jonas looks at you, the way he looks at Clementine… he wants so much more with you. Tell me you see it. Tell me you *feel* it. He flaunts his heart like a marquee sign."

I do sense the way Jonas cares about me. About both of us. Part of me is scared to take the next step. To get consumed by all that we feel. To open up, share my past, and let Jonas in all the way. Because if I open up, if I give him every little piece of my heart, and he crushes it… there is no coming back from such devastation. And if I fall that hard, that deep, and come out on the other side hurt, I can only imagine how my sweet, innocent little girl would handle it. Clementine should never have to experience such heartache. Not until she is strong enough, old enough, to deal with such anguish.

"Yeah, Pen, I see it." Probably because my heart reflects his. I pop up and glance at Rex and Reznor in the booths next to mine. "Boys?" They both perk up—eyes on their clients, ears on me. "Thoughts? Am I thinking too much into this whole scenario?"

Without a doubt, they have heard the entire conversation between me and Penny. Plus, they are family. Between all of us—Rex, Penny, Reznor, Iliana, and me—there are no secrets. Granted, Penny is the only one who knows every sorted detail about my past, but no one is out of the loop. They know enough I don't have to skirt around topics. Penny and Iliana generally work opposite days or shifts, so Iliana and I aren't as close as me and Penny. But we are all tight.

"Think if you explain it to the little princess the right way —staying over—it shouldn't seem abnormal to her. And yes, I think you should do it." Reznor pauses to dip the needle in the ink cap. "You deserve happiness, A. I love seeing you smile. And he makes you smile. All the time."

As if on cue, a smile perks up the corners of my mouth.

"I'm with Rez," Rex adds. "He seems like a great guy; legit. And if he isn't, your brothers will make it right."

I laugh and shake my head. "Oh god." But Penny gives

me a look that says *see, I'm right*. Yeah, yeah. "Alright, let me get back to work before the natives become restless."

The next few hours go by slower than desirable. With each line and dot and shading I etch into skin, I ponder over saying yes to Jonas. To his proposition of staying the night. A constant buzz courses through my body and it has nothing to do with the tattoo gun in my hand.

God, I cannot remember the last time I thought about spending the night with a man. Well, back then, they weren't men. Clementine's father and I had only been together six months when I found out I was pregnant. Pregnant at twenty. A single mother at twenty-one.

Sure, I had spent the night with other guys prior to Clementine's father, but during those days, most of us still lived at home with our parents. Spending the night wasn't so much an option, unless someone's parents were out of town. And that was almost never. At least, in the circle of people I knew then.

As an adult—a woman—this has never come up. That's what happens when you don't date. Seemed like the best decision at the time. Now, I wish maybe I would have given it a try once or twice. Just so I wasn't so inexperienced. Ugh.

When I wrap up with my final scheduled appointment, Penny skips over and watches me clean up. She doesn't speak a word. Just follows me with her eyes and pops her gum. But her gaze is loaded with questions. Questions I will answer, but not until she asks them. So, I continue to wipe everything down and dispose of my trash while she hovers like a grade A helicopter parent.

I laugh under my breath as she studies my every move out of the corner of my eye. Cracks me up how she waits—impatiently—for me to blurt out my decision. Penny has known me for years—I met her and the guys shortly before Clementine was born—and knows I won't freely hand out information. More often than not, someone has to ask for me to answer.

"You know, I thought maybe Jonas would've at least gotten you to be more forward. But it would appear otherwise," she says, narrowing her eyes.

Now I laugh out loud. "Old habits die hard," I answer.

"Well, that's one habit I hope he influences." She gives me a snide smile. "So, did you figure out what to do?"

I nod. "Yep." Penny waits for me to say more, but I stay tight-lipped. It's too much fun dragging it out and torturing the hell out of her.

"And?" She waves her hand frantically as she pops another bubble. "You live to mess with me, don't you?"

Shrugging, I bite the inside of my cheek and try to taper my smile. "It's fun. What can I say?" Her chin juts forward and her eyes widen. "And I decided to say yes."

"Eep!" Penny squeals, a body piercing sound from her throat as she jumps up and down in place. "Oh my god! Oh my god!" She looks between Rex and Reznor. "You guys hear that? She's going to say yes."

Heat creeps up my neck and fills my cheeks. "Penny, shh." Reznor and Rex give me subtle smiles. They are happy for me, but I'm glad they don't shriek and draw all attention my way.

"Whatever," she says. "So, is he coming over for dinner tonight? Should I be the annoying roommate? Or do you want me to act ignorant to all these details? Not clap when you tell him."

Oh Jesus. "Penny, please just be normal. No clapping or screaming or teasing. Please," I beg.

"Fine," she huffs out. "I'll be good." Penny puts on her cutest sulking face. "But when he leaves, I'm freaking out."

I snatch my purse and head for the exit. "I'm good with that. See you at home in a bit."

She waves. "Deuces."

I put the salmon fillets in the oven just as there is a knock at the door.

Clementine barrels down the hallway. "Mama, Jonas is here. And Sparty." Her excitement makes me smile.

"Hang on, pumpkin." Although we know who is at the door, I still don't let Clementine answer the door without an adult.

She bounces in front of the door, eager to see Spartan. As soon as I unlock and open up the door, I don't know who is more excited—Clementine or Spartan. He bounds inside and she leads him to the couch. They plop down and she starts telling him all about her day. The project her class has been working on. The icky cafeteria food. Everything. And it is too damn cute.

"Hey," Jonas says as he steps inside and kisses my temple. "How was your day, scarlet?"

His lips on my skin always make me forget whatever I plan to say. The only thought invading my mind now is the heat from his lips spreading across my skin. When I remember how to use my voice again, I speak up. "Long."

He chuckles against my hair, wraps his arm around my waist, and pulls me into him. "Mine too. Glad to be here now, though."

I breathe him in and melt at the scent I classify as one-hundred-percent Jonas. "Me too." I lean back and look up at him. "Want to help me finish up dinner? Pretty much done. Just have to plate it."

We move around the kitchen in symmetry. Yin and yang. Dark and light. Moon and sun. Opposing forces balancing the other out. Ebbing and flowing.

Penny joins us for dinner when she gets home. We each take turns talking about our day, but we all give Clementine more time than the rest of us. She talks animatedly about the seeds the class planted and how they started sprouting today. All of us zero in on every word she says and ask more questions to hear her enthusiasm about growing herbs.

Plates cleared; we load up the dishwasher then head for the couch to watch an episode of *How I Met Your Mother*. Clementine and Spartan sprawl out on a blanket on the floor. I curl into Jonas's side at one end while Penny sits on the opposite end. Halfway through the episode, Penny rises off the couch and fake yawns.

"Gonna head to bed. Night everyone," she says then tosses a wink in my direction.

I roll my eyes. "'Night."

After her door clicks shut, Jonas shifts beside me and finagles so we lay down. I scoot back and snuggle against his front as he splays a hand across my abdomen beneath my shirt. He kisses the spot beneath my ear and I close my eyes. Tingles ripple from his kiss on my neck to where his hand caresses my skin.

Jonas continues to explore my neck and ear with his lips, driving me wild. I lace my fingers with his. Tighten my hold with every other kiss. Breathe heavier with each press of his lips or nip of his teeth.

"Did you think about what I asked last night?" he whispers in my ear just before he takes my lobe between his teeth.

I clamp down on my lips and moan as quietly as possible. "Yes."

His lips pause at the curve of my neck. "Yes, you thought about it? Or yes, you'll stay?"

Chuckling, I spin around in his grip and face him. I lay my palm on his cheek and kiss him. "Both. Yes, I want to stay. For us to stay."

It takes a moment for my words to click into place, but as soon as they do, Jonas's eyes burn brighter. His hand skims up my spine beneath my shirt as he leans forward and presses his lips to mine. Consumes me. Gives me a piece of him.

When he breaks the kiss, I lift my gaze to meet his, and get lost in the intensity. In the volcanic eruption. Hot. Magnetic. Hypnotizing. It draws me closer and dampens my skin.

He glances over my shoulder to Clementine and Spartan on the floor. "Have you?"

I shake my head. "Wanted to tell you first. We can tell her together." He nods.

While the rest of the episode plays, Jonas and I lay facing each other, silent. And I have never been more comfortable in my life. Never more ready to share my life with another person. To let someone in and explore everything love has to offer.

And when we explain having a sleepover with Clementine, she seems nonchalant. Only excited she gets to spend the night with Spartan. It was all so easy. Simple. Perfect.

I hope our life stays exactly like this. Easy and blissful in our perfect little bubble.

twenty-four

JONAS

Autumn has been to my house before. Has seen every room. Traipsed her fingers on countertops and bookshelves and blankets. Stood at my stove and cooked alongside me. Cuddled with me on the couch and kissed me senseless.

But right now, I dash around the house as if none of that holds weight.

Tossing my clothes in the washer after moving the bedding to the dryer. Washing every cup, plate, and pan immediately after use. Wiping down the counters in the kitchen and bathroom. Scrubbing the toilet. And the shower. Dusting. Vacuuming. Mopping.

I woke before the sun came up. Made breakfast, then realized I needed to clean out the fridge. That very moment is when the manic cleaning marathon started. When I deep cleaned the entire interior of the house from top to bottom.

Spartan watches me with keen interest. Wondering what the hell is wrong with his dad. Tilts his head left then right as I dart from one end of the house to the other. But I don't have time to explain it all to him. Not like he would understand, anyway.

After making the bed and switching my clothes to the dryer around noon, I head outside and mow the yard. Thankfully, enough of my yard is landscaped that I only push the mower and thrust the weed whacker for an hour.

After a quick but thorough shower, I put away the last of the laundry and jot down some last-minute groceries. Out the door and at the store less than ten minutes later, I fill the cart with my normal weekly purchases plus some extras for tonight. During my last couple of grocery trips, I started picking up items specifically for Clementine. Little things such as her favorite juice and mini marshmallows, popcorn, and red licorice. The girl is fond of her movie snacks.

But today I plan to grab extras. Not just for Clementine, but all of us. Extra movie snacks and extra breakfast items.

Two nights ago, when Autumn agreed to stay over, my brain went frantic. I waited until yesterday to ask her what kinds of foods she and Clementine both liked for breakfast. Breakfast. A meal we haven't shared yet. A meal which could consist of hundreds of different options. Of all the meals, breakfast is generally the easiest. But only if you liked the standard breakfast foods.

With each day we spend together, I learn how much Clementine resembles Autumn. Appearance. Personality. And their love for food. I honestly have no idea where they pack it all.

After I check out at the grocery store and head home, the first thing I notice when I walk in the door is the strong blend of multi-purpose cleaner and generic pine. Once I put all the groceries away, I sift through a few cabinets in the utility room and locate a small tote of candles I have collected over the years. Candles I rolled my eyes at during the holidays when my sisters gifted them. Now, I need to remember to thank them during family dinner next week.

I remove the lid from the black candle, bring it to my nose, and inhale. Masculine. A blend of leather and teakwood. I light the wicks and place it as centrally as possible in the open floor plan of the house. Within minutes, the house smells less like a janitorial closet and closer to a men's clothing store.

A few minutes pass as I get lost in the flickering candle flames. Lost in the reality that Autumn and Clementine will be here in a couple hours' time. Since we have been officially seeing each other, shared dinners have happened almost nightly. But she or I always went home at the end of the night. And the thought of her not going home tonight has me unable to focus.

Tonight, Autumn will lay beside me. In my bed. Between my sheets. The heat of her skin pressed to mine.

Spartan barks and I snap out of my daydream. "Thanks, buddy. Time to prep d-i-n-n-e-r and dessert." He barks again. "Mine, not yours."

I get to work in the kitchen and prep the muffin-sized personal pies. Assembled in the pan, I cover and set them in the fridge until it's time to put them in the oven. Then I get to work on the baked macaroni and cheese, coconut chicken bites, and parmesan zucchini fries.

I move around the kitchen with ease and send silent thanks to my mom for teaching me how to cook and bake. Whether it was only for me or me and others, learning how to cook is one of the most valuable gifts she has bestowed upon me.

As I slide the pan of coconut chicken in the oven, Spartan perks his head up from his spot on the couch and barks like a loon. Jumping down, he continues to bark while running in circles. When there is a knock at the door, he practically rips it off the hinges. I laugh as I walk from the kitchen to the front door.

When I open the door, Spartan launches forward and licks every square inch of Clementine's face. She giggles and wraps her little arms around his neck. "Sparty," she giggle-squeals.

"C'mon, buddy. Let them in."

Spartan scoots back. Autumn and Clementine step in and I take a deep breath. We have done this many times before, but it suddenly feels as if this is our first time. Anxiety surges in my belly like a summer storm rolling in off the coast. I step into Autumn and kiss her chastely. And just as quickly as the storm rolled in, her warm lips against mine brings out the sun.

"Hey, scarlet," I croak.

She looks up at me from under her lashes, a shy smile on her lips. "Hey." Lifting the bag in her hand, she asks, "Where should I set this?" Her overnight bag.

This is really happening. Autumn and Clementine are here. And they are staying overnight. Not leaving until tomorrow.

"Let me." I take the bag from her and walk it back to my bedroom, setting it on the bed. When I spin around, Autumn stands in the doorway. Her eyes scan every inch of the room, stopping on me when she finishes.

Is she as nervous as I am? Maybe more. Neither of us has spent the night with another person in a long time. Not like this. Not with hearts out in the open and on the line.

In three short strides, I stand inches from her. Lower my mouth to hers and taste her again. Sweet and addictive. She grips the hem of my shirt and drags me closer. A soft moan spilling from her into me. My hands frame her face as I deepen the kiss. Consume her. Share one of the many ways I need her.

The timer on the stove beeps, letting us know a minute remains. Reluctantly, I break the kiss and inch back. "Help me finish dinner?" Autumn nods and presses her fingers to her lips.

"What're we having?" she asks as we stroll back into the kitchen.

The buzzer rings through the kitchen and I shut off the timer as I open the oven door. "Coconut chicken, baked macaroni and cheese, and zucchini fries," I tell her as I flip the chicken over and add the zucchini fries to the oven.

"Wow. Maybe I need to get cookies for your mom, too." I shake my head. "What? Not only are your parents generous, but your mom made you into every woman's dream man." She waves a hand toward the living room. "You clean. You cook. What other domestic duties do you fulfill?"

I cock a brow and smirk at her. "Hmm… I'll have to show you later." A blush I haven't seen on Autumn's skin in several days makes an appearance. And I love how her mind goes to exactly where I wanted it to.

She licks her lips and tucks them between her teeth a moment. "Later."

Soon, dinner is out of the oven and cool enough to serve. I pop in the muffin pan pies so they finish baking by the time we clear our plates. Autumn fills a plate for Clementine, then herself as I make mine. We sit at the breakfast bar and eat in silence for a few minutes. There is no unease. If anything, eating dinner with both of them feels like the most natural part of my day.

We all grab mini pies and ice cream after dinner and cozy

up on the couch. Spartan tries and fails to eat Clementine's dessert, but she giggles each time his snout gets close. "What are we watching tonight?" I ask Clementine.

"Mama bought *The Secret Life of Pets 2* for tonight," she says, dancing in her seat as the movie starts.

I laugh alongside Autumn as we watch the silly animated kid's movie and finish our dessert. An hour later, Clementine softly snores on the chaise section of the couch with Spartan as her pillow. Quietly, I rise from the couch, collect our dishes, and take them to the kitchen.

As I rinse the bowls, Autumn wraps her arms around my waist and kisses over my spine. "She'll be out for the rest of the night," she whispers into my shirt.

Spinning to face her, I glance over her shoulder and take in the sight of Clementine and Spartan cuddling. "Should we leave the light over the stove on? In case she wakes," I ask and Autumn nods.

I take her hand in mine and weave our fingers together. Without a word, I flip the light over the stove on and steer us out of the kitchen. After we turn off the television and drape the throw blanket over Clementine, I lead Autumn down the hall and into the bedroom.

This is it. The moment that will change our relationship. Add more definition. Sharpen the edges. Bring us closer. Closer than I have ever been with any other person. Make us never want to be apart—at least for me.

Autumn closes the door behind us, and I have never heard the latch click so loudly. Facing Autumn, I walk us to the bed, my eyes tracing the curves of her silhouette as we move. The back of my knees hit the mattress and I draw her close. Wrap her in my arms. Feel the tremble of her hands as they snake around my waist and under my shirt.

I drop my chin, bring my lips within a breath of hers. "We don't have to do anything you're not ready for. If you only want to sleep, then I'll happily hold you in my arms all night. Okay?"

She nods and pushes up on her toes. Our lips connect and I roll my eyes closed. Heat swelters in my chest and blooms across every lick of my skin. And the second she paints her tongue across my lower lip, I open for her and deepen the kiss. Her heat matches mine and ignites the kindling simmering low in my groin.

I groan, slip my hands under her ass, lift her up and spin around to toss her on the bed. She thumps against the mattress and I crawl up her body, slamming my mouth back to hers. Our hands fevered. Lips irrational. Breaths erratic.

Autumn slowly peels my shirt up my torso and over my head, then discards it on the floor. She trails her fingers down my pecs, my abdomen, and along the waistband of my jeans. Reading every dip and line and ridge of my skin like braille. I suck in a sharp breath as she charts new territory and memorizes the landscape. Her fingertips sear my skin, leaving a tingling trail of sparks in their wake.

Her fingers wrap around the button above my fly and I stop her. "Slow. There's no rush." I dip down and kiss her sweet mouth. "I want us to savor this. To savor us."

I roll us over and relish the sight of her straddling me, my palms cupping her hips. She strips her shirt off and tosses it in the same direction as mine. In the dim lighting, I make out the scalloped curves of her bra cups and sit up to get a closer look. The dark lace teases me. Taunts me. Sticks out its proverbial tongue and sneers.

I give her hips a quick squeeze before winding my hands to her backside and softly grazing them up the sides of her spine. She arches and presses her breasts closer to my face. And I can no longer resist the urge to taste her skin. Savor her uncharted territory.

Leaning in, I kiss the swell of her breast. Once. Twice. Lick along the lace edge of her bra cup. She rocks her hips against me, and I pin her in place as I grip her waist. Switch to the opposite breast and pay it equal attention. She threads her fingers in my hair, tips her head back, and moans at the ceiling.

As my tongue trails the swell of her breast, I unhook her bra and flatten my palms against her bare back as the lacy material falls between us. For the first time, the heat of her bare skin presses flush with mine. Fevered and damp and absolutely perfect. I stop breathing. Stop kissing her skin. Close my eyes and savor the moment. The heat, the longing, the absolute need for this connection.

After a beat, I roll Autumn to her back again. Kiss her lips. Kiss down the column of her throat. Along her midline to her navel. To her left hip, then her right.

She pants into the darkness as I unbutton her pants and drag the zipper down the teeth. As I peel the denim down her thighs, I spot her matching lace panties and smile. I pause to press my lips to the material. She groans and fists my hair.

I trace a finger along the waistband of her panties. "Did you wear matching bra and panties for me?" I rasp against her skin.

"Yes."

"You'll have to show them to me when the lights are on."

She moans. "Promise."

I kiss her hip and continue peeling away her jeans. Drop them to the floor, followed by my own. Pressing one knee, then the other, into the mattress, I crawl back up her body.

Hover above and lock eyes with her. With exception of her panties and my boxer briefs, we are skin to skin. Her eyes swirl like the Great Red Spot of Jupiter. Call out to me. Seduce me.

"Are you sure?"

"Never been more sure," she answers and lifts her lips to mine. Sucks my lower lip. Then clutches the back of my neck and draws me low, low, lower until my weight presses into her.

Her kiss rages and amplifies and turns white hot. Has me sweltering and begging for more. Rocking forward and grinding my erection against the junction of her thighs. Her nails scrape along either side of my spine. I hiss as she tucks them beneath the elastic of my briefs and shoves them toward my ankles.

We fumble and laugh as we maneuver the last scraps of our clothes to the floor. And when they drop away, all laughing stops. I kiss her gently. More tender than any time previous. Trace the curve of her jaw with my lips and pepper kisses down, down, down her body.

When I stop at the junction of her thighs, she sucks in a breath and holds it. I trace up the midline of her body with my eyes and revel in the sight of her. Fuck, she is perfect. "Is this okay?" I ask as it dawns on me that not all women enjoy oral sex.

"God, yes," she moans and I chuckle.

But it's the second she threads her fingers in my hair and thrusts my head between her thighs that I stop laughing. I clutch her hips, run my nose along the thin strip of hair, and inhale. *Fuck.*

As if a light flips on in my head and my primal nature surfaces, I lick up her center and taste her for the first time.

Sweet and salty and one-hundred-percent Autumn. Addictive and crucial. God, I could exist solely with the taste of her on my tongue.

I take my time. Devour her. Flick her clit with my tongue and lick up her seam. Insert a finger. Then another. Watch her writhe as I bring her higher and higher. Inhale her pheromones as she edges closer to orgasm. Groan against her skin as her whimpers escalate. Suck and lick her flesh when her release spills around my fingers. *Holy Christ.*

"Jonas…" she whimpers. "I need you. Need to feel you inside me."

I crawl back up her body and kiss her as if I never will again. She moans against my tongue as her hand dips between us and wraps around my erection. I break the kiss and gasp as her hand slides up and down my length.

Shifting closer to the bedside table, I open the drawer and grab a condom. I tear open the foil, slip out the condom and roll it on. Pressing my weight back over her, I line myself up with her entrance and wait.

In this monumental moment between us, there is one thing I want to say to her. Tell her. What this means to me. What *she* means to me. How much I cherish her. How I always will. But it might be too soon for her.

I lower my lips to hers. Kiss her tenderly. Tell her with my lips and not my voice. Sweep my knuckles lightly over her cheek as I slowly rock forward and push inside her. We both gasp into the silence. Lock eyes and hold. Don't flinch as her body adjusts to my invasion.

Her nails bite my upper glutes. "Please, Jonas," she pleas.

I rock back, then forward again. Her nails dig deeper and my eyes roll back. I drop my head into the crook of her neck and find my rhythm with her. Relish in her heat and the vice-like grip her body has on mine. I kiss and nip at the base of her throat. Stroke slowly in and out. Kiss my way back up to her lips and express how much she means to me with my body.

For the first time, Autumn breaks our kiss. Gasps and whimpers as her nails rake up my back. Her body hugs me like a glove. Squeezes. And Jesus fucking Christ... I bite my lip and restrain myself as I wait for her climax to peak. She pants sweet little whimpers into my ear as it hits. Takes her over.

White-hot heat snakes around my spine and fuses in my groin as her body milks mine and I lose all sense of reality. I slam my eyes closed as stars steal my vision. Blind me and help me see clearly for the first time in my life. I clamp down on her shoulder with my teeth and release inside her. My pulse throbs behind my ears. Pounds viciously and creates white noise.

I breathe her in as she strokes her fingers up and down my spine. *I love you.* The words are on the tip of my tongue, but I bite them back. Instead, I lift my head and lock onto her gaze. Drown in her fiery cognac irises. Get drunk in them.

A cluster of loose strands lay haphazardly on her face, and I sweep them away. Kiss her slow and sweet.

"Jonas, I..." She stares up at me with unsaid words on the tip of her tongue. Words I want to tell her too.

I brush my knuckles over her cheek and press another kiss to her lips. "I know. Me too," I whisper.

And without actually saying the words, we have both just said we love each other. The actual words may not have left either of our lips, but it's there. Pumping through the atriums and ventricles of our hearts. Ebbing and flowing with each breath we take. Rooted deep in the confines of our marrow. Consuming us.

After I dispose of the condom, I crawl back into the bed, curl up behind Autumn, and swathe her in my arms. She draws lines with her fingers over my forearms before rolling over to face me. Autumn inches as close as humanly possible and hugs me tight.

"Good night, Jonas." She presses her lips to the hollow point at the base of my throat.

I kiss the crown of her head and secure my arms around her. "'Night, scarlet."

I have no clue what time it is right now. Nor do I care. Only one thing, one person, matters right now. Jonas.

His still sleeping form lays peacefully beneath me. Chest rising and falling in a slow, rhythmic pattern. Disheveled hair I itch to comb my fingers through. Long lashes brushing softly against his sun-kissed skin. A peppering of stubble that makes my mouth water and has my thighs squeezing together.

Thin rays of sunlight dance across his bare chest as I lay with my chin on my hands just over his heart. *Tha-thump. Tha-thump. Tha-thump.* Steady and sure, I study the pattern of his heartbeat and lock it in my memory. A safe place. So any time we are apart, I can rest my hand over mine and imagine his is there with me.

And then the rhythm changes. Picks up speed. Wakes up.

His breathing becomes more noticeable. Not louder, just deeper. His body stirring to life as he leaves the land of dreams.

When his arm shifts and his hand slowly trails up my spine, I hold my breath. Relish in the warmth of his skin skirting over mine. The trail of fire his touch leaves in its wake. Watch as his eyes slowly open and notice me ogling him. The way his incandescent irises swirl with love and hunger and bliss. I lose focus as a soft, radiant smile lifts the corners of his lips. The lips I want to kiss all day. Every day.

He tucks his hands under my arms and slides me up his body. Brings us face to face. And it strikes a match low in my core. Roars into a bonfire. A wildfire.

"'Morning, scarlet," he whispers against my lips. His fingertips dance up and down my spine. Create a buzz in my veins. A hum low in my belly.

I press my lips to his and kiss him as if he is my lifeblood. Breathe him in as our lips break apart. Revel in the flutter swelling in my chest. "'Morning."

He turns his head and glances at the clock on the bedside table. Just after seven. Feels I have been awake hours. "I haven't slept this late in a while."

"Did I wear you out?" I tease.

He groans and brings his lips back to mine. Slips a hand into my hair and presses the other against my lower back. Curls his fingers in my hair as the kiss morphs from whole-some to libidinous. Rolls me over and pins me to the mattress with my hands above my head as he peppers kisses down my throat, my breasts, my belly.

Freeing my hands, he nips and licks a path down to the apex of my thighs. Inhaling deeply before his tongue darts out and sweeps a line up my slit. I bow off the bed, rock my hips into him, and fist his hair.

"Fuck, I love the taste of you."

A moan bubbles in my throat and spills from my lips. With every flick of his tongue, a new flash of euphoria glows in my vision. With each pinch and roll of my nipples, white noise fizzles my hearing. Fever blazes inside me and slicks my skin. Builds. Expands. Then constricts and erupts and renders me senseless.

Slowly, the room comes back into focus.

Jonas is above me on his haunches. He rips open a condom wrapper and rolls it down his length. I lick my lips.

One day, I will taste him on my tongue. Feel his silky hardness against my lips and down my throat.

Without preamble, he lines himself up with my entrance and rocks his hips forward. I tip my head back and gasp. Solid and thick and perfect. When I open my eyes, his are locked on the line of my face. Watching me. Memorizing me.

He slips a hand under my neck and holds me in place as he pulls out to the tip and drives back forward to the hilt. The entire time, his mesmerizing gaze stays locked with mine. An inferno of heaven and earth.

Then he rocks his hips again. And again. Eyes never straying. Speaking volumes all on their own as we make love. As he places a chaste kiss here and there.

And when his lips part, when I know he is close, a new sensation floods my veins. Red and potent and fervent. It fills my vision and expands the thumping organ in my chest. Intensifies. Surmounts every doubt in my heart. I allow it to consume me and hold me captive as I bend to its will.

Then I let go. Release and give in to the glorious vibration swimming in my bloodstream. Savor the ardor dominating Jonas as his body tightens and reddens and empties inside me.

Damn, he is beautiful.

We don't move. Don't look away. Not until our pulses settle and our breathing regulates. And even then, we don't stray far from one another.

Reluctantly, we rise from the bed and dress. I slowly crack open the bedroom door and see Clementine is still curled up with Spartan. I tiptoe to the bathroom and go about my morning routine. Jonas comes in, shuts the door, and does the same. As if we have done this time and again. The way we move around each other feels natural.

When we slip out of the bathroom, Jonas kisses me on the forehead. "Any breakfast requests?"

I shake my head. "Whatever you make will be perfect."

As Jonas heads into the kitchen, I wander over to Clementine and gently wake her. Even though I would love more individual time with Jonas, I don't want to disrupt her routine too much.

Any other time in history I have woken Clementine, she was a grump. But not this morning. And I don't know if it's due to her furry bedtime companion or she slept really well. Either way, I will gladly take the change.

"Can I watch cartoons?" she asks.

"Sure, pumpkin." I flip on the television and let her choose which show she wants to watch. And once Spartan comes back in from doing his morning business outside, he hops back on the couch and watches cartoons with Clementine.

Soon, we all sit on the couch—well, everyone except Spartan—and eat French toast, scrambled eggs, sausage, and hash browns. I peek over at Jonas and sigh. This all just feels so *normal*. Right. Perfect. As if everything in my life is finally falling into place.

In place with Jonas at my side.

Once Jonas loads the last of the dishes into the dishwasher, he suggests we go outdoors and enjoy the day. Although it's mid-January, the temperature hasn't dropped too much. And I packed options and jackets for me and Clementine.

The beach in January is an odd place. Odd because there aren't thousands of bodies covering every possible grain of sand. No beach towels stretched out or umbrellas shading patrons. No permanent perfume of shea and coconut floating in the air.

In January, most walk the beach in jeans and sneakers and long sleeves. Couples huddle close to one another for warmth. People sit on collapsible chairs in the sand and listen to the small waves crash along the surf. Occasionally, you spot a snowbird in shorts and flip-flops. Some in swimwear. One or two dipping their toes in the Gulf.

I shiver at the prospect of getting in the water this time of year. Unless it's in a heated pool or hot tub.

Jonas, Clementine, and I wander hand in hand on the white sands in Sand Key Park. Every fifty feet, Clementine begs us to lift her off the ground and swing her between us. Her resounding fit of giggles each time we do has me hoping she will ask again. Because her giggles match the happiness swimming throughout my body. A happiness I haven't known until now. A happiness I want forever.

Not that I never felt happiness when it was only me and Clementine. My daughter fulfills me in a way I never knew possible. She fills gaps in my heart. Makes me smile when I have a bad day. Gives me purpose when I feel as if I have none. Keeps my feet on solid ground. Makes me see the world in a new light.

But with Jonas, happiness feels different.

Jonas blankets me in warmth. Stirs passion in my soul. Resuscitates me after years of not experiencing a connection with another person. Bonds me to him with his lips and words and skin on mine. Grounds me when life feels off kilter.

For years, I wondered why I never had the urge to date. To spend time with someone romantically. I always told myself it was because of Clementine. Because she needed me, and my attention was best spent focusing on her.

Then Jonas stepped into the picture. With his sad heart and soulful eyes, he stole my breath from the start.

I tried to fight our connection. Tried to deny anything was there. But I knew. Knew I was lying to myself to guard my heart again. Guard it from hurt and heartache and abandonment.

But Jonas will never leave my side. Never.

"Let's go to the playground before we leave," Jonas suggests.

Clementine bounces between us like a kid on a sugar high. "Yay! Jonas, will you push me on the swings?"

He looks down at her and smiles. The way he adores her has me melting into a messy puddle of emotions. "Of course, I will."

For the next twenty minutes, Clementine hauls Jonas around the playground like a rag doll. Asks him to push her on the swings. Join her on the teeter-totter. Spin her on the merry-go-round until she dizzies and can't walk straight. Go down the slide after her.

And he does it all. With a smile on his face and without an ounce of hesitation.

I sit on a bench and warm myself in the sunlight as I watch my daughter and the man I *love* play together. I listen to their banter and laughter as she tries to outrun him and he chases her. Watch her squeal in delight as he catches her, swoops her off the ground, and tickles her into a fit of giggles.

Life couldn't be any more perfect.

All too soon, we hop in the Jeep and drive toward my apartment. The closer we get to my home, the less it feels as if I belong there. Penny and I have shared an apartment since the beginning. Turned housing into a home. But for the first time in my adult life, I don't feel as if I am headed home.

Jonas is home. Wherever he is, that is my home. And after spending the night in his house—in his bed—I don't know how I will sleep any other way.

As if he hears my thoughts, he lays a hand on my thigh and glances my way for a split second. "You okay?" he whisper-asks. "You've been awfully quiet."

I nod. "Yeah. Just thinking."

"About?"

I shift in my seat so I face him more. "How much your house feels like home," I mumble. Although Clementine is happily singing to the radio in the back seat, her little ears pick up so much. I don't need her partially hearing what I say and misinterpreting it.

A smile kicks up the corners of his mouth as he lightly squeezes my thigh. "Honestly, I've been trying to drag out the day. Didn't really want to make the drive back here." He lifts his hand from my leg, and I immediately miss his warmth. But I don't go without it for long as he cups my cheek. "As much as I'd love to drag you back to my house, I don't get to make that decision. My greed isn't what's important. What does matter is what you want for you and her." He nudges his head toward the back seat. "Whatever you decide, that's what I'll go along with."

He drops his hand to mine and lifts it to his lips, kissing my knuckles. Inhaling deeply, I ponder over his words. Smile at how lucky I am to have found such a wonderful man. Revel in the notion of how patient and kind he is, and how he will wait alongside me until I decide where we go from here.

How did I get so damn lucky?

Jonas steers the Jeep into the complex and winds around to my building. As my car comes into view, my heart bottoms out. I swipe at my eyes and squint as if I am not seeing things clearly. But I am. And I think I am going to throw up.

"Why is he here?" I mumble.

twenty-six

JONAS

Autumn tenses beneath my hand as I park the Jeep.

"Why is he here?" she asks no one in particular. Her eyes shoot daggers toward her car, where a man stands in a suit and tie with a cell phone glued to his ear.

I cut the engine and glance over at her. "Autumn, who is that?" Tears well in her eyes as she shakes her head. "Are you okay?"

She shakes her head again. "No," she whispers.

Leaning across the console, I frame her face in my palms. "Talk to me. You're scaring me."

"Mama, can we get out?" Clementine asks as she unbuckles her seat belt.

"Not yet, pumpkin. In just a minute." Autumn lifts her somber eyes to my concerned ones and I hold my breath. Fear and anguish and panic mar her features. She leans closer so her lips are at my ear. "That's Clementine's birth father," she whispers so only I hear her.

I lean back and stare at her wide-eyed. "What's he doing here?" At this point, Autumn and I talk in hushed tones. The only thing I know about Clementine's father is that he abandoned Autumn before Clementine was born. And that is more than enough to tell me what kind of human he is.

She shrugs. "Haven't seen or heard from him since he left years ago." Autumn shifts her eyes toward Clementine. "She doesn't even know who he is. Not his name or what he looks like. And I'd imagine the same in reverse."

Stroking a thumb over her cheek, I try to soothe away some of the worry Autumn must be experiencing. "Well, let's grab your stuff and go into the apartment. If he wants to talk, he can do it without her present." I nudge my head toward Clementine.

Autumn nods before we both open our doors and get out of the Jeep. She helps Clementine out while I grab their bag from the back seat.

As we meet at the front of the Jeep, the man starts walking toward us. I step in front of Autumn and Clementine and act as a barrier. The sight of him makes me sick, but I swallow it down and guard the two most important people in my world.

"Help you with something?" I ask as he approaches us.

The man does his best to look around me, but I tower over him and shield Autumn and Clementine from his view. "Who the fuck are you?" he bellows. "Autumn! A word. Now."

Who the fuck am I?

Well, asshole, I am about to become your worst fucking nightmare. Especially if you continue to talk to my girls like a dick. No man—or woman—disrespects my girls. No one.

I swing my face back in his line of sight. "Hey," I thunder and wave a hand in his face. "You need to step back. Now." I return his tone with a verbal punch. "Back. Up."

When he steps back, I look over my shoulder and signal Autumn to take Clementine inside. She complies without hesitation. Once Clementine is behind closed doors, once she is out of earshot and Autumn returns to my side, I get in this piece of shit's face.

"Who the *fuck* am I?" I belt out. "None of your damn business. And neither are they. Not since you jumped ship and left them to drown. What kind of man does that? What kind of man abandons his own child? You've got a lot of nerve coming here."

"You done, pretty boy?" He cocks an eyebrow at me. "Who I am and what I did have nothing to do with you. Matter of fact, you can be on your way. Seeing as this doesn't involve you."

I throw my head back and laugh. "Everything to do with them involves me. But you wouldn't understand such a concept. So get back in your car and drive off to wherever it is you came from."

Autumn grips my bicep and stands unified beside me. She hasn't said anything since we exited the car. Honestly, I think she is too afraid to speak. I don't know much about this guy, but from his demeanor I know he is a pompous prick. And if Autumn didn't want me to speak, she would have given me a sign or stopped me when I overstepped. She hasn't done either.

We stand five feet apart, glaring at each other. His clothes may scream money, but his expression yells piece of trash. As does his lack of human decency.

He takes a step back. Then another. Sizes me up with a snarl. Shifts his gaze to Autumn and his snarl turns mocking. As if he has a secret. As if he holds the key to her future.

"Sorry we couldn't have a civil conversation, Autumn. Seems lover boy does all the talking for you now."

"Say what you came here to say, Leo. Then leave and never come back."

The sneer returns to his lips. "Just thought I'd give you a heads-up. Being the nice guy I am."

A chill snakes down my spine that has absolutely nothing to do with the winter temperatures. I glare at this pathetic excuse of a man and try to read the hidden message in his words. But he holds his cards close. Waiting for the perfect moment to throw down.

I glance down at Autumn. She tilts her head as confusion mars her brow. "Quit being cryptic. Heads-up about what?"

My eyes dart back to him as he takes another two steps back. His sneer slithers into a smile that makes me uncomfortable. Autumn clamps on to my arm tighter and sucks in a breath. Both of us waiting for the other shoe to drop.

"I'm filing for sole custody of our daughter. Clementine, right? You should be served tomorrow."

And I can't breathe.

Love Buzz

BOOK TWO

To every reader who keeps choosing my books.
You mean the world to me! I love you!

One

AUTUMN

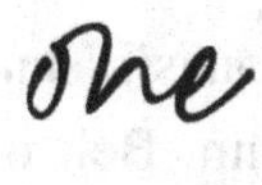

I can't breathe.

Did Leo just say what I think he said? That he has filed for custody of *my* daughter. Swear to God, I must be hearing things because Leo hasn't spent a day of his pathetic adult life near *my* daughter. Why would he suddenly want to now?

Leo waltzes toward his car, and I lose focus, gripping Jonas's arm tighter.

An evil cackle floats through the air and robs all but my hearing. His wicked laughter will no doubt haunt me for days and weeks and months to come.

All I want is to wake up from this nightmare. Because this has to be my mind playing a sick trick. An attempt to rip away the only true happiness I have in my life.

My vision focuses enough to see Leo slip into a white Mercedes sedan. He starts the car and revs the engine—which is a joke because the car isn't equipped to sound threatening. Then he rolls down the driver's side window as he rolls past us slowly. One corner of his mouth tugged up. Brow cocked. Hoity-toity sunglasses over his eyes.

"Until we see each other again." He throws a flippant wave and drives off.

For the first time in minutes, I breathe fully. But it doesn't last long. My deep, full breaths turn to short gasps. Come faster and faster. Pulse pounding so powerfully, I clutch my chest to smother the pain. Fist my shirt and tug at the cotton.

Then I lose it.

I drop my arm from Jonas's, stammer in place, then tip my face to the sky and scream. Belt out my anger and fear and frustration. I scream for all the bullshit I have dealt with since Leo up and abandoned me. Scream for all the pain and heartache I have endured. And I scream at the universe for doing this. For inflicting me with this level of misery.

What the hell did I do to deserve such duplicity?

From the moment I learned I was pregnant; I have been a good mother. A really good mother. I have given up everything for my daughter. Forfeited every part of life not revolving around her. Sacrificed everything so her life won't feel any less with only one parent. Given up on love—until Jonas.

Yet here I am, still on the receiving end of punishment. And I don't get it. Why? Why me? What past blunder has put me on the chopping block? Haven't I endured enough?

Jonas places a hand on my back—warm and comforting— and draws small circles with his thumb. My anxiety settles down a notch. Just barely. Every nerve ending sparks with unrelenting fury. And I hate it. Hate how easily Leo gets under my skin after so many years apart.

The worst of all... I have been so stuck in my head the last five minutes, I forgot Jonas stood less than a foot away. The man I care deeply for; I mentally abandoned him in a blink. If that doesn't make me a horrible girlfriend, I don't know what does.

Jonas steps closer—close enough, he is all I see—and frames my face in his palms. Brow pinching at the midline, he holds my gaze. His eyes a mix of concern and fear, strength and courage.

"Autumn, what can I do?"

The backs of my eyes sting as I slowly shake my head. "I don't know." Then the first tear spills and slips down my cheek. Jonas swipes it away. "Jonas, I don't understand why he is doing this. Why the sudden interest in her? He didn't care before. Threw us out like trash. So, why now? What triggered this?" As if the first tear granted permission for the others to fall, the floodgates open and flow uninterrupted. My body trembles crown to heel.

Jonas drops his hands to my waist and hauls me closer to him, swathing me in his strong arms. I snake my arms around his waist and cry into his shirt. He shifts one hand to the back of my head, strokes my hair, and shushes me.

"I got you. Just let it out."

We stand near his Jeep for minutes or hours. I cry gallons of tears as I bury my face in his cotton tee. My eyes puff up painfully. I fist Jonas's shirt, push off his chest, and add distance between us. Slowly, I peer up at him. His iridescent hazels hold my gaze and silently ask if I am okay.

No, I am nowhere near okay.

Honestly, I don't know if I will be for some time. But none of my feelings matter right now. Time to put my selfishness on the back burner. Again.

Inside the apartment, there is a little girl whose feelings matter more. Whose will always matter more. And I plan to do whatever it takes to protect that little girl. Protect her from a man who never cared for her or even the idea of her. Protect her heart from the pain this situation may inflict on her.

"We should check on Clementine," I say, emotionless.

Jonas nods then swipes at my cheeks. He studies me with worried eyes. "Yeah. Let's check on her."

I step up to the Jeep and check my reflection in the window. *Jesus, I look like shit.*

Taking a minute, I swipe at my cheeks to clear as much of the trailed mascara off them as I can. Then I slip my sunglasses on and smooth my hair. Not as if Clementine won't notice the difference in my appearance, but if I can make it as subtle as possible, I will. I need to.

Taking a deep breath, I square my shoulders and step back from the Jeep. Jonas wraps his arm around my waist and presses me into his side. Warmth and strength pass from his touch throughout my body. We walk to the apartment door, a couple united.

But in my head, I slowly lose my mind as I question every circumstance in my life. Including my relationship with Jonas.

For now, I shake it off. My focus needs to be on my little girl and no one else. Not myself. And not Jonas.

We walk inside the apartment and shut the door. Penny sits on the couch beside Clementine. Thankfully, Clementine is oblivious to any disturbance as she watches *The Nightmare Before Christmas* at a deafening volume. My guess is Penny turned it up after I brought her inside and she caught the ghostly expression on my face.

Bless you, my friend.

I slide my sunglasses to the top of my head and Penny's eyes widen. "You okay?" she mouths. Subtly, I shake my head and clamp my lips between my teeth to fight the tremor of my chin.

Jonas walks us over to the couch and we sit. For the first time since we strolled through the front door, Clementine peers over at us. Her sweet, innocent face nothing but smiles and love and cheer. She crawls across the small space between us and hugs me. I have no idea why—maybe she senses I need her little arms wrapped around me—but I hug her closer than ever.

When she unhooks her arms, she sits back and smiles up at me. "Mama, who was the man outside?"

In my periphery, Penny cocks her head and scoots closer to the couch edge. She picks up the television remote and turns the volume down. I peek over at her and give a subdued smile.

Inhaling deeply, I prepare for the grocery list of questions Clementine will have after I answer. "No one important, pumpkin. Just someone I knew a long time ago."

Ever the intuitive, Clementine gauges my expression. Studies my face longer than typical. But by some divine miracle, she appears pleased with my response. "Oh, okay. A friend?"

It takes every rational atom inside me to not rebut her terminology. But I remain tight-lipped. "Pumpkin, will you stay here and watch your movie? I need to talk with Jonas and Aunt Penny alone for a minute."

Clementine smiles up at me and nods. I swallow the emotion slowly building in my mouth. Bite back the tears that threaten to fall. And force it all past the boulder in my throat.

"Yeah. Can I turn it back up?"

I love how her sole concern lies in the volume of her movie. That her little seven-year-old mind knows no other worries. "Sure, pumpkin." I hand her the remote. "Stay here. We'll be back out soon."

Glancing at Penny, I tip my head toward the kitchen. The apartment isn't necessarily closed off in the main living spaces, but at least a partial wall blocks the conversation we need to have. Penny, Jonas, and I rise from the couch and head to the kitchen. In the small space, I drag us as far from Clementine's eyes and ears as possible.

"What is going on?" Penny whisper-shouts.

"Leo was by my car when we pulled up." I tuck my lips between my teeth and blink back the tears threatening to make an appearance.

Now is not the time to break down, Autumn.

"What the hell did he want?" Not too often will anyone ever meet a pissed-off Penny. But when she hits that point, people instantly know. Being on Penny's bad side isn't pretty. Not pretty at all.

I tip my head back and stare at the ceiling. For the umpteenth time since I spotted Leo outside, I fight the anger and frustration and fear boiling in my veins.

Hold it together, Autumn. Crying and screaming right now will not help anything. Just say what needs to be said.

Lowering my chin, I level my gaze with hers. "Said he's filing for custody of Clementine. I will be served tomorrow."

Penny slaps a hand over her mouth and slowly shakes her head as her eyes widen. After she marinates on the outlandish news, she opens her mouth. For a moment, she doesn't say anything. She snaps her jaw shut, then opens it again. "This makes no fucking sense. After all this time. After walking away without worry. So, why now?"

"Question of the day." I laugh without humor.

Beside me, Jonas remains silent with his arm around my waist. No doubt he is as baffled with what happens next as I am. His thumb draws lazy circles on my hip, his gentle reminder so I know he is here for whatever I need. That he supports my decision, whatever it may be. That he will be a leaning pillar of strength through this rocky time.

And I love how much he cares. Love how he will do anything for me, even after such a short time together. His level of love speaks volumes and resonates deep in my bones.

Penny continues to shake her head while tapping a finger over her lips. "Why?" she mumbles. The question not directed at anyone or meant to be answered. Just pure curiosity.

The three of us stand in the kitchen, staring at each other and nothing. My mind wanders as I search for some hidden reason or an obvious resolution. And honestly, I have no idea where to begin.

If Leo is filing a lawsuit through the court system, should I obtain legal counsel? Is an attorney my first step in handling this? Not as if I have friends or family who have been through this. Will I be able to afford an attorney? Especially on such short notice. How much does it cost to hire one? Will Leo drag out the matter and slowly drain my savings?

Panic hits my bloodstream anew and a tremor vibrates my body. Not enough for Penny to notice, but Jonas does. His hold on me is stronger as he leans in and kisses my temple.

Why the hell is Leo suddenly so interested in Clementine? After jumping ship close to eight years ago, telling me he had no idea how to be a father—nor did he want to be—why is he so eager to fill the role now? And how does he know where we live? What I named her?

Something had to have provoked his interest. It's the only logical explanation. But what the hell changed?

Then the answer hits me like a wall of summer humidity. Steals my breath and robs my heart. Jonas. Jonas is the only difference in my life after all these years.

What if Leo has secretly kept tabs on me over the years—kept tabs on Clementine—and recently learned Jonas and I started dating? Although he has no desire to be with me or be a father, is this his way of saying, *I don't want them, but no one else can have them either*?

My stomach balls into a knot and twists my gut.

If this holds true… one—this is fucking bullshit. And two—in order to not lose my daughter, I need to do something harsh. Something I may regret for the rest of my life. Something that has me queasy and on the verge of vomiting.

I need to distance myself and Clementine from Jonas. If my being with Jonas prompted this whole debacle, I need to back off. At least until I consult with an attorney and everything clears up.

Bile rises and burns my throat as I pinch my eyes closed. Jesus, I am going to be sick.

As if Jonas senses my dismay, he squeezes my hip and I open my eyes. I peek up at him and every molecule of love I hold for him slumps with sadness and heartache.

I don't want to do this. Can't do this. But what other choice do I have? Leo has dumped my worst nightmare in my lap and I see no other way out of it. Not yet, anyway.

"How am I supposed to handle this?" I whisper more to myself than to Jonas or Penny.

Jonas takes both my hands in his and lifts them to his chest. Beneath my palms, his heart thumps the rhythm I recently memorized. A rhythm I tucked away for safekeeping. And now it seems as if I will be unlocking that vault sooner than expected to play the recorded rhythm.

Because I am about to change everything. I am about to break both of us.

I stare at Jonas's chest as my fingers gently rumple his

shirt. He places a finger under my chin and tips it up until our eyes meet. Golden to hazel. In his eyes, I see promise and hope and love. The knife twists harder beneath my diaphragm at seeing his unconditional support.

I will miss him. So goddamn much. Every second and minute and hour. Every day and week and month. I mentally clench my fists and pinch my eyes.

"We will get through this together. Okay?" Voice soft and tender and barely audible. It shreds my heart further. "No matter what happens, as long as we have each other, we will survive this."

The backs of my eyes sting, but I don't dare let the tears break free. Tears may be what gives me away. And me putting distance between us won't happen if he picks up on my plan.

For now, I keep this tidbit to myself. I trudge forward and let him believe everything will be okay with us. I pray, in the end, it will be better than okay. So, I nod and force past the pain piercing my heart.

Regardless of my feelings, I must remain strong. Not just to get through whatever bullshit Leo is about to deliver, but also to protect my daughter. Above any person, Clementine matters most. And since the moment I learned I would be a mother, I swore to do whatever it takes to keep her safe and feeling loved.

Even if that means losing the only other person I have ever loved. Even if that means losing Jonas.

JONAS

The alarm clock wails on my bedside table and, for a moment, I ignore it. Ignore the blaring tone as it changes every ten seconds and becomes more frantic. When Spartan nudges my ribs, I roll my eyes and slap a hand in the general direction of the clock. After a few blind slaps, silence consumes the room again.

Silence and darkness.

After leaving Autumn's apartment last night, I couldn't shake the sudden pain in my chest. This sinking, drowning, I-can't-pull-in-enough-oxygen sensation. No matter how much I assured Autumn I'd be at her side, that we would get through this, a nagging pinch lingered beneath my sternum.

All night, I laid in bed and stared at the ceiling. Studied the minor imperfections in the plaster. On occasion, I drifted off. Only to be woken fifteen, twenty, thirty minutes later.

The pang beneath my ribs didn't exist solely from Clementine's father making an appearance—although he royally pissed me off. The stab persisted because something was off with Autumn. With us.

When Autumn, Penny, and I went to the kitchen to talk, I

felt the rift start. Our relationship may still be young, we may not know much about each other, but I have never been more hyperaware of anyone. Not even Cora. And seconds after we stepped into the kitchen, something in Autumn changed.

Can't pinpoint exactly what, but the ground shifted beneath us. The tectonic plates holding our hearts started slowly drifting apart. And the crack between us swallows me whole.

The snooze alert booms off the walls and I slap the clock again. As exhausted as I am, sleep evades me. No matter how many times I close my eyes, my mind refuses to shut down and let me sleep. But the energy to leave the bed won't come either.

Spartan noses my elbow and groans. "I'm getting up. Just give me a minute."

I roll over to turn off the clock, inhale Autumn's scent on the other pillowcase, and close my eyes. Fisting the pillow to my nose, I drag in the smell of her. Allow it to lessen the sharp sting between my lungs, if only for a minute.

When I drop the pillow and sit up, the pain throbs anew. This is going to be a long fucking day. I feel it in my bones.

Out of bed, I go about my typical morning routine. Taking Spartan for a walk—thank god he knows our route because I am mentally dead on my feet. Shower faster than usual. Dress for work robotically. As I take out items to make breakfast, I spot Clementine's juice in the fridge.

The knot in my stomach twists tighter. Has me nauseous. I cook half my normal breakfast and barely eat any of it. Before leaving the house, I brew a pot of coffee and fill my work thermos to the brim.

Today is going to snail by.

With Spartan secure in his crate, I turn on the radio for

him and head out. I opt to ride the bike today and, since it is still pretty early, drive aimlessly for almost an hour.

The cold air stings my skin as I ride around the city. I welcome the frigid burn. The bite of cold air better than the uncertainty clouding my every thought.

I drive aimlessly. Focus on the road. The vibration of the engine between my legs. The heat from the pipes near my calves. When I need to change gears and steer the bike, I focus on what I can control.

After an hour of aimless riding, I park behind the shop and amble into the office. Dad sits behind his desk, his stack of invoices thin as he peeks up when I enter.

I don't miss how he checks the clock above the door. How he scans my face after noticing I am only thirty minutes early rather than my typical hour-plus early. And I definitely don't miss the brief droop at the corners of his eyes and lowered edges of his lips when he scans my face and notes my sullen demeanor.

I never need to tell Dad something is wrong. He just knows. Until Autumn and I got close, I thought no one would be able to read me better than Dad. His parental superpower is sensing when his children aren't one hundred percent.

And right now, he more than senses something is off.

Giving a wave, I hold up the thermos. "'Morning. Coffee?"

He tilts his head slightly and gauges my stilted greeting. But he doesn't mention it. Doesn't shine a light on it and probe for further explanation.

"Please. Thanks, son."

I nod then turn my back to him, grabbing mugs, creamer, and sugar before parking it all on the desk. Filling the mugs with coffee from my thermos, I hand him his mug without meeting his eyes. Once he adds cream and sugar, I follow suit. It all feels routine… and robotic.

The slowest first ten minutes of my workday tick by. We drink our coffee in silence as Dad wraps up the last of his paperwork and I stare at a framed picture Mom suggested we add to the office. A mountainous landscape at sunset. *"You need more than bare walls and automotive posters in this place."* At least I have something to lose focus on while I sit here. A place to mentally get lost in.

"Want to talk about it?" Dad prompts after he stacks the day's invoices in a wire basket.

Dropping my gaze from the picture, I face him and shake my head. "Not yet."

Dad nods as his chair legs scrape the tile and he stands. Starting for the door, he pauses beside me and lays a hand on my shoulder. "Whenever you're ready, I'm here." Before I respond, he pats my shoulder, strolls out the door and into the garage.

I finish my coffee, wash the mug, and set it in the rack. Grabbing a fresh pair of coveralls, I slip them over my clothes, pick up the thermos, then mosey out to the garage. I survey the roster and see the majority of the schedule is full. A busy day is good. A busy day is exactly the distraction I need.

Three oil changes and a full set of new tires later, I would swear it should be closing time. No such luck. Still another thirty minutes until lunch. Then the back half of the day.

Dad has not so nonchalantly checked on me five times. At minimum. I understand his concern, but his constant over-shadowing doesn't make matters better. If anything, it constantly reminds me why my mood is sour.

After I replace a starter, Dad orders me to take lunch. My stomach growls for me to feed it, but my head shoots down the idea. Instead, I lie on the couch in the office and close my eyes. Although I won't sleep, my exhausted body will rejoice at being horizontal.

I jolt awake when Dad nudges my shoulder. "Jonas, you should wake up."

Rubbing my palms over my eyes, I stare up at him. "How long have I been in here?"

Dad glances at the clock on the wall. "Little more than an hour."

Shit. I may have needed sleep, but now I will be the chump not returning on time. The one screwing up everyone else's lunch break. The day just keeps getting better.

"Sorry. Be out in a minute." I drop my feet to the floor and sit up, propping my elbows on my knees as I further rub the sleep from my eyes.

"Take your time, son. Garage has been slow since you been in here. I sent one of the other guys to lunch shortly after you."

I nod. "Thanks, Dad."

Without another word, Dad pats my shoulder then exits the office. Once the door clicks shut, I drop my head in my hands and groan.

Why is it when life is going great, time whizzes by? But when life isn't all it's cracked up to be, time barely ticks. And to reaffirm the statement, I glance up at the clock and see I still have another four hours left to work.

Fuck.

I comb my fingers through my hair, tugging at the ends. "Just get off your ass and get the day over with." Besides, I still have dinner to look forward to. Dinner with my girls. Just the idea of dinner, of seeing Autumn and Clementine, perks me up.

Rising from the couch, I grab a cold bottle of water from the fridge and guzzle half of it before I head back to the garage. I will make the rest of the day better. Even if I have to fake it.

Dad and I roll down the bay doors and I sigh. The entire day crept by, but thank fuck all is said and done now. Dad checked on me just as much after lunch as he did before. And as we lock up the shop and head to our vehicles, he surprises me with a hug. Not just any hug, but one of his *I'm always here for you, son* hugs.

"Drive safe, son. See you in the morning."

"You, too. Thanks, Dad."

Dad hops in his truck, cranks the engine, and waves to me as he drives off. Once out of sight, I straddle the bike and pull my phone from my back pocket. As with the last hundred times I have checked my phone today, there are zero notifications. At least none I want to see. Which doesn't help the pang since leaving Autumn's apartment last night.

Inhaling deeply, I open our text history and type out a quick message.

> Hey, scarlet. Still coming over for dinner?

I hold my breath as I stare, stare, stare at the screen. Silently willing Autumn to read my message and respond.

The screen dims and I tap the glass to wake it. Twenty painstaking heartbeats later, the little gray bubble pops up and those three magical dots dance inside it. Finally, I exhale.

Too soon.

Not tonight. Got served today and I just
want alone time with Clementine.

Her rejection hurts, but I understand the reason behind it.

Want to talk about it?

Not tonight. Please. But soon.

God, I wish we were face to face. I desperately want to wrap her hand with mine. Want to comfort her and take away the heartache she must be suffering with all this. But I won't thrust myself in her face. Won't annoy her with my anguish. She has enough on her own plate; I shouldn't add to the list of things to worry about.

Sure. Talk to you later.

Later.

Can't imagine what Autumn must be feeling right now, but God how I want to hold her. Tuck her snug in my arms and reassure her everything will be fine. That it will all work out, in her favor. It has to. After everything she has endured as a single parent, how can this not end favorably for her?

I tuck my phone away, start the bike, and drive home. Mindlessly, I weave through the evening traffic. See other drivers on the road, but pay them no attention. The trip is a blur of early sunset colors and bright red and white lights.

The second I set foot in the house, Spartan barks incessantly and bounces around as per usual. Once out of his crate, I open the back door and let him roam the yard while I kick off my boots and grab a beer.

The entire day—and now the evening—feels forced. Mechanical. Lifeless.

I feed Spartan dinner and polish off beer number one. Every few seconds, Spartan stops eating to peer over at the door. His heart hopeful a specific small human will walk through the door and shower him with hugs and conversation.

"Not tonight, bud." I rough his fur up as I grab the throw blanket from the couch.

Spartan finishes eating in record time. I snag a fresh beer from the fridge and walk out the back door with him hot on my heels. He bolts past me and scavenges the yard for who knows what.

While he forages for lizards that aren't there, I grab the lighter from the cabinet beneath the fire bowl, crank the gas, and ignite the rocks. Kicking back on the lounger, I sip beer number two and stare up at the black sky.

Tonight, the sky is absent of bright, twinkling lights. No stars to guide me. To lead me in the right direction. To guide me down this new path.

It is just me in the darkness with only man-made fire to light my way. The irony isn't lost on me.

Maybe I should have called Autumn rather than texted her. At least I would have heard her voice. Gotten an idea where her head is after being served. After she read the painful lines on the scariest document. I may be reading the whole situation too deeply, but even her texts felt *off*. Clipped. Glum. Harsh.

God, I just want her in my arms. To be by her side and help make this all vanish. Figure out a way to fix this for her. Make it so she never worries about someone trying to take away the most important person in her world.

Long after I empty my beer, Spartan nudges my elbow.

His way of telling me he is bored and wants to go inside. I sit up from the lounger and extinguish the fire. "C'mon, bud. Let's go."

Woof, woof, woof.

Although the muscles in my face have refused to let me smile all day, this dog brings one out of me anyway. Never have I met or owned a dog like Spartan. Wild and crazy and my main man. Perfect.

And with the uncertainty revolving around Autumn, I am grateful to have Spartan to cuddle me when home. To keep me company and drive me up the wall on occasion.

I toss the brown bottle in the recycling bin then heat up a small portion of leftovers. I eat to satisfy my stomach—seeing as I have eaten next to nothing—and not my taste buds. After I clean my plate, I turn off all the lights and go to my room.

I tug my shirt over my head and toss it in the hamper. Then my socks and jeans. Spartan hops on the bed and settles where he normally sleeps when it is just us.

Statically pulling back the comforter and sheet, I slip under the covers. But as soon as I bring them to my chest, a waft of Autumn's scent hits my nose and takes residence. Her cherry vanilla perfume floats up my nose and drowns me.

And all I do is drag the bedding closer to me. Close my eyes and inhale deeper. Picture her in the bed next to me— hair loose and framing her face as she leans in to kiss me. The warmth of her skin as it melds with mine. Her soft lips as they brush mine and take me prisoner.

I groan into the darkness as the throb in my chest expands and I fist the bedding. No matter what it takes, I will make this better. Because, *fuck*, there is no way I can live without her.

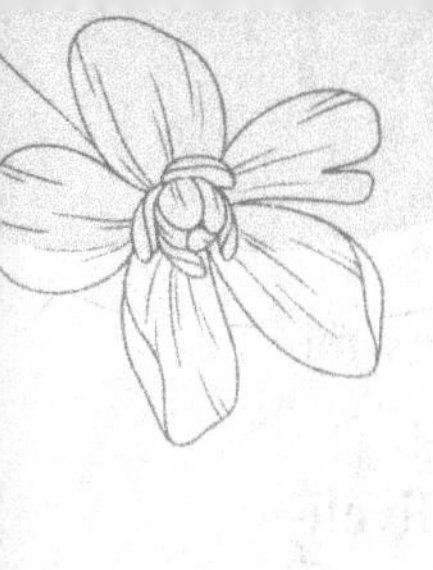

three

AUTUMN

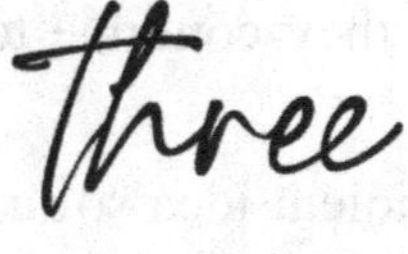

How does four days feel like a lifetime?

The whirlwind makes me dizzy. Sick to my stomach. The earth never felt this lopsided. This uneven and unpredictable. My life flipped upside down Sunday and I no longer know which way is up.

The day started out perfect. Full of warmth and love and everything I have missed out on as a woman. Waking up with Jonas beneath me in bed was nothing short of bliss. *God, I miss him*. Miss his heat and heart and whispered affection. His arms wrapped around my waist. We spent the day together like a normal couple. We enjoyed life. Simply being near each other—breathing the same air, sharing blissful smiles, and walking hand in hand.

Every facet of our weekend was sublime.

Then our bliss was stolen. Our bubble popped. Yanked out from beneath our feet and knocking us on our asses.

Leo. Fucking *Leo*.

Never have I been a violent person. Never have I sunk so low as to intentionally hurt someone. Physically, mentally, or emotionally. It isn't in my makeup. Inflicting hate makes me nauseous.

But since *Leo* waltzed back in and threatened my livelihood, threatened my sanity, I have conjured up countless ways to make him disappear from the world. Allowed my mind to adventure into some dark places.

None of the horrible ideas will come to fruition, nor will I speak them aloud, but they continue to pop up like an uninvited guest.

The funniest, nonviolent idea so far... tattooing "commitment issues" on his forehead. Or better yet, instead of his forehead, the best place is just above his dick. So every woman sees it when he strips bare. So every woman questions why. Questions him. No doubt Rex and Reznor would be up for the challenge.

Beside me, Clementine stirs and slowly wakes. And I envy this little girl right now. How she remains oblivious to what's happening with her sperm donor and the obstacle he threw our way. How she continues each day with a smile on her face and love in her heart.

And as long as there is breath in my lungs, I will keep her in oblivion. Keep her safe—physically, mentally, emotionally—from whatever tricks Leo has up his sleeve.

No matter what stresses life hands us, it should be me who loses sleep and worries about the outcome. In time, I will need to share everything with her—who her birth father is and what he is trying to do. But the time hasn't arrived. Not yet. And I plan to keep her life normal and full of the routine she knows.

Her eyes flutter open and peer up at me. "'Morning, Mama."

I love her sleepy voice. Sweet and raspy and innocent. Not a care in the world. A perfect mix of angel and groggy.

"'Morning, pumpkin. Did you sleep good?"

She nods, slow and steady. Then she stretches out her tiny hand and paints small semicircles beneath my eyes with her fingertip. Her lips turn down at the corners and sadness shadows her eyes.

"Mama, why do you look so tired?" My sweet, sweet girl.

Generally, Clementine is happy-go-lucky. Smiles and laughs and goofs off. But she has the biggest, empathetic heart. She may not understand the trials and tribulations adults deal with, but she senses when something is amiss.

"Just didn't sleep well." I bop her nose with my finger. "Nothing you need to worry about, though."

"Okay, Mama." A soft smile plumps her cheeks. "When will we see Sparty again?"

Over the last few days, I have dreaded the moment Clementine would ask about Jonas or Spartan. One of the reasons I didn't want her getting attached. Because if shit hit the fan—which it did, just not the shit I expected—she wouldn't understand why we didn't see each other anymore.

For now, as painful as it is, I just need things between me and Jonas to slow down. Dramatically. As in, press pause. For now, I need to spend all my time with Clementine. Because the possibility of Leo taking her from me seems inevitable.

Not that I will go down without a fight.

"Soon, pumpkin." And I hate how easily I make the promise to her. Hate how I don't know if I can fulfill said promise. "I have to take care of some special Mama-only tasks first. Okay?"

I love and hate how her little golden eyes narrow as she tries to read my mind. To find falsehoods in my words. I pray she doesn't. "Okay. But I really miss Sparty."

"Me too, pumpkin." I bite the inside of my cheek and

smile halfheartedly. "Now, though, it's time to get up and get ready for school."

And just like that, conversation over.

Clementine and I go about our morning routine of dressing and styling and eating breakfast. Thankfully, she doesn't mention Spartan again. Before long, we hop in the car and drive toward her school. She bops and sings to the music and I savor every moment from the corner of my eye. Her dark hair in a ponytail with a bandana tied around the elastic. The snug black long-sleeve top with cherry print, loose jeans, and saddle shoes. My sweet girl.

I will not lose her. I refuse to lose her.

After I drop Clementine off and watch her enter the school, I drive to the appointment I have dreaded all week. An appointment with a family law attorney.

After being served Monday morning, I read through the not-so-thin packet of paperwork. Overwhelmed doesn't remotely cover the whirlwind spinning in my head. I am no idiot, but legal jargon is not a language I speak. It was easy enough to decipher Leo requested sole custody of Clementine. The rest of the documentation was jibber-jabber.

Parking in the lot, I stare up at the building and read the large placard on the wall. *Theresa Chang, Esq. Family Law Attorney serving the community for over 20 years.*

Twenty-plus years has to count for something, right? No one flourishes and stays in business if they have no idea what they are doing. God, I hope so.

I double-check I have the folder of documents tucked in my purse, take a deep breath, then exit the car.

After setting an appointment over the phone, the receptionist gave me a rundown of what today's appointment would entail and what I needed to bring. My sole wish is this attorney will be the one to represent me. Time and money are tight. Bad enough I have to shell out thousands of dollars to deal with Leo in the first place. I don't need to waste any of the limited time I have.

The building is a subtle gray with large white pillars along the front, giving an outward appearance of a small courthouse. Two large oak trees shade majority of the building while ferns surround the trunks. An array of colorful flowers planted in large terra-cotta pots sit near the entrance and give an inviting vibe to an otherwise daunting structure. For a law office, it holds enough charm to appear less unnerving.

I fist the strap of my purse tight, take a deep breath, and stroll toward the entrance as I mumble self-assurances to settle my nerves.

Two feet from the door, I freeze and stare at the handle as if the metal will scald my skin. A delusion that holds no truth, but since Sunday evening, most of my thoughts have been a mishmash of chaos. How could they not be? Anyone in my shoes would freak out. Scream and tug at their hair. Ask why this was happening. Hell, plenty of people would behave much worse. Turn physically violent.

But I rein it in. I have to. For Clementine.

I clench my palms then release the tension and stretch my fingers straight again. You got this. No one will take Clementine from you. No one. Just breathe.

For days, this has been my mantra. What has kept me moving forward every time I want to crawl in a hole and wither. Fingers crossed this attorney will give me good news. I *need* good news.

Reaching out, I clasp the handle and open the door. *See, Autumn. Nothing to fear.* I step inside and meet the gaze of a young man behind the reception desk. His short blond curls bouncy. Periwinkle button-up undone at the collar. Bright smile on his face as he sits taller and faces me.

"Good morning. How may I help you?"

I step up to the counter. "Good morning. I have an appointment with Ms. Chang. Autumn Rooker."

He reads the computer screen and clicks the mouse a few times. He nods then faces me again. "Yes, Ms. Rooker. If you'll have a seat, Ms. Chang will be with you in a moment. Feel free to grab some water, coffee, or tea."

I thank him and amble over to the waiting area, taking a seat and foregoing the drink. Last thing I need is to fill my bladder then excuse myself in the middle of my appointment. Not only would I embarrass myself, I would probably pay for it—literally—since most attorneys are paid via time put into the case. Every minute counts. Every minute costs.

I weed through a handful of junk emails on my phone before I hear my name called. "Ms. Rooker?"

I lock my phone and shove it in my purse, then look up to meet a petite Asian woman. Her long black strands up off her neck and swirled into a prestigious bun just above the base of her skull. Although she appears of similar height, she stands taller. Fearless. Formidable. Her black pantsuit with an ivory silk top screams *powerful woman* and immediately boosts my confidence. She extends her hand.

"Theresa Chang. Thank you for waiting."

I shake her hand and rise from my seat. "Autumn Rooker. Thank you for seeing me on such short notice."

She guides us down a short hall and steers us into a conference room. At the opposite end of the room, a floor-to-ceiling window illuminates the room. Outside the window, plush green shrubs and colorful flowers add to the view. A hint of shade from one of the oak trees balances the bright morning sunlight. A large, refurbished oak table with a small potted plant in the middle occupies the heart of the conference room. The ivory walls decorated with framed art that has nothing to do with law and everything to do with family. A watercolor of a woman at the park pushing a child on the swings. A photograph of two men side by side, each of them holding a baby. Hand-drawn crayon pictures of stick figure families. And so much more.

My eyes blur. Pulse turns wobbly. Breath comes in jagged bursts.

I chose the right woman for the job.

"Have a seat Ms. Rooker and we'll get started."

Over the next hour, Ms. Chang—who insists I call her Theresa—reviews the documents I received. She asks several questions regarding me, Clementine, and Leo. After our thorough discussion, she addresses the financial end of things—which is hefty, but not as bad as I originally expected. All in all, the appointment wraps up with me less stressed and a strong woman standing at my side. A woman who has every confidence we will walk away from this better than before it began.

After I pay the retainer fee and sign documents to allow Theresa to start the proceedings, I walk out the door and unlock Betsy. I start the car and crank up the heat while I gather myself. For the first time since Sunday with Jonas, I smile. Not one worthy of awards, but a smile nonetheless.

Dealing with this lawsuit won't be easy. Fortunately, I found a woman who will fight to the bitter end beside me. Her confidence the exact boost I needed. And now, it's time to share the good news.

I dig through my purse until I locate my phone. Without

giving any thought, I open the text history between me and Jonas and type out a message.

> Spoke with an attorney. She is optimistic I won't run into trouble.

I hit send, tuck my lips between my teeth and stare at the screen, impatiently waiting for Jonas to respond. Glancing at the time, I remind myself he is at work and might not be able to answer. But as the thought crosses my mind, the indicator bubble pops up.

> Glad to hear. How are you?

He doesn't seem upset. Thank god. I have put him through the wringer since this started. And I worried my putting distance between us would upset him. Without a doubt, I'm sure he misses me as much as I miss him.

> Better now, but still a little frazzled. I miss you.

> Miss you too, scarlet.

As soon as the term of endearment flashes on the screen, I audibly exhale. With everything going on, I have been so laser focused on how to handle things with Leo. Meanwhile, I dropped all interaction with Jonas. Granted, I did it because I thought it was the appropriate thing to do. But Theresa told me to live life as we have been. Knowing Jonas still holds me close to his heart is a major relief.

> Can we have dinner tomorrow?

Definitely. Mine or yours?

Your house. Clementine misses Spartan.
And you.

See you tomorrow, scarlet.

Four days have passed since I last saw Jonas. Four very long, painstaking days. I miss him on an unhealthy level. A therapist would undoubtedly tell me this. Doesn't matter, though. Can't tell your heart what to feel. It also isn't wise to deny your heart what it wants. Even if what your heart desires may hinder your future.

Theresa told me to live life how I had been. And I want to. More than anything.

But something niggles at my subconscious. Tells me Leo will use my life and how I spend my time as a weapon. Hold it over my head and taunt me.

Sure, several factors of my relationship and history with Clementine weigh in my favor, but Leo—and his family— have money. More money than fathomable. If Leo wants something bad enough, he will have no issue paying the "right" person to get the job done.

I toss my phone back in my purse, grip the steering wheel, and take a deep breath. I stare at the jagged bark on the old oak tree and lose focus. Taking this fraction of time for myself, I let my thoughts roam free.

How do I live life normally? Is there a way to blend how life was before I dated Jonas with us being together? A middle ground.

The last thing I want is to alienate Jonas—and Spartan— from my and Clementine's life. In such a short period, they mean so much to us both. But I also don't want to become complacent. Don't want to rely on the assurances of my attorney—not that she isn't brilliant, but I haven't seen her in action yet—especially when the livelihood and well-being of my daughter is on the line.

Middle ground. At least for now.

Somewhere in the middle is better than nowhere at all. Right?

four

JONAS

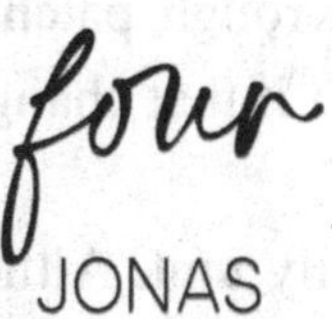

For the first time all week, the workday doesn't feel forty hours long.

I cash out the final customer of the day, walk them out, and give my practiced business goodbye. Once they drive off, I lock the office door and join Dad in the garage as we close everything up for the night. Currently, we stow one vehicle as we work on extensive repairs, but most of our recent clients have been easy same-day jobs.

As I stash the last of the tools in bay one, Dad coughs to get my attention.

After Monday, I have kept to myself most of the week. Conversations with me have been nonexistent. I arrive at work, spend fifteen or so minutes in the office, work until lunch, sleep on the couch at lunch, then work until the garage closes. I mind my own business and only speak when absolutely necessary. Today may have been the only exception. I probably spoke a few more sentences. And I blame it all on the fact I will see Autumn and Clementine soon.

I glance over my shoulder at Dad but don't say anything.

His cough was intended to get my attention. Attention does not equal spoken words.

"How're you holding up?"

I shrug. "Been a rough week. Haven't seen my girls since Sunday night. But they're coming over for dinner tonight, so…" I trail off and finish my task.

Unexpectedly, Dad sidles up to me and hugs my side. "Sorry you're having a rough patch. And I know you don't want to talk about it. But if that changes, you know we're here for you."

The Thompson family unit. Although all adults, we are a tight-knit bunch. We stand by each other no matter what. Mom and Dad instilled that in us. Even at their most annoying stages, Jasmine and Jillian have always been there when I needed them. Have given me the female perspective I some-times require. And vice versa.

"Yeah, Dad. When Autumn is comfortable with me shar-ing, I'll explain."

Dad gives me another hug, this one front facing and more constricting than an anaconda. And I let him squeeze the air from my lungs as I revel in the love he passes on. And for a brief moment, I close my eyes and embrace him with equal fervor. Then he pats me on the back and releases me.

"Just keep reminding yourself everything will work out in the end. All you need to do is be there for her, however possi-ble. Now get out of here and go home. I hear you have a date with two special ladies."

A small smile curves up one corner of my mouth. "Thanks, Dad. Tell Mom I say hello. Have a good weekend."

"Will do. You too."

After I strip out of the coveralls, I throw on my jacket, zip it up, and hop on the bike. Helmet on, I spark the engine to life and drive home. The road mild with traffic as the wind whips the exposed skin between my helmet and collar. I don't move to raise my collar and shield my neck. Instead, I let the bite remind me I am alive. Not only alive, but that I also get to see my girls tonight.

My girls.

Fuck, I have missed the hell out of them. Autumn's cognac eyes and natural radiance. Clementine's boisterous tendencies and sweet laughter. The way Autumn holds me close and breathes me in as if she never will again. How Clementine has full-blown conversations with Spartan as if they speak the same language.

Saying I miss them doesn't seem sufficient enough. More like an afterthought or brush-off. No, being apart from them has me missing a piece of myself. A huge piece. An absence. And I will do whatever it takes to have them back. To make us whole.

I park the bike in the garage, set my helmet on a shelf near the door leading into the house, then head inside. Spartan immediately loses his shit the moment I set foot in the house. But this is typical, even if I leave for fifteen minutes. Spazz is his middle name.

"Chill out, I'm coming." I shut off the radio and open the door on his crate. He flies out as if a wasp stung him in the hindquarters. "Wears the fire at, little man. Come on." I point to the door that leads to the backyard. "Let's go outside a minute. Then Dad needs to get to work."

Spartan bolts outside the second I open the door. He locates the perfect blade of grass, lifts his leg, and does his business. Typically, he runs off after, but tonight he dashes back into the house. Like he knows his new best friend is coming over and he needs to prepare himself.

Me too, buddy. Me too.

Back in the house, Spartan goes to the couch and grooms himself. Suppose licking his coat clean is his form of preparation. Whatever. If it keeps him out of my hair while I make dinner, I won't complain.

I get to work on dinner. Tonight's meal will be easier than usual, so I get more time with Autumn. From the freezer, I grab a bag of waffle fries. Then grab the turkey burger patties I set in the fridge to thaw. After setting the temperatures on the oven and stove, I toss the fries on a baking sheet and take the burgers out of the package.

Once both start cooking, I grab the pretzel buns and burger toppings. I slice up tomato, onion, and pickle, then tear up a few leaves of lettuce.

Just as I close the oven door after stirring the fries, Spartan barks like a banshee. *They are here.* I turn down the burner and head to the door. The second I open it, Spartan shoves past me, practically knocking me on my ass, and runs for Clementine.

"Sparty!" Clementine hugs his neck while Spartan licks her like a fiend.

"Let's go inside, pumpkin."

"Sparty, come on. You heard Mama, let's go inside." And just like that, Spartan runs into the house with Clementine on his haunches.

I open the door farther and let Autumn pass. She looks like my girl but exhausted as hell. Maybe more drained than me. The dark half-moons under her eyes appear tattooed like permanent makeup. Her cognac irises more transparent than usual; as if the fire in them almost burned out. And her frame seems thinner, cheeks more hollow, lips less pouty.

Seeing Autumn like this wrecks me. Tears me limb from

limb. Going forward, I don't care what the hell is happening, we won't spend this much time apart. Not when it slowly crushes us all.

I shut the door and turn to face Autumn. Before either of us says a word, Autumn steps into me and wraps her arms around my waist. Without hesitation, I snake one arm around her center while the other presses her close to my heart. Resting my cheek on her hair, I inhale deeply and bask in her perfume. One that has slowly faded from my sheets. One that reminded me she was here not so long ago. Time ticks on as we stand unmoving near the door. We shift to inch closer together but don't move otherwise.

Too soon, I lift my cheek from her hair and inch back slightly. Autumn peeks up, her lips a breath away from mine, and I see a hint of the fire returning to her intoxicating irises.

"Hey," I whisper, gaze locked on hers.

"Hi," she whispers back. "Missed you."

"Missed you more."

A small half smile perks up the corner of her mouth before she pushes up on her toes and presses her lips to mine. Warm and soft. Exactly as I remember.

Autumn kisses me sweetly as she curls her fingers in the cotton of my shirt. I frame her face and trace my tongue across the seam of her lips. As if we kissed thousands of times, Autumn opens up for me and tangles her tongue with mine. The kiss is slow and meticulous while we taste each other for the first time in far too long.

Far sooner than preferable, I break the kiss. Autumn slowly opens her eyes and stares up at me with hunger for something other than food. As much as I want to gift her that, now is not the time.

"Come on." I take her hand and start toward the kitchen. "Help me finish dinner."

I flip the burgers one last time and add cheese to each. Autumn gets plates from the cabinet and starts assembling toppings and condiments for everyone. Once the fries come out, we add the patties and fries to the plates and sit down to eat. Spartan whines as I go to sit, reminding me he needs his dinner too.

Over dinner, Clementine shares all the school stories I missed throughout the week. She tells me about one boy who always picks on her—says her clothes are weird or she doesn't have normal hair. I softly chuckle and tell her that is what boys do when they secretly like girls. The face she makes—as if a foul smell sits under her nose—is the cutest thing ever. Oh, how I missed my girls.

Once we finish eating, I set the plates in the sink and tell Autumn to ignore them. Clementine and Spartan get cozy on the chaise as we find a movie to watch. As the intro of *Finding Nemo* lights up the screen, I lie on the couch and create space for Autumn to lie beside me. Rather than lie with her back to my front, she settles in so we are face to face.

Minutes pass and neither of us says a word. We simply lie here and study the patterns of the others' irises. I get lost in the swirl of honey and cognac and love. Memorize the fan of her lashes and arch of her brow. Autumn leans in, lifts her hand to cup my cheek, and I close my eyes a beat before our lips connect.

The kiss is soft. Gentle. A reminder of the connection we share. It isn't lust driven. Not one ounce of it. The root of our bond is incomprehensible. Stardust and luster and vitality. An invisible force of life and love.

I break the kiss and hold her gaze. Although I could keep

my lips on hers for days, I also want more than just the physical. I need to know her heart. "How are you?" I whisper-ask.

Her eyes drop to my lips as she swallows. "Better now. Until my appointment yesterday, I couldn't catch my breath. Thought everyone I loved would be stolen from me."

I lift a hand to her cheek and stroke a thumb across her more prominent cheekbone. "Won't let that happen." And I mean it. With every ounce of strength I possess—mentally, emotionally, physically—I will not let anyone hurt Autumn. Or Clementine. Ever.

"How can you be so sure?"

I lower my hand and press my palm to the left of her sternum. For a moment, I stare at my hand as it cradles her heart. "Autumn, you and Clementine mean more to me than anyone. *Anyone*." Her eyes glass over as she tucks her lips between her teeth and swallows. "No matter what obstacles pop up, I will be here to help you, to help us, overcome them."

She releases her lips as a tear rolls over the bridge of her nose and splashes on the couch. "But what if he t-takes her?" she croaks out.

Leaning in, I kiss her forehead. "Between me and you and your attorney, and probably anyone who knows you and Clementine, no one is taking her from you. No one."

"God, I want to believe it. Been telling myself the same thing since Monday morning. But every once in a while, doubt creeps in. With his money, the possibility of him pushing me hard is plausible."

I tuck fallen strands of hair behind her ear. "Scarlet, all things are possible. Even the outcome being in your favor. Although it's difficult, you have to believe you will win. Put the positivity out into the universe. You are a wonderful mother. Have done everything right by Clementine. You may not have an overflowing bank account, but money does not make a good parent. Providing a loving and safe home for them does. Making sure she goes to school and smiles and is happy, those are what matter most."

"But..."

I press a finger to her lips. "No, Autumn." I tip her chin up so her gaze meets mine again. "You are a terrific mother. Please believe it. Tell yourself you are. Make a list of why you are and read it when you doubt yourself."

She nods as her eyes drift back to my lips. I close the space between us and press my lips to hers. They taste salty and sweet like kettle corn at the state fair. I savor the taste and remind myself this sadness is only temporary. A hiccup.

As long as Autumn and I are together, we can get through anything. And we *will* get through this.

five
AUTUMN

Being back in Jonas's arms again is nothing short of bliss. Not even a full week passed and yet it felt as if we spent months apart. With every brush of his lips, the idea of taking our relationship slower becomes more of a challenge. With every calloused caress of his fingers along my skin, I question how I will take a step back.

Then I shut down my inquisitive mind.

We should slow down. I *need* us to slow down. Spending less time with Jonas will be difficult. But fighting to keep my daughter supersedes my personal needs. I only hope I don't let Jonas drift too far and lose him in the process.

Seven-plus years have passed since I last saw or spoke with Leo. The Leo I knew in the past also didn't remotely resemble the Leo I met last weekend.

Thinking back, I don't recall Leo as pretentious and mighty. When we were together, he held a softer side. He had yet to be influenced by the patriarchy of his family. But life changes. Who you surround yourself with alters your perception of the world. And Leo has several larger-than-life people circling him.

What do I have? A group of overprotective tattoo artists, a goofy-ass friend, and a man who will do anything for me. Who will do anything for my daughter.

Is that enough? Is my small, yet consequential, circle of people enough to go up against Leo's army. In all honesty, I don't know.

Before visiting the attorney yesterday, I spent several hours online. Searching for anything and everything on Leo. News articles focusing on him and the business he and his family own. Is business good or bad? Has he been seen with women? His dating status was vital for several reasons.

One… if Clementine did spend time with him, who else would she be spending time with? What is Leo's family like now? In our time together, he never spoke much about them and introductions never happened.

Two… is he in a long term committed relationship or does he play the field? Important because my daughter does not need to be subjected to a revolving door of playmates. And after my history with Leo, I don't picture him committing to one woman for years.

Three… what types of women does he date? Are they bitchy and pretentious? Do they like children?

Ugh!

The questions constantly trickle in. The more research I did, the more questions I scribbled on paper. One photo of him, in particular, continues to throw gasoline on the slow-things-down-with-Jonas fire.

A professional photo of Leo alongside his father and two brothers, all wearing tailored five-piece suits that ooze money, smiling at the camera as they cut the grand opening ribbon on their fortieth luxury hotel in the state. Four-zero.

How do I compete with a family like his? How do I keep

the most important person in my life when I have nowhere near the same resources as he does? His net worth is more than I will make in my lifetime.

Jonas runs the tip of his nose along the side of mine before dropping a chaste kiss on my lips. My eyes refocus and lock with his.

"What has you thinking so hard? Your cogs are in overdrive."

A brief glance over my shoulder, I check on Clementine. In her own world, she curls up with Spartan, her head on his belly. Her little fingers wiggle in his fur as she watches the movie. And I take a mental snapshot of the moment. Of her happiness with her new best friend. Of her innocence.

For as long as I am able, I want to shelter her from the case. Shelter her from all the bullshit. The last thing Clementine needs is to stress over a battle she cannot fight. Or worry about a man she has never known.

I roll back to face Jonas again. His fiery hazels lock with mine, studying every move and expression. Gauge every fissure and twitch and almost spoken word, patiently waiting for my response.

God, I have never met someone so patient. Someone who will lie beside me, unspeaking for hours, and wait. Wait for me to find the strength and courage to speak or act in my own time.

How the hell did I get so lucky?

"He's so different from how I remember him," I whisper.

"How so?"

Where do I even begin? A major gap exists between now and then. Suppose the start is as good a place as any. How else can I explain the old versus the new Leo to Jonas? Explain how we met—two people from polar opposite lives.

Taking a deep breath, I dive in headfirst. "Leo and I met at nineteen. Neither of us knew much other than high school and a glimpse of adulthood. We both still lived with our parents. Parents who forced us to attend a fundraiser in Tampa." I pause to lick my lips, small snippets of the evening flashing in my memory. "Even then, Leo had the capability to get whatever he wanted. Always the smooth talker." I roll my eyes. "Mom and Dad insisted I attend the fundraiser with them. The church mentioned the event would raise proceeds to help a fellow member with MS. Each ticket cost a fortune, but the money went to a good cause. But the major influx of money came from auctions."

I close my eyes and take slow, methodical breaths. Jonas trails his knuckles softly over my cheek. "Stop anytime you want. Please don't feel obliged to tell me everything."

Nodding, I take another second to rein in my emotions. Meeting Leo wasn't necessarily all bad—when things were good, they were really good. Plus, Clementine wouldn't be the most astonishing part of my life if not for Leo.

Slowly, I open my eyes and study the staggering man in front of me. A man who wants nothing other than my happiness. My heart. I lean forward and press a tender, quick kiss to Jonas's lips.

"About an hour into the event, Leo approached me and introduced himself. We chatted briefly—two bored teens, forced to attend an event with their parents—before he asked me to dance." I didn't know how but agreed. It was better than sitting at the table with my parents.

"Before the night ended, we exchanged phone numbers. The first few weeks, we texted back and forth. Nothing important. Just idle chitchat. After a month, we went on our first date. He didn't ooze money then, but you could tell by his clothes and car he wanted for nothing. Not that my family was poor, but we didn't have anywhere near the same means."

I take a moment to catch my breath. To settle the bubbling anxiety beneath my diaphragm. "Anyway, we went on a date and really hit it off. One date led to another, and it wasn't long before we'd been together six months. It was close to New Year's, so we decided to celebrate. Although neither of us could buy alcohol, he had access to plenty. The both of us were so drunk, and we forwent a condom."

When I stop to gather myself, Jonas kisses the tip of my nose as his fingers toy with the length of my hair. I love his supportive nature. How he lets me set the pace while he holds me close. And the small gestures and touches to remind me he's still here.

Taking a deep breath, I mentally prepare to trudge through the ugly part of my relationship with Leo.

"A week before my twentieth birthday…" Jonas's eyebrows shoot up, silently asking the date. I chuckle. "Top secret. But I'll tell you soon." He shakes his head, kisses my nose, then gives me a nod to continue.

"A week before, it dawned on me I hadn't gotten my period since mid-December. Needless to say, I freaked out. Went to the store and bought every pregnancy test brand on the shelf, embarrassed as hell." I didn't have a job, unless you counted my measly pay from helping Dad at church, and I still lived at home. College was a bust because my parents convinced me art wasn't a notable major. The thought of becoming a mother with no future made me nauseous.

"Days before my birthday, we went on a date and I broke the news to Leo. At first, he remained quiet. Speechless. He didn't seem mad, except maybe at himself. The rest of the date felt awkward and ended sooner than usual. After that night, I never heard from him again. He either blocked me or got a new phone number. I had never been to his house, so I had no idea where he lived. By the time I pieced together he'd abandoned me—us—I told my parents. Telling them turned into a vicious cycle of one-sided conversations where they told me how disappointed God was with me. So, I packed up what mattered most and left."

As painful as I thought it would be telling Jonas this piece of my past, I harbor no apprehension. If anything, relief enters my veins. A major chunk of burden weighing down my shoulders lifts away. Some of the ghosts from my past vanish as the hurt I subconsciously held on to releases.

"How did you meet Penny and the guys?"

I close my eyes as love blooms beneath my breastbone. Although life hadn't been easy after I left home, I wouldn't change anything. Not even the times when I questioned whether or not I'd be able to eat.

"For a week, I stayed at a shelter for women. They had resources for jobs and provided me with so much love and support. With my love for art, I read over every art-related ad first. An ad for the shop popped up."

Clear as day, I see the ad in my head. *Tattoo shop seeking artist to help draw intricate pieces.* I had never set foot inside a tattoo shop. My parents would probably have a heart attack at the mere thought of it. Which is the exact reason I applied.

"Penny worked the front then too, and I instantly fell for her spunk and I-don't-give-a-fuck mentality. She may be a year younger than me, but even then, she had her shit together. The more we talked, the closer we got. I still lived at the shelter and she found out. From that day forward, we lived together. After Clementine was born, Reznor took me under his wing and taught me how to ink."

As weeks and months passed, everyone at the shop became my family. They cared more for me and Clementine than my actual blood relatives. For a time, this ideal made me sad. But as more time passed and I learned what it's like to care for someone else, the memories of them drifted. The way I see it… their loss.

Jonas holds my gaze. Intrigue and awe and admiration spark his fiery irises. "Wow." He doesn't say another word. Doesn't need to. His wide eyes and slightly parted lips say more than enough. His wonderment has the chambers of my heart working overtime as I fall a little more for the man a breath away.

"Leo made a choice back then. Whether it was out of fear or anger or selfishness, he decided. I shouldn't be punished—again—for his decision. Neither should Clementine. And I plan to do whatever it takes to make sure he doesn't hurt *my* daughter."

Jonas snakes his arms around my waist and draws me into his chest. I fist his shirt, inhale his familiar scent, and sigh as every muscle in my body calms. This man is my mojo. My lucky charm. The only person who soothes my soul just by being in the same room. When Jonas holds me in his arms, nothing else matters.

"He won't take her from you, scarlet. A judge would have to be insane to allow it. Especially with his past taken into account and everything you have done for Clementine. You may not have forty hotels and a couple commas in your bank account, but you are an exemplary parent. You always put her first. Always. And that counts more than anything."

I gather his sentiment, hold it close to my heart, and bask in the heartfelt meaning. Our relationship may still be fresh and young, but I savor every kind word and gesture from Jonas.

During my appointment yesterday, Theresa stated the same. Just using different words. She also emphasized most mothers maintain custody of children unless deemed incompetent. The fact that Leo popped up out of nowhere is suspicious and concerning, and Theresa plans to dig up as much dirt as possible. Plans to see if there is an ulterior motive to his sudden appearance.

I snuggle closer to Jonas and breathe in the peacefulness he exudes. Let it fill my lungs and add life to my veins. With each passing minute, I feel more serene, more at ease. My confidence may not be tipping the scales in my favor, but it certainly weighs heavier on my side now than it did hours ago.

The music indicating the end credits echoes throughout the living room. I sigh heavily as Jonas kisses the crown of my head. The last thing I want right now is the absence of Jonas's arms. Or to go home.

But a voice in my head has me hesitant to stay. Whispering ways Leo will use my relationship with Jonas against me to obtain custody of Clementine.

And how did Leo know where I live? Has he been watching me all this time? Following me? I shiver at the invasion. If that's the case, he more than likely knows where Jonas lives too. Where I work.

My stomach rolls as if I just stepped off the Tilt-A-Whirl. I swallow down the urge to vomit.

Every bone in my body opposes, but I pull away from Jonas and sit up. Rest my elbows on my knees and drop my face in my palms.

Why has this become my life? Why am I the one nauseous

over being with someone I care for? Deeply. This is horseshit. I shouldn't be made to feel guilty over wanting companionship and affection. And I shouldn't be punished—nor my daughter—for wanting more out of life.

I take a deep breath. Then another. And another. Jonas softly strokes up and down my spine. Soothes the pain a fraction. Again, I hate that we have to leave. But I suck it up and sit taller.

"Pumpkin, we need to head home."

Clementine snuggles closer to Spartan. "Why can't I stay with Sparty?"

"Not tonight. Maybe we can see Sparty again tomorrow."

Clementine groans and reluctantly slides off the couch. "Fine."

I watch my daughter pout as she puts her shoes on slower than any other time in her life. Occasionally acting as if the shoe doesn't fit her foot. She takes it off, loosens the laces more, then does it all over again. God, if she behaves this dramatically at seven, no telling what nonsense I will deal with when she is a preteen or teenager. Someone better rescue me.

Ten minutes later, Clementine finally has her shoes on and is ready to leave. She hugs Spartan so hard I hear him exhale. But he doesn't seem to mind. Jonas walks us out to the car. After Clementine hops in and buckles up, I start the car. As I shut the door to say good night to Jonas, Clementine mutters something about kissing and I shake my head.

Jonas tugs me close and bands his arms around my waist. "After having you here, I don't want to let you go."

"Me, either."

"Let me know when you get home. Would love to see you tomorrow. We can talk about it in the morning."

I fist the back of his shirt before leaning away and tipping my head back. Without hesitation, Jonas lowers his lips to mine and kisses me breathless.

In the kiss, he tells me how much he cares, how he will be at my side through thick and thin, and how we will get through this together. I match his fervor and pray he is right. Pray this ordeal with Leo ends quickly. That Clementine remains with me and comes out of this whole scenario unscathed.

Our lips break apart and Jonas places one last kiss on my nose. "'Night, scarlet. Talk to you in the morning. We'll plan the day then."

I nod, opening the car door. "'Night. Talk to you in the morning." And I almost slip up. Almost drop the *L*-bomb, but catch myself as I duck into the car.

Jonas closes my door and pats the roof. After buckling my seat belt, I throw the gearshift in reverse and back onto the street. Jonas waves and waits for us to drive off before going into the house.

I thought I should slow our relationship down, but I haven't the slightest idea how. And if I am honest with myself, I don't want to slow down. Quite the opposite, actually. The urge to sprint forward screams from every corner of my mind.

But the dark cloud that is Leo hovers over me with threats of robbing me of my joy. A joy no one can replace.

What the hell am I supposed to do? Standing at the proverbial fork in the road, I ponder which direction to take. As I steer the car left, I pray to whoever listens.

Please let this be the right decision.

six

JONAS

Coldness jabs my elbow. I groan and tuck my elbow more securely to my side. Just as I drift off, wetness replaces the jab. Poke. Nudge. Another round of moisture.

Argh!

I bolt upright, swatting the air. Spartan grumbles when I connect with his furry chest. With each breath in, disorientation fades as reality comes into focus.

I'm in bed. Spartan has been trying to wake me. And I actually slept. Not the best sleep, but sleep nonetheless.

"Give me a minute, bud."

I swipe a hand over my face and widen my eyes a few times. The sun bleeds through the curtains and brightens the room more than usual when I wake. What time is it?

Scooting out of bed, Spartan jumps down alongside me and races out of the bedroom. I grab my phone from the charger and click the side button. A little after eight. Wow. Sleeping past six thirty is a miracle on its own. Spartan doesn't always let me sleep in, but perhaps he knew I needed the extra time.

I set the phone down, shuffle out of the bedroom and over

to the door leading to the backyard, where Spartan bounces like a kangaroo. As soon as I open the door, he flies out and whips across the yard. And just as quickly, he runs back in the house and bolts to his bowl, knocking it with his nose.

"You have way too much energy for me today. Maybe we'll get some playtime in later." Adding a scoop of kibble to his bowl, I ruffle his fur. He stops vacuuming his food long enough to glance up and give me his best doggy smile.

I amble back to the bedroom and flop down on the bed after snagging up my phone. I type out a text to Autumn and hit send. Clementine's energy often matches Spartan's, so I doubt she is still asleep.

> Morning, scarlet. Up and ready to plan the day whenever you are.

I head for the bathroom and go about my morning routine. While brushing my teeth, I ponder what to do with my girls today. The cooler air outside may eliminate some options, but there are still plenty of alternatives. Indoor options are endless —movies, arcade, bowling, wandering the mall, trampoline playground.

I swish and spit out mouthwash as my phone pings.

> About to eat breakfast. Give us at least 30 and come by?

> See you soon.

After a quick shower, I let Spartan out and whip up scrambled eggs and toast. Autumn said thirty minutes, but giving her and Clementine extra won't hurt.

Finished eating, I wash the dishes then grab my wallet and keys. The second he hears my keys jingle, Spartan bolts inside his crate. I hand him a treat and turn on his radio then head out the door.

I type out a quick text to Autumn to tell her I am on my way.

Cracking the window, I shiver at the breeze blowing inside the Jeep. It should reach the upper sixties today, but with the sun beaming down, it will feel closer to mid-seventies. A day at the park may be an option if my girls are up for it. Perhaps a park Clementine hasn't visited yet.

I park outside Autumn's apartment and all but dash to the door. Seconds after I knock, Clementine squeals on the other side.

"Mama, he's here!"

Clementine's boisterous, joyful nature soothes me in an unimaginable way. Her radiant smile and sweet laughter cause my heart to swell in ways I never thought possible. It's strange. That exact moment you discover you were missing this odd-shaped piece of yourself. Not the piece that completes you as a lover. But the one that makes you whole as a man.

The door swings open and my girls stand a foot away with bright smiles warming their faces. And my heart.

"'Morning, girls." I step inside, squat down to hug Clementine, then stand tall and kiss Autumn.

"'Morning, Mr. Jonas. Where are we going?"

Door closed, I reach down to take Autumn's hand in mine and walk us to the couch. The simple gesture warms my skin and jump-starts my heart. This feeling—like the start of a summer rainstorm, when two energies collide and turn electric—will never get old. Will never fade away. Not for me.

"Thought I'd ask if there was anywhere you wanted to go. It's nice outside. The park could be fun."

Clementine bounces in front of us. "Ooh, ooh, ooh. The park, the park. Can we go to the playground?" Seriously, she and Spartan must have taken the same bouncy pill this morning.

Autumn leans into my side and I inhale her cherry vanilla scent. The fragrance hits me, and I close my eyes. Relish the perfume I have memorized. And delight in the way it relaxes every ache in my body.

"The park sounds nice. Let's go to a different one. Okay, pumpkin?"

"Only if there's a playground." Clementine gives Autumn a look that states she is not to be messed with. I bite the inside of my cheek to resist laughing. Last thing I need is to provoke her sassiness, which reminds me of Dad with Lex during Wednesday night dinners.

"Promise we'll find the perfect park, pumpkin. Go grab your jacket, just in case."

Clementine runs down the hall to get her jacket. Autumn spins to face me and smiles. The dark circles under her eyes not as significant today. Like mine. The luster in her cognac irises glows brighter today. Warmer. More inviting and intoxicating. Her lips perkier.

All from spending time together. One evening. Nothing extravagant. A small increment of time. Enough to see and touch and hold each other. To breathe life back in our hearts.

I reach up and caress her cheek with my knuckles. The second our skin connects, she closes her eyes, leans into my touch and sighs.

"Missed you. So much," I whisper.

Her eyes slowly open as she nods. "Me too." Autumn twists just enough to press her lips to my palm.

Clementine rushes back into the living room, jacket in her

clutches and a bright, toothy smile on her face. She grabs Autumn's hand and attempts to yank her off the couch. "C'mon. Let's go!"

The mini bubble of solitude Autumn and I shared seconds ago pops as we stand. Some people would be upset at the intrusion, but neither of us minds. Every moment with Clementine is a breath of fresh air.

"We were just waiting on you, slowpoke," she says, sticking her tongue out at Clementine as she grabs her purse and jacket.

Their banter continues as we exit the apartment and load up in the Jeep. All I think as they carry on teasing each other is how lucky I am. Lucky to have found this wonderful woman. And luckier that she came with a mini version of herself. Someone who makes us both smile, even on the darkest days.

I drive through Clearwater without direction. Unsure where to go. Until an idea pops in my head and I steer the Jeep toward Safety Harbor.

Clementine bops and sings to the song on the radio in the back seat. Autumn lip syncs the rock lyrics as she looks out the windshield and draws small circles on my upper thigh with her thumb.

Nothing has felt more right than the three of us. Nothing has made my heart thump as wildly than the three of us. Me and my girls.

Twenty minutes later, I maneuver the Jeep into Phillippe Park and drive toward the playground area. As I locate a parking space, Autumn spins in her seat to face Clementine.

"Hey, pumpkin." In the rearview mirror, I see Clementine perk up. "After we play on the playground a bit, I'd like to walk around the park. This park is special and I want to share it with you."

I cut the engine and turn to face the back seat. Clementine's eyes are wide as she stares out the window and looks at the trees.

"Why is it special, Mama?"

"A long time ago, this park belonged to the Native Americans. Their homes were here. They also cherished the earth and sun here, so there's a lot of special energy here."

"Really?" Clementine's brows shoot to her hairline while her jaw slackens. Her amazement is adorable. It makes coming here more memorable and special.

"Yep. We'll look at all the special places after we play at the playground."

We unload from the Jeep and Clementine runs to play. Autumn and I locate a bench in the sun and sit. Clementine climbs the ladder and slips down the slide several times. Then she goes to one of the mini rock-climbing walls and navigates the six-foot venture. Next, she hops on a swing and hurls herself back and forth to dizzying heights.

Autumn leans into my side, loops her arm in mine, and rests her head on my shoulder. Our fingers weave together and we both sigh at the contact. Not a single word exchanged. We simply sit here, in this peaceful place, with our eyes on Clementine.

Faster than anticipated, Clementine declares she is done playing and wants to go see the special part of the park.

The three of us wander hand in hand across a grassy patch. Within minutes, we reach a stairway made of large earth-colored flat stones. The couple dozen steps wide and shaded by moss-covered oak trees. We take the steps leisurely as we observe the park from a different vantage point.

On the landing at the top of the stairs, a large storyboard shares the history of the land with park visitors. We step up to the wooden sign and Autumn reads the story about the Tocobaga Temple Mound. The story of the Native American village that existed here before a conquistador arrived in the early 1500s. For a time, their cultures coexisted, but it wasn't long until European diseases caused their demise.

When Autumn finishes the story, Clementine's lips turn down as her eyes glaze over.

"That's so sad, Mama."

"Yes, it is. But many people say the energy from the Native Americans still lives here. That it gives them strength or soothes them or protects them."

Clementine peeks up at us, the skin between her brow bunching. "How?"

I squat down in front of her. "Well, the Native Americans prayed to the earth and sun and animals. Thanked them for shelter and food and life. Sang special songs to them and asked for their protection. The energy from their spirits is said to still live here."

Clementine stares off at the trees and whispers, "Wow."

Autumn takes Clementine's hand. "Come on, pumpkin. Let's walk around and see it all." Clementine nods, speechless.

We stroll without hurry down another, steeper set of stairs closer to the Bay. Every five to ten steps, Clementine stops and points to something fascinating her. A crooked tree, squirrels, birds. At a few trees, she steps up and places her hand on the bark as if trying to feel the energy. Who knows? Maybe she does. Children are more in tune with energy and the spiritual elements of the world.

When we reach the bottom of the steps, we walk along the

waterway and stop to admire the Bay. I see the appeal Odet Phillippe had to owning this land in the mid-1800s. A glorious view of the water and nothing but peace.

My stomach grumbles and I press a loose fist to my belly to quiet it. Beside me, Autumn laughs as she fishes her phone out of her purse and checks the time.

"Might be a good time to grab lunch. It's almost one."

Time flies when with people who make you happiest.

It's like pulling teeth to get Clementine to leave, but she concedes when we promise to bring her back on a different day. We trek back to the Jeep, hop in, and buckle up. Since we aren't far from downtown Safety Harbor, I suggest we find a restaurant there to eat.

Soon, we walk into a pizzeria on Main and get seated. After perusing the menu, we decide to share a Sicilian pizza. But it's no shock when Autumn orders mozzarella sticks, toasted raviolis, and garlic knots for appetizers. Maybe with three of us here, there won't be as many left-overs. But let's face it, who doesn't love leftovers. My girl definitely does.

The second the appetizers hit the table, we each dive in. Surprisingly, three-quarters of the appetizers are demolished before the pizza arrives. Thank goodness we didn't order a large. I see possibly two days of leftovers in the future.

After our bellies are full and half the pizza gets boxed up, we head out and window shop Main Street.

Our county only has a handful of cute downtown districts and Safety Harbor is one of them. Most of the shops and restaurants here are locally owned. Everyone is friendly as they stroll up and down the sidewalks and visit the shops. Trees drape several sections of street and sidewalk, keeping patrons cool on summer days. Some buildings are colorful and grab your attention. Eclectic and unique, as are most of the downtown areas near us.

Clementine walks a few strides ahead of us. Her eyes scanning every storefront, eager to see what's inside.

I lean in and kiss Autumn's temple. "Today has been wonderful. Especially after seeing you last night."

"Agreed. I slept better for the first time in days."

"Would love to do our dinners again. I miss my girls."

"Miss you, too." I hear the dejection in her voice. Catch the minor twitch of her lips.

All day, I considered mentioning the party Cora and Gavin are throwing me for my birthday tomorrow. More than anything, I want to celebrate with Autumn and Clementine. But something keeps me quiet. Autumn's somber mood has me hesitant.

In all seriousness, why would she want to celebrate anything when her life feels as if it's being ripped out beneath her?

So, I don't bring up the party. As long as I get time with my girls—like today—I am happy.

"But?"

She tucks her lips between her teeth and watches Clementine as she stares inside a candy shop. "But I don't know if us being together right now will hinder things. While this case with Leo lingers, I mean. I can't lose her, Jonas," she whispers at the end.

I haul Autumn into my arms, bundle her close, and hold her as if she could slip from my reach. "No one will take her from you. Ever."

"How can you be so sure?" I hate how small her voice sounds. Fragile and vulnerable.

I make a silent vow, once this case ends, to never let her

feel this way again. To never let another person make her feel helpless or frightened. No one hurts my girls. No one.

"Call it intuition or instinct or a vibe. You have enough love surrounding the two of you to protect you for a lifetime. No way someone like him will tear it down."

Autumn takes a deep breath and fists my shirt beneath my jacket. "Hope you're right."

Clementine dashes over to us and jumps up and down. "Mama, can we get candy from there?" She points to the shop. The all-window storefront displays hundreds of chocolates and taffy and tons of other confections.

"Sure, pumpkin. But not too many."

"Yay!"

And just like that, we mosey about as if our conversation was background noise since we don't discuss Leo and the case around Clementine. I just pray Autumn doesn't continue to believe shutting herself and Clementine away from the world is the best solution.

I will never leave her side but fear she may try to abandon mine.

Seven

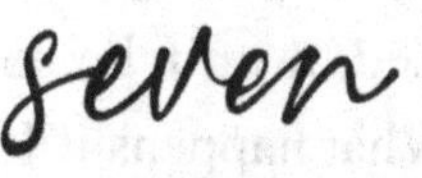

AUTUMN

Our day has been absolutely wonderful. But also offbeat.

Spending time with Jonas lifts my spirits and eases some of the agony festering in my head. In the same breath, time with Jonas leaves me exposed. Wide open to what-ifs and dreams. Unfortunately, with all the shit Leo is stirring up, I cannot afford to live in the world of what-ifs and dreams.

Jonas parks in front of my apartment. After our conversation outside the candy shop, neither of us has spoken much. He means well and speaks the truth when he says I have a small army of people ready and willing to help me. But how will my family compete against Leo? Against everything his family has to offer? Money may not buy love, but, for the right price, it buys other things—including legalities.

When he cuts the engine, Clementine unbuckles her belt. "Wish we could have dinner at Mr. Jonas's house so I can see Sparty." The blend of sadness and sarcasm in Clementine's voice doesn't go unnoticed.

I twist in my seat and half smile at my daughter. "We'll see Spartan again. Just not tonight, okay?"

She huffs in the back seat and turns away from me. Why is it every time I feel I am making the right choice—not just for me, but also for Clementine—I appear the bad guy? Yes, she has bonded with Jonas and Spartan. Their connection should make me smile like a fool. And it did until Leo popped up. Now, their connection adds another pang in my heart because I have kept them apart.

But how do I tell her it's just until the case concludes? Which, fingers crossed, won't be long. What happens if I throw in the towel? What happens if I live "normally?"

If I live life as I did before Leo made an appearance, I have a sneaking suspicion my and Clementine's relationship with Jonas will be dragged through the mud. Become tainted and damaged. With his money and resources, Leo has the ability to dig up dirt—or create his own. The last thing I want is for me or Jonas to question each other. Our pasts or some fabricated version.

Seems easier to lay low and dial our relationship down until everything passes. Theresa never gave a specific timeline as to when this would end, but the way she explained the process, I foresee it wrapping up sooner rather than later.

Would I miss the hell out of Jonas? Undeniably, yes. In such a short period of time, he has become so much more than the man I date. He has brought me back to life. And with this minor hiccup of time apart, at least we will come out clean on the other side. Or so I hope.

I peer over at Jonas; his fiery hazels stare back at me with questions. Questions I wish I had the answers to. Sentiments I hug close to my heart.

Will you and Clementine come to the house again? What can I do to help? You know you're not in this alone, right? Please, let me help. Please, don't shut me out.

Before I open my mouth and say something undesirable, I twist in my seat and exit the Jeep. As soon as I do, Clementine opens her door. I extend a hand to help her down. She glances at it briefly, ignores it, and shimmies her way down without assistance. "I'm a big girl and can get down by myself. I don't need your help."

Knife to the heart.

Once her feet hit the concrete, I reach for her hand and stop her. "Excuse me, young lady." I drop down in front of her and wait until she looks me in the eye. When she does, I see fire and heartache. "You're upset, I get it. But that is no reason to be lippy with me. Was I mean to you?"

She bites the inside of her cheek. Behind me, Jonas comes around and stands near us. His stance and energy project his agreeance with me. *Thank, god.* He doesn't say a word, but provides me with the strength to hold my ground.

"No, Mama." Clementine hangs her head. "Sorry."

"Thank you for apologizing. Sometimes emotions make us say and do things we normally don't. So, remember to think about other people before you say mean things. Words hurt too, pumpkin."

She sniffles. "I promise to think harder next time."

Rising to stand, I hold my hand out to her and she takes it within seconds. Clementine is frustrated with the wishy-washy too. One week, we see Jonas every night. Then, without warning, I strip it all away. I recognize this wasn't fair of me to do. Maybe with more time and better explanation—not today, but soon—Clementine will understand my reasons.

Inside the apartment, Clementine dashes for the room we share. More than likely, she will be in there until dinner. She apologized for her behavior but now needs solitude to understand it all.

I step into Jonas and wrap my arms around his waist, peering up at him. "Want to help me in the kitchen?" I ask, praying he says yes. My cooking isn't horrible, but Jonas cooks pasta better.

He plants a quick kiss on my nose. "Sure. Have anything in mind?" I shake my head. "Okay. Well, let's go investigate our options."

We head into the kitchen and riffle through the fridge and cabinets. Within minutes, Jonas has chicken, carrots, potatoes, onion, garlic, and green beans on the counter. After I show him where to find the pots, pans, and cutting boards, he gets to work. He puts me in charge of cleaning and cutting the vegetables to roast in the oven. Then he gets to work on cleaning and cutting the chicken into smaller pieces.

Being in the kitchen with Jonas feels routine. Right. A part of who we are. The way we move around each other. How easily life flows when we are together.

In no time, we have a pan loaded with vegetables and olive oil, and a sheet pan covered in barbecue glazed chicken. We pop them in the oven—which I didn't realize Jonas preheated—and start cleaning up. He makes dinner seem so effortless. I would have given up sooner and probably eaten the leftovers from lunch. Or found something that required less preparation.

Once the dishes are clean, Jonas dries his hands, steps into me and draws me close. My hands automatically wind around his backside while his rest on my lower back and shoulders. And for a moment, we stand stock still. Silent. Nothing but our uneven breaths and pitched heartbeats filling the room.

I love being in Jonas's arms more than anything. Love how his warmth blankets me, protects me. Love the erratic tick of his heartbeat beneath my ear as I lay my cheek to his chest. I snuggle into him farther, not wanting this moment to end.

Which is the exact moment the voice of uncertainty in my head whittles at my happiness. Eats away at my smile. Steals the hope and joy in my heart. And I hate that I listen to it. Hate that the moment it creeps in, I drop my arms from Jonas and take a step back. That I let it overpower me. That I let it fill my head with hesitation and doubt.

"You okay?" he asks, lines marring his forehead.

I nod, although my internal voice screams *what the hell are you doing?* "Yeah. Shouldn't we check the food?" My excuse is lame, and Jonas is no fool. Since the day we pulled up to my apartment and spotted Leo, everything between us has been off-kilter.

"Set the timer." He peers around me. "Still have another five minutes before I flip the chicken."

And because I am irritated with my unsure mind, I remain tight-lipped and nod. When Jonas steps up to me again, I don't resist his embrace. But I don't give myself over to it as much as I long to. Don't melt into him. Don't clutch on to him as if my life depends on it—which is partial truth.

Until dinner finishes cooking, we hold each other in an awkward embrace. If I sense how odd the energy in the room is, he does too. But he doesn't say a word. He just holds me; his cheek resting on the crown of my head.

Dinner is quiet. Not even Clementine speaks up. The vibe while we eat is stifling.

Clementine is upset and pouts for good measure. I push food around my plate like a picky child, eyes glued to my fork. But even with my eyes downcast, I *know* Jonas is staring. I feel his gaze deep in my bones. Every other minute, he spears food on his plate in my periphery but does so blindly. When I lift my chin and catch his eyes on me, my assumptions are answered.

Before I open my mouth to stupidly ask what is wrong, Clementine speaks up. "May I be done, please?"

I glance at her plate, which is mostly clear. "Sure, pumpkin. Go pick a movie and we'll be there in a minute."

The moment Clementine is out of earshot, Jonas locks onto my eyes. "Did I do something wrong?" His voice so soft, I barely hear him. But in his tone, I decipher hurt.

Gah! I have been so worried and distracted with Leo and the case, I am already messing this up.

This is why separation—temporarily—is the best idea. Because I am screwing up the best relationship, the best man, in my life. All because I don't know how to balance our time together along with raising my daughter and dealing with an ex who gave zero shits about me or Clementine then suddenly does.

What *is* the right choice here? Feels as if there isn't one.

God, I like Jonas. Considering I almost slipped and said the *L*-word, I more than like him. He possesses every great quality I desire in a partner—kindness, affection, warmth, and he cares for Clementine as if she were his own. No matter how you spin it, I am lucky to have Jonas in my life.

But I can't stop thinking about Leo using Jonas as a weapon. What if he tells the courts I didn't give him a chance to be a father to Clementine because Jonas assumed the role? Although the idea is far-fetched, I wouldn't put it past Leo to say such things. Which is why I need my relationship with Jonas to slow down a bit. Not full-fledge stop, but ease off until I have better reassurances from Theresa.

Could the teeter-totter balance in the middle for just a bit.

"No, you've done nothing wrong. But I need you to understand how torn I am right now."

His chair scrapes against the tile before he rises and takes his and Clementine's plates to the kitchen. I follow in his wake, adding my uneaten food to a leftover container with the rest. Once all the dishes are rinsed and in the dishwasher, he spins to face me again.

"Can you please tell me what has you so divided?"

I take a deep breath and step within inches of Jonas. Reaching forward, I fist his shirt and peer up. "I feel... stuck. Like no matter what decision I make right now, it won't be the right one. If we go about things as if nothing has changed, what if Leo digs up stuff and pins us against each other."

"Autumn, I have told you about my past."

"Romantically, yes. But Leo's family can get dirty when they want something. No doubt he picked up the habit. He may not dig up something bad about either of us in the romance department, but what if you got into a physical altercation before? He may claim to the courts you have a history of violence."

"That isn't true, though."

"Yes, but his money will make it true long enough for him to win. Do you understand where I'm coming from now? Why I have been so tossed up? Jonas, I lo— care about you. A lot. And I don't need Leo ruining your life just for the hell of it."

Jonas closes the space between us and swathes me in his arms. "I care about you a lot too, scarlet." He kisses the crown of my head. "The only way he can ruin my life is to take you away from me."

Knife in the heart, twisting and digging deeper.

"Can we talk about this later? Let's go watch the movie with Clementine."

Jonas kisses the crown of my head again, then releases me. "Sure."

We weave our way into the living room and plop down on the couch. Clementine is a good twenty minutes into *The Nightmare Before Christmas* already. She lays sprawled across pillows and blankets on the floor, twirling the length of her hair around her finger. In no time, Clementine will pass out. She fights sleep by twirling her hair.

And as we do every time a movie plays while we are together, I curl into Jonas. Sometimes we spoon—his front to my back—but tonight I want to nestle into his chest. I burrow my nose where his neck and shoulder meet, and inhale his scent. A blend of working in the garage, sunscreen, and Jonas. My favorite smell.

His arms snake around my backside to press me closer while I hold on to him for dear life. Legs tangle. Breathing spikes little by little. Hearts thump, thump, thump to a vicious rhythm. But we don't move. We remain close, encased in our own little bubble of bliss.

When the familiar jingle plays for the credits, I quietly huff into Jonas's chest before separating us.

"Stay here," he says. "I got her."

I scoot to sit up. Jonas eases off the couch, crouches down, and gingerly scoops a sleeping Clementine off the floor. As he tucks her close to his chest and her little arms cling to him, I melt into the cushions. When he rises from the floor and snuggles her closer to his chest, Clementine reaches for his hair and plays with what her little fingers reach.

I stop breathing. While Jonas walks her down the hall to the bedroom, he whispers in her ear and she hugs him tighter.

My heart melts and puddles on the floor. Doesn't matter what he said to her. His whispered words were meant solely for my daughter.

Jonas is so good with her. Cares for Clementine more than I ever imagined possible. More than I pictured any man caring for my daughter.

Which makes my indecisiveness that much more difficult.

A moment later, Jonas returns to the living room empty-handed. He sits on the couch beside me and picks up his shoes with hesitance. Jonas doesn't want to leave. I don't want him to leave. But until we know what type of Leo fire we need to extinguish, us sleeping apart is for the best. At least this is what I continue to tell myself.

When he finishes tying his laces, we rise from the couch as I walk Jonas to the door. We stop a foot away and Jonas closes the space between us. He brings one hand to my cheek, then the other. For a beat, he just holds me there, his gaze locked with mine. His face inches away, I swear he will kiss me any second.

He brushes the tip of his nose along the length of mine, and I close my eyes. Then his lips drop to mine. Warm, soft lips press to mine as I wrap my fingers around his forearms. His lips caress with such tenderness and devotion. Our breaths swirl in the air as we gasp between every other kiss. Then he slowly brushes the tip of his tongue over my lower lip. A shiver ripples through me before I open up and invite him in.

A hand slides into my hair while another drops to my hip and squeezes. I skim my hands up his chest, over the column of his throat, and into his hair, fisting the dark locks. We kiss until we need to come up for air. Even then, I need more of his kisses.

Foreheads pressed together, we work to settle our erratic

breathing and hyper heart rates. I wish for this blissful bubble to never burst. Wish me, Jonas, and Clementine could stay in this happy place forever without disruption. But, right now, this wish won't be coming true.

I pinch my eyes closed and wish I felt confident enough to *not* do what I am about to do. Maybe I will get lucky and someone will smack the obvious against my skull. Until then, this is the only way.

"Jonas," I whisper between us. He inches back enough to see my face. To see the worry lines marring my forehead. The pain in my pinched eyes.

"Scarlet, open your eyes." It would be so much easier if I didn't have to *see* his pain when I say this. But I deserve to feel the impact. "Talk to me."

I tuck my lips between my teeth, take a deep breath, and swallow. "Until I get more details from my attorney, about Leo and any possible leverage he may hold, I think it's best we slow down more."

Jonas flinches as if I slapped him. "Slow down more? Yesterday was the first time I saw you in almost a week. After we…"

Now I flinch. I deserve the virtual slap to the face. He was going to say after we made love over the weekend. More than once.

"Please, Jonas. I can't lose her, or you. But I don't know how to navigate down this path. The only person who can guide us safely is the woman I just handed half of my savings to. And she's currently digging to find me answers. Until she does, I shouldn't jeopardize any chance I have of keeping my daughter."

Jonas drops his hands to his sides and steps back. The

second step back hurts worse than the first. His eyes dart between mine, looking for any semblance of misunderstanding. When he doesn't find any, he shakes his head and takes another step back. God, why won't he say anything? His speechlessness kills me just as much as the pain smeared across his face.

He pats his back pockets before pulling his keys from the front. "I need to go," he mumbles.

"Jonas, please tell me you understand," I croak.

The longer we stand like this, the more pained Jonas appears. The backs of my eyes sting. I blink and blink, begging my eyes not to betray me while he stands here. Why did I believe this was the only viable solution? I need answers. Now. But all reasonable thought has left the building.

"Wish that was possible, Autumn." He shakes his head. I don't miss how he calls me Autumn instead of scarlet. Twist the knife a little more to the left. "Not like I have a choice. I'll be waiting in the wings. Let me know when I'm allowed to care for you and Clementine again. Hope it's not too long."

He steps around me, opens the door, and storms out. The door hangs open and I follow him with my eyes as he unlocks the Jeep, jumps in, cranks the engine, and whips out of the complex.

What did I just do? What the hell was I thinking? He's gone. Jonas is gone. And I did this.

I shut the door, lean my back against it, and slide down until my butt hits the ground. As soon as it does, a torrent of tears lets loose, soaking my cheeks and shirt.

Don't know how, but I need to resolve this mess. Quickly. I need answers from Theresa. Because this isn't like last weekend when Jonas and I parted. This isn't like after the bowling alley when I told him about Clementine.

No, this is a million times worse. And I fear I permanently messed us up. Ruined the best thing, other than Clementine, to happen to me… all because I am too scared to take a risk. Too scared to let love stand up and fight.

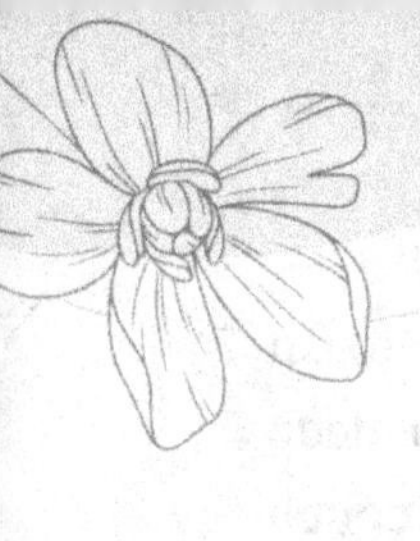

eight

JONAS

"Did you actually pay attention in body shop class, Ken? Or did you just watch videos on YouTube?"

Ken shrivels under my harsh criticism, but I don't give a fuck. Feels as if it has taken him ten times longer than usual to replace the rear quarter panels on the sedan he's working on.

"Jonas," Dad barks from the door leading into the garage office. "Office. Now." He doesn't wait for me to answer. Just pivots on his heel and heads inside.

I throw the wrench in my hand in the general direction of the toolbox, the metal on metal clangs and echoes off the concrete walls. Just as I open my mouth to snap at Ken again, Dad hollers from the office. "Now, Jonas."

Weaving between the cars in the bays, I head into the office. I shut the door and huff as I cross my arms. "What, Dad?" I bite out.

Dad steps up to me and points a finger in my face. "Don't you take that tone with me, son. You may be a man, but I don't deserve the shit coming out of your mouth."

I flinch, not used to hearing my father speak to me in such a harsh manner. He lowers his finger, then walks over to the couch and sits down. Eyes on me, he doesn't ask me to sit down, but his narrowed lids imply I do so. Taking a deep breath and dropping my arms, I amble over to the couch and sit.

"You need to talk to me, Jonas. I have put up with your foul mood for more than a week now. I've let some things skirt by because you are obviously upset. But yelling at the employees for no reason, I draw the line there."

I rest my elbows on my knees and drop my head in my palms. *Fuck, fuck, fuck.* I am a goddamn mess.

The last time Autumn and I truly spoke was when I left her apartment… ten days ago. After the way we left things, I haven't reached out. She texted once to say she missed me but left it at that. What did I say in return? Nothing. If she still wants to spend time with me, if she still wants our relationship, Autumn needs to be the one to take the leap. She needs to say something more than *I miss you.* Show me some indication she wants to see or spend time together.

"Haven't talked to Autumn in almost two weeks," I groan. "She said things between us needed to go slower because of her ex making an appearance and filing for custody." Beside me, Dad gasps. Not loud, but enough for me to hear. "Autumn thinks if we're together, the ex will use our relationship against her. I don't get her reasoning. And considering the guy ditched her before Clementine was born, I don't think he has a leg to stand on."

Dad pats my shoulder. "For obvious reasons, I didn't go to law school. But after seeing how friends of ours handled divorces and custody battles, I would side with you on this. If the man has never been around, his case probably holds no weight."

I lift my head from my hands and sit up straighter, peering

over at Dad. "This is what I've tried to tell her. Even her attorney said to live life as she had before he showed. There has to be something she hasn't told me. Something else about him that scares her. Which bothers me more."

"Son, all you can do is support and be there for her. Even if it's sporadic. If she hired a good lawyer, this will work itself out soon. And although she asked for distance, don't keep hiding in the shadows. Reach out to her. If she doesn't want to talk, she won't."

This has been one of my fears. After this much time apart and no real interaction, will she just shrug me off? She has handled this without me for more than two weeks since it all came to light. Does she need me for anything at this point?

"Dad, if she doesn't want to talk to me… I don't think I'll handle that well. At all. You think the last ten days have been bad?" I shake my head and leave it at that.

"I don't doubt it, son. But stop for a moment and put yourself in Autumn's shoes. Imagine all the stress and uncertainty she has to deal with right now. Until not too long ago, her life was normal and boring. She went to work and spent time with her daughter. Then you came into the picture and stirred things up." I give him the side-eye and he holds his hands up in surrender. "In a good way. But she was still adjusting to a new way of life with you, then her ex blindsides her and threatens to take away her daughter. Son, she went into protection mode. Like any good parent would do. And I attest to doing irrational things while in parent mode."

"Okay. So, how do I insert myself into her life then? I don't want to overwhelm her. But I want to be there. Right now, it feels as if I don't matter. Like she could live without me."

The more days we spend apart, the deeper the ache in my

bones. I can't seem to catch my breath. And the pain in my chest grows stronger each day. Worst of all, I get next to no sleep. So, all I have is time to think. And I just want my brain to shut the hell up. Just one night.

"Text or call her. Without too much detail, tell her how you're feeling. Don't make your chat a guilt-trip. Don't make it all about you. Ask her how things are going. If she's gotten any updates." Dad clasps my shoulder. "Son, it's okay to go at her pace. Just don't lose sight of her."

I nod. *Go at her pace, but don't lose sight of her.* Got it.

We sit in the office in silence for a bit. Dad knows I am marinating on his words. Trying to absorb and digest them. Dad may not have a wall full of college degrees or any special initials after his name, but he has always been a good listener and an even better advice giver. He has the patience of a saint. Who wouldn't after dealing with us Thompson kids?

Dad claps my shoulder and stands. "Heading back out to the garage. Stay in here as long as you need. Come back out once you're levelheaded enough."

"Thanks, Dad. Be back out shortly."

Once he exits the office, I fish my phone out from my coveralls. Unlocking the phone, I open my text history with Autumn and read her last message for the millionth time.

I miss you. Same, scarlet.

I take a deep breath and poise myself to type out a text. My fingers tremble above the screen and I close my eyes and take a few more deep breaths before I type.

> Sorry I didn't answer before. Miss you too. Terribly. How are my girls?

After I hit send, I question whether or not it's okay to still call Autumn and Clementine "my girls." But as soon as the three dots dance in the gray bubble, my doubt gets shoved aside.

> Clementine is a grump. Me too. I have another appointment with my attorney Thursday. Hoping for good news.

I don't know much about attorneys and the timetables for legal matters, but two weeks have passed since Autumn last spoke with them. Shouldn't there be updates already?

> Fingers crossed. I'd love to see you. No pressure, though.

Adding the last part was painful. As if I have ever pressured her into spending time together. If anything, I have been more relaxed than most.

> Me too. I promise. Soon. Gotta go - client.

I want to text her back and say more, but I stop myself. She wouldn't see it until later anyway. Maybe I should write her another letter. Her work hours are earlier now, so I would have to either drop it at her apartment or give it to Penny or one of the guys at the shop. Maybe I will just leave it at her door.

In the meantime, I should get all the advice I can right now. With my phone still out, I open up another text history and type.

> Busy tonight?

CORA
No, what's up?

GAVIN

Just watching Lord of the Rings for the
361,722,908,639th time.

CORA

Shush, mister.

Mind if we hang? Could use some advice.

CORA

Come over when you're done with work. I'll
cook.

GAVIN

Eat meat ahead of time, if that's your thing.

I laugh out loud, and it feels good to smile a moment.
Although my time with Cora isn't as frequent as it once was, I
still remember her no-meat diet.

Not worried about it. I'll be there a little
after 5.

CORA

See you.

GAVIN

It's your stomach. Later, bro.

I stuff my phone back in my coveralls and amble out of
the office. Work is the last thing I want to do, but I need to
pass the time with distractions. Later, I will ask Cora and
Gavin the hundreds of questions brewing in my head. Hopefully, they will have answers.

~

After going home to let Spartan out and feed him early, I ride over to Cora and Gavin's house. At times, I still find it odd calling it *their* place.

Not a full year has passed since Gavin returned to Florida, and yet it feels as if several years have flown by. So much has happened since last April. Most of the monumental moments have occurred in the last two and a half months. In my eyes, anyway. Between Cora and Gavin getting married and me falling for Autumn and Clementine, life has been a whirlwind. And now with the custody case, seems I can't catch my breath.

I pull onto the paved driveway and park my bike behind Cora's car. Kicking the stand out, I rise off the bike and remove my helmet. For a beat, I stare at the small patio area just outside the back door. Most of the decor is small pieces Cora had before Gavin returned, but every now and then I spot new touches. Pieces that reflect Gavin's taste or their combined taste. As similar as the two of them are, I notice the small nuances after knowing my best friend for a decade.

If I get lucky, one day I will see pieces of Autumn in my life.

Taking a deep breath, I head for the back door. Although my family would be more than happy to give me advice with what's happening, my friends are what I need. People who are family, but in a different light. That have no bias because they know my childhood or want to soothe my wounds. Cora and Gavin may not have experienced the same hiccup in their relationship, but they have had hardships.

Just as I lift my hand to knock, the door swings open and a smiling Cora stands on the other side. "Hey." Without warning, she lunges toward me, grabs my hand, and hauls me forward. Her slender arms wrap around me and squeeze with unimaginable strength.

I welcome the embrace and return it. A year ago, Cora's hugs held different meaning. They once held the hope of something beyond friendship. Now, hugging Cora is like hugging Jasmine or Jillian. Full of warmth and tenderness and love, but familial.

"Hey," I say as I peel my arms away.

Gavin steps past Cora and pulls me in for a half hug and shoulder slap. "Hey, man. Come in."

My relationship with Gavin shifted quicker than imaginable. Since our conversation at Dave and Buster's, after he packed up his life in California, Gavin and I developed a slow but great friendship. Until I met Autumn, I remained envious of him. Now, I envy the bond he shares with Cora. A bond I believe lies buried deep between me and Autumn too.

The back door closes and I step farther into the house, Cora and Gavin following in my wake. As I make it past the short hall, hints of basil, garlic, tomato, and an unfamiliar savory scent flit through the air. After I set my helmet in the living room, I join Cora and Gavin near the kitchen on one of the barstools. Cora stands at the counter, slicing up a baguette. I follow her hands as she saws the serrated knife across the crusty bread. Watch as she mixes olive oil, herbs, garlic, and parmesan.

"Want a beer?"

I snap out of my daze and turn toward Gavin. "Yeah, thanks."

He twists the cap off and hands me the brown bottle before resuming his seat beside me. "So, what's going on, man?"

I lift the bottle to my lips and sip the local brew, the flavor more bitter than I'm used to. Setting the bottle down, I pick at the corner of the label. "Did you know Autumn has a daughter?"

Gavin says "no" at the same time Cora says "yes." Well, at least I am not spilling too much if Cora knows. I assume Autumn sharing with Cora would mean it is safe for Gavin to know.

"I haven't met her," Cora states. "But Autumn has mentioned her when we hung out—just her and me."

After another sip, I take a few breaths. "Her name is Clementine, and she is the cutest little girl."

Across the counter, a soft smile perks up Cora's lips. "What a sweet name."

"Yeah," I mutter as I continue to pick at the label. "I hope you meet her soon. You'll both love her."

"Would be great. Is Clementine the reason you need advice?" Gavin asks before sipping his own beer.

I nod. "Not the only reason." Peering up from my bottle, I glance between my friends. "Also regarding Clementine's estranged birth father's return."

Cora's eyes widen at the same time Gavin's jaw drops. *My thoughts exactly*. The timer on the range buzzes and we all jump.

After Cora extracts a hefty pan of lasagna from the oven, she sets it on trivets to cool before returning to the counter. "Are they back together?" Cora asks, hesitant to hear the answer.

"No," I answer with obvious relief. "He jumped ship while Autumn was still pregnant. Now, more than seven years later, out of nowhere, he has filed for sole custody of Clementine."

"Are you serious?" Gavin stares at me with fire in his

eyes. The same fire that roars in my veins every time I mull over this whole scenario. "Why the hell would anyone even give his case merit? He hasn't been around."

"Right there with you, man. But Autumn isn't looking at it the same way. She believes his family's money will hold enough ground to take Clementine away from her. So, she's trying to be the supreme model parent. Which includes spending no time with me."

Without a word, Cora rounds the bar top, sidles up next to me, and hugs me. "So sorry, Jonas." She drops her arms and steps back. "How can we help?"

This is my dilemma. I don't know how anyone can help. Autumn is so stuck on thinking Leo will use our relationship as a weapon. I have yet to figure out how. So what if Autumn is in a relationship with someone other than the father of her child. This is not an abnormal occurrence in the world. If I were a piece of shit, then sure, it would make sense for Autumn to be concerned. But I care for my girls like no one else. They mean everything to me.

"Autumn is convinced the more I am in the picture while the case is open, the likelihood of her losing Clementine is greater. But I don't understand why. She needs someone to literally write it out that her ex has no chance of winning. And I don't know where to go from here. Dad tells me to be patient, but I'm losing it."

Cora shuffles back into the kitchen and starts portioning out lasagna for the three of us. "Do you want me to reach out to her? See if I can get a girls' day with her? Maybe she will explain her fears to me differently."

"Give it a try. Not sure she'll spend time away from Clementine, though. You may only get her on the phone."

Cora carries the plates to the dining table while Gavin

brings the bread and dipping oil. I slide off my stool and join them at the table.

"I'll send her a text first. Check in. Haven't seen her since bowling, so it wouldn't seem odd for me to ask for updates. I won't mention our conversation."

I nod. "Thanks. Appreciate it."

Scooping a portion of lasagna onto my fork, I let it cool a moment before tasting it. The hot cheese melts over my tongue as I bite into something resembling meat. My brows pinch together as the flavors hit my taste buds.

"What do you think of the lasagna?" Cora poses the question with obvious curiosity.

After I swallow the bite and take a sip of my beer, I answer, "Thought you didn't eat meat?" Across from me, Gavin snickers.

"I don't."

I point my fork at the heaping square of layered pasta on my plate. "Uh, this states otherwise. Not sure if Gavin snuck it in, but there's meat in this." Now, Cora giggles and confuses the hell out of me.

"Nope. No meat. In fact, this lasagna is one-hundred-percent vegan. You like it, don't you?"

I startle with a slight shake of my head. "No denying it, but you better tell me what I'm eating before you expect me to eat more."

Gavin full belly laughs before shoveling another forkful in his mouth. Traitor. Not that I expect anything else. He loves Cora enough to eat whatever she cooks.

"Pasta, red sauce, plant-based meat, and cheese." She says the ingredients as if everyone eats them.

"And how exactly do plants equal meat or cheese?"

For the next half hour, Cora goes into a long drawn-out

explanation of plant-based substitutes. Although it's not something I see myself switching to, I don't dismiss it either. If I would have eaten this lasagna anywhere else, I'd have guessed it was traditionally made.

The rest of our night is filled with light conversation and talks about upcoming projects Cora and Gavin have. And when I leave their house after watching something other than *Lord of the Rings*, I feel a little lighter. My relationship with Autumn may not be better, but sharing with my friends has helped. Plus, Cora reaching out to Autumn is perfect. Although Autumn has Penny, sometimes talking with someone outside of the situation makes a difference.

I hope it does. Hope it helps Autumn look at the case and us in a different light. That being with me won't hinder her chances. Hell, it might help.

But most of all, because I need her, maybe more than she needs me.

nine

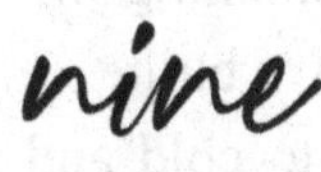

AUTUMN

Swiping the dampness from my cheeks, I slip out of bed and tiptoe out of the room. I have another thirty minutes before Clementine has to be up. I intend to use the time to shower away the tears staining my cheeks.

Steam billows throughout the bathroom as I step under the hot spray. Under the stream, I cry for the umpteenth time since this nightmare began. I cry for my daughter—who has been affected in this whole scheme, although she still has no idea what is happening. I cry for the man who cares more for me than anyone, who cares for my daughter as his own, and who I have sidelined.

Damn, I miss Jonas.

I miss the way he presses me against his chest and holds me close to his heart. Miss the warmth of his lips on mine, kissing me breathless and waking up my soul. Miss the fire in his magnificent eyes and the inferno he creates when we are skin to skin. But most of all, I miss having him beside me. His strength and heart and smile.

I am sick and tired of crying. Sick and tired of being punished for someone else's choice. Why the hell am I the one who suffers in all this? Why do Clementine and Jonas have to suffer? None of us have done anything wrong. I may be far from perfect, but I am a good person. Do good things. Make good choices.

The tears stop flowing as I rinse the suds from my skin. Before the bubbles swirl down the drain, anger replaces the tears. Anger for a man who has no right to disrupt my life. To insert himself after abandoning me and his unborn daughter. Uprooting the life we have built.

I crank the shower to cold and allow the frigid water to diminish the fire boiling beneath my skin. Because I need to remain as levelheaded as possible around Clementine. Even if just for show. Once I cool down to a simmer, I shut off the water and towel dry. Wrapping the towel around my torso, I tiptoe back into the bedroom.

As I tug a shirt over my head, the alarm clock buzzes on the bedside table. Clementine groans, rolls over, and slides under the comforter, as if hiding will make the need to get up vanish. I laugh under my breath as I turn off the alarm.

"Time to wake up, pumpkin," I singsong. "Gotta get ready for school." I rub the comforter where her back is and she wiggles.

"I don't want to get up."

"Neither did I, but we both have things to do today."

"Why can't I stay home from school today?" Clementine never stays home from school unless she feels sick, which is next to never.

"Because you can't stay home unless you're sick. Those are the rules," I remind her.

Beneath the comforter, Clementine starts coughing. "I don't feel so good, Mama," she croaks. *Nice try, kiddo.* I whip the comforter off of her and she yelps. Then, I tickle her. "Stop." Giggle. "Please, Mama. Stop." Snort laugh.

I pause the tickle fest. "Are you going to get up and get ready?"

Who knew a seven-year-old could scowl? Not me. But Clementine scowls for two beats before replacing it with another forced cough. "But I said I don't feel good."

"And you didn't mention not feeling well until I told you it was the only reason to miss school. Plus, you don't have a fever and you wouldn't be laughing if you were sick, even if I tickle you."

In the same fashion as she has for the last couple of weeks, Clementine jerks upright and storms out of the bed. She heads straight for the bathroom without a word. At least I convinced her early on to not slam the doors with Penny sleeping. My daughter may be upset, but she isn't heartless.

Once dressed, she meets me at the table to eat breakfast. I whipped up some quick cheesy eggs and toast. She sits down and eats. After a few bites, she peers up at me.

"When can I see Sparty again? He misses me."

I love how each time Clementine brings up Spartan, she mentions how he misses her and not vice versa. No doubt it holds true, but Clementine misses him more than she cares to admit. And I hate that I have separated them this long.

Yesterday, out of the blue, Cora texted me. When my phone dinged, I half expected it to be Jonas. Especially after he left another note on my car sometime between Tuesday night and yesterday morning. The note simple—*I miss you*. And I have a sneaking suspicion Cora's sudden interest in talking was sparked by Jonas. Either way, I was happy to talk with her. Penny is supportive, but she has too much inside information to give me an outsider's perspective. Which Cora did with perfection.

Our texts weren't anything spectacular, but she started it off with "heard you might need someone to talk with." An hour later and I had spilled my fears to her. In return, she told me I should share the same with Jonas if I hadn't already. Not until the end of our texts did she mention Jonas, and even then it was just that I should talk to him. Cora opted to play the neutral party to help steer us back toward each other.

"I bet he does, pumpkin. After my appointment today, I might stop by Jonas's work to talk with him." Clementine's face lights up. "But no promises." Her face falls again.

For a few minutes, we remain quiet. Clementine scrapes the fork tines across her plate between bites. After she finishes her breakfast, I take our plates to the sink and wash them. While she stomps around the apartment to grab her belongings, I ponder explaining to her why we haven't been to see Jonas and Spartan as often. She may be seven, and her little mind might not grasp all the ins and outs, but she has every right to know why everything has changed so drastically in such a short period of time.

Glancing at the clock on the microwave, I note we don't have to leave the house for another fifteen minutes. I walk into the living room and sit on the couch. Clementine should be out here in a moment with her backpack. And like clockwork, she stomps out and sits to my right.

"Pumpkin, I want to talk to you before we leave. About why we haven't seen Jonas or Spartan as much."

She peeks up with worry lines drawn across her face. "Is Sparty okay?"

"Yeah, pumpkin. He's okay." The lines on her face smooth

out as she exhales. "You remember the day we came home from the beach park with Jonas and there was a man outside?"

She looks up and to the left while bunching her lips. After a moment, she nods. "Kind of."

I take a deep breath and prepare for the most adult conversation with my seven-year-old. "The man who was outside when we came home that day, he is your father." I don't use the term dad because I have always seen a dad as someone who participates and spends time with their children.

"Mama, I don't understand."

"Before you were in my tummy, I met that man. Back then, he was nice. And we spent time together like I have with Jonas now. And after we dated a while, he became my boyfriend. When grown-up people date for long periods of time, they do certain grown-up things to show each other how much they care."

"Like what?" Clementine interjects.

Kind of walked myself into a corner with this one. "Things we will discuss when you're closer to being a grown-up. Anyway, after we showed each other how much we cared, you started to grow in my belly. But your father didn't want to be a daddy, so he stopped being my boyfriend and didn't talk to me anymore."

"He didn't love you?"

My poor sweet girl. Voice so soft and frail. If I tell her he no longer loved me, then she will assume it was her fault.

"Pumpkin, I'm not sure if either one of us really loved each other. We liked each other a whole lot, enough to make a beautiful little girl." I bop her nose. "But there are just some people in the world who don't want to have children, and that's okay. There are still plenty of other people who do."

The skin between her brows bunches. "So how come he

was here that day?"

Here is the part I dread telling her, but I need to be open and honest with my little girl. "He said he wants to be your daddy." The confusion still sits on her face as she stares at me with unfocused eyes. "And he wants you to live with him and not me."

At this, Clementine jumps up from the couch and balls her little hands into fists. "He's not my daddy," she screams. "I won't let him be. I hate him." She snatches her backpack and storms to the front door, cutting our conversation off.

Penny comes out of her room, wiping her eyes. "Everything okay?"

"Peachy," I deadpan. "Tell you later." She waves and goes back into her room.

I grab my purse and head for the door. A few feet from Clementine, she unlocks the door and stomps out. Nothing like starting the day with a moody seven-going-on-seventeen-year-old. Can't wait to see her temperament when she actually gets closer to her teens.

The drive to her school lacks conversation, but at least she sings and bops to the music while staring out the window. As soon as we get to the drop-off point in the school car line, she hooks her backpack over her shoulders, grumbles out an *I love you*, and exits the car. I stare after her as she steps on campus and smiles at some of her friends. Sighing, relief fills me that she can at least smile with her friends.

Leaving the school, I steer the car in the direction of the attorney's office. Theresa said she had some updates she wants to discuss, plus a document I need to sign. After dealing with morning traffic for forty minutes, I park in front of Theresa's office. Today, the building isn't as intimidating as on my first visit.

I head inside, wait a few minutes, then am escorted back to the conference room. Over the next hour, Theresa explains how Leo holds no weight in the case. Since he intentionally left before Clementine was born, has never spent time with her or attempted to, and has never contributed to her well-being, the judge will side with us without question. Theresa assures me no amount of money will sway a decision in his favor. There is no justification or evidence to back up such a ruling.

The document I sign is for the court hearing toward the end of the month. *Sooner than expected, thank god.* I sign on the line and Theresa steps out of the room to make me a copy. During the minute of her absence, I go back and forth on an idea I have toyed with. She enters the conference room and I decide to heck with it.

"As I stated at our first meeting, I have no intention of giving up custody of Clementine." Theresa nods. "But I am okay with her meeting Leo's family, if they would like that. Supervised, of course. She would be so scared if I wasn't there."

Theresa smiles. "A kind gesture. Not many would be so nice. Not after everything you've had to deal with on your own."

"I like to offer second chances. We all make mistakes. If Leo's family would like to meet her, it's only fair of me to allow it."

"I will make note of it in your file, but we won't be mentioning this until the hearing. If we bring it up now, they may push for more."

"Sounds good. Thank you for everything you've done so far. Don't know where I'd be without you."

She offers another smile. "I'm here to help you win and

relieve you of legal stresses. In the meantime, don't let this wear you down. Enjoy your life. You're an excellent mother and don't deserve any undue strain."

At this, I question my being with Jonas. Now is the perfect time to ask the proper person. "Theresa, I have a personal-ish question."

"Shoot."

"Does it look bad for the case if I am in a relationship with someone other than Clementine's father?"

Theresa cocks her head and studies me a moment. "Why would you think that?"

At this point, I don't know. "Honestly, I wasn't sure how the court would perceive it. Leo's family has money and can no doubt provide for Clementine. I didn't know if me being in a relationship would make me vulnerable. An easy target. If they could say my time is divided and not solely focused on Clementine."

Theresa scoots the paperwork aside, laces her fingers, and sets her hands on the table as she leans in. "Autumn, you are allowed to be in relationships. Long term or short, doesn't matter. You are allowed to continue living. Allowed to be happy, as is your daughter. I encourage you to be in a relationship. Lean on someone. Share the burden of this situation. Don't take it on alone if you have others willing to stand by your side."

Several people tried to tell me the exact thing Theresa said, but an unsettled part of me needed to hear it from her. Someone who knows the outcomes of cases like mine with different variables. In her twenty-plus years of practicing, she has surely seen every possible case out there. Has fought for women with similar circumstances.

"Thank you. You have no idea how much I needed to hear that. Especially from you."

We stand and she walks me out. "Don't worry about a thing. Do what is best for you and your daughter. If that includes you being in a relationship, then you do it."

I give her a quick hug and am a bit surprised when she returns the gesture. Theresa is more than my attorney; she's a friend too. And more than anything, I am grateful to have her fighting my case.

Leaving her office, I drive down the road with a smile on my face. Minus Clementine's outburst this morning, it has been a great day. Better than the previous twelve. And I hope it continues to get better.

I make a quick stop at the sub shop Jonas and I ate at during one of his lunch breaks. After I study the menu, I order us both sandwiches. Even if I didn't remember the correct sub, he won't care. Once the food is ready, I hop back in the car and drive up the street.

As I pull in the lot of Thompson's Garage, my pulse whooshes behind my ears. My breathing morphs from a walk to a sprint. With the car in park, I close my eyes a beat and work to settle my nervous body.

Our texts have been so abrupt—my fault, if I am honest. And he was so upset when he left my apartment a couple weeks back. Will he forgive me for my irrational fears? Will he take me back with open arms?

God, I hope so.

I turn the key until the engine quiets and look over at the bays, spotting Jonas right away. His gaze locked in my direction. I swallow hard, grab the food bag, and exit the car.

Here goes nothing.

JONAS

A familiar rumble echoes across the lot. The rumble any mechanic would automatically recognize as a classic car. When cars are created different ways, with different components and materials, they just sound *different*. Most newer cars are quieter—unless they have major issues or added upgrades. But classics have this low purr-like roar.

I roll out from under the pickup I work on and scan the lot. Sure enough, a black Bel Air I know all too well is parking near the office.

Rising off of the creeper, I stand, pull the red rag from my coveralls, and wipe my hands. I stare through the windshield at Autumn as she locks eyes with me. Feels as if I haven't seen her in years.

She breaks eye contact when she fetches something on the passenger seat and gets out of the car. Without a side-glance, I toss the ratchet in the general direction of the toolbox. When a loud clang rattles, I give myself a mental high five.

Autumn walks my direction—cute as fuck in a dress that makes concentrating impossible. The navy material V's at her bust, but doesn't dip too low. It hugs all her curves and stops at her knees. Large white buttons start to curve from her left hip to the base of the fabric at her midline. White accents the base of each sleeve, the neckline, and the waist. And like a cherry on a sundae, two houndstooth bows rest near her shoulders.

Not sure if this is her dressy look—since she had an appointment with her attorney—but I love it.

I meet her halfway. "Hey, scarlet," I whisper. "Happy to see you."

She smiles and my heart hiccups. "Brought us food." She swings a bag in the air.

I glance back at Dad and he tips his head toward the office. "Let's go inside." She nods and I direct us to a more private place to talk.

Once we reach the office, I strip out of my coveralls. "Jonas, what…" Before she gets another word out, I wrap my arms around her and breathe her in. She drops her purse and the bags of food to the ground and winds her arms around me, squeezing me as if I may disappear any minute.

We stand like this—unmoving, not a word spoken—for minutes. Autumn presses her ear to my chest and listens to my heartbeat. With one hand around her waist, I stroke the length of her hair with the other. I close my eyes and rest my cheek on the crown of her head. Breathe slow and steady as I reacquaint myself with her perfume, the feel of being in her arms, her warmth. Everything about this moment feels like returning home after years apart. No matter what, there is no way in hell we are spending so much time apart again. I may have said as much last time, but I don't care. She means too much.

"God, I've missed you," I whisper.

Her arms squeeze me tighter as she fists the back of my shirt. "Me, too. So much."

I lean away and she tips her head back, her cognac irises swirl as she soaks me in. Without hesitation, I lower my lips to hers. As soon as our lips meet, I am home again. Every tear, every spit of anger, every hair pulling moment since I last saw her disappears. Wiped away with the press of her lips.

The kiss isn't lusty or intense but expresses every emotion we experienced in our time apart. Deprivation. Anticipation. Hope. Love. It spins in the air, surrounds us, like a gyroscope.

Reluctantly, I break the kiss and press my forehead to hers. "Can we please not torture ourselves like this again?"

Autumn lays her palm on my cheek and strokes her thumb over my stubble. "No more torture. Promise."

I exhale and pull back to look in her eyes. "Thank fuck." I kiss the tip of her nose. "Let's sit down so we can talk and eat."

After picking the food bag up from the floor, I guide us over to the couch. Rummaging through the bag, I note she went to the sub shop I took her to months ago. And she ordered the exact same sandwich I got that day. Either she has a fantastic memory or she made the perfect wild guess. Either way, I smile at the notion.

We unwrap the brown paper from our subs and dig in. After each of us has a few bites, Autumn sets hers down, wipes the hint of mayo off her lips, and faces me.

"I'm sorry for how things have been between us since all this chaos started. It wasn't fair of me to not include you. Thought I was doing right by Clementine."

I reach for her hand and hold it between mine. "You do not need to apologize for loving your daughter. For wanting the best for her. And with her father showing up, neither of us knew what the best looked like."

She nods. "True. But I have a better grasp now." Autumn

tucks her lips between her teeth as her jaw wobbles. "Jonas, it has been terrifying. Not knowing what will happen from one minute to the next." Her eyes glaze over. "I had it drilled in my head that if I wasn't the picture-perfect parent—and who knows what that looks like—I would lose Clementine. And although I have always been there for her, done everything to provide for her, I feared me being with a man other than her father would look bad in the court's eyes."

I give her a minute to catch her breath before speaking. "Not to come across in a derogatory way, but why would you think they'd look down on you for being with another man?"

Autumn sighs as her head slumps an inch forward. "I don't want to get into it too much because it rehashes bad memories, but my parents would be the reason." She closes her eyes a moment and swallows. When she opens them, I see the tears ready to spill. "Long story short, my parents don't believe a woman should be with any other man except the father of her children. Most people call my parents extreme. I didn't know any different until my late teens. In their eyes, when I told them I was pregnant, I should have married Leo. Of course, I got lectured several hours a day and handprints on my cheeks for having premarital sex. Until I left."

Just wow.

Yes, I have heard of people behaving like this. Only seeing the world as one way. Expecting or assuming every man and woman lived their life in this way. But I have never personally known anyone with such perceptions. I haven't met Autumn's parents, but if I ever do—after what she just said—I don't imagine the meeting will be pleasant.

"I don't know what to say. Sorry doesn't seem appropriate."

"It's okay. You don't need to say anything. I haven't seen

or spoken to them in almost eight years. But every now and again, small tidbits of how they raised me creep in and fill me with doubt or fear. Make me wonder if I made the right choice when I left their house. Eventually, I remind myself why I chose to leave and the questions and uncertainty fade. But when Leo made an appearance, it was the first time since leaving I let all their hurtful words seep back in. Let them overrule every rational thought. And I don't want it to happen again."

I want to assure her it won't happen again. Not with me supporting her. But now is not the time to make such proclamations. Not when the case with Leo still looms over her like an angry thunderstorm.

"You know I'm here for you, right?" Autumn nods. "Good. Nothing will change that. You and Clementine are my world. My girls." A delicate smile tugs at the corners of my mouth. "Just don't shut me out again. Please."

I have never been the type of man to beg or grovel, but I will do whatever it takes to keep Autumn and Clementine close. Being without them for the last couple of weeks has been torture. The sleepless nights and lack of laughter and joy. My purpose had been stolen. Robbed by someone who holds no significance in any of our lives.

Autumn shakes her head. "I won't. It's been hard dealing with all this Leo stuff. When I sat down and really thought it over, dealing with it all without you to support me is harder."

I take the sandwich in my lap and set it on the table, followed by Autumn's sandwich. As soon as they are out of the way, I scoop her into my lap and just hold her. Hold her until my arms grow tired. Hold her until she melts into me and I melt into her. For as long as I live, I will never have my fill of this woman. Of the love she gives.

A soft knock raps at the door. "Come in," I grumble against Autumn's neck, refusing to let her go.

"Sorry to interrupt. We just had a few more clients pull up," Dad informs.

He won't come right out and say he needs my help. But he needs my help. "I'll be out in a minute." Without another word, Dad exits and closes the door.

I groan against Autumn before kissing the spot where her shoulder and neck meet. "Why isn't the workday over yet?" I grumble.

Light laughter shakes Autumn's frame and I lean away from her. She lifts her hands to frame my face and leans in. Her lips close enough to kiss. "Soon." Eyes open, she closes the space between our mouths and presses our lips together.

Her intoxicating eyes locked on mine while we kiss makes me dizzy. In the best way.

"Come over tonight. Have dinner at the house. You and Clementine. Spartan has been a mess without his new favorite person."

Autumn laughs. "Clementine keeps telling me Spartan misses her, and not the other way around. Although I know she misses both of you. And yes, we'll come over tonight."

I grab Autumn's hips and slowly shift to stand, planting her on her feet. Then I kiss the hell out of her. Kiss her like oxygen feeding the flame. Kiss her to make up for all the kisses we have missed ever since this fiasco began. And as much as I don't want to stop kissing her, I do. Because I am at work and she probably needs to go to work too.

"See you tonight, scarlet." I kiss the tip of her nose. "Let me walk you to your car."

We wrap up the rest of our uneaten sandwiches, put mine in the fridge and hers in the bag. Then I walk her out. On the way to her car, I catch Dad smiling as he fakes busywork. Somehow, he knew everything would work out. I had doubts, probably because my emotional scale went from jovial to freaking out in point-five seconds.

Everything is better now. I have my girls back. In my arms. And no one will take them away again. No one.

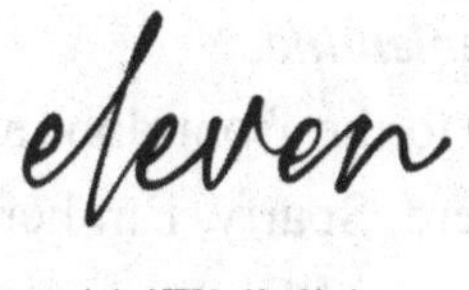

eleven

AUTUMN

All in all, today has been better than any day in the last few weeks.

When I picked Clementine up from school, her pouty face dwindled slightly when I told her we were going to Jonas's house tonight. She wouldn't show or admit it, but this news made her day better. Knowing she would see Spartan later, that she would get to cuddle with her favorite furry friend, made a smile tug at the corners of her mouth.

The first question out of her mouth was why we couldn't see them before, but can now. I didn't have a short answer for her, so I just told her I needed my friend—meaning Theresa—to assure me everything would be okay. For the first time ever, Clementine rolled her eyes.

And I gave her a one-time pass.

On the drive to Jonas's, I work to wipe away the discontent Clementine has felt through all this. "Blinding Lights" by The Weeknd comes on the radio and I crank up the volume.

Usually, she sings at the top of her lungs and dances in her seat when the song plays. At one point, she tried to convince me to make a TikTok video with her to this song. Didn't happen, of course. I hope to get a little bit of her typical energy going. And she doesn't disappoint. Clementine doesn't belt the lyrics out like usual, but she sings loud enough for me to hear it and dances in her seat slightly.

A small win that I gladly take.

Before long, I park behind Jonas's Jeep. The second we exit the car, Spartan starts yipping from inside the house. *He really has missed Clementine.*

Clementine bolts to the front door as fast as her short legs will take her. "I'm here, Sparty. I'm here." Just as she reaches the door, it flies open and Spartan attacks her with slobbery dog kisses. And my little girl giggles and giggles. The most perfect sound in the world. A sound I missed these last weeks.

When I reach the door, Jonas looks up from the Spartan-Clementine hugfest and smiles. "Hey, scarlet." He takes my hand and tugs me into his chest, hugging me as if we hadn't seen each other earlier. And I welcome every second of it. "Come on, let's go inside."

We head inside and go separate ways—Clementine and Spartan to the couch while Jonas and I go to the kitchen. The simple routine something I more than missed. While Clementine whispers to Spartan on the couch, catching him up on all the stories he hasn't heard over the last two weeks, Jonas and I cook dinner.

"What's on the menu tonight?"

A smile kicks up Jonas's lips. "Thought I'd keep it easy tonight. Pizza."

Across the open floor plan, Clementine hoots. "Yay for pizza!"

"Dad told me about a new take-and-bake place that opened. We'll see how it is. Clementine..." Jonas calls across the room to her and she perks up. "I got you a four cheese pizza. Hope that's okay."

"She loves all cheese," I mention.

Clementine scowls at me a second before looking at Jonas and smiling. "Cheeses is my favorite. Thank you, Mr. Jonas."

"You're welcome, cutie." After Clementine focuses her attention on Spartan again, Jonas turns to me. "What just happened there?"

I purse my lips. "Caught that, did you?"

"Kind of hard not to."

"She's been upset with me for days." Understatement of the decade. Upset doesn't begin to cover how Clementine has acted. I don't blame her, but it also means she has become very much attached to Spartan and Jonas. In some respects, I love the idea of her connecting so easily with them. But I fear the worst if something bad happens. "Today hasn't been as bad since I told her we were coming over."

"Sorry you've had a teenage seven-year-old on your hands." He leans against the counter and pulls me to stand between his legs. "Hopefully the dramatics fade soon, now that we'll see each other more."

"Fingers crossed."

The timer buzzes and Jonas checks the pizzas. As soon as they are out of the oven, the air fills with the delicious scents of cheese, bread, and herbs. After they cool a moment, Jonas cuts the pizzas and sets them on the breakfast bar.

"Time to eat, pumpkin."

Clementine huffs, walks from the couch to the breakfast bar, then pulls out the stool on the far end. She doesn't say a word before she swaps the pizzas—hers and Jonas's. In the past, Clementine sat between us. But she is still upset, and her payback is to not sit next to or acknowledge me unless absolutely necessary.

After Jonas feeds Spartan, we all sit down to eat. Dinner is quieter than any previous time. Part of me worries my former decisions have screwed up my relationship with Jonas. As if he hears my wayward thoughts, he nudges me with his elbow. I peek up from my pizza and meet his gaze. He shakes his head.

"Your thoughts practically scream from your head. Stop. It'll be okay."

"Maybe we should both talk with her after dinner. Since I seem to be the enemy, maybe she'll listen to you."

He nods. "Good idea. Better to nip this in the bud now."

I swoon a little at how effortless it is for Jonas to want to speak with Clementine. How he assumes a fatherly role with her without overstepping. How he wants the best for her—for us—and has no issue doing whatever it takes to make it happen.

We finish eating our pizza in amicable silence. When Clementine finishes, she hops down and runs back to the couch. After Jonas and I clean up our plates, we join her in the living room.

"What movie are we watching, Mr. Jonas?"

"Not sure. Before we watch a movie, your mom and I need to talk with you."

She rolls her eyes and I lose it. Although this entire ordeal has been nothing but painful, I don't deserve to be treated as the villain in all this.

"That's enough, young lady." Clementine's eyes go wide. "The eye rolling stops now. It's rude and disrespectful."

She crosses her arms over her chest. "Well, you haven't been very nice either."

I have to remind myself that Clementine is seven and not an adult. The way she reacts to situations will be different than me or Jonas. Juvenile. All her little mind knows is I took away someone she cared about, and it hurt her feelings. I take a few deep breaths and calm my nerves.

"Yes, I have made some choices that have upset us all. And I apologize."

Jonas rubs his palm over my thigh. "Clementine, your mom did what she thought was best for you at the time. She didn't know another way yet. Now she does and we can be together more. But you have to stop being mean and hurtful. Being that way will only make everyone stay upset longer, and we want to be happy." Jonas's tone is gentle and nurturing.

Clementine looks between me and Jonas, unsure. She wants to believe him. Wants to believe he wouldn't tell her lies. But after all the back and forth over the last few weeks, it's like grasping at air. My poor girl.

I did this to her. Let her get close to someone. Someone I care about deeply. Then I pulled the rug out without warning. Left her in the dark because I didn't want to burden her with topics a young child shouldn't have to worry about. But it still didn't work. I still messed up. My only hope is it won't take long for her to smile at me again.

"But what if that man takes me away?"

Twenty-four hours haven't passed since I went into a better explanation about Leo to Clementine and she is already worried about the outcome of the case. A burden I did not want for her.

I scoot closer to her and, thankfully, she doesn't back away. "You know all those appointments I've been going to, pumpkin?" Clementine nods. "Those are so I can talk to my attorney friend, Theresa. When I saw her today, she gave me good news." At this, Clementine leans an inch closer. Eager to hear more. "She said because I have been such a good mom and your birth father has never seen you, the judge will let you stay with me." Partial truth. Still have to wait until the judge puts his seal of approval on the paperwork. But Clementine doesn't need semantics. "We just have to wait for the special meeting later this month. But Theresa also said it's okay for you and me to be with Jonas and Spartan. Before, I didn't know if spending time with them would make it harder for you to stay with mommy."

All of this is a lot for Clementine to process, but I need for her to understand that I haven't done all these things to be mean. Being apart from Jonas hurt us too. Since seeing him earlier today, after agreeing to not be apart again, the ache I experienced since this whole nightmare started has lessened.

I may not *need* Jonas to get through this, but I want him by my side. Without effort, he makes me whole. Lifts me up and keeps me standing strong. Has my heart beating vigorously. My lungs flooding with oxygen. He gives me life.

After a moment, her eyes dart between me and Jonas. "Okay, Mama. Can we watch a movie now?"

"For a little bit. Not too late. We still have to get up early tomorrow." She nods.

And just like that, the conversation ends. We turn on the television and find something to watch on Netflix.

Jonas and I curl up on the couch facing each other. Neither of us says a word, we just lie there, get lost in each other's eyes, exchanging the occasional touch or kiss. Everything about the moment feels right. Meant to be.

Before long, the show ends and I decide it's time to head out. Not that I want to. More than anything, I want to stay in this house, crawl between Jonas's sheets, and never leave. But not tonight. Probably not tomorrow either. But hopefully soon.

Clementine hugs Spartan and whispers in his ear before letting go. As we walk to the door, a smidge of her sulkiness lingers. But this version is much more tolerable.

Jonas walks us out to the car. After Clementine is in her seat, I start the car and turn the heat on low. "We'll go in just a minute," I tell Clementine. She nods and turns up the radio. Good sign.

With Clementine situated, I close the door and face Jonas. He wraps his arms around me and hugs me tight. "Come over again tomorrow. Feel like we have so much time to make up for." He kisses the crown of my head.

"Yes, we do. And we'll be here."

Jonas brings his hands to either side of my face and holds me as if I am the most precious person in existence. He lowers his lips to mine and lights a fire under my skin as he kisses me senseless. No matter how much time passes, I will never get enough of Jonas. Not his hugs. Not his kisses. Nor his love. Call me addicted, I don't care. All I know is, Jonas is the only person who has completed me. Made me whole. A better version of myself. And I don't want another day without him in my life.

Jonas breaks the kiss and inches back. "Text when you get home."

"I will. See you tomorrow."

"Tomorrow…" And I swear he wants to say more. I see it linger in the air. But he bites his tongue.

Me too, I say to myself. Because I swear Jonas was just about to say he loves me.

twelve

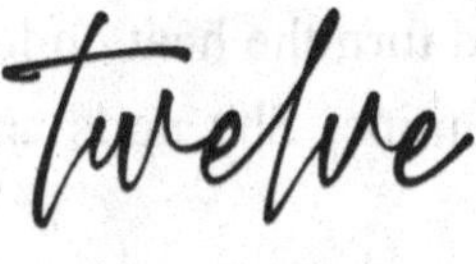

JONAS

"Not sure what happened yesterday, but it's good to see a smile on your face again," Dad says as I stroll into the office early.

For the first night in weeks, I slept without disruption. Yesterday, the stars in my and Autumn's constellation realigned. Everything wasn't back to before Leo made an appearance, but I don't imagine it will be exactly that way again. If I had to guess, I would say our relationship will be better. Stronger. More potent and appreciated.

After our time apart and the heartache we both endured, neither of us will take our relationship for granted. We will cherish it more. Every touch—big or small—will hold more meaning. Every kiss will have deeper sentiment.

"Autumn and I had a lengthy discussion after her appointment at the attorney's office. The attorney gave her the reassurance she needed to be comfortable in our relationship while dealing with her ex."

Dad sets his pen down on a stack of invoices. "Glad to hear things are on the upswing. We all enjoyed meeting her and Clementine. Hope to see them again, when the dust settles."

I brew a pot of coffee and bring the cream and sugar to the desks. "Me too. She loved meeting everyone."

Once the brewer finishes, I pour a mug for us both and sit at my desk. The stack of paperwork on my desk has gotten taller and taller with each day I didn't see or hear from Autumn. Thank goodness I am not in charge of billing, otherwise we would be too far behind. My job is to file away invoices for record keeping. No big shake. Usually finish the prior day's paperwork before the garage opens each morning. But seeing as how I haven't filed paperwork for several days, I may be spending my lunch breaks playing catch up.

I use every minute possible before the garage opens to file invoices. When the time comes to roll up the bay doors, Dad and I head out to the garage.

One after another, customers clamber in with their vehicles. Oil changes. Tire replacements. Dent removal. Windshield replacement. The day whizzes by. The entire time, a painful smile stretches across my cheeks. Nothing can ruin this day.

The back half of the day goes by just as fast as the morning. It boggles my mind how easily my mood changes the pace of the day.

About an hour before closing, I glance up from an engine I'm working on. A familiar white Mercedes drives into the lot and parks near the office.

How can my blood boil and turn to ice simultaneously? I set the ratchet down, grab the red rag from my coveralls, and wipe my hands as I step toward the car.

"Jonas," Dad calls from a bay over. "Everything alright?"

I tip my head toward the car. "Autumn's ex."

Dad sets down the wrench in his hand and steps closer in my direction. "What's he doing here?"

"Hell if I know. Probably stirring up shit. Seems to be his thing."

"You need me with you?"

I subtly shake my head. "No, but stay within earshot in case he causes problems."

Dad pats my shoulder. "I'm here."

Leo steps out of his pricey car wearing an even pricier suit. He scans the garage as if he doesn't see me twenty feet away. When his visual perusal stops on me, a smug grin lights his face. He closes the door and presses the fob, locking it as if someone might steal his precious car with him feet away.

Ten feet from him, I stop. The distance between us intentional. I know next to nothing about this man, but he has done nothing but piss me off and upset my girls. No telling what I will do if I get within a foot or two. So, for now, it is in the best interest of us all if I keep my distance.

"What can I help you with?" I continue wiping the oil and grease from my hands to keep my mind distracted.

He takes another step closer. I don't move. But if he gets much closer, I will have to divert him. Distance from him is best no matter what goes down.

"You need to back off."

I know he refers to my relationship with Autumn and Clementine, but I plan to play coy. "Don't know what you're talking about."

"Maybe you're as dumb as you look."

"Best if you think before you speak."

He cocks his head. "Like I said, you need to back off."

Less than five minutes has passed and I already want to punch him in the face. In my periphery, Dad takes a step forward but doesn't say a word. He will go to bat for me—and the girls—without hesitation. Dad may be a kind and forgiving man, but no one steps on him or his family.

"Well, *Leo*, seems as if you're confused." The skin between his brows bunches then relaxes. "Seeing as you have no claim."

This pisses him off. Within seconds, his posture shifts. He leans in closer. Takes another step forward. Balls his hands into fists at his sides. Curls his upper lip. "Hate to break the news, lowlife. I have more claim than you'll ever have. That little girl… she's mine." His voice climbs an octave. "And if I want Autumn again, she will be mine."

I grind my molars and breathe through my nose. I don't give a fuck what this prick says, he will never get Clementine and he was too chickenshit to stick around for Autumn. His loss. All my gain. And that knowledge alone fuels the beast within.

Throwing my head back, I laugh. When I meet his eyes again, he looks even more pissed. *Good. Asshole.* "You may have donated sperm to the cause, *Leo*, but you have zero claim on that little girl. You lost that privilege when you left her mom high and dry. Pregnant and alone." I point my finger at him and inch closer. "Your money won't win this war. Best if you leave and crawl back in the hole you squirmed out of."

Leo's face turns a brilliant shade of red. The color nothing to do with the sun beaming down on us. He is livid. Furious I called him out in front of other people. Made a mockery of him. He should be angry—at himself. No one but himself put him in this position. He has no one else to blame.

"Best if you watch your back, lowlife. You think money can't win this war? Who knows, maybe you're right. But it sure as hell can make things highly uncomfortable. Unpredictable. Unsafe."

Now I step forward. Resist every urge inside me that says to knock him to the ground. I have to—for Autumn and Clementine. I lean in closer and laugh when he jolts back. "You threatening me? Threatening Autumn? I'd watch what I say next, if I were you."

He takes a step back. Then another. His shitty smile dons his face. "See you around, lowlife." He unlocks his car, gets inside, and drives off a moment later.

Until he is out of sight I don't move, don't breathe. Dad steps up to me and rests his hand on my shoulder, and I inhale for the first time in too long. "Go sit in the office and cool off. I'll close everything up." I close my eyes and nod. When I open them, Dad stands inches to my left. "Everything will be fine. Just keep Autumn and Clementine safe. Keep them front of mind at all times." Dad gives my shoulder one last squeeze and heads back in the garage.

I go to the office and pace. Think over how I will explain this to Autumn. She needs to know her ex is threatening people. Threatening her and Clementine. She needs to inform her attorney. No way this is acceptable or allowable, especially with the case open.

I will tell her. Later. Not yet. Not when my synapses are firing on overdrive. After I calm down and can properly articulate what just happened. Last thing I need to do is freak Autumn out after we have just returned to a better place. Either tonight or tomorrow, once I have had time to let his words simmer and digest.

Until then, though, Autumn and Clementine shouldn't be alone. Not with him tossing threats around like beads at Mardi Gras. Leo is scrawny. But who's to say he won't pay someone else to do the dirty work. Isn't that what people with money do?

I fish my phone out of my coveralls and unlock it. Pulling up the text history with Autumn, I type out a message.

> Hey, scarlet. Almost done at the garage.
> Any dinner requests?

We may have only just decided to pick things up where they left off, but I have to ease into asking things of Autumn.

> Breakfast sounds fun. Doesn't matter,
> though.

Breakfast. Perfect segue.

> What if my girls stay over and we can have
> 2 breakfasts together.

A minute passes while I stare at the screen. She hasn't responded yet. The indicator bubble to tell me she's typing hasn't popped up. Was it too quick for me to jump on the "stay the night" train again? Things have been off, but I don't think she has reservations about staying. Maybe the doubt her parents cause crept back in. The last thing I want is for her to slow things down again.

Before she responds, I send another message.

> No pressure. I'd just love to have my girls
> stay over. Think about it. I'll see you in a
> little while.

And with that, I leave the decision up to her. Until she answers, though, I am a live wire. Thank god, I have plenty of stuff to preoccupy my time between now and when Autumn and Clementine arrive at the house. Grocery shopping. Spartan. Dinner/breakfast.

Dad steps into the office and tells me everything is taken care of. After we strip out of our coveralls, we lock up and exit through the back. He gives me a hug and pat on the back. "Just stay levelheaded. It will all work out." I nod. "And if you need me, you better call."

"Thanks, Dad."

"Those girls are family. And Thompson's protect their own."

I love how easily Autumn and Clementine have won the hearts of my family. Even through all the craziness, Dad recognizes what I feel. That the love I have for them won't fade. And that I intend to keep Autumn and Clementine for the long haul.

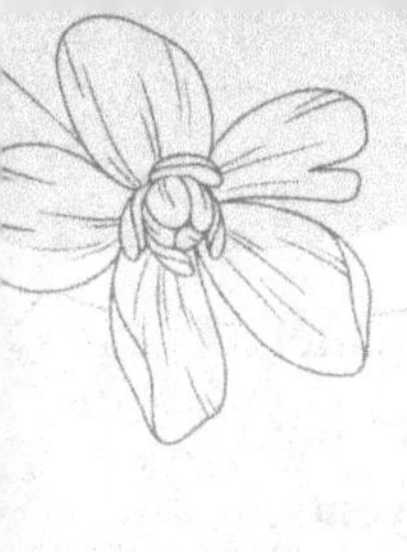

thirteen

AUTUMN

Penny strolls into my booth and plops down on my chair. "What's up with you? Look like someone just shredded your favorite dress."

In all the madness, I have been a bad friend and roommate to Penny. Between my grumpy antics and Clementine's tantrums, we have to be driving her insane. If so, she hides it well.

"Jonas just asked me and Clementine to stay the night."

Her brows shoot up as she continues to smack her gum. "So, what's the big deal? You stayed over before."

True, but that was before Leo waltzed back in and trampled over my life. "Things have been off since Leo showed up. Do you think it's too soon? Again."

Penny blows a bubble and pops it. "No. You guys have it bad for each other. Plus, your attorney said to do you. Don't let *him* dictate your life, Auti. That isn't fair to you, Clementine or Jonas."

I huff, tossing the wad of paper towels in my hand in the trash bin. Nothing about Leo returning has been fair. From the second I saw him standing next to my car, I knew nothing good would come from his sudden appearance. And no matter how I try to let it go, I continue to question why he materialized out of thin air. After no communication in years, why now?

None of it makes sense. Every sleepless night, my mind orchestrates countless possibilities as to why he wants custody of Clementine. Publicity, perhaps? But giving the appearance of a family man to the media, claiming a little girl as yours when no one has seen her previously, would pose more questions and issues than Leo probably wants. So, why?

"It isn't fair. But I just don't get it, Penny. I don't understand his motivation."

She jumps off my chair and skips around it to stand where I see her better. "Auti, maybe you aren't meant to understand. Not yet. But have patience. You have a kick-ass attorney who will dig. And if she doesn't find anything before the hearing, maybe the judge can pull out his reasoning. You have a right to know, but quit letting the whys and what-ifs rule your life. Don't give him your power."

I shift ink bottles around on the shelf in my station. Organizing the bottles then rearranging them. Anything to keep me busy while I mull over Penny's advice. She stares at me while I stall, but I don't rush my reaction or answer.

Every time the topic of Leo and the custody case comes up, it always cycles back to the same result. Everyone telling me to let the attorney do her job and for me and Clementine to go about our lives. God, am I trying. Some things are easier said than done.

But I don't want to regret missing out on life. Of being happy, of Clementine being happy. Regret will eat at my joy more than Leo.

"Guess you're right."

"Damn straight I am. And as far as staying over at Jonas's house, I say do it. You never know what will happen tomorrow, Auti. Live today, and don't have regrets tomorrow."

I throw my arms around Penny, hugging her close and squishing her more than normal. But she gives as good as she gets and has me tapping out of the hug first.

"Love you, Pen."

"Love you, too." Penny slaps my ass and winks. "Now finish cleaning up and get out of here."

Once I finish wiping my booth down and everything is back in place, I snatch my purse and say bye to the guys. Before leaving, I give Penny one last hug. "Thanks again. See you tomorrow."

When I release the hug, she narrows her eyes before tossing out another wink. "Have a good night," she singsongs.

~

"You ready to go, pumpkin?"

Clementine comes barreling out of the bedroom with a tote bag hooked over her shoulder. Shortly after I got home, and Iliana left, I told Clementine we would stay at Jonas's house tonight. Not a second after the words left my lips, she bolted from one corner of the apartment to the next. When I started packing an overnight bag for us, she asked if she could pack her own.

Mama, I'm a big girl. I want my own bag.

How could I deny her sunshiny smile? Too much time had passed since I last saw that smile. And the fact I stole that from her stabbed me center chest.

"Yep." She pats the overstuffed bag. "Got all the goods."

"What on earth did you put in there? Looks like it weighs more than you."

She purses her lips and narrows her eyes. "My clothes, some movies, and some stuff I want to show Sparty."

I laugh under my breath. Spartan has become her brother, their bond unrivaled. "Okay. If you have everything, let's go. Jonas is making breakfast for dinner."

Clementine's eyes go wide and she scurries for the door. "Come on, Mama. Let's go."

As soon as Clementine learns the dinner menu, she rushes us. Has me shoving our bags in the back and all but snaps her fingers for me to start the car. Thankfully, it's a quick ride to Jonas's house. Music and singing pass the time faster.

I park in Jonas's driveway and cut the engine. Clementine hauls her bag from the back and bolts for the front door. I dash to keep up with her sprint. Before either of us can knock, Jonas opens the door with a wide grin splitting his cheeks. Spartan tackles Clementine with kisses. It all just feels normal.

"Let me take your bags," Jonas offers, taking Clementine's off her shoulder before holding a hand out for mine.

The start of our evening goes much the same as before. Except now, Jonas and I discover every possible moment to touch each other. In the kitchen, while we eat, when we curl into each other on the couch. His fingers sweep stray hairs off my cheek. Arms around me as he demonstrates how to cut the fruit "easier." My knees grazing his over and over as we eat our meals. And now, his fingers splayed on my belly, thumb drawing small circles, reminiscent of the movie night we shared in the park.

The movie plays on the screen, but I don't see or hear any of it.

Eyes closed, I focus on my breathing. His breathing. The rapid uptick in each pattern. From shoulders to toes, our bodies mold as one. Heat radiates off him, burning through layers of clothes, and scorches my skin. And a rhythmic cadence I memorized, one I called to mind several times while we were apart, beats fierce in his chest and thumps between my shoulder blades.

A light sheen of perspiration prickles my skin as Jonas skims his palm higher and higher, slow and steady up my abdomen. When he traces the underwire of my bra, I stop breathing. When he kisses the sensitive skin behind my ear, I grind my hips into him. Jonas exhales a soft growl, his breath hot on my neck.

"Cannot wait for this movie to end," he whisper-growls in my ear.

I open my eyes, peek at the screen before shifting my gaze to Clementine. The movie is almost over, but she is wide awake. Time to offer alternative solutions.

Rolling over to face Jonas, I bring my hand to his cheek and run my palm over the stubble. "She's still awake. Might need to put on another movie to watch, flip the lights off, and we can go to bed." He lifts his head to spot Clementine then nods.

For the last fifteen minutes of movie one, Jonas and I kiss and touch and reacquaint ourselves with simpler contact. When the movie ends, I pop off the couch. "Pumpkin, what other movie do you want to watch? Jonas and I are going to bed, but you can stay up and watch."

"*The Nightmare Before Christmas*." I should have known.

"You got it. Go change into your jammies while I set it up."

She jumps off the couch and bounds down the hall with

pajamas in hand. While out of the room, I start up the movie while Jonas sets up the couch for her to sleep. A few minutes later, she plops back on the couch in her movie-themed pajamas with Sally on her limbs and torso. She wiggles her way under the blanket, Spartan curls up beside her, and we kiss her good night.

Jonas and I stroll back to the bedroom, hand in hand. The second the door clicks shut, the energy changes. Grows heavier. Potent. Feverish. I freeze and Jonas steps up to my backside. Hands on my biceps. Fingers traipsing down until they weave with mine. He inches closer. Heat swirls in the air, licks my skin, and blankets me. His breath comes faster, hotter, sweeping across my neck.

He brings one of our joined hands to my abdomen and grazes the skin above the hem of my jeans. Presses me into him. Rocks his hips against my butt. I tip my head back and rest it on his shoulder. A slow moan on my lips.

"Missed you so much," he growls and trails kisses up my neck. Along my jaw. Consuming my lips.

I unweave my fingers from his and spin to face him. "Missed you more."

Pressing my hands to his pecs, I trail my palms down his chest, relishing the dips and ridges beneath my fingertips. When I reach the hem of his shirt, I fist the material and tug up. The cotton hits the floor as I lean forward and press my lips to his skin.

He hisses in the dimly lit room, hands clutching my hips as I navigate the terrain with my lips. Each clavicle, left then right. The dip at the base of his throat. Down his sternum— paying extra attention to the flesh protecting his heart. I kiss my way across his left pec, drawing circles with my tongue around the nipple before pulling it between my teeth. Mimicking the same on the right.

As my lips pop off his flesh, he tugs at my shirt and whips it over my head. Before the fabric hits the floor, his fingers tug at the button and zipper of my jeans. In a blink, we flip from hungry to famished. Hands pawing, fingers grasping, lips groping.

When the only thing separating us is underwear, Jonas guides me to the bed. Slides me toward the headboard then yanks the comforter down. He crawls up the mattress, hazels locked on my golden irises. Kisses my knee, my thigh, the waistline of my panties before trailing his lips and tongue up my center to the base of my throat. He nips at my jawline as my back bows off the bed.

My bra unfastens as Jonas trails a finger along my spine. I wiggle out of the lacy material and drop it to the floor just as Jonas takes one nipple between his lips, then the next. A firestorm rages beneath my skin. Scorches me from crown to toe. Builds. Faster. Needier.

"Jonas…" I moan, grabbing at the waistband of his underwear. "I need you inside me."

He rocks his hips and grinds his erection against my apex. His lips crash to mine and he devours me as if he will never taste me again. I shove his underwear down his legs, using my feet to push them off completely.

Jonas breaks the kiss and trails his lips down my center again, painfully slow. When he reaches my panties, inch by slow inch, he peels them away. He crawls back up the bed, locks his thermal gaze with mine, and kisses me with reverence. Cherishes me. Worships me. Then rocks his hips forward and fills me. I gasp and knead his firm glutes.

"Fuck." He rears back and rocks forward again. And again. Building a rhythm until my body remembers his girth.

He flips us over, grabs my hips, and guides me up and down his length while I flatten my palms against his chest and ride him. I pick up speed, rock my hips as he meets me thrust for thrust. Energy builds in my chest, hot and heavy and powerful. Trailing down my spine and seating low in my pelvis. It's liquid fire and hunger and lust and love. And as I dig my nails into Jonas's pecs, body rocking to a feverish rhythm, I shatter around him.

In a blink, he flips me on my back, lifts one of my legs over his shoulder and pistons his hips. His lips crash to mine and I weave my fingers through his hair, fisting the strands. He braces one hand at my shoulder while the other holds my hip, pinning me in place, hitting me deeper and deeper with each thrust forward.

And my body climbs up that mountain one more time. My breath coming in short bursts. Heart pounding. Orgasm building. Heat scorching. Body dripping.

Then my body finds oblivion. And Jonas is right there with me. Kissing me. Caressing me. Whispering how beautiful I am. Holding me in his arms. Stirring me back to life. Loving me.

And that's exactly how we fall asleep. In each other's arms. Blissfully replete.

fourteen

JONAS

Cherry and vanilla waft around me in a cloud of bliss as I wake from the best sleep in weeks.

On my back with eyes closed, I bask in the heat of Autumn's body draped over mine. Bare skin pressed to my chest and limbs. Cheek nestled between my shoulder and pec. Arm draped across my torso. Leg tangled between mine. Her soft, shallow breaths painting my skin as her chest rises and falls. Heartbeat steady beneath her breast bone pressed to my ribs.

I want to open my eyes, shift an inch or two, and memorize the lines and curves and peaks of her face while she sleeps. In the early morning light, I want to take in the shape of her brows, where they arch and end. Study her lashes as they fan out over the small area just above her cheekbone. Trace my eyes around the edges of her lips until I follow where they join in the center. Navigate the soft edges of her jawline. Regard the movement of her eyes behind her closed lids as she dreams.

But I don't dare move an inch. Don't jostle her awake.

Because everything about this moment is as perfect as it should be.

As I listen to the soft cadence of Autumn's breathing, I notice it changes. Takes on a new rhythm. Grows in tempo. Her fingers twitch on my chest. Toes wiggle beneath the sheet. Jaw flexes as she licks her lips. Breasts press against my side. Hips wobble just above mine. Unhurried, she lifts her head to peek up at my face.

When she catches my eyes already on her, a brilliant smile plumps her cheeks. Seeing her like this—not a lick of makeup on her face, hair messy in every direction, lips plump and perky, irises glittery in the morning sun—steals my breath. Jolts the chambers of my heart. Robs me of every rational thought. Has me in a trance.

I return her smile as my fingertips dance up and down her spine. "'Morning."

She wiggles up my body, leans in and presses her lips to mine, slow and sweet. "'Morning. How long have you been awake?"

"Not long." I skirt my fingers up her side, from hip to the curve of her breast.

Her fingertips stroke the stubble along my jaw before she brings her lips to mine again. This kiss hungrier as she lifts her hips and straddles me. Nipples hard, scraping against my pecs. Hands planted on both sides of my face, caging me in. Her hips rock over mine, skimming my erection with her slick lips.

I take hold of her hips. Squeeze them with inexplicable roughness. Match the intensity of our kiss as I rock her core over my erection. A heatwave ripples through my body, scorching every inch of me in its wake. Dampness slickens me from root to crown. The heat converging, pooling, settling in my groin.

I bolt upright, her legs encircle my waist as her hands glide around the back of my neck, into my hair. Curling. Fisting. Tugging at the strands. I scoop my hands under her ass and lift her enough to rock back and glide the crown of my cock against her slick folds. For one, two, three strokes, I tease her entrance. On the next stroke, I lower her on to me with precision and fill her fully.

Autumn tips her head back and gasps at the feel of me inside her. Presses her breasts against my collarbones as she yanks my hair with such force, the ceiling comes into view. I don't move. Not an inch. I wait for her to let me know she is ready. Until she drops her chin, until her addictive cognac irises lock with mine.

Her fingers loosen their grip, just slightly. But I keep my head back. I stare up the column of her throat, lock on to her pulse as it pounds beneath her ear, watch her swallow and drag in a deep breath. Her chin drops lower, lower. Our eyes meet. The tip of her nose brushes the bridge of mine. Lips lock and claim. Licking, sucking, consuming.

Bundling her in my arms, I harden my hold on her and rock my hips. She moans against my tongue, down my throat, and it's a bolt of lightning to my cock.

Her fingers release my hair, ankles unhook behind me, and before I protest, she pushes me down into the mattress. Pins me, fingers digging into my skin. Grinds her hips, moves against and in time with me. Nipples pebbled. Jaw slack as soft whimpers spill from her lips. She tucks her chin, her hair falling forward and framing her face.

I bite my lower lip and groan as every nerve in my body sparks like heat lightning. The electrical current ebbs and flows. Fuses together. Slithers down my spine until it settles in my groin. Expands and pulses with each rock of her hips.

She buries her nails in my flesh as her body constricts. I flip her on to the mattress, lift her legs to rest on my shoulders, grip the back of her neck, and slam into her. Autumn tucks her lips between her teeth before turning her head and biting the pillow. One, two, three more thrusts and my vision hazes as I release. Ringing echoes in my ears as bright lights sparkle behind my lids when I slam them shut.

I release Autumn's legs and press my weight into her. Kiss her fiercely as she combs her fingers through my hair. When I break the kiss, I press my forehead to hers and breathe her in.

"God, I love waking up with you in my arms," I confess.

"Couldn't agree more." She brings a hand to my cheek and strokes her thumb over my stubble. "I don't want to, but we should probably get up. Before Clementine."

I sneak in one last kiss before leaving the comfort of the bed. Autumn sticks out her lower lip, pouting, and it is one of the cutest fucking things I have seen. She rolls on to her belly and groans into the pillow before reluctantly abandoning the bed.

"I want to take my girls out today," I declare as I shrug a shirt on.

"Oh, yeah?"

"Yep. Don't know where. Not sure what we'll do. But we should make today adventurous." Autumn giggles at my proclamation. "And cake should be involved more than once."

"Cake?" Autumn's eyes widen. "Clementine won't disagree with you."

"Lots of cake. We'll call it a belated birthday celebration."

Autumn freezes, hand hovering over the zipper of her

jeans. "When was your birthday?" Her question comes out squeaky.

"Couple weeks back." Autumn's face pales as her eyes glaze over. I frame her face in my palms and shake my head. "No, scarlet. No tears. We will have plenty more birthdays to celebrate together. And I'm not upset. Just because we didn't celebrate on the exact day doesn't mean anything."

Autumn works to blink away her tears before taking a deep breath. "I promise to make it up to you."

I lean down and kiss her briefly, tenderly. "You being here, staying with me, has more than made up for missing the day."

Just as Autumn opens her mouth to rebut, the soft sound of little feet padding on the floor, followed by a knock, halts any further conversation. Autumn pats her head in an effort to tame her sex hair before opening the door.

"'Morning, pumpkin. We were just coming out to see if you were awake yet."

Clementine hugs Autumn's waist, then mine. "Sparty needs to go potty," she says as she releases me and walks out of the room.

Just like that, our morning has officially begun. The three of us—plus Spartan—in the same space feels *normal*. And I love every second of it.

After our previous visit to Phillippe Park, Clementine immediately suggested us spending the day at a park. Although I love revisiting parks, I asked her permission to go to a different location since we were celebrating my birthday.

When she cocked her head and pondered, it was the cutest thing ever. But she agreed with one condition.

We have lots of cake and ice cream.

Sold!

Foraging through the garage, I locate the cooler and carry it inside. Once we are ready to go, I toss the cooler in the back of the Jeep and we all pile in. On the way to the park, we stop at the grocery store and buy subs, drinks, snacks and a small bag of ice. With everything packed in the cooler, I drive us to a nature preserve at the northeast corner of the county.

Clementine kicks her feet while she sings along with the song on the radio. She sports a pair of black wingtip sunglasses and stares out the window at the passing scenery. The closer we get to the preserve, the less buildings we see. In our part of the state, most of the land is packed with streets, malls, shopping plazas, and homes. More concrete than trees. Thankfully, though, some beautiful stretches of land have been preserved.

As I steer the Jeep into the preserve, Clementine sits up straighter. Scans the land with curious eyes. "Is this the park?"

"Yep," I say, turning down the music. "But this park is different than most parks by us."

"Why, Mr. Jonas?" I love it when she calls me Mr. Jonas.

"This park is ginormous. Bigger than any other park close by. With lots of big trees and trails to walk on and a nature center to learn about the animals."

"Will we see animals here?" she asks as her pitch bumps up.

"If we're lucky. We might see some deer or rabbits or other animals."

She gasps and stares into the passing trees. "I hope we see a deer. Would be so cool."

I glance over at Autumn and match her ear-to-ear smile. Seeing her this happy, seeing Clementine this happy, it brings new meaning to love and life and joy. Clementine may not be my daughter, but she is as equally precious to me as Autumn. *My girls*. I never knew I could be this enamored by a woman and her daughter.

As I park the Jeep, Clementine bounces in her seat, eager to jump out. We hop out and leave the cooler in the back. For the next few hours, we wander through the education center and along the trails of the preserve. The sun beats down on us and keeps us warm in the cool February air. Every once in a while, Clementine has us swing her in the air as we walk.

When our stomachs begin to rumble, I grab the cooler and we sit at a partially shaded picnic table to eat our lunch. For the most part, the preserve has minimal people here. At most, we have seen ten people. During our visit, we see one deer, a few rabbits, several squirrels, and a snake that slithers away. Clementine has been fascinated with it all.

All in all, it's been a peaceful day. Which is exactly what the three of us needed.

With full bellies and tired feet, we decide to head back to the house. But as promised, on the way back, we stop at the store to pick up cake and ice cream.

We stroll into the store and beeline to the bakery. "If I get to pick the cake, you can pick the ice cream," I offer to Clementine.

She taps her lips with a finger and narrows her eyes a moment. How can someone be this adorable? "Deal." Clementine extends her hand and we shake.

After I select a small vanilla and chocolate cake with chocolate frosting, we go to the frozen section. For the next ten minutes, Clementine studies the ice cream selection as if her decision will end a war. Autumn holds her up every other minute so she can see the higher shelves better. I don't rush them.

Instead, I stand back and observe my girls. *My girls.*

Clementine points at a container and Autumn whispers in her ear what the flavor is. Clementine shakes her head and they move down the line. This happens over and over, and yet, it doesn't bother me. Doesn't make me impatient.

If anything, I ask for more time like this. More time to bask in the joy of being a part of their lives. More time to watch the woman I care about dedicate herself to her daughter. To help her with tasks most adults consider menial. To focus on her daughter and forget everything else. Autumn is a phenomenal mother to Clementine. I envy her devotion. Having them in my life… I have never been so lucky.

After Clementine chooses, we check out and leave the store. "Happy birthday, Mr. Jonas."

I peek in the rearview mirror at Clementine. "Thank you. Hope you're ready for cake and ice cream."

She gives a confident nod. "Born ready."

Autumn laughs, slips her hand into mine over the console and squeezes. "Today has been wonderful. And it's still somewhat early."

At the red light, I meet her eyes. "Maybe we can take a nap after cake." I cock a brow.

"A nap, huh?"

I simply shrug and focus my eyes on the road again. A few minutes later, I park in the driveway and we all hop out.

In the house, Clementine tells Spartan about the preserve while we dish up cake and ice cream. And after our plates our clean, I mention napping again. Clementine says she will watch a movie with Spartan while Autumn and I take a short nap.

Once we land on my bed, I close my eyes. Although I can't see her, I *feel* Autumn observe me. "You really wanted to sleep? Interesting. Thought you were using a nap as an excuse for birthday sex."

I laugh and pull her down to the bed. "We can do that later. For now, I just want to lie here and hold you. That okay?"

Autumn snuggles into my side. "Yes, but we should set an alarm. Just in case."

After we set an alarm for forty-five minutes, we just hold each other. And for the first time since yesterday evening, I think of Leo's visit to the garage. I need to tell Autumn what happened. Not just for the sake of telling her, but also because I worry for her and Clementine both. Plus, she should forward the incident to her attorney.

Tonight, I will tell her. After dinner.

"Stay with me again tonight," I whisper against her hair. "I love having you both here."

Autumn stays quiet a moment and I wonder if she fell asleep. Until she gently fists my shirt. "Yes." She lifts her head and rests her chin on my chest. "We love being here."

I sweep a few wayward strands from her brow and tuck them behind her ear. Then lean up to kiss her. We lie in the bed until the alarm buzzes. For the rest of the day, we take it easy. We order Chinese takeout and laugh over fortune cookies, and another helping of cake and ice cream while watching *The Secret Life of Pets*.

When Clementine falls asleep, I extend my hand to Autumn. "Come sit out back with me for a bit." She takes my hand as I lead her to the patio.

I light the fire bowl before sitting on the lounger and nestling Autumn between my legs. We stare at the flames and weave our fingers together. I close my eyes and breathe in her cherry vanilla scent, letting it center and soothe me as I muster up the courage to tell her about yesterday.

Inhale. Hold it. And exhale. I do this a few times. "Autumn," I say softly. "I need to tell you something, but don't want you to freak out."

As the words leave my lips, she locks up. Not moving for ten rapid beats. Then she breathes again and twists to look at me. "What is it?"

I swallow, trying to dampen the sudden dryness in my throat. "Leo stopped by the garage yesterday."

She sits up straighter and spins to face me full-on. "What?" she exclaims, eyes wide with fear. "Why? What did he want? How did he know where you work?"

All questions I wanted answers to as well. Honestly, I think he was looking to start a physical altercation with me to make Autumn appear bad in the court's eyes. Too bad for him, I am not a dumbass.

I relay everything that happened. How Leo flaunted his tail feathers and acted possessive. How I kept my cool but put him in his place. And how Dad stood in my peripheral the entire time and had my back. When I finish, Autumn shakes her head. Not because she doesn't believe me, but more as if she doesn't understand his sudden interest.

"Just let your attorney know as soon as possible. Sometimes, little things add up in the end."

We stay out by the fire a while longer, enjoy the quiet as our minds run wild. When I extinguish the flame, I guide us back in the house and to the bedroom. As soon as we step over the threshold, I pull Autumn into my arms.

"In here, we don't talk about anything but you and me and, occasionally, that little girl in the other room." I trace along Autumn's jaw and tip her chin up. "Okay?"

She nods. "Yes." Pressing up on her toes, she leans in and kisses me. On her next breath, she says, "Let's go to bed." And I let Autumn guide me to the bed as we peel away our clothes.

fifteen

AUTUMN

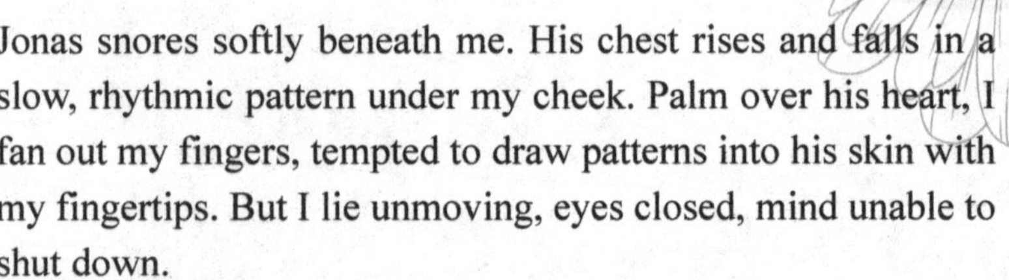

Jonas snores softly beneath me. His chest rises and falls in a slow, rhythmic pattern under my cheek. Palm over his heart, I fan out my fingers, tempted to draw patterns into his skin with my fingertips. But I lie unmoving, eyes closed, mind unable to shut down.

New questions run wild in my head. Questions asking what Leo aims to accomplish with his relentlessness. What is his endgame in this scenario? What is he out to accomplish? I just don't get it. If he would have stepped back into the picture within the first two years, I might have understood the desire to be a part of Clementine's life easier.

But too much time has passed. Too many circumstances in both our lives have changed. For someone who ditched me—us—without a backward glance, Leo's newfound persistence worries me. His pursuit of sole custody of Clementine is tied up with something. Something just out of my reach. And it twists my insides in a nauseating pretzel.

I *need* to learn what's behind his motivation and soon. I need the truth behind his sudden desire to be a father. Not just for the sake of knowing, but because Clementine's well-being hangs in the balance.

Curling farther into Jonas's side, I work to match my breathing pattern to his. Inhaling his unique scent, my body relaxes more. And before long, I dream about Jonas at my side until we are old and gray.

~

What's better than a great night of sleep? Waking up with Jonas's lips on my skin. God, if every day starts like this, I will never leave this bed.

After he ignites every inch of my skin and liquifies each molecule in me—three times—we stumble out of bed and dress. My legs are noodles walking on gelatin as we exit the bedroom and I slap a hand over my mouth to stifle my laughter.

Clementine lays curled in a semi-fetal position with Spartan as a partial pillow. But it won't be long before she wakes.

Jonas and I step into the bathroom, brush our teeth, and groom enough to not look as if we have spent the last hour trying to yank each other's hair out. I skip putting on makeup and twist my hair into a topknot.

Stepping up behind me, Jonas locks eyes with me in the mirror over the vanity. His hands secure on my hips, lips grazing the shell of my ear. "I love waking up with you in the morning. Seeing you like this." He kisses the spot below my ear, grinds his hips against my low back, then locks his gaze with mine again. "Natural and perfect and more stunning than ever."

I spin around, tip my head back, and lace my fingers at the nape of his neck. "You trying to flatter me, Mr. Thompson?"

His intense, addictive hazels lock me in place and I stop breathing. Heart thrashing against my ribcage. Limbs tingling as heat courses through my veins and sparks new life. Jonas drops his chin an inch, his lips so close I practically taste the peppermint on his tongue. He traces the tip of his nose along the ridge of mine and I stutter an exhale.

"How can I not?" he whispers against my lips. "Hope you let me flatter and compliment and kiss you every day."

I press my lips to his in answer just as a knock on the door disrupts the moment. "Are you almost done? I need to go potty," Clementine states from the hall.

"Just a second, pumpkin." I peek up at Jonas. "As long as you can handle the two of us, you may dote upon me any day of the week."

"Wouldn't want it any other way." He steps back, adjusts himself in his sweatpants, and opens the door with a smile on his face. "'Morning, sunshine."

Clementine narrows her eyes with suspicion. "Why are you both in the bathroom? That's weird."

"We didn't want to wake you while we brushed our teeth," Jonas answers without delay.

And as if his answer needs no further questioning, Clementine shrugs and relaxes her expression. "Okay. Can I go now?" She points toward the toilet.

"Sorry, pumpkin."

We scurry out of the bathroom and leave her be. Heading into the kitchen, we start our morning like a family. Jonas and I take out ingredients to make chocolate chip pancakes, cheesy scrambled eggs, and turkey bacon. We move seamlessly in the small space as if this normal task happens daily.

While I whisk the eggs, he ladles batter on a hot skillet and sprinkles it with mini chips. The bacon sizzles in the oven as I pour the eggs into a pan.

Jonas deposits the first batch of pancakes on a plate, butters the skillet again, and adds more batter. Spatula midair, he glances my way. "I don't want this to come out the wrong way, but you and Clementine shouldn't be alone. Not until the case ends."

I stop scraping the eggs from left to right and peer over at him. He means well. Wants to protect me. Protect us. But if I am supposed to live my life normally, that means I will be alone from time to time. Or with only Clementine. How can I not be?

"Jonas, I get where you're coming from. I understand it. But how am I supposed to follow a regular routine—work, school, errands—if I" —I pause and take a deep breath— "we need a bodyguard all the time."

He flips the pancakes, sets the spatula down, and steps closer. I peek over my shoulder and check Clementine isn't eavesdropping. "We'll find a way. Between me, Penny, everyone at the shop, and our friends, we can make it happen. We need to." I roll my eyes and shake my head. Jonas grazes his knuckles down my cheek. "It's only temporary. And if something happens to either of you, I won't be able to live with myself."

I turn the heat on the stove to low and face him fully. His eyes bore into me, glassy and a tinge red. Concern written in the underscoring on his forehead. I snake my arms around his waist and rest my cheek over his heart. Warm arms envelop and hug me with renewed strength. "It won't be easy."

"Doesn't matter," he mumbles into my hair.

"How will we get everyone in on the plan?" A legitimate

question, considering not everyone knows the details of my past.

Jonas kisses the crown of my head and releases me, stepping back to the skillet. "The shop is closed today?" I nod. "Let's invite everyone over for an impromptu cookout. We can use my birthday as the initial excuse."

Not a bad idea. The guys will definitely be down for a gathering if we involve food and drinks. Penny will get Iliana on board. The last time we all did something outside of work was too long ago. Years ago, we'd hang out a Sunday per month. Nothing special, just enjoying life and seeing each other somewhere besides the same four walls.

"Okay. After breakfast, I'll get the ball rolling with everyone from the shop. What time?"

"Is five good? We can chat a bit while I get the grill going. Eat around six."

"Should be fine. Clementine will also get to play with Ashton, Rez's little boy."

Jonas cooks the last of the pancakes while I take the bacon from the oven. We plate up the food and sit at the breakfast bar with Clementine, sharing our plan for the day. A lazy morning, followed by house cleanup and a trip to the grocery store before having friends over. She chimes in with food she wants added to the grocery list and tells Spartan he will meet one of her friends today.

After texting our friends and watching hours of Sunday morning cartoons, we decide to vacate the couch and get to work. The inside of the house sparkles within the hour. A candle lit in the living area wafts the scent of fresh cotton around the house. Jonas goes outside to check the grill, making sure we have enough charcoal.

The trip to the grocery store goes quicker than expected,

but we walk out with more than our list of items. Every time Clementine pointed to something and begged, Jonas caved and added it to the cart. Thankfully, she only did this a handful of times. She picked good things, though—s'mores making supplies, a couple movie night candies, and berries to go with our leftover cake.

Back at the house, Jonas marinates chicken and forms burger patties while I cook pasta and potatoes for salads. Clementine digs out colored pencils, crayons, and a coloring book from her stuffed overnight bad. Sneaky girl brought everything.

We finish prepping whatever possible. Every opportunity we get, Jonas and I exchange touches. A forearm graze. A kiss on the cheek as he reaches for a gadget. His front brushing against my back as he moves past me. My fingers tracing his low back as I set the strainer in the sink.

Will it always be like this? The constant need to touch each other. For me to feel his warmth and strength and love. To be near him, to see him, to smile with him. Some may consider our attachment unhealthy. Clingy. I say, when you find the person who connects all the dots perfectly, the person who makes you see the whole constellation and not just a mess of stars, do what makes your heart happy.

Yes, I pushed us apart when Leo made an appearance. But it was maternal instinct to shut everything down and protect my daughter. Little did I know, Jonas was equally willing to go to battle for her to stay. And no matter what is thrown at us going forward, I won't make the same mistake.

The doorbell chimes and snaps my attention to Clementine, who peeks out the window and waves like a loon. "People are here."

That she doesn't mention names has me heading for the

window. Glancing out, I spot Cora and Gavin. Walking up the drive is Erin, Shelly, and Micah. "Those are my and Jonas's friends. The ones we went bowling with." Clementine nods.

Jonas opens the door and invites everyone in. I introduce Clementine to everyone and she gives each of them a hug. The guys loiter in the kitchen and catch up while us ladies sit in the living room. Less than five minutes pass before Clementine bolts up from her spot at the coffee table and peeks out the window. The recognizable low rumble of Reznor's car echoes outside.

"They're here," she exclaims, jumping in place. "Can I open the door?"

"Wait until they walk up, so Spartan doesn't run out."

Jonas excuses himself and joins us at the door. Clementine peeps up at me and I nod. She flings the door open and runs up to everyone, giving them hugs. I stare after her a minute, watching as she plays mini hostess. "Come on, guys. Let's go inside." She takes Ashton's hand and helps him up the porch stairs.

Once everyone steps inside, I introduce my tattoo family to everyone already here. Gavin shakes Reznor's hand and gives a more in-depth introduction to Cora. I learn Reznor inked Cora's name on Gavin's chest before I inked bands on their fingers. Small world. Reznor introduces Tatyana—his long-term girlfriend—and Ashton, their son. Before everyone settles, Jonas suggests we head out back and start grilling.

Cora deposits a small cooler on the counter and takes out a few items. When she sees me staring, she explains. "Vegan burger and sides."

"You should've said something. We would've got stuff at the store."

"No worries. Kind of used to bringing stuff when we go

places." She hands the patty to Jonas and says to cook it like a normal burger.

Everyone heads out back, Spartan on Jonas's heels, praying for him to drop something. The kids share a lounger and pull up a side table to color. Spartan runs around the yard, sniffing the grass and searching for lizards. I light the fire bowl while Jonas mans the grill. Beforehand, we brought out extra chairs from the garage, and now have more than enough seating for the large group.

The guys shoot the shit by the grill while us ladies talk on the outdoor L-shaped couch. Cora tells me about an upcoming wedding she and Erin are shooting. Erin has slowly transitioned from an assistant to a photographer over the last year. She continues to learn, but Cora is the perfect teacher. Since the change, the two of them have tweaked the business. A fresh name—Hunt-Wallace Enterprises—and new faces. They reach more clients, hired assistants, and have the ability to take time off. Cora says she couldn't do it without Erin, while Erin disagrees.

Shelly talks about the floral industry in ways I have never heard. Quotas and sales and deadlines. Sounds like a nine-to-five corporate office gig. But I suppose all industries have this. I never think of the tattoo industry like this, but I suppose Oscar—the shop owner—does. He pops in once a month to check on us but leaves us be for the most part. He owns several shops in the state but designates a manager for each location to make on-the-spot decisions. That would be Reznor for us. He keeps the shop going with ease.

Penny chimes in on occasion, but otherwise chills beside me with our arms hooked at the elbow.

Once the food is ready, we all gather around the fire bowl and eat. Smiles and laughter and shoulder bumps flow like the beer in our bottles. When people start leaning back and patting their stomachs, I glance up at Jonas and nod.

"Thanks for coming on such short notice, everyone," Jonas announces. "We brought you here under the guise of a makeup birthday celebration. While that's true, there's more to it."

All eyes turn my direction. The men with an air of concern and the women silently questioning what the hell is going on. Penny glances down at my abdomen before meeting my eyes again and I shake my head. She laughs.

"Some of you know," Jonas continues, looking to Penny before scanning the group, "and some of you don't. But Autumn's ex has started stirring up trouble." This causes Rex and Reznor to sit taller. "He filed for sole custody of Clementine and has since made verbal threats to both of us. We have maintained our cool and done everything through the appropriate channels. But it seems he is stepping up his game. So…" Jonas smiles and my favorite dimple appears. "We are enacting Operation Don't-leave-Autumn-and-Clementine-alone."

Everyone nods except the children.

"What does this look like?" Penny asks.

"Basically, someone is with them around the clock. Doesn't matter who. Even together, someone should be with them. Obviously, when here, they'll be with me."

"And with me at the apartment and work," Penny chimes in. "But if our schedules don't align, we'll sort it out ahead of time."

The conversation flows for another hour before people leave. Beforehand, we all exchange phone numbers and sort out tomorrow's schedule for now. Since Penny rode with

Reznor, Tatyana, and Ashton, she stays to ride home with me and Clementine.

We clean up the back patio and kitchen. The closer we get to clean, the tighter my stomach twists. After a wonderful weekend with Jonas, I don't want to leave. I want to crawl into bed and snuggle with him. Listen to his soft breaths as he sleeps. Fall asleep to the thumping cadence of his heart beneath my ear. Wake up to the scent of his skin and the warmth of his embrace.

But we aren't there yet. Aren't to the point where we spend several days straight in the same place. Should we be? Would it be odd this early on? Some would say yes while others would suggest there is no correct timeline.

Reluctantly, Clementine and I gather our bags and trod to the door. Penny holds out her hand for my keys. "I'll start the car so you can exchange good nights." After I hand them over, she walks to the car and starts it.

Clementine hugs Jonas around the waist. "'Night, Mr. Jonas."

He hugs her small frame. "'Night, sunshine."

She clings to Spartan a moment. "Night night, Sparty. See you soon. We can have more slumber parties." Giving him one last squeeze, she trots down the drive and gets in the back seat of the car.

"I don't want to leave," I confess, peering up at Jonas.

He pulls me into him, wraps one arm around my waist while he braces the length of my spine with the other, fingers in my hair. "Don't want you to go either. After we figure out schedules, we'll be together more nights. Guaranteed." He kisses the crown of my head.

"Music to my ears."

We inch apart. Jonas frames my face in his palms and

drops his lips to mine. He kisses me sweet at first, then traces my lower lip with the tip of his tongue. I deepen the kiss, devouring him as if I won't see him for days again. When he breaks the kiss, I brace myself on his forearms.

"See you tomorrow, scarlet."

"Tomorrow." I give him one last kiss before walking to the car.

I toss my bag in the back, then get behind the wheel. As we back out, Clementine and I wave goodbye.

A block from Jonas's house, Penny twists in her seat to face me. "I foresee needing a new roommate in my future."

I slap her arm without looking. "Shut up," I joke. But I don't fight the painful smile. Nor do I dispute her accusation. Because I see it too.

sixteen

JONAS

Nothing like startling awake to a cold nose and wet tongue in your armpit.

"Argh! What are you doing?" I croak, arms flailing in a desperate attempt to stop Spartan.

Woof, woof, woof.

I peek up at the husky hovering an inch from my face. "You don't behave like this with Clementine," I accuse.

Woof, woof.

"I see how it is. Well, I'll remember this conversation next time you beg for treats."

The alarm buzzes and Spartan jumps off the bed. I slap the clock and roll into Autumn's pillow, smothering myself with her scent. Not quite the same as her in my arms, but it will make due for now.

I fall out of bed, slip on sweatpants and a hoodie, and use the bathroom before clipping Spartan's leash on. We trod out the door and walk our normal route around the neighborhood.

Five houses down, an odd sensation washes over me. A fluttery twitch in my solar plexus. I stare down the sidewalk and across the street but spot nothing out of the ordinary. When Spartan stops to sniff a mailbox, I glance behind us and scan where we came from. Being five in the morning, I don't usually see neighbors during our morning walk. And this morning is no exception as I spot nothing. But the uneasy tremble in my gut begs to differ. The sensation screams at me that I am not alone.

Unable to shake the feeling, I cut our walk short.

Back in the house, I go about my morning weekday routine. After eating a quick breakfast, I pour the pot of coffee in my thermos, grab my wallet and keys, then put Spartan in his crate and turn on his radio.

"Be good. See you later, bud." I ruffle his fur through the grate.

I lock up the house and walk to the Jeep. As I peer up and press the fob to unlock it, I notice a slip of paper pinned beneath my windshield wiper. Approaching the Jeep, I scan up and down the street for signs of anyone but see nothing odd or notable.

Once the paper is within arm's reach, I tug it out. I check the street one last time before unfolding the paper and looking down.

She doesn't belong to you.

What the actual fuck?

My fingers curl as I start to ball up the note. But before I wad the note or rip it to shreds, I take a deep breath and relax my digits. I walk to the end of my driveway and scan the street again as I stuff the note in my pocket.

I scrutinize every car along the street. Peek through the windshields for people or movement. Scan the length of the sidewalk, searching for anyone on foot. Glance up the nearby trees and stare through every shrub within a fifty-foot circumference.

Not a goddamn thing.

"Come at me, motherfucker," I growl. "You won't touch her."

Not sure who this asshole thinks he is, but there isn't a chance in hell he will lay his hands on Autumn. He is damn lucky I restrain myself from beating his ass.

I get in the Jeep and start it. While the engine warms up, I take out my phone and type a message to Autumn.

> Morning. After you drop Clementine at school, please call me.

I send the message, connect my phone to the Jeep, and drive to work.

When I step into the office, I stash away my concerns about the note for now and smile when Dad looks up. He matches it with one of his own. "'Morning, son. Glad to still see a smile on your face. How are the girls?"

"Good. We had a nice weekend together. Created a plan to make sure they're safe."

Dad rises from his desk and walks to the dish rack to grab his mug for coffee. After mixing our morning caffeine, we sit behind our desks. "Glad you're taking care of them. Raised you right," he states with pride in his voice.

Shortly after the garage opens for the day, my phone rings. I wipe my hands and retrieve it from my coveralls. "'Morning, scarlet," I say, walking toward the office.

"Good morning. Everything okay?" Concern laces her words and I hate that I have to deliver more unsavory news.

"Are you driving?"

"No. Penny is. We just dropped Clementine off."

Once I step inside the office and close the door, I tell her about the note. "As I left for work this morning, I noticed a piece of paper under my wiper blade. It was a note." The line goes silent for too long. I check the screen to make sure the call didn't drop and see it hasn't. "Autumn?"

"Yeah, sorry." I picture her with her eyes closed, taking deep breaths. "What did it say?"

I swallow and relay the message. "When I took Spartan for a walk earlier, I felt as if someone was following me. But I never saw anyone."

"This is ridiculous," she mumbles. "Will you take a picture of it and send it to me, please?"

"Of course." At this point, I have no idea what steps we should take. But she should definitely tell someone. "Should you send it to your attorney?"

She huffs into the line, exasperated over the whole scenario. "Probably. I don't know. When we get off the phone, I'll call her."

I don't want to upset Autumn with how I feel right now, but I refuse to hide or run from the stabbing pain in my chest. When it comes to Autumn and Clementine, everything needs to be out in the open. She needs to hear where my head and heart lie. "Autumn, please be safe. Both of you. Keep your eyes open and stay vigilant."

"I will," she whispers. "Promise."

"Thank you." I sigh. In some respects, I am glad Autumn and Clementine didn't stay over last night. They would have been witness to the note this morning and Autumn might not have been able to keep her cool in front of Clementine. Then again, maybe the note wouldn't have been there if they stayed. Who knows? "Call me back when you know more."

"Okay." Her voice travels from miles away, quiet and somber. "Talk to you soon."

The need to tell her I love her hangs from the tip of my tongue now more than ever, but I don't say the words. I want to. God, do I want to. But now feels so far from appropriate. Her thoughts are probably all over the place with worry. I don't want the first time I express my love for her to be during a moment of stress. I don't want it to be over the phone, where I cannot see her face and vice versa. Plus, I don't want her to feel obligated to return the sentiment just because I put it out there.

So I bite my tongue and project my love into the universe in her direction. Send her every ounce of positivity and love she has stirred in my veins.

"Soon. Stay with Penny."

"I will. Bye."

"Bye, scarlet."

The call disconnects and I stand staring at the wall a moment. I zone out, close my eyes, and beg to the heavens for all of this madness to end soon.

Then I remember to take a picture of the note and send it to Autumn. Once she receives it, she texts her thanks.

I stay in the office a moment to drink another mug of coffee. When I head back into the garage, Dad catches my eye and waves me over.

"Everything alright?"

I nod. "Just more drama. Autumn is calling her attorney to figure out what we do next." I tell him about the plan for the girls to not be alone and about the note this morning.

"Keep me up to date."

I agree and amble over to the car I was working on before the call. Picking up the socket wrench, I get back to work.

Thankfully, I can work on the engine without one-hundred-percent focus. Because my mind is far from this garage. My arms mentally around Autumn as we navigate through this nightmare.

seventeen

AUTUMN

"What's going on?" Penny asks when I get off the phone with Jonas.

I huff and drop my head back on the seat. "Jonas found a note on his car this morning." My phone pings with an incoming text. I open it and see the note. The handwriting too boxy, as if someone put extra effort into disguising their penmanship. "And he just sent a picture of it."

"Can I see?"

"In a minute. Let me call Theresa first."

I scroll through my contacts and tap on the attorney's office, bringing the phone to my ear. On the second ring, the young man at the front desk answers. "Good morning, attorney Theresa Chang's office. How may I assist you?"

"Good morning. This is Autumn Rooker. I need to inform Theresa of some new information regarding my case. It's somewhat urgent."

"Let me check if she's available, Ms. Rooker. I need to place you on a brief hold."

"Thank you." Jazzy café music floats through the phone line while I wait. Not a minute later, Theresa answers.

We exchange pleasantries, then she turns all business. Asking if Clementine and I are okay. Once I assure her we are physically safe, I share the incident of Leo stopping by Jonas's work on Friday afternoon and the note on his car this morning. She asks me to send her the picture, but to get the actual note from Jonas. When I have it, I am to bring it to her after I file a police report.

Not that I didn't foresee this happening, but dizziness starts to swallow me whole. Everything whirls around me in the passenger seat as I take deep, relaxing breaths. Beside me, Penny reaches over and clutches my arm.

"Auti, you good?"

I nod, slow and unsure. Lifting the phone away from my mouth, I whisper, "Go to Jonas's work." She gives me a thumbs up.

Theresa informs me she will spend the day trying to get the hearing moved up in light of this new information. I thank her and promise to see her soon.

"Talk to me," Penny states as soon as I hang up with Theresa.

"The note says *she doesn't belong to you*. Jonas thinks it's about me, but I think it refers to Clementine." I take a deep breath then continue. "We need to get the note from Jonas, go to the police station and file a report, then take the note to the attorney as evidence." I press my palms to my eyes. "How am I supposed to work today? And how am I supposed to get around if you have to work today and I shouldn't be alone?"

"Call Rez. He'll understand. As for me, I'll tote you around as long as possible. My shift doesn't start until noon. Hopefully, we can knock this out in the next couple of hours."

While Penny drives, I call Reznor and explain the situation. He waves off my worry and tells me to take the day off.

With everything going on, his empathy is bar none. At least I have one less stressor to bog me down.

Penny parks in front of Thompson's Garage and I jump out. Jonas dashes over to me and we exchange a brief kiss.

"Hate to cut this short, but I need the note to file a police report and take to the attorney's office."

Jonas fishes the note from his jeans pocket beneath his coveralls. When he hands it to me, he kisses my forehead. "Let me know how it goes." He waves at Penny. "And if you need me later when Pen goes to work."

"I will." We exchange one last kiss. "Call you when I know more."

Penny whips out of the parking lot faster than she pulled in. We speed down the road, but I miss the blur of the buildings and trees.

I stare down at my hands in silence. Stare at the ivory paper between my fingers. Rub the vellum with the pads of my thumbs. The subtle roughness familiar, but can't place from where. I unfold the paper with ease, eyes glued to the shaky block letters. Tracing the slight swoops and lines and edges of the letters, I study the print for any indication of who wrote it.

The answer is there. Just out of reach. On the tip of the tongue. But it retreats back into my mind, mimicking a frightened child.

Folding the note back together, I tuck it in my purse before eyeing the road. We are blocks from the police station now. Any other day, I would reprimand Penny for her lead foot. But today, grateful doesn't begin to cover her speediness.

She parks the car in the police station visitor lot and stands at my side the moment we step out of the car. For a beat, I contemplate telling her to wait in the car but know I won't win the battle.

After checking in with a receptionist too bright-eyed and smiley to work in a police station, we sit in the waiting area. With the early hour, I pray we get in and out quickly. Minutes later, the gods answer my request and send an officer to call me back. Since we're in the station, Penny opts to sit in the waiting area while I speak with the officer.

I have never seen the inside of a police station but didn't picture it looking like an open area call center. Cubicle central with low glass walls dividing clusters of desks. Weird.

The female officer directs me to have a seat. Unyielding plastic digs into my hips as I sit down. Minus a few framed photos of her with fellow officers or superiors, her workspace appears as sterile as my booth at the shop.

She extends a hand across the desk and I shake it. "Officer Martinez. I was told you need to file a harassment report."

"Yes. I'm in the middle of a custody suit and my daughter's birth father has begun harassing my boyfriend." Opening my purse with shaky hands, I retrieve the note. "Friday, the birth father went to my boyfriend's place of business and provoked a verbal altercation. This morning, when my boyfriend left for work, he found this on his car." I hand the note to her. "My attorney advised me to come here and file the report before giving her the note."

Officer Martinez takes the note and studies it momentarily. "Bear with me, I need to ask you questions and document everything. Shouldn't take long. Please answer as openly and honestly as possible."

For the next thirty-plus minutes, Officer Martinez prattles off question after question. Some in regards to Jonas, others in reference to Leo. I provide her with as much detail as possible. She scans the note into the digital file and hands it back. With the note being touched so much this morning, she said the likelihood of lifting prints from someone other than me or Jonas is low. Before she walks me to the front, she prints off a copy of the report and hands it to me along with her business card.

"If anything else pops up, reach out." She points to her contact information on the card. "I may not respond immediately, but will as soon as possible." I nod. "In the meantime, I suggest being vigilant. Stay aware and steer away from any possible interactions unless your attorney is present."

"Thank you, Officer Martinez." We shake hands again.

"You're welcome. Stay safe." With that, she leaves me in the reception area.

Penny peeks up from her phone, locking it and rising when she spots me. "Done?"

"Yeah. Now, to Theresa's office."

I tuck the report and note in my purse on our way to the car. The second I click my seat belt in place, Penny backs out of the parking space. I prattle off the address for the office and direct her where to go. Thank goodness, the drive to Theresa's office takes less than ten minutes.

Inside, Penny does the same as at the police station and waits out front. In the conference room with Theresa, I relay what Officer Martinez said, then hand over the police report and note. An unfortunate side effect of no prints or detectable handwriting, the police cannot point the finger directly at Leo without further evidence.

Theresa keeps the original documentation but makes copies for my records. "I submitted a request for an earlier hearing date. Should receive a response soon. As soon as I do, I'll reach out to you. Meanwhile, steer clear of Leo, if possible. If he approaches you or Jonas, call the police. With a report filed, it will reflect poorly on him if an officer arrives on scene." We rise from our seats, and before leaving the conference room, Theresa gives me a hug. The embrace comforts me and I return it. "We'll get through this. Until then, stay strong and lean on people you trust."

"Thank you," I say, breaking the hug. "Doing my best."

She walks me back to the front and reminds me she will be in touch. Stopping here hasn't wiped away all the anxiety and stress, but knowing I have a team of people on my side helps ease it slightly.

Penny and I stroll out to the car, the adrenaline buzz from the morning fading as it inches closer to midday. We get in the car and sit quietly. Penny doesn't start the car or turn the key to kick the radio on. For a moment, we just breathe in strength and exhale the bullshit.

Until Leo reappeared, life had been low-key and kosher. Yes, my romance life was snore-worthy until Jonas came into the picture, but I had been content with sharing all my time with Clementine. She is the most important person in my world and her happiness is more important than my own. Little did I know, me being in a loving relationship boosted her happiness.

After a deep breath, Penny starts the car and steers us out of the lot. "Don't know about you, but I'm ready for this day to be done."

"Me—" My phone buzzes in my purse and I dig it out. Clementine's school name flashes on the screen. I rush to answer. "Hello?"

"May I speak with Ms. Rooker, please?"

"This is she."

"Hi, Ms. Rooker. This is Daniel in the front office of

Clementine's school. We have a gentleman here, not on the approved list, who is trying to take Clementine out of school early. He will not identify himself. We have denied him, of course, but need to notify you."

I stop breathing. *What the fuck is going on?!* I have no clue what the hell is going on in the world, but all the walls are caving in. Seems if it isn't one thing, it's another. Like my and Clementine's life are some big game to toy with.

"Is the man still there?" Penny glances at me, wide-eyed.

"Yes, ma'am. He refuses to leave without Clementine."

I inhale deeply and ball the hand not holding the phone into a fist. My nails bite the skin and I welcome the reality check. "If possible, don't let him leave. I'm on my way. He is *not* to leave with her."

"We will keep him here as long as possible."

"Thank you." I disconnect the call and face Penny. "We need to get to Clementine's school. Now. A man is trying to withdraw her from school."

"What the actual fuck?" Penny belts out as she changes course and speeds toward the elementary school.

"My thoughts exactly."

I scroll through my contacts and tap on Jonas. He answers on the second ring. "Hey, scarlet. That was quicker than expected. Everything go alright?"

For a beat, I stay silent. I clench and relax my fingers a few times. "Jonas, please don't freak out. Because I'm freaking out enough for the both of us."

"You're scaring me. What's going on?"

I pinch my eyes together so tight, a sharp jab shoots from the midline out. After a deep breath, I answer. "Penny is driving me to Clementine's school right now. An unidentified man is trying to withdraw her."

Deafening silence. Then a bang so loud I hold the phone away from my ear. "Motherfucker," Jonas growls. He remains quiet a minute. "Want me to meet you there?"

Part of me wants to say yes. To ask him to meet me there and help protect me and Clementine from all this craziness. But it isn't sensible. More angry tempers will not fix this. And without seeing his face, I *feel* the pain and anger radiating off Jonas. He loves my little girl as much as he does me and is willing to do whatever necessary to protect us both.

"No. We're pulling in now. I'll check in soon. I—" I cut myself off. *Not the time, Autumn.*

"Me too, scarlet."

The call disconnects just before Penny parks the car. I jump out while she waits in the lot. My feet carry me faster than ever before as I run for the office. Daniel from the front desk buzzes me through a locked door and I step inside the warm office.

"Autumn Rooker. You called about a man trying to withdraw my daughter from school."

Daniel smiles as if a stranger wasn't just here trying to steal my child. And it pisses me off. But I bite my tongue and breathe through my anger and frustration.

"Yes. He left a few minutes ago after we wouldn't comply."

"Did you get a name?"

"No, ma'am."

The heater kicks on and ruffles papers on the countertop between us. Daniel's clipped answer bumps my irritation up a notch. The whole situation isn't his fault and I don't want to take my problems out on him, but the fact he seems so nonchalant about this annoys me further.

"Can you tell me what he looked like?"

"A few inches taller than you, gray hair, balding on top. Short-sleeve dress shirt. Khaki pants. Older, but I'm not good with age." He winces. "Until I asked for his identification, he was overly polite."

"Did he say anything else? Besides asking to pick up Clementine?"

He shakes his head. "No, ma'am."

Well, at least my daughter is still here and safe. "Thank you, Daniel. While here, I'd like to review and update who may pick up Clementine."

"Sure thing."

With each tap of the keys on his keyboard, I lose my cool a little more. Why the hell is this my life right now? Why are people trying to steal my daughter? Whoever came to the school today was not Leo. His father, perhaps. No one I know fits the description Daniel provided. Nicely dressed fits Leo's family.

All I want to do is tip my head back and scream at the sky. Scream loud and violently. Scream until my throat becomes sandpaper and my larynx shrivels.

As I update Clementine's approved pickup list to include Jonas—just in case—I decide to withdraw her from school early. At this point, she has less than half the day left. Once she arrives in the office, I take her hand and hold it tighter than usual.

When we walk out of the building, she glances up at me. "Why did you pick me up early, Mama?"

My daughter doesn't need my stress, so I choose to skirt around the truth. "Today has been a crazy day. Just need to have you with me." She hugs my side but doesn't say a word.

I open the back door for her and she hops in. Sitting in the passenger seat, I face Penny. "Not there," I mumble. "Left before we got here. But it wasn't him. Someone older." Parallel lines wrinkle Penny's forehead. "Will you drop us off at Jonas's work? You can keep the car."

"Of course."

In my short-lived life, I have experienced a lot. Not in regards to travel. But actual life experiences. Hope and adoration. Despair and worthlessness. Love and joy.

Today, in this very moment, is the first time I encounter extreme vulnerability. Today is the first time I feel my and my daughter's safety is at risk. And I have no clue where to go from here.

eighteen

JONAS

When I plucked the note off my Jeep this morning, fury slithered in my bloodstream. When Autumn stopped here earlier to collect the note to take to the police and her attorney, her red eyes and withered stature nearly crippled me. But when Autumn called forty-three minutes ago to tell me an unknown man was trying to remove Clementine from school, I lost my shit. Literally.

Once our call disconnected, I threw a wrench at the back wall of the garage. Then, stormed into the office, grabbed a pillow off the couch, and screamed into the stuffed material. More than once. Although the action was cathartic, relief didn't follow.

The measures this man takes to hurt Autumn, emotionally more so than physically, blows me away. Disgusts me more than comprehensible. Makes me violent and irrational. I aim my rage at inanimate objects, but it boils beneath the surface, begging to seep out. I remind myself this is probably all a ploy. A way for him to provoke me or Autumn. And as much as I am dying to take my aggression out on him, I won't.

I refuse to stoop to his level and be a lesser man. Money

may buy you fancy things, but it doesn't make you a decent human. People choose to be decent. From what I have seen so far, Leo has made his choice and it is nowhere near respectable.

For the last five minutes, I have laid on the creeper and stared at the same oil filter. If today were a good day, I would have removed it four and a half minutes ago. I have yet to lift a finger.

Just as I do, the familiar rumble of Autumn's car garners my attention. I roll out from under the car, point to James and ask him to finish the job. After my outburst earlier, everyone here is on edge. So James nods and shifts his attention. After this is all over, I need to treat the staff to beers and burgers.

I jog over to the car. Autumn and Clementine both get out, opposing expressions on their faces. Autumn looks as if she just went ten rounds in a fight and came out visually unscathed. But I know her insides are pulverized. Clementine is all smiles and sunshine. Obviously, she has no idea what all has happened today. Which is good. Children don't deserve to bear the brunt of adult issues.

With as much enthusiasm as I can muster, I haul both my girls in for a hug. "Hey," I whisper in Autumn's ear. "Been worried about you both."

Autumn squeezes me with more oomph. "Can we stay here until you're off work? I-I don't feel safe going anywhere else right now."

"Don't even have to ask." I unravel my grip on them and squat down in front of Clementine. "Hey, sunshine. Let's go sit in my office for a bit. Is that cool with you?"

Clementine nods and scrunches up her nose. "It smells funny here."

Autumn and I laugh. "Yeah. Sometimes the stuff in car

engines smells weird. But I promise the office smells nice." I cup a hand around my mouth and lean into her. "My dad sprays flower air freshener in there sometimes." She giggles and I love how unaware she is of the chaos.

I lead them into the office and tell them to use whatever they need. Before I head out to the garage, I order lunch for the three of us and promise my girls to be in when it arrives.

Back in the garage, Dad wanders over. "Everything okay?" He tips his head toward the office.

There is no use in sugarcoating it. Because shit is definitely *not* okay. "Not really." I relay what happened at Clementine's school. Relay how unsafe Autumn feels. Share how she is doing her best to not let Clementine hear all the nitty-gritty details because it isn't fair to worry her over something she ultimately can do nothing to fix.

Out of nowhere, Dad hauls me in for a hug. "Sorry you're both dealing with this. Let us know if you need help. Even to watch Clementine so you two can run errands or go to appointments."

I nod. "Thanks, Dad."

Taking back over my job, I thank James and work until lunch arrives. Now that Autumn and Clementine are here, I breathe easier. Focus without difficulty. Relax with less effort.

When the food is delivered, Dad tells me to take as much time as I need. I carry the bag into the office and enjoy the next hour with my girls. Clementine has been busy doing schoolwork while Autumn occupied herself with the internet, reading old magazines in the office, and occasionally helping Clementine with her work.

We munch on sandwiches while Clementine tells us about the art project they are doing—a collage made from magazine clippings where each image must represent a letter of their name. Needless to say, her collage will have lots of pictures. While Clementine eats french fries and does a sheet of math equations, I take the opportunity to talk in hushed tones with Autumn.

"Might be a good idea if we update everyone later. We can visit the shop after work, then text everyone not there."

Autumn nods and leans on my bicep while resting her head near my shoulder. "Good plan." I kiss the crown of her head and she closes her eyes. "Just want this to be over."

"Me too. Soon." I take one of her hands between mine in my lap. "Until then, definitely don't want either or both of you alone. Not even at home."

May seem like drastic measures, but when it comes to my girls, no measure is too extreme. I will protect them until my last breath. And that breath won't come anytime soon.

Wetness hits my collarbone, and I tip my chin to look at Autumn. She stares at Clementine with silent tears rolling over the bridge of her nose and down her cheek. I drop a hand from hers to reach up and wipe away her tears. She leans in to my touch and kisses my palm.

Autumn tilts her head on my shoulder, pressing her lips to my neck, my jaw, beneath my ear. My eyes roll back as my jaw falls slack. We have kissed several times with Clementine in the room, but right now, I want to kiss her fiercely. Much stronger than any PG suggested rating.

I cup her jaw and meet her lips in the middle. Warmth and tenderness and intimacy collide as our lips move in time. Soft and gentle at first. But the moment she paints the tip of her tongue across my upper lip, I gasp and tug her closer. Inhale her heady cherry vanilla aroma. Taste the cola on her tongue. Tremble as she adjusts her position and fists my hair. Scoot her closer when she moans down my throat. Groan in return when I brush over her pulse and feel how viciously her heart thumps for me. For us. For this kiss.

When her hands untangle from my hair and drop to my chest, I break the kiss but don't lift my lips from hers. "If she wasn't here right now…"

Autumn presses her lips to mine again. "Same."

Reluctantly, I inch away from her and groan. "I have to get back out there, but only a bit longer. Do you need anything? You can use the computer if you want." She shakes her head. "Be done soon." I kiss the tip of her nose before getting up, adjusting myself as I do.

When I get back to work, Dad and James take their lunch. For a Monday, the garage is slow. Then again, we are caught up on the few labor-intensive jobs we had, which helps other jobs go quicker. While Dad has lunch, I finish a routine oil change James started, plug a tire in no time, and schedule body repair for a crumpled fender.

As a new customer pulls up, Dad exits the office/customer waiting area. I check the wall clock between two of the bay doors. He took twenty, maybe twenty-five minutes for lunch. At minimum, we take thirty. Been that way since day one of Dad buying this place.

After collecting basic information from the customer, I show them to the waiting area while we work on their car. When I walk back into the garage, Dad is gearing up to take over.

"Hey, old man. I got this. You should finish your lunch."

He laughs and shakes his head. "When James gets back, you head out for the day."

What? Although I'm grateful for the offer, I don't want to ditch everyone and overwhelm them. "Why? I can stay longer."

Dad steps closer and rests a hand on my shoulder. "Of course, you *can*. Doesn't mean you *should*." He points his thumb over his shoulder. "They need you more than me right now. And we'll be fine here. Been slow." He taps my shoulder one, two, three times. "Son, there are times when the people you care about are more important than work. You need to recognize those moments and do what's right. And being with them while all this is happening, it's the right choice."

Who knew my dad was philosophical? He is a good man. Always has been. Puts those he cares about above everything else. Which is exactly what he tells me to do now. How can I not be proud of the man who raised me with heart? Hopefully, I meet his expectations when it comes to being a good man. Tough shoes to fill and all.

I pull him in for a hug and hold him longer than our typical hugs. "Thanks, Dad. For everything you've done and always do."

"Love ya, Jonas. Now, stop being all sappy. We have work to get done before you go."

I laugh and slap the back of his shoulder before I release him. We work in sync for almost thirty minutes before James returns. Once he jumps in, I say my goodbyes and collect the girls from the office.

We make a quick stop at my house—which is easier said than done when Clementine and Spartan get together. Once Spartan has done his business, we pile back into the Jeep and drive toward the shop. Autumn has been quiet since we left the garage. More than likely, overwhelmed with everything happening. If my nerves are shot over this whole Leo debacle, I only imagine how crazed she must feel. I just wish there was more for me to do to make it go away.

Monday appears to be an all-around slow business day

when I park the Jeep behind the shop. Autumn leads us inside through the back entrance. When we round the front desk where Penny sits, she pops her gum, bolts out of her chair, and hugs Autumn with undeniable strength.

Penny steps back, holding Autumn at arm's length. "Any updates from earlier?" Autumn shakes her head, still silent.

"We thought it might be a good idea to come update you guys in person."

She nods. "Rex should be done in a few. Rez is indisposed."

Autumn walks us over to her booth and plops down on her stool. I pick Clementine up and sit with her in my lap. Understandably, Autumn is upset and frustrated. But since the day we met, I have never seen her like this. One hundred percent in her head. I would give anything to know what she's thinking right now. To help her trudge through all the *what-if*s and *why*s and *where do we go from here* moments. None of us have all the answers, but we will find them easier together.

Rex finishes up and wipes down his booth. Once everyone comes together, we give the simple version of what happened today. Clementine acts as if she isn't listening, but I notice her ear perk up on occasion.

Everyone is on the same page when it comes to Autumn and/or Clementine always being with someone. The only exception is work and school, which happen by default. For the first time since I met her, Penny stopped chewing gum. Her face never more serious.

"Why don't the two of you stay with me until this settles," I suggest.

Autumn turns to me, eyes wide and jaw slack. "Don't you think that's extreme?"

"Quite the opposite."

"Jonas, I love being at your house. But being there nightly, without everything I need, or everything Clementine needs, it's more of a hassle."

Ouch. I see her point—us picking up their belongings frequently—but it still stings. "Can we at least compromise?" Last thing I need to do is give Autumn something else to worry over.

She tucks her lips between her teeth and rocks her jaw side to side. Her cognac irises have dulled today. Darkened. They dart between mine, glassy and indecisive. I hate that she has to make these choices. I hate that she fears stepping foot outside, worried who might be waiting. Hate that she questions every decision about their lives.

"We should do at least two to three nights a week at the apartment." Her decision lacks confidence. She may change her mind. Make it more time at her apartment. Or… possibly more time at the house. Fingers crossed for the latter.

"Whatever you feel most comfortable with, scarlet. You good with Spartan tagging along?"

Clementine bounces up from my lap. "Sparty!" She rushes Autumn. "Please, Mama."

Autumn tucks a strand of Clementine's hair behind her ear. "Sure, pumpkin." She meets my gaze. "Tonight, let's stay at my place."

I lean in and kiss her forehead. "Fine with me. We should grab dinner soon."

The group disburses. After saying our goodbyes, the three of us pile into the Jeep and pick up a quick bite to eat. We stop at my house, feed Spartan, and gather everything we need for the night.

No matter how many trips it takes, no matter how uncomfortable the arrangement, I will protect my girls.

nineteen

AUTUMN

I told Jonas we would alternate between staying at my apartment and staying at his house. That was Monday. Monday, we stayed at my apartment. Now it is Thursday, and we haven't been at my apartment since, with the exception of packing stuff to bring to Jonas's. To be honest, I would more than love to stay here every night. Question is, am I ready?

Two very different voices clamber inside my head. Take up space and want to be heard. One claims to be reason, while the other claims to be reality. Both make me seem certifiable.

Believe it or not, reason is the temperamental one. The loudest and most annoying voice. Reason spews off all the what-if questions. Reason makes me second-guess myself and the choices I have always made. Makes me paranoid and uneasy. Before reason came into play, I never felt this uncomfortable in my own skin or mind.

Now, reality… she sits in the corner. A quiet spectator. She only speaks up when reason gets a little out of hand. But when reality voices her opinion, everyone stops to listen. Reality stands tall and fierce. Is a force to be reckoned with. Reminds me I deserve to live a life full of love and passion and exultation. I deserve to smile and laugh and joke around with people who lift me up and stand strong beside me. I deserve to live the life of my choosing, not what someone else deems fit.

Some days, reality rises above. Other days, reason stomps her foot and knocks reality down a notch.

Since the note and incident at Clementine's school on Monday, nothing else has happened. Seventy-two-plus hours without a peep. I want to be excited, but worry something crazy will happen if I get ahead of myself. Celebration is an invitation for chaos.

Clementine sits beside Spartan on Jonas's couch, reading her book to him as part of her homework assignment. Jonas stirs a pot of pasta sauce on the stove while the noodles boil and meatballs bake in the oven. I offered to help, but he shooed me away.

"Need me to pack anything for you? Seeing as I have nothing to do."

He side-eyes me over his shoulder. "Already packed. You just stay on the stool. It's okay to just be sometimes."

I roll my eyes at him. "Says the man who hasn't sat still in days."

When Clementine and I stayed over on Tuesday, the house looked different. At first, I had difficulty putting my finger on what changed. Wasn't until we headed to bed, walking down the hall, that I noticed more light in the second bedroom on the way to Jonas's room. I never toured the office set up in the room, but the desk grabbed your attention when walking by. Now the desk was gone.

I just stood in the hall and stared into the room. Jonas stepped up behind me, wrapped his arms around me, and told me he hadn't used the desk in a while. So, he donated it. The bookshelf had been moved to the living room, which is what was different.

But that wasn't such a big deal.

Nope.

Not by a long shot.

I rest my elbow on the breakfast bar, chin on my palm, and smile at Jonas—well, his backside. The man who took it upon himself to clear out a room less used. To repurpose it and put it to better use. Not better for him, though. Better for Clementine.

Two nights ago in the hall, he steered me into the second bedroom, closed the door, and flipped on the light. I didn't see the white-framed twin bed in the dark, but with the light on, I saw it perfectly. It wasn't only a frame and mattress. It was so much more. *Is* so much more.

"Do you like it," he had whispered in my ear. "It's for Clementine. So she has her own bed here. But don't tell her yet. I want to surprise her."

When Jonas told me this two nights ago, I cried the happiest tears of my life in his arms. With the exception of the day Clementine was born.

In that moment, when Jonas confessed his selfless act, I fell even harder for him. Me telling him I love him was there. Right there. Ready to dive headfirst off my tongue. But reason slapped me in the moment and I didn't profess anything.

But the resistance in me is fast fading.

Yes, it terrifies the hell out of me to tell Jonas I love him. It terrifies me to cut myself open, expose my heart, and pray he knows how to handle the beating organ with compassion and tenderness. That he won't abandon me when times get rough. That he won't jump ship because something doesn't go according to plan. Since Leo appeared, Jonas has stood strong at my side. Fought for me, even when I pushed him away. But reason whispers doubt in my ear. Tells me different circumstances create different responses. Maybe next time around, whatever pops up will push Jonas over the edge.

"If you think any louder, I may actually hear what's brewing in that head of yours," he teases as he strains the pasta.

"Just thinking about the room." As promised, I have not told Clementine. If I refer to it as *the room*, she won't make the connection if she eavesdrops.

Still, Jonas glances over his shoulder at her. She flips the page of her book and points out a picture on the page to Spartan. Oblivious.

"Anything in particular?"

"No. Just the room itself." I tuck my lips between my teeth. "What might look good in there."

Jonas blends the pasta and sauce together, then takes the meatballs out of the oven. He sets the pan on the stove, then steps my way while they cool. "Throw some ideas my way."

He tosses me a wink. A wink. Have I ever seen him wink in my general direction? Not so much. Smile? Yes. God, I love his smile. Especially when his dimple makes an appearance. But winks are not a Jonas thing.

I narrow my eyes. "What are you up to?"

"Just making dinner," he says, a wide smile plumping his cheeks and displaying my favorite dimple. *Way to distract me —for now.*

We plate up dinner and eat earlier than usual. Spartan crunches on his kibble and tries to get Clementine to sneak him pieces of meatball. Thank goodness, she doesn't give in to his cute whines and grumpy groans at her feet.

Once we finish dinner and clean up, I check my email

while Jonas grabs his things. An email from Theresa is the bearer of good news.

"Guess what," I say as Jonas walks back out to the living room.

"What's up?"

"The hearing has been moved up. Monday, the twenty-fourth." I smile, glad to have some form of happy news.

"This month?" I nod and Jonas pulls me in for a hug. "Thank god. That's less than two weeks."

His realization swirls in my head. *Less than two weeks.* Before the end of the month, all this will be over. I hope. *Please, let this be over.*

Maybe the hearing adjustment is the reason for all the quiet. No more signs of Leo. No threats or unannounced appearances. I have no plans on jinxing this, but I will take all the good news and positive energy I can get.

"Come on, let's go."

We file out to our cars. Although Operation Don't-leave-Autumn-and-Clementine-alone is still in full swing, it has been deemed safe for me and Clementine to be in my car if someone in the trusted circle follows us. A smidge more freedom while remaining safe.

At the apartment, we crash on the couch and settle in to watch a movie with Clementine. On the nights we stay at the apartment, Jonas sleeps on the couch. Initially, I protested and said he could sleep in bed with me. The gentleman his father raised him to be, he refused to uproot Clementine's normal bed space. It wasn't fair to her.

In the same breath, he also said if she fell asleep on the couch curled up with Spartan, he may reconsider my offer. I don't believe him.

While Clementine watches the movie, Jonas and I watch

each other. He lays on his side—back against the cushions—while I lie on my back. With the softest touch, he slowly traces his fingertip over my skin. Following the motion with his eyes.

Over my collarbone, from shoulder to sternum. Up the column of my throat before brushing my hair aside. Along the sensitive skin beneath my ear. Around the shell of my ear. With each direction change, a shiver rolls through my body. When he reaches my temple, he draws small circles there. Drags his finger down my cheekbone. Encircles my lips, then presses the single digit in the middle before bringing his gaze back to mine.

Have you ever watched your lover as they intimately touch you non-sexually? I have never been so enamored with another person.

Without effort, Jonas loves me. Gives me every non-materialistic gift a woman desires and needs. Worships me. Cares for my daughter as if she were his own.

And he does all this without a single word said. His love is in his actions. The way he cannot keep his eyes off me. How he reveres me as a woman and a mother—strong and capable and exceptional. How he touches me—gentle and rough. The way he kisses me—as if every kiss may be our last. The way he breathes me in and hugs me close.

He leans down and I close my eyes as he presses his lips to mine. Slipping a hand behind my neck, he presses more of his weight into me. I pant when he sucks on my lower lip. Roll my eyes back when he dips his tongue in. Fist his hair when our bodies tangle like wild teenagers.

I really want to take him to bed. Strip him bare. Feel his steely-soft erection between my lips. Taste him on my tongue and swallow every drop when he releases down my throat.

Grind my hips against his face and scream his name as I gloss the stumble on his jaw. Kiss him like a savage and taste my saltiness on his skin.

I want to do all of this and more. But not tonight. Not here.

In my apartment, we exchange simple touches. Touches that imprint your skin more than any tattoo ever could. Touches that express our fierce connection in other ways. The emotional and mental and spiritual.

Reason says all things never stay. But reality gives a swift kick in the ass to reason, telling her to shut the hell up. Because Jonas… he will always be around.

twenty

JONAS

As an adult, I have never celebrated Valentine's Day. Not in the sense of buying flowers and chocolates and gifts for a person I care about. My mom and sisters do not count in this equation. I'm strictly thinking of romantic interests. Considering the only other woman I thought of romantically never reciprocated, I never bought her anything.

For the first time, Valentine's Day is a big deal.

After I leave Autumn's apartment, I drop Spartan off at home and head to work. I relay my plan to Dad when I get to work and he tells me to take a half day so I can get everything done in time. I debate with him a moment, but give up after he tells me he will close the garage for the day if I don't.

Twist my arm.

Before arriving at work, I pictured the day going by slow. Excitement has me jittery and on edge. So, when lunchtime rolls around, I freak out. I let everyone take lunch, with plans to leave when they return.

"What if I don't get everything done in time?" I ask Dad.

"Most of the stores are right next to each other. Unless you have no idea what you're getting, you'll do just fine."

Dad pats my shoulder. "Proud of you, son. And I'm glad you found someone who makes you happy. You deserve it."

"You trying to make me cry, old man," I tease.

"Would be a beautiful thing if you did. Shows how much they mean to you. Never be ashamed to show how you feel." Dad gives my shoulder another pat. "I'll be done in a bit. Then you get out of here and surprise those girls."

Dad takes his lunch and returns in no time. When I try to protest his twenty-minute break, he shrugs and tells me he ate. Conversation done. I finish the car I'm working on then prep to leave. After the tools are back where they belong, I ditch my coveralls and wash up.

"Sure you're good with me heading out this early?"

Dad shakes his head on a chuckle. "If you don't get out of here, I'll spill your secret plans to Autumn." He reaches for his phone.

The second time I brought Autumn and Clementine over for family dinner night, Dad gave her his number in case she ever needed help and she couldn't reach me. She reciprocated. Not only did the exchange shock me—our relationship still so young—it stirred up new admiration for my father. A man I hope to live up to.

"God. Fine. I'm leaving."

"Enjoy your weekend," Dad shouts as I exit the back of the garage.

"You too. Buy Mom some flowers."

I hop in the Jeep and drive toward the mall. Every store I need to hit is within a mile or two. And since it's still early in the day, traffic is light. Altogether, I have five stops. Only one stop will be challenging. So, I make it the first.

The second I set foot in the store, I question every reason behind the choice. But when a woman walks up to me and asks to help, I breathe a little easier. She asks open-ended questions and lights up when an idea strikes. In less than thirty minutes, I swipe my card as she bags up my purchase.

With an extra bounce in my step, I leave the store and go to the next. Fifteen minutes later, I exit the mall with the hardest part of my shopping done. I am in and out of the next stop faster than either shop in the mall. When I reach stop four, Shelly greets me with a goofy smile.

"Feel like I haven't seen you in years," she teases.

"Were you not just at my house last weekend? I swear you hung out, ate the food I grilled, and chatted with my girl."

A breezy smile kicks up her cheeks. "I love how happy you are."

The last time I remember blushing is middle school. So, the sudden heat on my neck and cheeks comes as a surprise. "Thanks, Shell."

After a quick hug, she slips into business mode. "What can I get for you?"

"Obviously, I'm here for flowers." Shelly rolls her eyes at me. "But I don't know what flowers Autumn likes. Or Clementine. I'd prefer to not get roses."

"Too cliché?" she jokes, but continues. "Do you want to get the same for both of them?"

"No. Think it would be nice for them to have flowers they call their own."

Shelly taps her lips for a beat before her eyes light up. "Wait here."

She dashes around the floral shop so quickly it dizzies me. After stopping at several bins, she meets me back at the counter. One hand overflows with flowers while the other holds greenery. This is why I come here. Because Shelly and Elizabeth, Cora's mom, don't mess around when flowers are involved. I love their passion and how easily they can make an arrangement look like art.

"Blush ranunculus and eucalyptus greens for Autumn," she mumbles, setting them on brown paper. "And red poppies, baby ranunculus, daisies, and kumquats for Clementine." She secures the flowers for Autumn in the brown paper with black ribbon. Clementine's flowers are artfully arranged in a mason jar with the same black ribbon tied around the jar threads. Shelly sets a vase on the counter. "When you get home, add water to the mason jar. After you give Autumn her flowers, put them in this vase and do the same."

Although I am thankful for her step-by-step instructions, she talks to me as if I have never bought my mom or sisters flowers here. I let her do her spiel, though. "Thanks, Shell. They're perfect."

I pay for the deeply discounted flowers and we exchange one last hug before I leave.

Next and final stop before home; the grocery store. I breeze through the aisles, man on a mission, and pick up all the ingredients for the dinner and dessert I have planned. Once I check everything off the list, I load everything on the belt at the register and exchange Valentine's chitchat with the cashier. She tells me my lady friend is a lucky woman. *I consider myself the lucky one.*

Minutes later, I haul everything into the house and let Spartan out. I stow the food and flowers while I set up one of the gifts. Finished, I package up the only other present that didn't have a gift wrap option. I set out several candles and light them before filling out a card I bought for Clementine and writing a love letter to Autumn. Once that task is complete, I straighten up around the house and prep dinner and dessert.

Cutting the last of the strawberries, I check the time. Just after four.

"Whatd'ya say, Spartan. Should I tell the girls they can come over now?"

Woof, woof, woof.

"Will do."

I wipe my hands on a towel, then snag my phone from the counter.

Whenever you're ready, come on over.

Almost done prettying ourselves. Be over soon.

I smile at the screen. Neither of you needs to pretty yourselves, I mumble.

The buzzer on the stove goes off and I take the angel food cake out of the oven. I adjust the temperature of the oven and blend the ingredients for the baked five-cheese macaroni. Sprinkling it with bread crumbs, I place the deep dish on a sheet pan and slide it in the oven.

As I deposit the mojo chicken in the oven, Spartan barks like a loon. Which can mean only one thing… they are here.

I open the door to see my girls walking up and Penny waving behind the wheel of Betsy. My cheeks grow painfully tight as I wave back at Penny. *She's letting Penny take the car.*

Spartan tackles Clementine before they reach the door. "Come on, bud. Let them inside." After another lick or two, he runs back in the house, barking for Clementine to follow.

"Hey," Autumn whispers as she sidles up to me.

I lean down and kiss her. "Hey, scarlet." Another kiss. "I have surprises for you both."

We walk into the house. "Oh yeah…" Her voice trails off

the moment she spots the flowers on the breakfast bar. "Jonas." My name rolls softly off her tongue. "You didn't have to buy me flowers." She pivots to face me, a gentle smile on her lips. "You didn't have to buy us anything."

I snake my arms around her waist and draw her closer. "True. But I wanted to." I drop my lips to hers and bring her hips flush to my body. "And there's still more." I step back and weave my fingers through hers, walking her to the bar. "For you." I point to the ranunculus and letter. "For Clementine," I say, pointing to the mason jar of flowers next to a card.

"Thank you." She lifts the flowers to her nose and inhales. "They're beautiful."

"You're welcome. Glad you love them."

"Clementine?"

Her head pops up from the couch where she and Spartan appear to be having a serious conversation. "Yeah, Mama."

"Come see the flowers Jonas got you."

I kiss the crown of her head. "You two enjoy those a moment while I check on dinner."

Autumn and Clementine ogle over the flowers and read the notes I left them. When I peek over my shoulder to see if they are still reading, I spot a tear roll down Autumn's cheek. Normally, I would worry. But the constant smile on her lips tells me the tears are happy ones.

"About ten more minutes until dinner," I announce. Autumn lifts her gaze to mine and I stop breathing. Her cognac irises swirl with admiration and passion and something powerful. Love. *She loves me.* The confession plain as day in her eyes and on her face, but I won't force the words from her lips. She will say the words when she is ready. "In the meantime… Clementine?" She glances up at me from her card. "Would you like your other Valentine's present?"

Her face lights up as she hops off the stool and bounces. "Yes, please."

I walk over to Autumn and lace my fingers with hers. "C'mon, scarlet." She slides off the stool and I lead us to the second bedroom. When I open the door and flip on the light, Autumn gasps and lifts her free hand to her mouth.

"Jonas…" she mumbles.

"Clementine." I squat down and look her in the eye. "This room is for you when you're here. Decorate it however you like. Hang out in here with Spartan. Whatever you want. This is your space."

Her little jaw drops as her eyes widen. "Really?" she asks in disbelief. I nod. She squeals and lunges forward, wrapping her arms around my neck. "Thank you, Mr. Jonas."

She releases the hug and I stand up. "You're welcome. Hope you like it."

She spins around and stares at the oak-framed twin bed. A khaki comforter with a punk version of Alice from *Alice in Wonderland* drapes the mattress. Two matching decorative pillows rest against normal bed pillows. On the floor, a shaggy five-by-seven red rug adds a pop of color to the room. The room still needs more work, but for now, it will do.

"I love it," she exclaims, running and hopping on the bed. "C'mon, Sparty." She pats the bed beside her and he jumps up.

My work here is done.

Autumn and I leave the room and return to the kitchen. She parks on a stool while I check the last of the food cooking.

"You didn't have to do all this," Autumn whispers.

I take what is left in the oven out and set it on trivets before facing her. "Yeah, I did." I circle the bar and step into her. "You and Clementine deserve to be doted on." Leaning down, I kiss her. "And I'm not done yet."

Once dinner is plated up, we call for Clementine. I have a sneaking suspicion we won't see much of her or Spartan, now that Clementine has her own space. While eating, we discuss what movie we should watch tonight. Being Valentine's Day, Clementine suggests a love movie. I laugh at her exaggeration of vowels in the word love.

While I clean up dishes and assemble dessert, I tell my girls to find us a *love* movie to watch. I tote dessert out to the living room and receive oohs and awes from Clementine when she spots my mom's version of chocolate-dipped strawberry shortcake—aka strawberry shortcake with chocolate drizzle. But before either of them reaches for their plates, I hold up my hand.

"Another present. Then dessert." Surprisingly, neither of them says a word. Hands folded in their laps, both smile and bat their lashes. "Actually…" I point to Autumn. "I have two more for you."

I take two velvet bags from my pocket and a small box. Autumn follows every move I make as she tucks her lips between her teeth. I hand the satchel tied with a red ribbon to Clementine. She opens it up and plucks out the silver link chain with a heart charm in the center.

"Look how pretty this is, Mama." Clementine holds up the necklace for Autumn to see. Autumn nods before tipping her head back and blinking rapidly. "Open your presents."

Autumn levels her gaze with mine. "You really didn't have to."

I cup her cheek and nod. "Both of you deserve nothing less."

She clamps down harder on her lips, then swallows. I tip

my head at her gifts and she opens them. Inside her satchel is a matching necklace. The linked chain matches a charm bracelet I spotted on her wrist a time or two. I help them both don the necklaces before Autumn opens the final gift. The one I worry over more than the rest.

With trembling fingers, she peels back the paper and removes the lid. The second she sees the key inside the box, she grabs my wrist. Tears flood her eyes and spill down her cheeks.

"I'm not suggesting anything you may or may not be ready for. But I want you to have a key. In case you need to be here when I'm not. Or just to let yourself in. But Autumn…" I wait until she looks up at me. "There is no pressure. Please don't think I'm pressing you to move in. Not that I wouldn't love to have you both here every day."

She gingerly sets the key back in the box and replaces the lid. Leaning forward, she places it on the table without a word. Then she whirls around and hops in my lap, peppering me with kisses. I wrap my arm around her waist and haul her closer.

"Guess this means you're okay with having a key," I joke.

"Best gift ever." She crushes her lips to mine until Clementine pipes up and asks if we can eat dessert yet.

And just like that, life is perfect. Autumn and I scarf down dessert so we can touch and kiss and do anything except watch the movie. When Clementine passes out, I carry her to bed and we tuck her in. Spartan jumps up and lays at the foot, guarding her.

As we walk out, I leave the door cracked. Weaving my fingers with Autumn's, I guide us down the hall to the bedroom. *Our room.*

The moment our door closes, I step into Autumn. Frame

her face in my hands. Kiss her without reservation. Her fingers trace up my biceps, along my clavicles, winding up my neck and into my hair.

Without hurry, we strip away our clothes. I guide her onto the bed and crawl up until her cognacs line up with my hazels. Sweeping the hair from her face, I press my lips to hers.

Today has been a whirlwind of adoration. Every glimpse, every touch, every kiss, every word. All of it swirls together in kaleidoscope fashion. A pattern of me and Autumn and Clementine. A life full of exhilaration and laughter and love. One I don't want to live without.

My heart gallops into a full sprint as my breathing spikes. Autumn reaches up, traces her fingers from my temple to my chin. I close my eyes and absorb the tingle she ignites under my skin. The burn that never fades away. The fire she blazes beneath my sternum.

I open my eyes and lock on to hers. Her breathing shifts; grows heavier. She sees it in my eyes. Feels it in my touch. Tastes it on my lips. And I won't keep it in any longer.

"I love you, Autumn." The admission soft and strong on my lips. "More than imaginable."

Her eyes glass over and she lifts her lips to mine. The kiss gentle. Heady. A proclamation. And for the first time, she breaks the kiss.

"I love you, too," she whispers against my lips.

"I love you, too," I whisper against his lips.

Beneath my breastbone, the chambers of my heart contract in a vicious rhythm as the rest of my body catches up to this revelation. I drag in a lungful of air and tremble. Jonas ghosts his lips over mine and I close my eyes. A low-frequency buzz radiates off him and spills into me. I have never felt so completely vulnerable and alive in my life.

"You feel that?" he murmurs against my lips. "The energy vibration between us." I nod as the vibration sparks every nerve in my body to life. "Know what that is?"

"No," I confess, breathy.

"Love buzz." He presses his lips to mine. "The energy of two forces merging into one."

I slide my hands down the sides of his torso, past his waist, until I take hold of his glutes. Lean and muscular. I hold him in place as I gently rock my hips up. "Make love to me, Jonas."

His forearms planted on either side of me, he slowly drops his mouth. The soft caress of his lips on mine incinerates something deeper inside me. Love buzz, as Jonas called it.

Deep in my bones. A low-frequency hum simmers in my marrow. Rocks my frame. Jars my strength. Stimulates every nerve ending from head to toe. The sensation starts at the epicenter between my lungs. Radiates until it reaches every possible end point. Then boomerangs back and blooms with fire and zeal and hunger.

I claw my way up Jonas's back. Rock my hips and grind against his length. He trails kisses along my jaw, sucking on my earlobe.

"Wanted to take this slow. Show you how much I love you. But you're making that a bit challenging."

Trailing my hands down his back, I squeeze his ass and press his erection between my thighs. "You do show me. Slow and sweet sex isn't the only way to express love. Sometimes, rough and fast is just as powerful."

"You're going to be the death of me."

"But what a good way to go," I growl in his ear.

Confession. I have never had rough sex. At least not what most people constitute as rough. Considering the last person I had sex with was barely twenty, neither of us had much experience at the time.

With Jonas, though, I don't imagine rough sex being something unenjoyable. I welcome the experience. Welcome the tinge of pain that marries with the pleasure. I may be less experienced in the partner department, but all women have needs. And I have done whatever necessary to satiate those needs over the years. But they don't hold a match to Jonas.

Jonas licks and sucks his way from my ear to my collarbone. Nips and marks my skin. Takes hold of my breast and kneads it in his palm. Drops his mouth to my nipple and sucks with teeth.

The pressure skirts the cusp of pain. Heightens the buzz

low in my belly. Has me rocking my hips up, seeking relief. When he doles attention on the other breast, my eyes pinch shut as my back arches off the mattress. I fist his hair and yank. Hard. His responding growl with teeth has my breath coming harder. Faster. Heavier.

He kisses his way down my midline. Sucking and biting and marking me as his. When he drops between my thighs, I clutch his hair like a horse's reins. Rock my hips up to meet his tongue. Mewl as he teases and tastes. Moan as he builds me up and lets me fall.

And when he crawls back up my body, when he hikes my legs over his shoulders and locks me in place, when he clamps down on my neck... I groan.

He enters me slowly. Inch by glorious inch. And his eyes never veer from mine.

"Good, scarlet?"

"God, yes," I moan.

"Hold on. And let me know if we need to stop."

Stop? Holy hell. What did I get myself into?

Jonas leans in closer. Presses my thighs closer to my belly. Knees almost to my face. The position more awkward than uncomfortable. He kisses my calves as he palms my thighs. Then he rocks his hips forward. Fills me fully. And I bite my fist to stifle my cries.

In and out. In and out. Every movement fluid. Pulsing. With each new thrust forward, he picks up speed. Adds more weight. Hits that spot inside me harder. Builds me up and makes me cry louder.

He slides his hand from my throat to cover my mouth. Presses hard but doesn't mask my nose. "Let go, Autumn."

Sweat drips from his chin to my chest. My eyes roll back and I focus on every sensation he creates. The heat from our skin on skin friction. The sweat slickening our flesh. His girth and strength and stamina. His weight pressing down on me, pounding into me. But most of all, I focus on the love we share.

I fist his hair. Bite his palm. Cry out against his skin as my body has him in a viselike grip. And as soon as my muscles relax, he leans back. Drops my legs to the mattress. Peppers kisses wherever his lips reach until he lands on my lips.

And then he moves again. Slower. Measured. His palm caressing my cheek, my temple, my brow. Down my neck, my breast, the side of my belly, my hip. He makes love to me. Unhurried. Every touch and stroke and caress deliberate and tender.

"I love you, Autumn." He rocks forward. "More than I ever thought I could love another person." Forward again. "And I don't want a day without you by my side."

Reaching up, I frame his face in my palms. Meet him stroke for stroke. "I love you, Jonas." My eyes roll back. "Never thought anyone would matter the way you do." I moan as he drops his lips and delivers an evocative kiss.

Our bodies move in synergy. Steady and unyielding. Constant and loving. Building. Blooming. Higher and higher.

"Look at me, scarlet."

I open my eyes and lock on his gaze. The orange near his pupil glows wild. My body on the brink and he knows it. Feels the way my body starts to grip his tighter.

"Love you, Autumn." His admission all I need to set myself free.

I quiver as my body grips him tight. "Love you, too." And Jonas releases inside me. Lips on mine. Our love sealing every crack our hearts ever held.

Jonas shifts to lie beside me, tugging me close. He

envelops me in his arms and kisses my forehead, my nose, my lips. His touch adding a new layer of timbre or resonance to the buzz swimming in my veins.

No other time in my life compares to this. Loving Jonas is magical. Sublime. Irreplaceable. Before him, I never pictured myself happy with someone else. My priorities were set in stone and immovable. Or so I thought. Now, I never want to picture a day without Jonas. Without his joy and warm heart in my—and Clementine's—life.

I snuggle farther into Jonas's frame. Grip him tighter. "Good night," I whisper against his chest. "Love you."

He gently strokes my hair before kissing the crown. "'Night, scarlet. Love you, too."

The house is unbelievably quiet when I wake. No snores or tip-tap of dog nails or whispered conversations from a little girl and her dog. Which surprises me with how bright the sun filters through the blinds. Has to be past nine, although I have zero intention of moving to check.

While everyone sleeps, I decide to daydream. Fantasize over what life would be like with Jonas. Dream of sharing a bigger home and maybe the pitter-patter of more little feet. Going to weekly Wednesday night dinners and gaining a family. A family much larger and more loving than my own knew how to be. Affectionate people who love to see me and ask how my life has been. Remarkable people who don't criticize or judge who I am or what I enjoy.

They just care for *me*.

I picture a life with Jonas full of endless smiles and hearty laughter. Of sitting on the patio, cuddled in each other's arms, and listening to the cicadas chirp and fire crackle. Of teaching Clementine—and future children—how to ride a bike or grow gracefully into adulthood. I picture all of this and so much more.

And it stirs me to life. Heats my blood and quickens my pulse. Has me desperate for Jonas. To taste him on my tongue. Feel him skin to skin. Hear the hitch in his breath as he climbs higher and higher.

Without second-guessing, I dip beneath the sheet and wake Jonas with my tongue on his flesh. And I feel it. The moment he rouses from sleep. The moment it dawns on him I have my lips wrapped around him.

The more I lavish him with my tongue, the wetter I get. He swells in my mouth; close to climax. But before he releases down my throat, he hauls me up and positions my hips over his. Just as I start to protest, he lifts his hips and pushes inside me. The most unladylike groan rips from my throat.

I slap my palms to his pecs and rock back. Every thick inch of him stretches my walls. Strokes with precision. Drives me wild.

With his grip firm on my hips, I lift my hands to my breasts and palm them while I ride him. We set a relentless tempo. My fingers pinch and tug my nipples as I tip my head heavenward.

"Fuck, you're bewitching," Jonas grunts out.

Then he sits up, hands still on my hips. I wrap my limbs around him like tentacles and lock him in place. He fists my skin tighter, slams me up and down his length. Paints my skin with his breath. Groans in my ear. Dampens my skin. Presses his forehead to mine and holds my gaze. The room smells of sex and forever.

I weave my fingers in his hair, clamp down, and yank his head back. "I want you dripping down my legs."

He groans louder as his eyes roll back. *Slap, slap, slap.* Our hips collide with violence. His jaw slackens; opens wider. His cock grows impossibly thicker inside me. *Slap, slap, slap.*

Then he lets go. As do I.

Eyes open. Breathing stops. Mouth wide. He wraps his arms around my waist and bear-hugs me. Holds me still as he spurts inside me. Fills me. Marks me—again—as his.

And as our breaths quiet down and our heartbeats resume their normal pace, I imagine what it would be like to spend forever in his arms.

twenty-two

JONAS

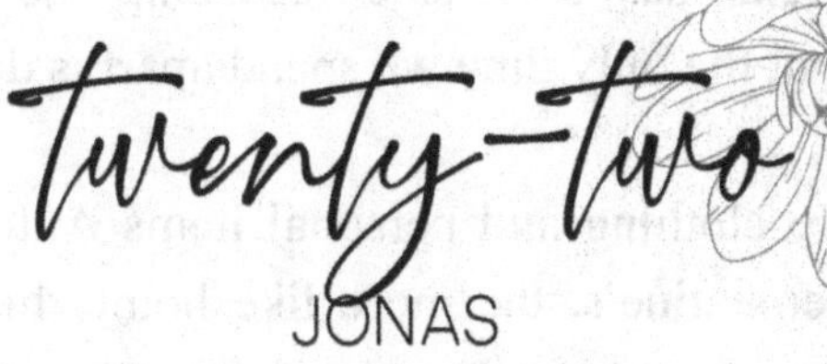

I toy with the ends of Autumn's hair as we lie on the lounger in the backyard. She sits nestled between my legs, her back on my chest as we watch Clementine and Spartan run around the backyard.

She sips her coffee before setting it down and twisting in my arms. Chest to chest, she bends her legs at the knee and crosses her ankles in the air while propping her elbows on me and resting her face in her palms. She looks like an old-school pinup girl. *My pinup girl*.

I sweep a few wayward strands from her cheek. She leans into my touch before kissing my palm. "I love sitting out here. It's peaceful."

"Lounging with you makes it a hundred times better than when I sit here alone."

"What, Spartan wasn't a good lazy day companion?" she teases.

I glance over to where Clementine points out flowers to him and tells animated stories. "He's only ever chill with her. Early on, I was worried he would knock her over being a spazz." I shake my head and laugh. "Guess he only reserves that for me."

Autumn smirks. "Maybe."

A week has passed since I redecorated the second bedroom and gave Autumn a key to my house. And not a day since has Autumn slept anywhere other than my bed. *Our bed.* Nothing official has been said regarding the two of them moving in, but the only time we spend apart is during working hours.

The more clothing and personal items Autumn brings of hers and Clementine's, the more like home this house feels. Small touches in the kitchen or living room. Clementine's *Jack Skellington* cookie jar on the counter. Autumn's current paperback is on the coffee table. A soft throw blanket draped over the back of the couch. Shifting my clothes in the closet and dresser to make room for Autumn. Her scent thick in the air no matter which room I enter.

"Did you want to do anything today? Go anywhere?"

Autumn shakes her head. "Just want to take it easy. With everyone coming over to hang out tomorrow, we should kick back today. Maybe go grocery shopping."

I hook my hands under her shoulders and drag her up my body. A half smile kicks up her cheek before she leans in and kisses me. She drops her hands to my chest and supports herself as we press our foreheads together and breathe each other in.

Having Autumn and Clementine here every day has been incredible. Not everyone pictures themselves cohabitating, but falling asleep and waking up next to Autumn every day feels natural. Right. How it always should have been.

"Might be a good idea to plan what to make for tomorrow," I suggest.

With the hearing on Monday, we thought it would be nice to have everyone over again tomorrow. A chance to hang with our friends and mentally escape the anxiety of the potential outcome.

As far as the case goes, things have been quiet. Too quiet. Almost eerie. Leo had thrown so much drama at us in the beginning, it was easy to assume his theatrics would continue. But since the note on my Jeep, there hasn't been a peep. Part of me hopes Leo has learned his surprise appearances, verbal threats, and shady notes won't rattle us the way he expects. But I am not naïve enough to believe he doesn't have other tricks up his sleeve. Men like Leo don't show up out of nowhere, make a scene, then drop off the face of the earth.

I stare up at my girl and check for any signs of worry. Look for tension in her jaw or the occasional twitch in her eye. Don't need her bottling up anything when it comes to Leo and this case. But as I study the smooth lines of her skin and fiery swirl of her cognac irises, I see nothing off-putting. All I see is happiness and warmth and love.

"Maybe we should do a themed cookout," she states with enthusiasm.

"Did you have something in mind? It is a party for you, after all."

A few days ago, Clementine came to me when Autumn stepped away to use the bathroom. She talked in hushed tones and asked what I was getting Autumn for her birthday. I asked what day her birthday was because it had been top secret. Clementine eagerly shared everything. Not only was Autumn a leap day baby, but she also rarely celebrated her birthday.

That changes this year.

So, when the idea of having everyone together again came up, I suggested we do it as a birthday/we're-going-to-win-the-case party. The shocked expression on Autumn's face when she realized I had top intel on her birthday was priceless. She may not have enjoyed celebrating her birthday before, but I promise to make each and every one of her future birthday's memorable.

"Since it should be warmer tomorrow, let's do something tropical."

Winter in Florida lasts two months, if we are lucky. And this year is no exception. Winter may not officially be over, but the sun warms the air a little more each day.

"Tropical sounds perfect. Do you want to decorate? Or only make tropical foods?"

"Definitely food. Not so much of the decor. I'd rather spend the money elsewhere."

An idea sparks. "Let's figure out the food and drinks, then stop and pick up tiki torches. They're tropical and we can use them year-round."

"Deal."

We lounge out back a little longer before heading in and planning the menu for tomorrow. Once the shopping list is made, we shop early on so we can relax the remainder of the day. We purchase several tiki torches at the home improvement store to strategically place around the yard. Then leave the grocery store with four armfuls of bags.

The back half of the day is spent lounging on the couch with movies and books and cuddles. Lazy weekends had never really been my thing, but they are growing on me fast. Who knew just being around the right person made everything perfect?

After dinner and more movie time, we shuffle off to our rooms and call it a night.

Once Autumn and I wear each other out between the sheets, I tug her against my chest and easily fall asleep.

Bam! Bam! Bam!

I startle awake and glance at the clock. Four in the morning. Autumn shoots up and holds the sheet to her chest. "What was that?"

Bam! Bam! Bam!

Spartan runs out of Clementine's room and barks in the living room. Is someone breaking in?

I jump out of bed and throw on pants. "Stay here," I tell Autumn. Bolting to the living room, I peer through the blinds and scan the porch and yard. But I don't see anyone. The motion light kicked on and illuminates most of the yard. I scan every inch thoroughly, stopping when I see Autumn's car.

"What the fuck?"

Autumn peeks her head out of the bedroom but doesn't step out. "What is it? Is someone out there?"

I walk back toward the hall and point toward Clementine's room. "Go lie with her," I tell Spartan. He jogs past me and runs into her room, jumping back on her bed. When I reach the bedroom, I search for a hoodie and my phone. I step into Autumn and frame her face in my hands. "Please stay inside while I check your car. Looks like someone busted your windshield."

Her chin wobbles as her eyes glaze over. "Please be careful."

I lean down and kiss her. "Always. Stay inside." She nods, following me to the living room and sitting on the couch.

Walking toward the front door, I grab the baseball bat I stash in the corner. I stare out the peephole before opening the door and stepping out. Everything is quiet as usual. With each step I take, I scan my surroundings again. The motion light flips on as I step into the sensory field. My eyes dart left and right. Ears zero in on the slightest sound. The closer I get to Autumn's car, the more the hair on the back of my neck rises.

"Fuck," I mutter as I get within feet of her car.

The windshield isn't just busted. In all honesty, it looks as if someone pummeled it with a sledgehammer. The glass isn't just webbed. It is thoroughly destroyed. Hammered so many times the glass is caving in. Bashed to the point that the glass is as clear as a blizzard.

I grab my phone from my back pocket and open the camera, taking several pictures. Pocketing my phone, I reach for the note under the wiper blade. Walking to the end of the drive, I glance up and down the street and see nothing out of the ordinary.

I unfold the paper and growl.

I warned you.

Throwing my hands up, I shake my head. "Too chicken-shit to come at me? Not man enough to discuss this face to face? Breaking shit and leaving notes doesn't scare me. And you're no man. Just a fucking coward." I want to scream and pound my chest, but I maintain my composure before heading back inside.

In the house, Autumn runs up to me. Eyes scanning me head to toe. "What happened?"

I explain what happened to her car and the new note. She covers her mouth and shakes her head. "Come here," I tell her, opening my arms. I hold her a moment before bracing her at arm's length. "Need to call Dad in a bit, so we can tow your car to the shop. Should also update the police report with the incident."

"Why?" Autumn whispers. "Why do this? What does smashing my windshield gain?"

I take a deep breath and circle my thumbs over her shoulders. "Probably trying to rile us up."

Does this piss me off? You better believe it. Will I cave to this juvenile behavior and the cowardice threats? Not a chance in hell. There is too much at risk to allow my emotions to take over. No, I need to remain levelheaded. To be the real man in this scenario.

After checking the locks on the doors, I guide us to the couch and lie down. "Let's rest a little longer. Then we'll get up and take care of this."

I pull Autumn against my chest and hold her. Soon, her breathing levels out and I close my eyes, drifting off.

~

"Miss me already?" Dad says when he answers his phone.

"Ha ha, old man. Actually, wanted to ask a favor."

"What's up?"

I take a deep breath. "Someone smashed in Autumn's windshield last night. I need it towed to the shop, but I'm not comfortable leaving them alone at the house."

"What the hell?" When Dad starts cursing, you know a nerve has been struck.

I relay the alarming wake up in the early morning and explain the condition of the glass and the note left behind. He mumbles unintelligible words into the phone. Dad and I are similar creatures and right about now, he's working hard to keep his temper in check. Autumn may not be his daughter,

Clementine not his granddaughter, but he protects and stands up for them just the same.

Dad agrees I shouldn't leave and tells me he will head down to the garage and drive the flatbed over.

"Really appreciate it, Dad. Thank you."

"We're family, Jonas. Wouldn't have it any other way."

After breakfast, we hang on the couch until Dad shows up. We chat while he loads the car on the flatbed. He tells me he knows where we can get a windshield to replace Autumn's and not to worry. Before he drives off, he promises to secure her car in the body bay of the garage. Thankfully, we have security cameras around the shop. If anything happens while we aren't there, we have "eyes" on the place.

When Dad drives off, I head back inside and sidle up to Autumn on the couch. "All taken care of." She tucks her lips between her teeth and nods slowly. I bring my thumb and forefinger to her chin and lift her gaze to mine. "Hey, there isn't much else we can do right now. So, as best we can, let's try to enjoy the day and our time with everyone later. Okay?"

She blinks back the tears fighting to escape. "Okay," she croaks out.

I press a chaste kiss to her lips. "This will all be over tomorrow. Let's focus on that and celebrating you."

We spend a little longer on the couch before hopping into action. We have a long list of things to do before everyone arrives—food, cleanup, setup—and divvy up the list so no one is overwhelmed. For obvious reasons, we give the simpler tasks to Clementine. But she will also help Autumn with a few recipes.

In no time, the house is clean and the kitchen counters are littered with bowls and platters of food. Going with the tropical theme, everything we have on the menu contains either fruit or Polynesian flavors. Autumn also messaged Cora before we went shopping yesterday and asked what to buy, so she didn't have to bring separate food.

Our friends slowly arrive at the house. No one asks where Autumn's car is, and we don't bring up the topic. Instead, we spend hours with our favorite people. Our family. We smile and laugh and enjoy ourselves.

Gavin, Rez, and Micah man the grill with me. Cora, Shelly, Penny, and Tatyana lounge on the outdoor couch with Autumn. Rex, Erin, Iliana, and Trevor chat near the cooler and banquet table of snacks. And Clementine plays tag with Ashton and Spartan in the yard.

I love how we have all easily blended together. Four months ago, I never would have pegged this as my life. In love. A backyard packed with people who care about me as much as I do them. None of those people my kin. Each and every one of them there for me in a heartbeat.

Couldn't ask for a better life.

After we devour dinner, Clementine lights the candles on Autumn's pineapple upside-down cake and everyone sings "Happy Birthday". Cake is eaten and gifts are handed over. Autumn blooms under the attention and I vow to make each of her birthdays going forward better than the previous. She had no expectations of being showered with gifts, but doesn't turn a single one down.

One by one, our guests give us hugs and say good night. Penny, Cora, and Gavin hang around long enough to help us clean up. After the last farewells are given, we tuck Clementine in and get ready for bed.

"Thank you for today," Autumn says as she peels away her clothes.

I step into her and wrap my arms around her. "My pleasure, scarlet." I kiss the tip of her nose. "Next year will be even better."

She holds my gaze a moment. "As long as I have you, every year will be perfect." Her gaze drops to my lips as she licks hers. "Now, I'm ready for my favorite present," she whispers.

"Oh, yeah?" She nods. "And what's that?"

"You." She peels my shirt over my head and pushes me down onto the bed.

As she crawls up my body and presses her skin to mine, I wish her a happy birthday and lose myself to her.

twenty-three
AUTUMN

I scoop cheesy scrambled eggs onto a plate and add a slice of buttered toast. Setting it on the breakfast bar for Clementine, I pour her a glass of orange juice.

Clementine swings her dangling feet as she eats her breakfast. To her, today is just a typical Monday. Breakfast before school. Getting dressed and gathering her backpack of school supplies.

But today is far from a typical Monday. Quite the opposite, actually. Today, my daughter's future is in the hands of a judge. A judge I have never met and know nothing about. A judge who reads over a stack of papers and listens to our attorneys as they plead our case. And there is nothing I can do except try to remain calm. On the outside, at least.

Jonas strolls into the kitchen in jeans and a T-shirt. Last night, we decided to dress as we normally would in the morning. We didn't want Clementine to go to school asking why we were dressed up or with worry in her heart. So, for now, we go about the morning as if nothing is different.

"'Morning, scarlet." Jonas steps up behind me, wraps his arms around my waist and kisses my temple.

"'Morning. Hungry?"

He nods. "Little bit."

I portion out the last of the eggs and make us each some toast. After we finish eating, we gear up and drive Clementine to school. She bops and sings in the back seat, and I can't help but tear up a little. But I resist the urge to cry and swallow the wad of emotion lodged in my throat.

Just before we reach the drop-off point in the car circle, I spin around in my seat. "Hey, pumpkin. Hope you have a good day at school. Are you doing any fun projects?" Jonas rubs small circles on my thigh, trying to soothe me as I engage with Clementine.

I don't want to consider this my last opportunity with my daughter, but what if it is? What if the judge sides with Leo and I am ordered to hand custody over to him before the end of the day? Doesn't seem logical, but I have also never been in a situation like this. I have never had to think about the possibility of losing my child to someone who never cared until eight weeks ago.

"We're making aliens in art class today," she says with exuberance.

"How cool. Do you know what you want your alien to look like?"

Until we reach the drop-off, Clementine goes into animated detail on how she plans to create her alien. When it's time to say goodbye, I choke back my words and hug her harder than normal.

"Have a good day, pumpkin. See you later."

"Bye, Mama. Bye, Mr. Jonas. See you after school." She hops out of the Jeep and walks past the gate into the school.

I stare after her until she heads into the building. As soon as she vanishes, I lose it. Tears spill down my cheeks and I sob at the plausibility of not doing this every day. Of not dropping my daughter off at school. Of not hugging her whenever I please. Or being able to enjoy the little moments. The animated conversations. Watching a movie with her every night. Witnessing her evolve from a girl into a young woman.

"Know it's not easy, but try to stay optimistic. Keep telling the universe you *will* get to keep her. Put it out there."

And I do. I pray to whoever listens and ask them to let today end well. To let Clementine stay with me, where she is loved and happy and healthy. To let today be the last day I hear from or speak to Leo again.

We get back to the house and rush to get ready. Jonas changes into gray dress slacks and a black button-down. Considering I see him in jeans and a T-shirt most days, I look forward to peeling his clothes off later.

"Quit looking at me like that," he states.

"Like what?" I play coy.

"Like you want to rip my clothes off." He chuckles when I shrug and my favorite dimple makes an appearance. "We'll have time for that later. When we're celebrating."

"Celebrating," I mumble. "Yes."

I finish getting ready. Apply a light coat of makeup and pin the top half of my hair back while letting the rest hang in loose waves. I lint brush my knee-length black and red dress, shifting the skirt a little to make sure the small pleats at the base sit over my knees.

"You look beautiful," Jonas says from the doorway. "We should get going."

We head out the door and drive toward downtown. The traffic is light heading toward the beach this time of day. Most residents are heading out, and it's still early for the snowbirds to drive to the beach.

By the time Jonas turns on Court Street, my palms are clammy. As he pulls into the parking lot, locates a space to park, and feeds the meter, my nails dig into my skin. My heart beats out of my chest as Jonas opens my door and holds his hand out.

"I've got you. Don't worry about what's going on around us."

He guides us into the courthouse and we go through security. Past the screening area, I spot Theresa and wave. Once we catch up to her, she shakes Jonas's hand before pulling me into a hug.

"Today is a big day. I know you're nervous, but I need for you to compartmentalize it as much as possible. Show your strength. Wear it on your sleeve. Do not bow or bend or show vulnerability. It won't matter to the judge, but if his defense sees it, they'll use it as ammunition."

I take a deep breath and shake my arms at my sides. "Okay. I can do this."

Theresa turns to Jonas then. "Glad to see you here, Jonas. Autumn will need your support here today, but do me one favor." Jonas's brows shoot up in question. "While in or near the courtroom, do not speak for Autumn. Although you may have good intentions, she needs to display her strength and not be outshone." Then she bounces her eyes between the both of us. "And both of you, try not to engage in any unsavory behavior. Don't speak to Leo or his attorney. Better to err on the side of caution."

Once we both agree, Theresa walks us through the courthouse and leads us to the courtroom where the case will be decided.

As we approach, Jonas speaks up. "Theresa, there was

also another incident." Jonas looks to me briefly. "Autumn's windshield was smashed and a note was left."

Jonas pulls his phone from his pocket and shows Theresa shots of Betsy and the note.

"Were the police notified?"

"Yes," he responds, stowing his phone.

"Perfect. Hopefully we don't need it, but the evidence ways in our favor."

We sit on a bench just outside the room and hold each other's hands. No words are exchanged as I lean into Jonas. He draws small circles on my skin and soothes the anxiety ripping through my bloodstream.

Theresa clears her throat and we both look up in time to spot Leo and an older man at his side. I release Jonas's hand and sit up straighter. For the next however long, I shove every insecure thought about myself and losing Clementine in a closet in my mind. Leo's attorney steps up and shakes hands with Theresa. I suppose most attorneys in the area know each other and are cordial, even when they are on opposing sides.

Leo stares at me and Jonas. A wicked gleam on his face. He doesn't say a word, just stands beside his attorney with his hands shoved in his overpriced suit pockets.

The door to the courtroom opens and a man in security attire steps out. "You may come in now. Judge Walton will be ready to proceed momentarily."

Leo's attorney heads for the door, Leo on his heels. Before Theresa moves to enter, an older couple steps in line to go inside.

The moment I get a good look at them, I stop breathing. *What the actual fuck?*

Every muscle in my body turns to stone. I clutch Jonas's arm to stabilize myself. My throat runs dry and my mouth feels tacky. I blink a few times, wondering if my mind is playing tricks. But they are still there.

And when they sidle up to Leo, his wicked gleam grows tenfold. They enter the courtroom, and I hold us outside a moment longer.

"What the fuck," I whisper.

"Who are they?" Theresa questions.

"My parents. They kicked me out after learning I was pregnant and that Leo and I were no longer together."

"Why would they be here?" I shake my head at Theresa. "Either way, shove aside whatever you're feeling. Remember what I said earlier?" I nod. "Okay. Take a deep breath. Loosen your grip on Jonas. And let's go in there and win this."

I inhale deeply, over and over. When I loosen my grip on Jonas, I shake out my hands. With a few minutes left, we stroll into the courtroom and I keep my eyes forward, away from Leo and my parents.

A moment after we sit and Theresa takes out a thick binder, Judge Walton walks out. We rise from our chairs and stand.

"Be seated," she says. Judge Walton scans the documents in front of her. "Today's case is a petition of custody for Clementine Arianna Rooker." She glances at Leo and his attorney, then us. "Ms. Rooker. If I'm reading the documentation correctly, you have had sole custody of Clementine since birth?"

I glance at Theresa and she nods. "Yes, Your Honor."

Judge Walton nods then looks to Leo. "Mr. Parker. It is my understanding you have not formally met your daughter. Please tell me why."

Part of me jumps for joy when Judge Walton puts Leo on

the spot. Although, no doubt he has been schooled in his responses.

"Your Honor, I was a young man when I learned I would become a father. I made a juvenile decision and walked away. I am here today to correct said decision."

Judge Walton hums and shuffles through the documents in front of her. She pins Leo with her gaze again. "Mr. Parker, your daughter is seven and a half years old. Why are you suddenly interested in her well-being? Why are you filing for sole custody when you have never interacted with her?"

Leo swallows. Beneath the table, I catch his leg bouncing. I give a mental victory fist pump at his nervousness.

Since this all started, these are the exact questions I have asked. No normal person files for sole custody when they have never made attempts to be in a child's life. When they have never shown signs of caring or wanting to get to know the child.

"Your Honor, there aren't many decisions in my life I regret as much as abandoning my daughter." His knee bounces faster. "I would like to make amends. Provide her with whatever her heart desires. Make sure she wants for nothing." He fidgets with the hem of his jacket under the table. "I want to get to know her."

Judge Walton purses her lips and doesn't look away from Leo. "I see." I don't miss how Judge Walton's eyes shift back to my parents before coming my way. "Ms. Rooker. Would you be open to shared custody with Mr. Parker?"

Theresa glances at me before speaking up. "Your Honor, when the initial suit began, Ms. Rooker agreed to allow joint custody so long as she maintained majority. She also wanted to include Clementine's opinion in the matter, seeing as she has never met her father and may be frightened to be left unattended with a stranger. Ms. Rooker stated she would allow supervised visitation with Mr. Parker and his family until Clementine felt comfortable being alone with them."

Judge Walton faces Leo. "Mr. Parker, did you refuse these terms?"

Sweat beads on Leo's temple and I beam inside. This is not going according to his plan. *See, money doesn't always work in your favor.*

"I did, Your Honor."

"Why?" Judge Walton asks, bluntly. "Why do you feel your daughter needs to be fully removed from her mother's custody? Has Ms. Rooker done something untoward?"

"No, Your Honor. I just…" Leo shifts his face enough to side-glance my parents. And that glance answers every question I have asked since the day he stood in front of my apartment. It isn't Leo who wants Clementine. It's my damn parents. Again, what the actual fuck?

"Mr. Parker. May I ask your relationship to the man and woman behind you?"

Leo fists his suit jacket. The bead of sweat rolls down his temple and drips from the angle of his jaw. I am dying to hear his answer. "This is Burton and Kathryn Rooker. Autumn's parents."

"Ah, I see. And why are Ms. Rooker's parents sitting behind you and not her?"

This just keeps getting better and better. If I asked these questions, Leo would give me an angry rebuttal and storm off like an adolescent. But he can't be a loose cannon with Judge Walton.

"I'd like to rescind my petition for custody," Leo belts out. I gasp at the same time my parents turn beet red and sneer.

"My choice to file for sole custody was irrational and hasty. My apologies to everyone."

"Well, this makes my day run a bit smoother," Judge Walton states. "But, you're not off the hook yet, Mr. Parker. We will not discuss the details today, but your attorney will be receiving documentation from my office regarding missed child support."

Leo hangs his head. "Yes, Your Honor."

Judge Walton looks to me. "Ms. Rooker. I hear by award you sole custody of Clementine Arianna Rooker." She lifts her gavel and claps it to the base. "This hearing is adjourned."

We all stand as Judge Walton exits the courtroom. As soon as she enters her chamber, I spin around and hug Jonas.

"See, scarlet. Nothing to worry about." He hugs me tight to his chest. "It was great to watch him sweat, though."

I laugh. "It was, wasn't it."

twenty-four

JONAS

Autumn stands tall beside me, and I have never been prouder to have her on my arm.

While we wait for Leo, his attorney, and Autumn's parents to leave, Theresa talks softly about next steps. Paperwork that will follow in regards to back child support and any future support. Autumn disputes the notion, stating she doesn't want a dime of the money. But Theresa comes back with a better solution—a future savings for Clementine. Whether for college or a first car or when she decides to move out.

Leo and his attorney, as well as Autumn's parents, start for the door, but Leo pauses before exiting.

"Autumn, I apologize for all this." He rocks back on his heels. "And I want to forego any visitation. With me and my family. Sorry to have put you through all this. I will pay your attorney's fees."

Well, well, well. Mr. Hotshot is just full of surprises today. Either way, I am glad he had a change of heart. Not sure what provoked it, but maybe his morality kicked in. Thank god it did before the judge made a decision.

Autumn nods and gives a gentle smile. "Thank you."

The four of them leave the courtroom. Autumn's parents still appeared perturbed by the outcome, but I really don't care. We hang back for a few minutes and allow them to get a head start on leaving.

"See, nothing to worry about," I say, squeezing Autumn to my side. "I knew everything would swing in our favor."

Autumn peers up at me with a sparkle in her intoxicating eyes. "Oh, did you now?"

I nod. "Yep."

After a few minutes, we exit the courtroom. Before parting ways with Theresa, she tells Autumn she will reach out to her as soon as she receives the paperwork. Should be straightforward and only need signatures.

We walk down the steps outside the courthouse, hand in hand, smiles plastered on our faces. "We should definitely celebrate," I suggest. "A nice dinner, or maybe a special dessert. Something."

"I…" Autumn stops short and I follow her line of sight. To my Jeep. Where her parents stand, arms tight across their chests.

Not sure what their game is, but I kept an eye on them the entire time in the courtroom. They sat behind Leo, hands folded in their laps, expressions blank. Mostly.

As soon as Autumn told me who they were, something didn't sit right with me. Why the hell would they show up to a custody hearing for Clementine? One—Autumn hasn't spoken to or seen them in almost as long as Leo. So, it's not as if they heard the news from her. Two—they sat behind *Leo*. Her parents sat behind *him* in silent support.

Why?

Not as if he and Autumn had been dating for several years and her parents developed a loving relationship with him. From what Autumn said, she and Leo had been together less than a year. During their time together, not much of it revolved around time spent with either of their families.

And then it clicks into place. The puzzle pieces lock together and form the bigger picture. I see it now. When their faces turned bright red in the courtroom as Leo forfeited. The way Autumn's father gnashed his teeth as the judge announced Autumn the sole custodial parent of Clementine. Their balled fists as they rose from the bench. The disgust in their eyes as they left the courtroom.

They did this. They went to Leo and orchestrated this whole mess.

Her father steps closer. "She doesn't belong with you," he seethes.

Pissed, I step protectively in front of Autumn and point a finger at him. "You need to back the fuck up."

"What are you going to do, boy." He steps closer. "You gonna hit me? Go right ahead. Plenty of cops around here to haul you to jail."

"Actually, I won't hit you. That's what you want. To see me hauled off in cuffs."

Autumn's mother comes to her father's side with a sneer on her face. "That's what you deserve, lowlife."

Behind me, Autumn's body tenses. Her nails dig into my biceps. Before I can stop her, she steps around. "No," she shouts. "You don't get to come here and act high and mighty. Not after sending your daughter to live on the streets. Not after you shielded yourselves behind a man who abandoned his child. Who the hell do you think you are?"

Her father steps within feet of Autumn and I shove him

back. "Don't test me."

He throws his head back and laughs. "You don't scare me, boy." Then he faces Autumn. "You don't deserve her. What kind of mother works in a tattoo parlor and dates a mechanic? Don't you realize the damage you're doing to that girl? She won't live up to her potential."

"Think you can do better, *father*?" Autumn breathes heavily. "Because, in your eyes, I didn't turn out so great."

Her remark meant to make him falter has me wondering if she sees herself this way. As a failure. But I don't dwell on it now. There isn't time. Because he steps closer. Too close.

"How dare you speak to me with such petulance. Your mother and I raised you with good morals and faith. You best respect me, girl."

"Respect you?" Autumn inches closer to him. I remain on her heels. "Respect is earned, not handed over. Clergy collars don't make you righteous, *father*. Nor do they mean you *deserve* respect more than someone else."

"I warned you," he sneers. *I warned you.* The note on Autumn's car yesterday. Moments ago, he said *she doesn't belong with you.*

Holy shit. Holy. Shit.

"It was you," I mutter.

Autumn faces me, brows pinched. "What?"

I meet her eyes. "The notes, your windshield. It wasn't Leo." I point at her father. "You did this." His smug smile all the response I need.

But before I react, Autumn's mother storms forward and backhands her. Autumn falls to the ground and everything around me goes red. I won't hit a woman, but I sure as shit won't stand for anyone hitting Autumn.

I reach out and grab her wrist. "Get your filthy hands off me," she screams. But I refuse to loosen my grip.

Her father steps forward and I glare at him. "Don't test me. I won't hit her, but I will gladly knock you out."

I glance around the lot, scanning for a police vehicle. Spot one in the distance, an officer sitting behind the wheel, and wave my arm high. The police cruiser veers our way and stops a few car lengths back. After talking into the radio on her shoulder, the officer steps out of the car and approaches us.

"What seems to be the problem?"

I lift Autumn's mother's arm. "This woman just assaulted my girlfriend. She, and this man, approached us in the lot after our hearing in the courthouse."

The female officer steps closer to Autumn, who hasn't stood up yet, and squats in front of her. "Are you alright, ma'am?" Autumn nods and the officer extends a hand to help her up. "Tell me what happened here." Her question directed at Autumn.

Autumn explains the reason we came to the courthouse today. How she was shocked to see her parents with her ex. Then, she gives a small backstory regarding her parents before explaining what happened as we approached the Jeep.

Before the officer begins questioning Autumn's parents, I interject about the harassment and police report she filed. I add how Autumn's father basically confessed to the notes and damage after I put the pieces together.

"You can't prove shit, lowlife," her father hisses.

Autumn steps up to her father. Gets in his face. Emboldened with the officer at her back. "Did you do this? Did you write those notes and trash my car? Try to take my daughter away from me by using her birth father as a scapegoat?"

His lip curls. Eyes narrow. He leans in, inches from her face. "You don't deserve to be her mother. Gallivanting around like a whore. Living a trashy life. No sign of God in your life. Worthless." He inches back and spits at her feet. "You're no daughter of mine."

The officer steps around Autumn, grabs his hands and yanks them behind his back. She reads him his rights and steers him to the back seat of her car. All the while, Autumn's mother thrashes in my grip.

"Who do you think you are?" she hollers at the officer. "How dare you arrest a man of the cloth. You'll burn in hell for this." She shifts her gaze to Autumn. "As will you. You disgust me. At least your sister knows what it means to be a good Christian woman. At least I don't regret her coming from my womb."

I tighten my grip on her wrist. "Best if you stop speaking now. Before you dig yourself in a deeper hole."

Autumn sidles up to me, takes my free hand and shakes her head. "No, it's okay. Let her say whatever she wants." Autumn turns her attention on her mother. "I've always known who you are, mother. Always known I wouldn't live up to your expectations. As a child, it hurt when I never made you happy or proud. As a woman…" she sighs, "I don't care. There has never been a day in my life where I felt your love. Ever. Growing up under your scrutiny made me feel small and meaningless. The day I left… that was the day I woke up. Came to life. I may have lived in a shelter for a short time, but even those people cared for me more than you ever did." Autumn wraps her hand around my waist. "And finding Jonas, discovering true love, has wiped away every ounce of hurt you and father inflicted upon me."

Caught up in her proclamation, I miss the slight shift as

Autumn's mother swings her free hand forward. A crack ripples in the air as her hand connects with Autumn's face.

"You ungrateful little witch," her mother hisses.

The officer jogs over from the cruiser, yanks Autumn's mother's wrists behind her back, and cuffs her. As she walks her to the cruiser, she prattles off Miranda rights.

I face Autumn, framing her cheeks in my hands. "Are you okay?"

Her eyes glaze over as she stares up at me. "Yes. No. I don't know."

On the verge of tears, I hug her to my chest and turn her face away from the police cruiser. "Got you, scarlet." She fists the back of my shirt, trembling against my frame. "Shh, shh, shh. I got you." I sway her slowly in my arms.

As her grip loosens on my shirt, the officer approaches us. "Ma'am, I need to know if you'd like to press assault charges."

Autumn peeks up at me, seeking guidance. I want to tell her yes. Want to tell her she should not allow them to get away with everything they have done. But I don't. Instead, I give her a soft smile that says the choice is hers. I will never rob her of her choices. And this decision, although it weighs heavily, is one she should make on her own.

She swallows and meets the officer's gaze. "Yes." Her frame relaxes in my arms. "I want to press charges."

The officer takes out a business card from her breast pocket and writes on it before handing it to Autumn. "The case number is on the card. As soon as possible, we need you to come to the station and give a formal statement." Autumn nods. "If anything else occurs, call the number on the card." The officer smiles, the corners of her eyes crinkling. "Sorry this happened to you. Try to enjoy the rest of your day."

Turning on her heel, she walks to the cruiser, gets in, and drives off.

Autumn sighs and I steer her toward the Jeep. "C'mon. I know exactly where to go."

What the hell just happened?

Jonas helps me up into the Jeep. I buckle my seat belt and stare out the windshield, the world around me a clouded haze.

Today has been a roller-coaster ride from hell. And it isn't noon yet.

When my parents appeared outside the courtroom, confusion set in. The last time we spoke was the day they banished me from their lives. *"No daughter of mine will have a child out of wedlock."* Those were my father's final words to me. Literally disowning me with my mother at his side. She hadn't even flinched at his words. If anything, she appeared relieved I was leaving.

What kind of people do that?

Jonas gets in the Jeep but doesn't start it. We sit in silence as the last thirty minutes process. Their cruel words. Bringing a hand to my cheek, I rub against the sting beneath the surface. I zone out and scan memories over the last seven and a half years. Plucking out every oddity I couldn't explain. Wondering if my parents had been preying on me—preying on my daughter—all this time.

"How are you?" Jonas asks, breaking the silence. He reaches across the console and weaves our fingers.

I twist in my seat and face him, leaning against the headrest. "Freaked out. Puzzled. Hurt." I shake my head. "Relieved. Glad this is all over."

He brings my hand to his lips and kisses my knuckles. "Sorry you had to deal with all this in the first place."

"Not your fault."

"No, but no one deserves to deal with what just happened."

We stare at each other, his thermal pools a swirl of emotions. Sadness. Worry. Happiness. Hope. I grab hold of the last two and hug them to my heart. I fear the first two will linger if I don't tell him more about what happened with my parents. And the way I was raised.

"Hate to say it," I croak, my throat like sandpaper. "But I expected nothing less."

Jonas juts his bottom lip out, the corners of his eyes turning down. I lift my free hand and trace his lower lip from corner to corner.

"Growing up in the Rooker house was not like being around your family."

"You don't need to explain, Autumn."

I nod. "That's one of the things I love about you, ya know. How you don't hold expectations over my head." He smiles as I stroke my thumb over his cheek. "But I need to get this out."

"Okay. Just don't feel obliged."

I close my eyes and take a deep breath. Jonas turns into my palm and kisses the center. His touch buzzes under my skin and shoots a current straight to my heart. When my eyes open and lock on his, peace washes over me. Even with the pain of the past thrown in my face minutes ago, Jonas settles every anxiety-ridden memory.

Swallowing, I take one last deep breath and dive in head-first. "When you're only exposed to one way to live for the first thirteen years of your life, it's difficult to believe another way exists. As a little girl, I looked up to my parents. Did as I was told. Took the beatings when I disobeyed. Listened to the constant verbal beatdowns. How did I know being treated as such was wrong? I had nothing to compare it to. Father enrolled me in the church's private school at age three. It wasn't a bad place. The teachers were wonderful, as were my classmates. With my father giving sermons several times a week at the church, everyone looked up to him. Saw him as a role model. Even me."

I close my eyes a moment and collect myself. Jonas tightens his grip on my hand, showing silent support.

"Even when he hit me. I was taught to believe disobedi-ence equals punishment. Punishment in the Rooker household equals a hole-laden wooden paddle against your bare butt. Obviously, I avoided this as much as possible. But, some-times, I received punishment simply because father had a bad day."

I tuck my lips between my teeth. Jonas caresses my cheek with his knuckles. "Sorry this happened to you, Autumn." His voice soft and sad.

"Wasn't until I went to public high school that I learned how different my life was. Compared to my new friends, I was sorely lacking. Yes, I had intelligence. But only from textbooks. And even then, my education had been tweaked around scripture. Wasn't necessarily a bad thing, but it secluded me. Put me in a box with the teens labeled as weirdos or freaks by the popular students. I didn't let it bog me down, but I wished to make at least one friend who didn't look at me like I traveled through time from the 1950s in my handmade dresses."

Jonas laughs and my brows shoot up in question. "You still dress like someone from another era. Just look sexy as hell now."

I join in his laughter. "Touché." He makes a fair point. "Anyway… the longer I spent in public school, the more I opened up. Not just verbally, but in the way I expressed myself. Clothing, makeup, hairstyle. My parents never spent a dime on any of it, though. I had to earn it working at the grocery store near the house." Taking a deep breath, I lick my lips. "I remember the first day I wore makeup and my mother called me a whore. The first time I wore clothes that showed my curves and she backhanded me so hard I had a bruise on my cheek for a week. Every time I painted over it with concealer, I cried."

Jonas stares at me, glassy-eyed. "Wish I would've found you sooner." I love the way Jonas wants to heal all of my scars. Wants to replace every action that has blemished my life.

"Me too. But if you had, I may not be who I am today. And I love who I am. Especially with you."

He leans across the console and kisses me. So tender. So sweet.

"Esther—my sister—never received punishments. For whatever reason, she did no wrong. She was the daughter my parents always wanted. Obedient, quiet, subservient. When my parents threw me out, she stood by their side with disgust on her face. My parents had learned to keep her in private school after seeing how it changed me. Last time I spoke with her was about a year ago. Although she still feels my parents were doing what they thought was best, she is slowly being exposed to the world. Hopefully, in the future, we'll be in a better place. I'd love for Clementine to meet her cousins. And I pray one day to get to know her again."

"You will," Jonas states with confidence.

I exhale and release it all. My mother and her twisted version of love. My father and his rigid outlook on life. I breathe in fresh air and expel every ounce of the hurt they inflicted upon me.

"Thank you." Jonas scrunches his brows. "For letting me get that off my chest. For allowing me to shed weight I didn't know I still held on to."

He strokes his thumb over my cheek. "You're welcome." Leaning in, he kisses my forehead. "Can I take you somewhere?"

"Yes."

He kisses my lips. "Nowhere fancy. But after the day's events, I think it's the perfect place to be."

Jonas starts the Jeep and drives away from downtown. Billie Eilish croons through the speakers as the city zips past us. Every minute of the last two hours flashes in my mind. The worry and anxiety, joy and fright. Then I relax. Melt into the seat and close my eyes as realization hits.

This is over. And Clementine won't be going anywhere. Relief washes over me and I bask in it. Let it heal me and steal all the pieces of my past that threaten my well-being.

Before long, Jonas parks in front of his parents' house. I glance over at him and tilt my head.

"Only Mom is here. She wanted me to call as soon as the hearing ended. Since I didn't have the chance, thought this might be better."

For whatever reason, my nerves skyrocket. The few times

Clementine and I have been over for family dinner night, his parents—the entire family—have been lovely. Treated me like I belonged. Hugged me like their own daughters.

So why are my palms sweaty?

We go inside the house and Jonas calls out for his mom. I clamp onto his arm, mirroring a timid child. His mom steps out of the hall, her smile bright, wide, and welcoming.

"Hey, you two." She pulls Jonas in for a hug, then me. She holds me at arm's length, eyes searching mine. "How'd it go?"

Jonas guides us to the living room and we all sit. Over the next hour, we share the craziness of the morning. Along with the good news. More than once, Jonas's mom tugs me into her arms and just holds me. The second time she does, I cry on her shoulder. She holds me close, strokes my back softly, and tells me to let it all out.

Irene Thompson may not be my birth mother, but she is the most maternal person in my life. And she embraces me as her own. For that, I have never been more grateful.

When I finish spilling my heart, she drags us to the kitchen and we make lunch together. The simple sandwiches taste better than any meal I ate in my youth. We sit at the dining table and enjoy each other's company.

As it nears time to pick Clementine up from school, we exchange hugs and goodbyes.

"Hope to see you all on Wednesday."

I curl into Jonas's side. "We'll be here," I answer for us.

"See you then. Give that little girl a hug for me."

We say one last goodbye before leaving. Jonas drives us through the city and in the direction of Clementine's school. And the entire time, I ogle him.

How did I get so lucky? How did I land a guy as sweet

and caring and desirable as Jonas? A man who doesn't just love me, but also my little girl. A man who goes above and beyond to make us happy. Who doesn't hesitate when it comes to our hearts and our happiness. Who will drop everything to be there for us.

I don't know what I did to deserve Jonas, but I will never take him or us for granted.

"What're you thinking about so hard over there?"

"How lucky I am," I answer without hesitation.

He reaches for my hand and brings it to his lips. "Think you're mistaken." When I continue to stare at his profile, unspeaking, he fills in the blank. "I am definitely the lucky one."

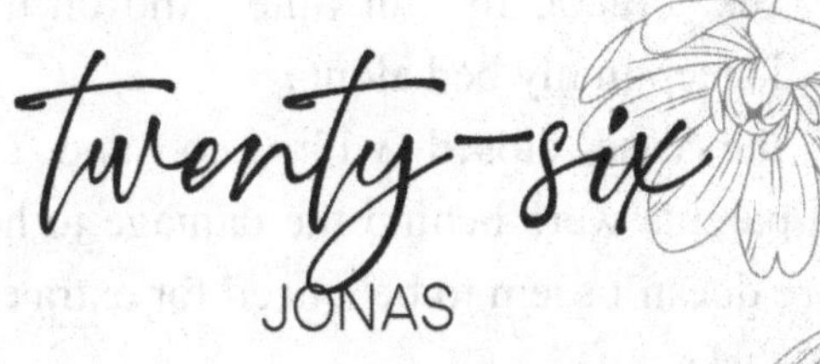

twenty-six

JONAS

Clementine darts across the house, Spartan hot on her heels as they search for Lex. Giggles echo from the pile of blankets on the other side of the couch as Clementine keeps calling his name. When she finally lifts the blankets away, they both run off laughing.

I help Jasmine and Jillian make dinner while Autumn sets the table with Mom. They chat while placing plates and silverware and napkins on the table. But their conversation is too quiet for me to hear.

"Really good to see you smiling so much," Jasmine says, bringing my attention back to the kitchen.

"Thanks, I guess."

How can I not smile when Autumn and Clementine are near? They bring a joy into my life I never imagined possible.

Yet, it seems as if Autumn still has hesitations about living together.

Almost a month has passed since I gifted her a key to my house. Since I set up a room for Clementine. And yet, I still don't have her in my bed every night.

Is it wrong for me to expect such things? Yes, I suppose

so. Considering we have only been together roughly four months, asking Autumn to uproot her and Clementine's life for my own selfish needs would be a dick move.

Doesn't mean I don't want to, though.

Anyone else in my shoes would be grateful to have what I do. Autumn and Clementine stay at the house four or five nights a week. Practically full time. And on the nights they don't stay, I sleep in my bed alone.

Since the case closed with Leo, and since learning Autumn's parents were behind the damage to her car and the notes, there doesn't seem to be a need for extra eyes.

And it sucks.

Don't get me wrong. I am beyond grateful she and Clementine are safe. In fact, they are more than safe. Safer than before the trial began.

When Leo and Autumn's attorneys spoke after the hearing, something unexpected and surprising happened. Not only did Leo pay back child support, interest, and Autumn's attorney fees; he also signed away his parental rights. Theresa had to explain it to Autumn several times. We also learned Autumn's father threatened to throw Leo into a shitstorm with local media about his abandoned child. Leo is by no means a celebrity, but when you own a massive hotel chain, news spreads quickly in the community. The news may have ruined the life he'd built.

Basically, Leo told his attorney he didn't want a similar occurrence to happen to Autumn or Clementine in the future. He didn't want someone to try and use his paternity to hurt either one of them. He never had ill intent and honestly didn't realize what he was getting himself into. I don't know how much of that I believe.

Either way, at least Autumn sleeps better at night knowing no one can take her daughter from her.

"Is the roast ready?" Jillian asks as she finishes smashing the potatoes.

I open the oven and jab the pot roast with a thermometer. After the needle hits the temperature Mom deems as the perfect roast, I grab the potholders and take it out. "Ready."

We carry the food dishes to the table then holler for everyone to come eat. Dad, Anton, and the kids rush to the table. Once we are in our usual seats, Mom tells everyone how grateful she is to have them at the table again. Then everyone fills their plates.

Dad encourages Lex to be mischievous while Clementine giggles. He nonchalantly picks up a green bean with his finger and pretends like he will throw it at Mom. A minute later, Lex tosses a green bean and Jasmine snaps at Dad to not goad him. I don't remember Dad being such an instigator when we were kids. No matter, he loves making the little ones laugh.

Although it's only March, Jillian rambles on to Mom about the fall fashion line the store will receive soon. Turtlenecks and scarves and gloves. Wool jackets and thermal-lined pants. Honestly, fall and winter attire in Florida is a strange concept. The actual fall season feels like a mild summer. And winter resembles what northerners experience as fall. Most clothing stores in Florida sell swimsuits year-round. No joke, we could get away with wearing fall attire in the winter without discomfort.

Beside me, Autumn focuses her attention on Jillian. Every now and again, Jillian pipes up and asks what she wears during different seasons with her rockabilly style. Genuinely intrigued by Autumn's fashion. How she wears it with ease, although not many local stores carry her style of clothes.

I lean back in my chair, eat my dinner, and absorb the ease with which Autumn talks with my family. Autumn and Clementine both. As if they have been sitting at this table and sharing meals with the Thompsons for years. Watching them blend in without effort has my heart stuttering before it takes off in a sprint.

With each passing day, our relationship grows stronger. Our bond more inseparable. We gravitate toward each other like the moon does the earth. As if finally where we are meant to be. In synergy. Two halves of one soul coming back together.

In the same breath, I miss her. On the nights she and Clementine don't sleep under the same roof as me. When Autumn doesn't lie next to me in bed. I miss her weight on my chest and her breath on my skin. Miss her soft snores and the twitch of her fingers when she dreams.

Do I wish the two of them lived with me full time? Hell yes. Do I question why they aren't? Also, yes.

The last thing I want to do is pressure Autumn. Especially after the debacle with Leo and her parents.

But I also can't stand not knowing if she wants to take the next step. If she wants to move in together. Or if she wants to keep things as they are.

Is it too soon to live together? This question has popped into my head more times than I care to count. Perhaps timing keeps her hesitant. Four months isn't long in the grand scheme. Some couples live apart for years before moving in together. But some move in within weeks.

"What do you think, Jonas?" Mom asks, and I have no idea what I missed.

"Sorry, was zoned out a minute. What'd you ask?"

"If you wanted to join us for Easter. Nothing fancy. Egg hunt, sugary treats, and dinner."

I glance over at Autumn to see her watching me with a shy smile. "Sounds like fun, Mom. Just tell us when to be here."

She claps and rubs her hands together. "Wonderful."

Autumn curls her hand around my bicep and leans into my side, resting her head on my shoulder. I kiss her forehead then press my cheek to her hair. Taking a deep breath, I close my eyes and absorb every ounce of love she radiates.

Move in with me.

Beside me, Autumn stiffens. Minus Clementine and Lex, the entire room goes silent. *Shit.* "Did I just say that out loud?" I whisper, although everyone hears.

Autumn sits up straighter and faces me. She tucks her lips between her teeth, eyes darting between mine. "You did," she croaks.

Dad sparks random conversation with Mom, thank god. Soon, everyone else chats among themselves again and pretends to ignore us.

I lean in closer to her, in the hopes of shielding our conversation somewhat. "Wasn't trying to put you on the spot. Sorry. The idea has crossed my mind before. And I'd love you both to be with me every night. But I didn't realize it came out of my mouth until you froze."

Passion mixes with fear and swirls like wildfire in her intoxicating irises. She clamps down on her lips harder and I have to fight the urge to graze my thumb over her chin, just beneath her lips. Beneath the table, her knee begins to bounce. Body stiff, her eyes dart toward everyone in her periphery.

"Can we discuss this later?" she whisper-squeaks. "In private."

I nod. "Of course. Like I said, it was a slip of the tongue."

Clamping down on her lips one last time, she releases them and spins in her chair to face everyone else again. She picks up her fork and pushes food around her plate, but doesn't eat much else. And for the next hour, she resumes prior conversations as if the subject never came up.

Just before eight, we exchange hugs with everyone and head out. Before heading over tonight, Autumn agreed to stay at the house. As she sits silently in the passenger seat, I pray she doesn't regret the decision.

I reach across the console and take her hand in mine. She weaves her fingers with mine and I breathe a little easier. *Thank goodness.* Not sure how I would handle it if Autumn shirked away from me.

After I park the Jeep in front of the house and we wander inside, Clementine gets ready for bed while I let Spartan outside. The nightly routine goes much the same as usual. Autumn and I give Clementine kisses and hugs good night and ruffle Spartan's fur before we turn off the light and close the door halfway.

In our room, blanketed in darkness, I reach for Autumn and pull her into me. Kiss her forehead, between her brows, the tip of her nose, her lips. Her body goes lax, melts into my touch, my lips. She fists my shirt then releases the cotton, sliding her palms up my chest to my neck, lacing her fingers at the base of my skull.

Apple lingers on her tongue from dessert and mixes with the taste of her. Her cherry vanilla aroma billows around me. From shoulder to hip, she eliminates any measure of space between us. I hum against her lips, her tongue, as she threads her fingers through my hair and tugs at the strands.

With my slipup tonight, I worried—still worry—she

would pull away. I have no intention of taking back what I said because I meant it. Just didn't mean to say it aloud. Yet. So much has happened since we started seeing each other, the last thing I want is for Autumn to believe I'm pressuring her into something she isn't ready for. Although, in my eyes, she is more ready than she realizes.

We take our time stripping off clothes and falling in to the bed. Tonight, our kisses and touches and whispered moans weigh heavier in the shadows. Our bodies move slower, with more intention and adoration. This isn't just sex. Not just a physical need for release or routine activity. And when we climax, the energy around us radiates heart and heat and traces of forever.

My front to her back, arms holding her snug against my skin, we start to drift off. The last thought floating in my mind is how we never brought up the conversation from dinner again. Either of us. And I wonder if that is a good thing or bad.

Before Jonas and I started dating, I rarely went out. Not that I didn't want to. Penny tried several times to drag me out of the apartment to let loose. Clementine had always been more important. My sole focus.

Now with the custody case closed, I sleep better and breathe easier. Leo signing away his parental rights was the most selfless and unexpected act. Burton and Kathryn Rooker now have assault charges on file and are undoubtedly being ridiculed in their community with a restraining order on record. I have never been a vindictive person, but I do believe in karma. And several years' worth has unleashed upon them.

"Sure you're good watching her tonight?"

Penny tilts her head. "You act as if I've never had girls' night with Clementine before." A palm rests over her heart as her eyes go wide. "You wound me."

I throw my eyeliner at her. "Such a drama queen."

"Be glad your makeup's done, otherwise I'd be holding this hostage until you groveled for forgiveness."

After applying my lipstick, I spin around and latch on to

her neck. "You love me." Penny shoves me as laughter spills from both of us. "Say it. Say you love me."

"Will you get off me if I do?"

I peer up at the ceiling and pucker my lips, feigning contemplation. "Hmm… only if you mean it," I tease.

Penny surprises me and throws her arms around my waist, hoisting me off the floor. "Love you, Auti," she coos, delivering air kisses near my face and hair—careful not to mess up either.

With my feet firmly planted on the ground again, I blow her a kiss. "You're the best." Penny being Penny, she curtsies then saunters off to the living room.

In front of the full-length mirror in the bedroom, I do one last scan, hair to heels. The black and white plaid-print strapless crop top sits high enough to cover the girls, but shows two fingers of skin above my waistline. Charcoal slacks hug my skin from navel to ankle. A simple pair of black heels shine at my feet. My signature scarlet lips for an added pop and hair in a ponytail.

Jonas steps in the room and closes the door. He sizes me up, licking his lips. "Not sure if we'll make it out tonight."

I push out my lower lip and bat my lashes. "But I got all dressed up."

"Fuck, scarlet. Don't pout. I might mess up your makeup." He comes up behind me, staring at me in the mirror over my shoulder, arms slithering around my waist, hips flush against my low back. "Sure I can't convince you to stay in?" Jonas kisses beneath my ear and I roll my eyes closed.

"Our friends are waiting for us," I rebut huskily.

He kisses farther down my neck, hands roaming my abdomen. "They'll understand."

God, I want him to keep going. Explore my skin with his

lips and tongue. Taste me. Heat ravages my skin as he kisses along the curve of my neck. "Jonas…"

"Yeah, scarlet."

"I want to." Spinning in his arms, I lock on to his otherworldly eyes. "But after we go out."

My favorite dimple appears as his lips kick up at the corners. His lips hover over my ear. "Hours of torture." He groans then releases me.

"It'll be worth it."

Before I change my mind about going out, I rush us out of the room. Jonas chuckles, his hand on my hip. Hugs and good nights are exchanged with Penny and Clementine. We buckle up in the Jeep and drive toward Tampa.

We crack the windows enough to let the cool night air sweep inside the cab. Salt and sand and earth perfume the breeze. Brilliant shades of tangerine and magenta dust the horizon as the sun dips below the water. "Level of Concern" by Twenty One Pilots plays on the radio as Jonas draws circles on my thigh with his thumb.

My eyes drift closed, amplifying every sense but sight. The whorl of Jonas's calloused thumb swirls on my thigh and stirs heat low in my belly. Hints of sunscreen mixed with Jonas's scent float in the Jeep cabin, and I take a deep breath. A brisk gust whips across my cheek and tampers the heat slowly building from his touch. And as the song on the radio fades from one to the next, I picture dancing with Jonas tonight, sweat dripping off our bodies.

Tonight celebrates a first, of sorts. Not the first occasion going out without Clementine. Jonas and I have gone on several dates. Gone out to hang with our friends and have fun —which is where we are headed now.

But tonight is different.

Because when we all go our separate ways tonight, Jonas and I will go home to his house. Alone. Without Clementine.

Part of me screams inside and waggles a motherly finger in my face, berating me for not being under the same roof as my daughter when I go to sleep. Another part of me hoots and hollers and jumps on the bar top whirling a towel over her head. She praises me, tells me *it's about damn time*, teases I won't get any sleep tonight.

"Should be there in five," Jonas states as he exits the highway.

I shoot a text to Cora and let her know our ETA. She replies and indicates where they parked. A few more turns and Jonas parks the Jeep one row back from Gavin's Range Rover. We stroll to the Rover hand in hand and meet up with everyone. After hugs and quick hellos, we enter the club.

Although I never experienced the clubbing stage of my late teens/early twenties, I suddenly *feel* years younger. A rush of excitement fuels me as we walk through Roar. Bass and occasional treble pour from the speakers and rattle my bones. Sporadic flashes of colored lights illuminate the dark club while dim lights softly brighten the bars. Sweetness and salt filter through my nose as we pass people bumping and grinding on the dance floor. Jonas guides me through the club with his hands on my hips, provoking the urge to dance.

Gavin maneuvers the group toward a table near the bar. As we circle around, Micah waves then signals he will be over in a minute.

Jonas stands flush to my back, not a breath of space between us. His hands clasp at my belly as his fingers tickle the sliver of visible flesh near my navel. Light caresses fan the flame already heating my skin. Lips lightly nibble at my ear as I roll my eyes back and press my butt against his thighs.

"Mmm... definitely dancing tonight," he muses, breathy on my ear.

I tip my head back, rest it on his shoulder, and meet his gaze. His lips lower to mine and break away far too soon. When I display my best pouty face, Jonas shakes his head and chuckles.

Micah joins us at the table, exchanging hugs and bro back slaps. Although he works tonight, he promises to hang during breaks. He goes around the table and jots our drink orders on a napkin.

After he scratches the last drink down, Micah steps between two people at the bar and hollers. "Peyton." A woman midway down the bar, blonde hair loosely pulled back in a ponytail glances up. Close to our age. She's tall—closer to Shelly's height than the rest of us. Her eyes scan the bar to find who called out. When her eyes land on Micah, she grinds her jaw. He tosses the napkin on the bar and slaps it. "Drink order," he yells.

She drifts down the bar to stop in front of him. From my vantage point, I can't hear the exchange. But hostility rolls off the two of them. Or is that sexual tension? He says something else to her and she shakes her head while grabbing a glass. When he spins around, she aims her middle finger in his direction.

I laugh and Jonas peers down at me. "What's so funny?"

He leans in close and I cup my mouth to his ear. "Little love-hate relationship between Micah and the woman behind the bar." Jonas looks to the woman in question and nods. "Not sure if they're dating or have dated, but there's definite tension."

Micah delivers the drinks to the table then darts behind the bar to help. We sip our drinks and catch up on life. Before long, everyone drifts out to the dance floor while Jonas and I hang back at the table.

Jonas faces me, snakes his arms around my waist, and hauls me closer to him. "Want to dance when they wear out?" Lacing my fingers behind his neck, I nod.

His gaze holds mine for a beat before dropping to my lips. Without preamble, he kisses me breathless. The flashing lights and thumping music fade away. Wet heat traces the seam of my lips and I open up. With hundreds of people nearby, Jonas kisses me wild.

Our lips break apart, but he peppers kisses along my jaw. When he reaches my ear, he sucks the lobe between his lips and growls. "Autumn." My moan in response vibrates my chest. "Move in with me."

I fist his shirt and bite near the collar at the base of his throat. He growls again, fueling the flame in me. "God, I want to."

Jonas leans back and I immediately miss his weight on my nipples. Finger under my chin, he tilts my head back. "Then say yes."

Music blares from every corner and hidden speakers in the ceiling. Sweaty bodies gyrate on the dance floor and near the tables. Upbeat energy bounces off every surface. And yet, it all disappears as I study how the blue marries gold in Jonas's irises.

This is the second time Jonas has proposed Clementine and I move in with him. The first was a slip of the tongue at his parent's a few nights ago. After I told him I wanted to discuss it in private, rehashing the subject hasn't happened. Until now.

Will Jonas be upset if I tell him I decided the very same night? That as he drifted to sleep, I imagined—not for the first time—what living together would be like. Waking up next to him every morning and falling asleep in his arms. I wanted to rouse him from sleep and tell him yes. But so many people say making rash decisions isn't smart. So, I simmered on it.

With each passing minute, hour, day, the desire to say yes expanded in my chest. Consumed me. Begged to be let out.

I lift up on my tiptoes and press a kiss to his lips. "Yes," I whisper, breathy.

Leaning back, his eyes dart between mine. "Yes?"

I nod and, in a blink, he hoists me off the floor and spins me in circles. Glad I haven't drunk much. My feet hit the floor and he crashes his lips to mine. Tasting me. Devouring me. I fist his hair. Moan when he kneads my hips and grinds me to him.

"Get a room," Micah yells from the bar. Catcalls and wolf whistles echo around us as we peel apart.

As Jonas flips Micah off, the blonde bartender yells something at Micah I don't hear. But if the curl of her lip is any indication, she probably told him to shut up or mind his own business.

As our group trickles back to the table, we share our news. Cheers erupt as the ladies crowd around me and squeal. The guys exchange fist bumps or shoulder hug-slaps. Once the congratulations die down, we lose ourselves to the music.

Jonas threads his fingers with mine and walks backward toward the dance floor, tugging me along. His smile illuminates the dark club as he pins us chest to chest, palms flat on my low back. Our bodies grind and sway. Sweat slicks our skin and drips from our temples. Jonas drops his forehead to mine and holds my gaze.

"I love you," he mouths. His silent declaration louder than the thumping music.

"Love you, too."

He dips his chin and tastes my lips. One song bleeds into another. Then another. All the while, Jonas and I sway in the middle of the dance floor, lips locked, tongues tasting, oblivious to the world around us.

When he breaks the kiss and we come up for air, he whispers in my ear. "Let's go home, scarlet."

Better words have never been said. "Let's go home," I repeat.

twenty-eight

JONAS

For someone who cohabitated in a small apartment with another adult and a child, Autumn has more shit than imaginable.

"We may have to add another room to the house," I tease, heaving another box from the floor.

Autumn sticks her tongue out. "Ha ha. If we fit everything in here" —she waves her arm around the bedroom— "we can fit it into the house."

My house—our house—may be small, but I have upgraded majority of it over the years. Done my fair share of walks through the Ikea showroom for innovative ideas in small spaces. Learned how to make the best of unused wall space. And although my belongings don't fill all the shelves and cubbies and rods in the closet, I made the most of the space when updating it.

Which means Autumn will have plenty of space for her clothes and shoes and purses and whatever else she owns. And if the closet fills, there is plenty of room in Clementine's closet.

Back seats laid down in the Jeep, I wedge the box between

two others and go back for more. Everything leaving the apartment is small enough to fit in the Jeep or Autumn's car. After talking with Penny, Autumn opted to leave the furniture in the apartment for whoever rooms here next. Better it go to use than sell it.

In the apartment, I wander to the Jenga pile of odd-sized boxes. "This the last of them?"

Autumn pops up behind the open kitchen counter and brushes a stray hair out of her face. "Just packing up the last of the kitchen items. Everything else is done."

One by one, I carry out the larger boxes, followed by several small boxes labeled *bathroom*. As eager as I am to share the same living space with Autumn and Clementine, the number of personal care items going into the bathroom intimidates the hell out of me. What do I have? Maybe less than ten hygiene/personal care items in the bathroom. By the looks of it, Autumn owns the entire beauty care department in Target.

The bathroom may need revamping. Again.

Not that I am opposed.

Once everything is crammed inside the Jeep and Bel Air, we drive back to the house and haul everything inside.

The house looks like a war zone. Boxes in every room. Piles of wadded newspaper from unwrapping fragile pieces. We pile the boxes according to room then disburse accordingly.

Clementine spends the day in her room, putting away her own belongings as Spartan supervises. Every once in a while, we hear her direct him where something goes—although he isn't capable of putting it away. Or so I thought. At one point, I peeked in her room and watched Spartan carry a stuffed animal on the bed and place it by the pillows. Huh. Only for her.

We spend all of Saturday unpacking. Only taking breaks to eat and sleep. When Sunday morning rolls around, I glance around the house with fresh eyes. It's the same space, but not. The energy vibes differently. Feels more lived in. Comfortable. A home.

While the girls are still asleep, I cook breakfast. Our first official Sunday living under the same roof. And I plan to treat my girls.

Clementine wanders from her room first. Balled fingers rubbing her eyes as she yawns big. Spartan ambles lazily beside her. Before Clementine, Spartan was this wild child. Barking and running like his ass was on fire. Now, he peers up at her, docile and at her beck and call.

"'Morning, sunshine. Did you sleep good?"

She nods. "Can I let Sparty out?"

"Sure. Just open the back door. He'll bark when he's ready to come back in."

After she lets Spartan out, she sidles up to me in the kitchen. "Whatcha making?"

"French toast, sausage, eggs, and fruit."

Spartan barks to come back inside. Clementine tends to him as I finish cooking. When I spin around to grab plates from the cupboard, Autumn stands at the opposite end of the kitchen, ogling me.

Sleepy eyes rake over my bare chest and sweats. The hunger in her eyes is a delicious assault that lights me on fire. Her tongue sweeps out and licks her lips. Chest rises and falls quicker. And I love how easily she is affected by me. Just as I am her.

Each morning, I am rewarded with her natural beauty. Although I love seeing Autumn styled to the nines—hair pinned to perfection, lips and nails scarlet red, outfit glamorous even when casual—seeing her fresh from sleep is my favorite. Tank top and pajama shorts hugging her curves. Face free of makeup. Hair frizzing in every direction. Feet and legs bare.

I saunter over to her, grip her hips to bring her flush to my chest as I kiss her. "'Morning, scarlet."

Eyes closed, a warm smile curves her lips up. "'Morning," she says, breathless. "Smells good."

"Was about to plate everything. Pull up a stool." I kiss her nose and smack her ass as she heads for the breakfast bar.

Maple, herbs, and citrus waft in the air as I deliver breakfast to my girls. As we eat, the topic of tonight's gathering comes up.

Although I have owned the house for some time, having Autumn and Clementine here makes it feel new. Our recent Sunday get-togethers with friends have been wonderful, so we opted to do a housewarming. As I see it, tonight's shindig is just another of our Sunday gatherings, just using the guise of Autumn and Clementine moving in as a reason to ask everyone over.

Once we clear our plates, I clean up the kitchen. Autumn and I sit down to write a shopping list while Clementine showers.

If there is one thing that will take time adjusting to, it's the fact I now have to share one bathroom with two additional people. Thankfully, the water heater holds enough to let us all shower without the water running cold.

Though we are slowly settling in to the idea of living together, I wonder how long we will be able to stay in this small house. Does it have everything we need? Absolutely. Will it be a struggle to live in a small space with one bathroom as Clementine approaches her teen years? More than likely. But we will cross that bridge when we get to it.

With the list made, we gather clothes for the day while waiting for Clementine to finish.

I sit on the edge of the mattress and follow Autumn around the room with my eyes as she plucks a shirt from the hanger and tugs jeans from the dresser. She lays them beside me and returns to the dresser for bra and panties. She twirls the minimal material lace panties around her finger and saunters over to me.

I look between the sexy as hell panties and her eyes, swallowing. "Don't think I've seen those," I squawk like a hormonal teenager.

Her knees bump mine before she plants each on the bed, straddling me. I stare up at her in complete fascination as she licks her lips. "You haven't. Bought them online a few weeks back."

My hands go to her hips, knead once, twice before dipping to her ass. I cup her cheeks and drag her closer to my chest. "Can't wait to see them on you." Her plump lips tug at the corners. "And to peel them off later."

She drops her mouth to mine and kisses me with fire on her lips. "Later." Hopping off my lap, she tosses the panties to the bed and takes my hand. "Let's go shower."

There are pros and cons to having a single bathroom and shower in this house. Con—you have to wait your turn. Whether to shower, brush your teeth or use the toilet. Con—you never know how long the wait will be. Pro—more joint shower time with Autumn to "conserve" water or time. At least that is the excuse we give Clementine.

Until today, I'd never had shower sex. Movies and television make it look easy. In reality, it's awkward and slippery and complicated. Guess we will have to practice until we get it right.

Won't find either of us complaining.

～

Lifting the beer to my lips, I swallow down the hoppy brew and glance around the back patio.

Everyone being here feels almost dreamlike. Six months ago, if someone would have told me I'd be head over heels in love with someone other than my best friend, I would've laughed in their face. If they also told me the love of my life came with the cutest little girl on the planet, I would've laughed harder.

Sometimes fate surprises you. Throws a wrench in your ideal plan because it has something better in store. Seeing my friends and family together tonight proves you can't stay single-focused forever. You have to learn that people enter your life for a purpose. To show or teach you love so you recognize it when it enters your life. To tear you down so you learn how to rise and be the strongest version of yourself. And how to locate your own path.

For some, it takes a lifetime. Thankfully, I didn't have to wait so long. But I thank fate for the years I traveled down my path. Through the heartache and uncertainty. The friendship and laughter. Without them, I might not have met Autumn. I might not have been ready to meet her. Unwilling to open up or see the big picture. Feel the way my soul hums when she enters the room.

Tonight wouldn't be what it is without her.

Cora, Erin, Shelly, and Penny lounge on the outdoor couch with Autumn, laughing. Watching them whisper like school girls is a sight. Autumn snorts then smiles and I can't take my eyes off her. That woman belongs to me, and I am damn lucky.

Mom and Dad play with Clementine, Ashton, and Lex in the yard, chasing them around until they squeal with delight. Spartan is hot on Dad's heels, barking playfully. With Clementine living here now, I contemplate adding kid-friendly fun to the backyard. A swing set or trampoline or treehouse. Maybe Jasmine will bring Lex over to play more if I do.

Gavin, Rex, Anton, Micah, and Reznor are in what looks like an all too serious conversation. Anton animatedly tells them something and I am certain it is in regards to finances. Anton has always been a great guy, but as soon as someone mentions saving for the future or making significant life changes, he flips into the most passionate numbers man.

Jasmine, Jillian, Trevor, and Iliana sit opposite the couch near the fire bowl and talk softly. And, if I am not mistaken, Trevor glances a little longer than typical at Jillian, but I won't call him out on it. Trevor has been through some shit with his ex. Considering how long we have been friends, I know he wouldn't hurt my sister. Especially if he wants to keep his dick intact.

Cora rises from the couch and walks my way. Sidling up to the grill, she refills her drink then faces me.

"I'm happy for you."

After I flip the chicken, I glance at her. A smile I used to think I couldn't live without stretches across her face. The appearance brings me joy, but a form much different than it once did. So much has changed between us. It isn't often men and women remain friends. Usually, relationships or emotions meddle. At one point, that was almost the case for us. But it never felt right. Although I love Cora, my love for Autumn is a million times more powerful.

As Autumn once told me, maybe Cora came into my life so I could experience love and see it firsthand with her and Gavin. Cora was never fated to be mine, just a teacher to prep me for the future. For Autumn and Clementine.

"Thank you. Never thought this would be my life." I wave my beer bottle around. "But I'm damn glad it is."

Cora leans in and hugs me. "Knew she was out there. She was waiting for you too."

I break the hug and smile. "Yeah." I glance over to Autumn, who peeks up and smiles back. "Lucky I found her."

epilogue

AUTUMN

One year later

"I miss your face," Penny whines as she wanders into my booth.

"Just my face?"

She pops her gum and plops down on my freshly cleaned client chair. "Would you be mad if I said yes?"

"What's the matter, Rex not as pretty as me?" I tease.

A month after I moved out of the apartment with Penny, Rex and his girlfriend at the time got in a huge fight. Seeing as they were living together and her daddy paid the rent on their apartment, Rex got the boot. Thankfully, Penny hadn't found anyone to occupy the second bedroom. When Rex came into work "sobbing like a baby" as Penny so gracefully stated, she took pity on him and let him move in.

Over the last few months, I noticed a slight shift in how they act around each other. Small things.

The way he glances over to the reception desk more often than before. Her obvious avoidance of him at work—overtly intentional. And anytime we all hang out, they stay as far apart as possible.

If I didn't know any better, I may believe they are sleeping together. Either that or they fight the urge.

Penny rolls her eyes on a huff. "Definitely not. He also isn't the cleanest human on the planet. And is it too much to ask for him to put the damn toilet seat down?"

I chuckle and she narrows her gaze at me. Taking a step back, I hold my hands up in surrender. "Sorry, but you have to admit, it's kind of funny."

She pops off the seat, plants her hands on her hips, and shoots me a pointed glare. "It isn't funny, Auti." Her hot pink fingernail aimed at my chest. "And you're supposed to be on my side."

"I am on your side," I cajole. "Sorry Rex is a bad room-mate. Have you talked with him about it?"

Slowly, over the last year, I have lightened my schedule at the shop. Now working four lighter shifts, Tuesday through Friday, so I have more time with Clementine and Jonas. On a typical day, Jonas works until five and Clementine attends an after school martial arts program. And if I pick her up earlier than four thirty, I regret the decision all night.

In the not too distant future, I see myself working even fewer hours. But we will play it by ear.

"You're joking, right?" She shakes her head while tapping her Mary Jane on the linoleum. "Talking to Rex about anything is a lost cause."

I tuck my lips between my teeth to stop myself from laughing and focus on finishing my cleanup. "Pen," I start with a headshake. "You need to talk with him. Even if he's a pain in the ass, you need to sit down and hash this out. It won't get better otherwise."

Tossing my gloves in the trash bin, I grab my purse from the cabinet and exit the booth with Penny on my heels. She plops down in her chair behind the reception counter on a huff.

"I hate it when you're right, Auti."

"Glad you still love me." I bend and bear-hug her. "Let me know how the talk goes. Love you."

"Yeah, yeah. Go be with your man." She shoos me away.

I hop in the Bel Air and drive to the dojo to pick up Clementine. As she gathers her belongings, Clementine brags about the instructor's praise on her kata technique. As girly as my daughter is, I never expected her to love martial arts the way she does. But it warms my heart she discovered something she is not only good at, but also loves enough to flaunt.

On the way home, I remind her we're going out for dinner. In the past year, having Jonas as a father figure and Spartan as a daily companion has been a good change for Clementine. Her sass has knocked down a notch and she interacts more with us than being glued to screens. Undeniably, my little girl has grown up so much.

As soon as I cut the engine, she darts in the house, loves on Spartan a moment, then takes off for a quick shower.

Not a foot in the door, Jonas has his arms around my waist and his lips pressed to mine. "How was your day?"

"Uneventful, unless you count Penny flipping out because Rex is a slob."

He chuckles and shakes his head. "When I went out with the guys last weekend, he went on a tirade about her nagging. Seems like some love-hate going on there."

"Agreed."

We break apart as Spartan bolts past us and we stumble

into the couch edge. Jonas scolds Spartan, then frames my face in his palms. "You alright?"

I nod. "Yeah. Just stumbled a bit. The house gets smaller the bigger he and Clementine get." Nonchalantly, I hint at needing more space for the second time this week.

Jonas shrugs it off and repeats the same line he said last time. "We'll figure something out."

Once Clementine finishes getting ready, we pile into the Jeep and drive to Red Robin. Instead of bopping and singing in the back seat, Clementine prattles on about how eager she is to earn her next belt in karate. Her hands animated while she talks about the new kata she learned today. Her enthusiasm pastes smiles on our faces. He clutches my thigh a little tighter as he steers us into a parking space.

No matter how gentle or firm, I love Jonas's touch. Live for the warmth and tingle it provokes. In the last year, every touch has held more meaning. Lit me on fire further. Had me falling more and more in love with him.

After a table full of appetizers, three burgers, and a few drinks in funky cups, we decide to wander the mall to burn off the obscene number of calories we consumed.

In one of the department stores, we wander to the kid's section and stare after Clementine as she scrutinizes every item on the racks. As we steer closer to where her sizes butt up against the baby clothes, I get lost in the soft gray and subtle green onesies, sleepers, and outfits. Before I stop myself, my hand reaches out and grazes the delicate cotton.

Jonas steps up behind me, snakes his arms around my waist and whispers in my ear. "Everything okay?" His voice riddled with questions. "You've been quiet the last few days."

I drop my hand from the sleeper and spin to face him. "Yeah. Just been thinking."

His fiery hazels lock on to my goldens and study me with great intensity. "About?"

Clementine bounces over toward us with a rock band shirt in her hand. "Can we get this? Pleeeease."

I nod. "Sure, pumpkin. But that's it." As she skips away from us, I peer up at Jonas. "When we get home."

After we pay for Clementine's new "Girl bands rock!" shirt, we walk back to the Jeep. The ride home is quiet and heavy with questions. Out of the corner of my eye, Jonas peeks my way every opportunity he gets. I keep my eyes forward and my fingers curled with his.

At home, Clementine and Spartan lock themselves away in her room, leaving Jonas and I alone.

It's now or never, Autumn. Just tell him. No need to worry yourself sick. Everything will be fine.

Jonas guides me to the couch and we cuddle the moment we plop down. He strokes my hair and I close my eyes to focus solely on his touch. The heat of his skin on mine. His jagged breath as he hugs me closer to him.

"You can talk to me, scarlet. About anything," he croaks against the crown of my head.

No doubt my silence has him worried. Roles reversed, I would feel the exact same.

I tuck my lips between my teeth and take a deep breath before releasing them. "I'm late." Jonas goes still beneath me. Too still. I close my eyes and pray this won't be an issue. "And I took a pregnancy test a few days ago."

After a yearlong minute, Jonas scoots away an inch. I pinch my eyes until the corners hurt, until the warmth of his palms rest on my cheeks. Slowly, he tilts my head back until his eyes meet mine.

"Autumn…" he breathes my name as if it is his last breath. "Why didn't you tell me sooner?"

Tears sting the backs of my eyes and I question myself as to why I waited so long. Who the hell knows? I shrug and swallow the emotion swirling at the back of my throat. "Don't know. Guess I was worried how you'd react."

"Autumn, I love you. No matter what." He leans in and kisses me soft and sweet. "What did the test say?"

A tear spills down one cheek, then the other. "That you're going to be a daddy." I smile as his eyes dart between mine.

"Really?" he questions with wonderment in his voice. I nod with my eyes on his. He kisses me again, this time greedier. "I-I don't even know what to say."

I grip his forearms and study his ear-to-ear smile. "Tell me that you're happy and you want this. A baby."

"Hell yes, I'm happy. And damn right I want this." He crashes his lips to mine and makes me breathless. When he breaks the kiss, he glances around the open floor plan before coming back to me. "Guess we will need more space after all."

I trace from his temple to the angle of his jaw before cupping his cheek. "I love you, Jonas."

His thumbs stroke my cheeks a moment before he drops his palm to rest over my lower abdomen. "Love you, too." His glassy eyes meet mine. "Thank you," he whispers.

"For what?"

My favorite dimple makes an appearance. "For loving me." He presses my hand to his sternum and covers it with his own. "And for giving me something I never thought I'd have." I scrunch my brow. "A family of my own."

～

Want more Jonas and Autumn? I have four chapters of bonus content on my website!

Ready for the next duet? The Insomniac Duet is an enemies to lovers, workplace romance packed with witty banter. Start Micah and Peyton's story now!

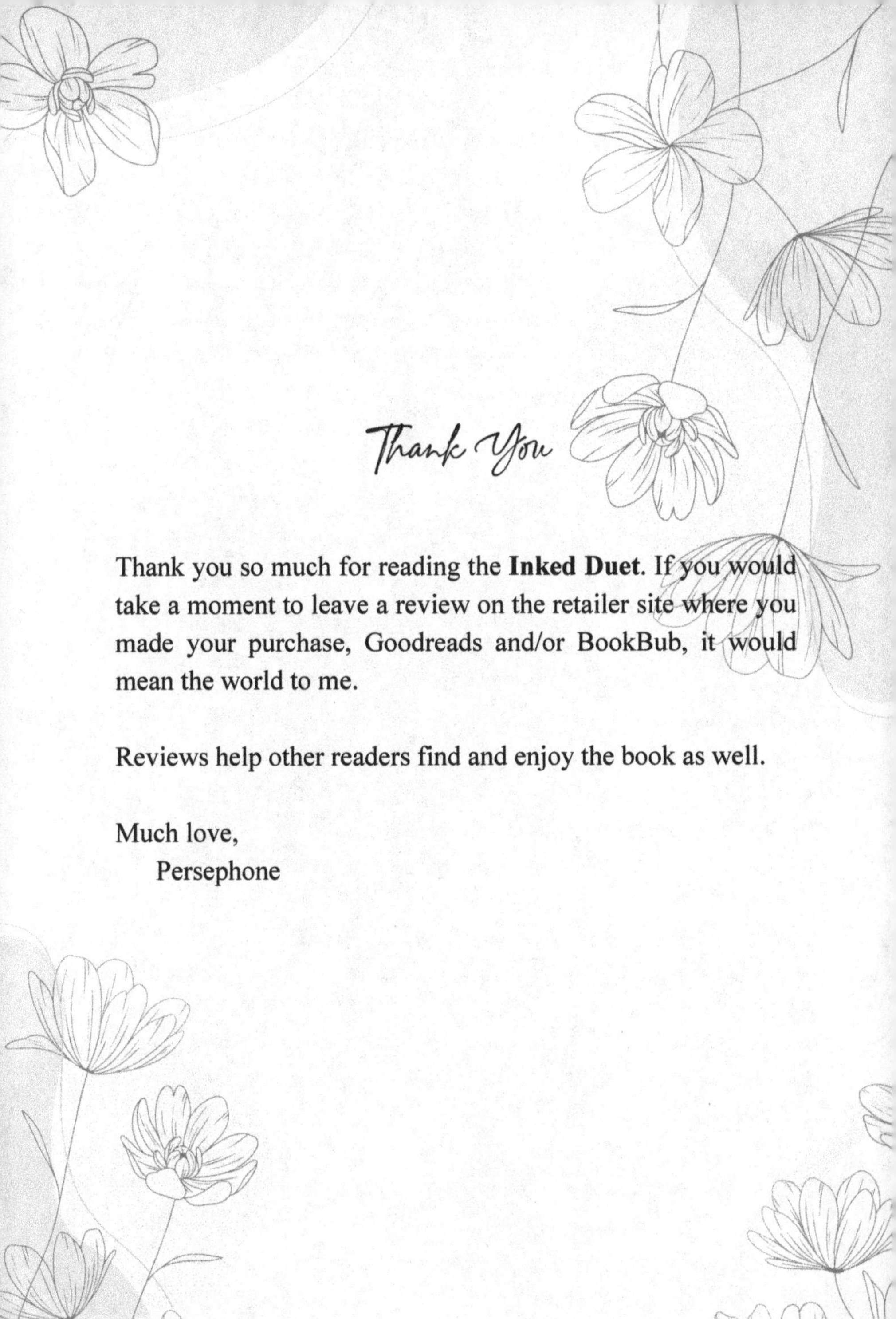

Thank You

Thank you so much for reading the **Inked Duet**. If you would take a moment to leave a review on the retailer site where you made your purchase, Goodreads and/or BookBub, it would mean the world to me.

Reviews help other readers find and enjoy the book as well.

Much love,
Persephone

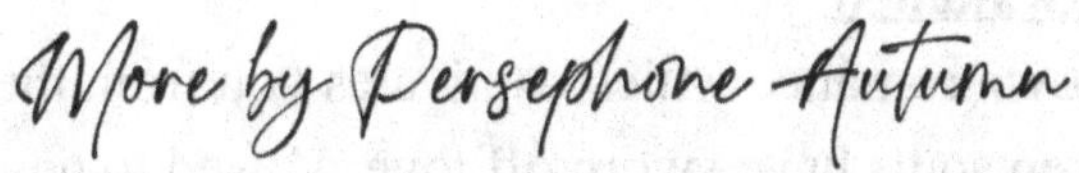

The Click Duet

High school sweethearts torn apart. When fate gives them a second chance, one doesn't trust they won't be hurt again. Through the Lens (Click Duet #1) and Time Exposure (Click Duet #2) is an angsty, second chance, friends to lovers romance with all the feels.

The Insomniac Duet

He was her high school bully. She was the outcast that secretly crushed on him. More than ten years later, he's her boss, completely oblivious to their shared past, and wants no one but her. More importantly, he doesn't understand her animosity toward him.

The Artist Duet

A tortured hero with the biggest heart and a charismatic heroine with the patience of a saint. Previous heartache has him fighting his desire to be more than friends with her. But she is everywhere, and he can't help but give in. The Artist Duet is an angsty, friends to lovers slow burn.

Transcendental

A musician in search of his muse and a woman grieving the loss of her husband. Two weeks at an exclusive retreat and their connection rivals all others. Until she leaves early without notice. But he refuses to give up until he finds her again.

<u>Depths Awakened</u>

A small town romance which captivates you from the start. Two broken souls have sworn off love. Vowed to never lose anyone else. But their undeniable attraction brings them together and refuses to let go.

<u>One Night Forsaken</u>

One night. No names. No romance. Just fun. Nothing more–at least, that's what she tells herself. Until he appears in her coffee shop months later with that addictive smile. She swore off commitment. He vows to never love again. But the more they fight it, the more life brings them together.

<u>Every Thought Taken</u>

As young children, an unshakable friendship brought them together. As teens, they discovered an undeniable love. Then life pulled them in different directions–into darkness and light–and slowly ripped them apart. Years later, he returns home in the hopes of a second chance with his first love and to conquer the demons of his past.

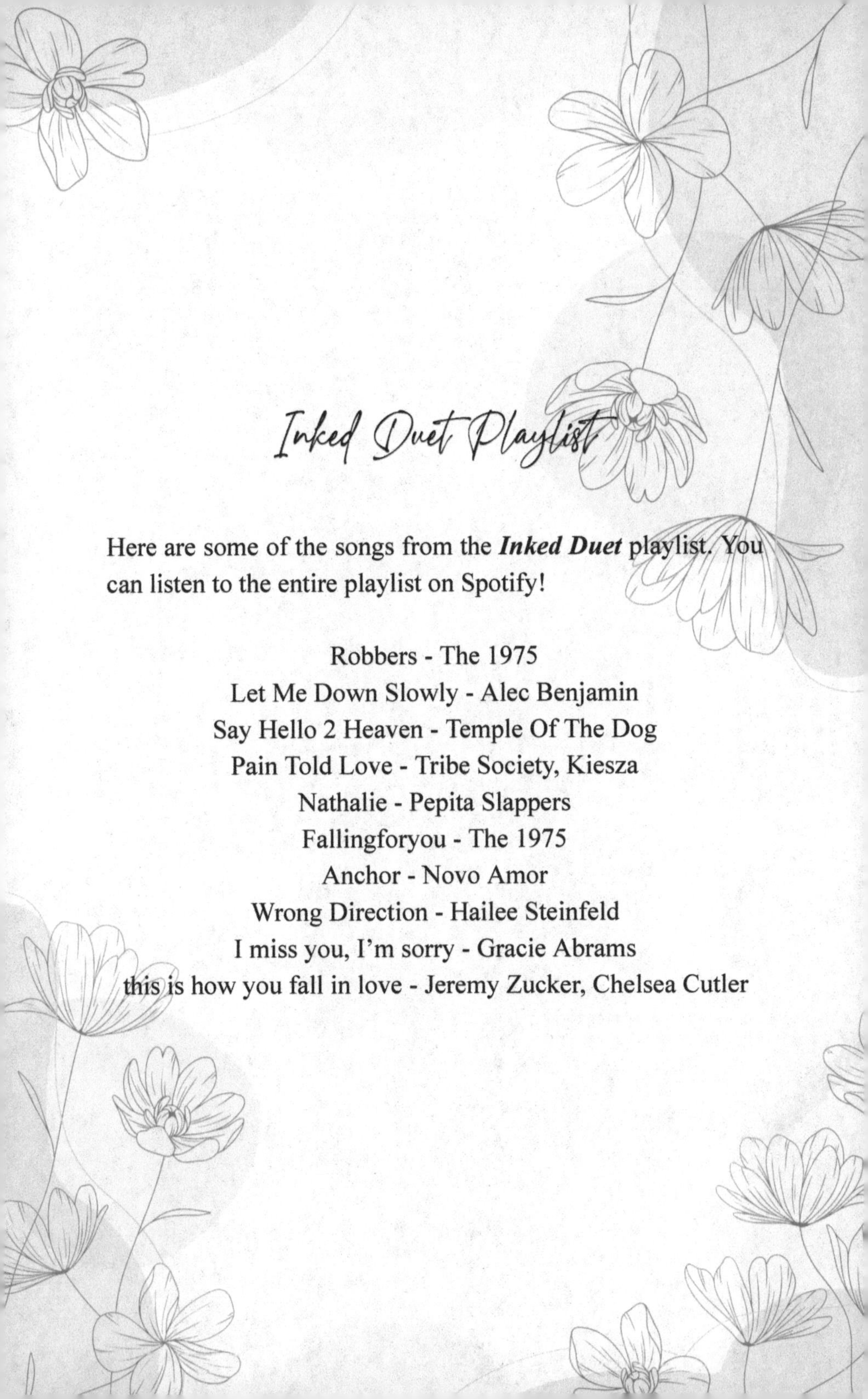

Inked Duet Playlist

Here are some of the songs from the **Inked Duet** playlist. You can listen to the entire playlist on Spotify!

Robbers - The 1975
Let Me Down Slowly - Alec Benjamin
Say Hello 2 Heaven - Temple Of The Dog
Pain Told Love - Tribe Society, Kiesza
Nathalie - Pepita Slappers
Fallingforyou - The 1975
Anchor - Novo Amor
Wrong Direction - Hailee Steinfeld
I miss you, I'm sorry - Gracie Abrams
this is how you fall in love - Jeremy Zucker, Chelsea Cutler

Acknowledgments

Loved ones first!

Thank you to my wife, dad, and daughter for constantly being my biggest fans, cheerleaders, and motivators. Without your support, my writing journey wouldn't be where it is now. We've had ups and downs, but every time, we come out on the other side. I know I do because of you three in particular. I love you!

To the best kickass editing team a lady could ask for… Ellie and Rosa, you always make my manuscripts beautiful and perfect. At least with this one, my commas were practically spot on. Must've been a good day lol. Rosa, your insight and feedback is invaluable. You always pick up on stuff I miss or don't wrap up 100%. All the fucking hugs!

To Kat… thank you for being an amazing friend and making my covers stunning every time. And thanks for putting up for my craziness every once in a while.

To Theresa… First, I miss your face. Most importantly, thank you for letting me use your first name and physical likeness for a tertiary character in this book. When I wrote her, I tried to picture you (minus your super tall heels). All the hugs! And I can't wait to hang out again when the world is less chaotic.

To my author friends… I look forward to squeezing you all one day. Thank you for any and all support you give. For letting me share my covers and releases in your groups or on your pages. For sharing my books in your newsletters. For answering any questions whenever I bug you. We have to stick together through all this author madness, and I'm glad to have you in my corner.

To everyone who's read my previous books… THANK YOU! Thank you for loving my work enough to read more than just one. Thank you for not throwing my book away. Thank you for looking forward to the next book.

To every person new to my books…. THANK YOU! Thank you for taking a chance on me and reading my work. Writing is wonderful and crazy and frustrating. But for every person who reads my words, writing is worth it every single time.

Connect with Persephone

<u>Connect with Persephone</u>

www.persephoneautumn.com

<u>Subscribe to Persephone's Newsletter</u>

www.persephoneautumn.com/newsletter

<u>Join Persephone's Reader Group</u>

Persephone's Playground

<u>Follow Persephone Online</u>

instagram.com/persephoneautumn

facebook.com/persephoneautumnwrites

goodreads.com/persephoneautumn

bookbub.com/authors/persephone-autumn

amazon.com/author/persephoneautumn

pinterest.com/persephoneautumn

USA Today Bestselling Author Persephone Autumn lives in Florida with her wife and psycho cat. A proud mom with a cuckoo grandpup. An ethnic food enthusiast who has fun discovering ways to vegan-ize her favorite non-vegan foods. Most days, you'll find her with a tea latte or fruity concoction in her hand. If given the opportunity, she would intentionally get lost in nature.

For years, Persephone did some form of writing; mostly journaling or poetry. After pairing her poetry with images and posting them online, she began the journey of writing her first novel.

She mainly writes romance and poetry, but on occasion dips her toes in other works. Look for her non-romance publications under P. Autumn.